Atlantis Rising

A Fantasy Kingdom-Building Adventure

by David Lingard

<u>A note from the author</u>

I just wanted to say here, thank you, whoever you are for however you have arrived at this book and my story. It makes a big difference to authors like me, who like to feel as though their hard work and dedication is appreciated when our work is read.

Your investment of your own time and money is as always, well appreciated. It takes a long time and a lot of effort to write, edit and release a book, so please, I ask that you **rate** and **review** everything that you read – and not just this book, so that lesser-known authors can grow their audience and gain the credibility that they deserve.

Also, I have a website that is usually kept up to date with current works, reviews and a few extra little bits. You'll find it at: www.davidlingard.com

Chapter 1 - Mutiny

"Fire the cannons!" I bellowed at the top of my voice, over the sound of the turbulent seas crashing against the wooden hull of my ship and over the sounds of my dedicated band of free men engaging sword to sword with the oppressive soldiers of the Royal Navy. We always fought with our hearts when it came to the Royal Navy because they were the ones who sought to remove us from the seas and to take our freedoms away.

The deck shook violently as my ship's cannons roared in unison, belching fire and smoke, sending a hail of iron towards the enemy vessel we had turned to come alongside. It had taken years of training and dedication, but we had become feared by the Royal Navy. They sent ship after ship to send us to our watery graves, but ship after ship we had destroyed and pillaged. Now it seemed that their tactic was to send larger vessels after us, with more guns and crew.

But we keep sailing.

The Iron Will was the name of my ship, and crewed by the very best free men that I had ever known; we would never shy away from a fight.

The deafening booms of the cannons were swiftly followed by the tortured screams of wood splintering and metal tearing as the heavy cannonballs found their mark. Amidst the chaos, the salty sea air was thick with the stench of burning wood and gunpowder and filled with the screams of injured and dying sailors.

My crew fought with unmatched ferocity across all the oceans; their eyes burned with the passion for freedom and vengeance against the tyrannical rule they had long suffered. They swung from ropes, boarded the enemy ship, and clashed with the Royal Navy's soldiers, their cutlasses and straight swords slicing through the air with deadly precision. It was almost sad to watch; the soldiers of the Royal Navy looked the part, but when faced with an opponent who had spent their lives killing, stealing and pillaging, they simply didn't match up. The saying goes that only a Free Man can dethrone a Free Man, and these sailors were anything but. They were slaves to their commanders, slaves to the Commodore, and slaves to the Crown.

The enemy ship, now listing from the damage inflicted by our cannons, became a brutal battleground as both sides fought tooth and nail for survival and victory. The groans of wounded men mingled with the triumphant cries of those who found their mark, the sound of steel meeting steel ringing out like a chaotic symphony. I stood on my upper deck with one hand on the giant wooden wheel and the other holding my sabre to the ready. As Captain of the Iron Will, I would seldom be called upon to jump to an enemy vessel, but I had been known to do so if the situation had called for it, or if I felt the call of battle.

"Captain Reid," one of my sailors approached up the steps. "The Royal vessel, she's turning away from us, trying to escape!"

The wind whipped at my long, dark hair, stinging my weathered face as I surveyed the enemy ship. She was damaged and limping, and I could already see that there would be no escape for her, no matter how hard her crew tried to urge her away from the battle.

"Grappling hooks, Mr Blackwell!" I announced loudly to my man. "Make them regret the day they decided to come looking for Marcus Reid and his Iron Will!"

The ever-faithful Gideon Blackwell then quickly turned and ran back towards the deck, where my men had started firing their rifles and flintlock pistols across the widening chasm between the two vessels. I wasn't worried for my crew aboard the Royal Navy ship; they were experts in keeping together and causing maximum havoc with minimal casualties, and friendly fire really hadn't ever been a problem for us.

"Grappling hooks! Grappling hooks!" I heard the man cry out as he ran the length of the Iron Will. Then in a flurry of activity, a number of my crew ran back and forth to the cannons atop the deck with long iron hooks attached to ropes that they loaded into the muzzles of the heavy weapons. A moment later, the cannons boomed again, though this time, they fired the hooks into the flesh of the enemy vessel, and the ropes quickly pulled taught. The Royal Navy ship had tried to turn, but our hooks had pulled it fast. The enemy was now stuck within range of our broadside cannons, but as she had already partially turned, she couldn't hit us back with anything at all.

As with every fight I had ever been in charge of, with each passing moment, the tide of battle swayed further and further in our favour, our indomitable will driving us ever forward.

The Iron Will held the enemy ship firmly in her grasp, and I couldn't help but feel a sense of pride in my crew and our unwavering determination. The Royal Navy had underestimated us once again, and they were now paying the price with their ship and their lives. Our reputation as a formidable force grew stronger with each battle we won and with each ship we sank, and with each victory, the whispers of our exploits spread further and wider afield.

My men continued to rain pellets and cannon fire down on the enemy from the deck of the Iron Will, but the battle was all but won. With that in mind, I let the ship's wheel fall where it may and made my way down into the fray. Three of my crew followed me as I made my way along the ship and to the boarding lines, and as a group, we swung across to the Royal Navy ship and landed with a loud thud when my boots hit the hard wooden deck.

My sailors had done a fine job at pushing back the enemy, and I found myself able to take a deep breath, inhaling the smell of smoke and victory before I readied my sabre and let out an ear-piercing scream, running towards the closest engagement to me with my small boarding party closely behind.

I was into the battle in an instant. My sabre cut through my opponents as though they weren't even attempting to defend themselves. These weren't well-trained military men; they were peasants, beggars and teenagers forced into servitude for the Royal Navy and her long-reaching arm.

I scowled at the insult.

"Send me real men, or you all will sleep at the bottom of the ocean!" I cried as I cut down another unworthy foe. I parried a slow, lumbering overhead strike with my cutlass and planted a well-aimed boot into the stomach of my next attacker. By now, the enemy had started to back away, and as I, my new group of bodyguards and the boarding party that was already here decimated the enemy ranks, it was clear that they wanted nothing to do with us.

A large sailor suddenly charged at me through the crowds of other battles, his sword raised high. I parried his opening attack with my own weapon, the metallic clang echoing through the air. With a swift kick, I knocked him off balance, creating an opening to deliver a decisive and deadly blow. As he crumpled to the deck, I turned to face my next opponent. This time it was a smaller, more smartly dressed man.

This one, I was sure, was an officer, and he, too, lunged at me, his rapier glinting in the sunlight. I narrowly dodged his quick thrust, feeling the wind whistle past my ear as the blade missed its mark. I countered with a swift slash, but he deftly sidestepped my attack. We danced around each other, each seeking an advantage, threatening to lunge, but both affording respectful distance to each other. Our blades clashed over and over as we tapped them, testing them, and finally, I feigned a strike to his left, and when he moved to block it, I changed direction and landed a solid stab to his right shoulder. He staggered back, dropping his rapier and clutching his wound. I feigned a sidestep again and delivered a swift punch to his face that sent him sprawling.

Meanwhile, my crew fought fiercely against the enemy sailors. The air around me was ringing with the sounds of steel on steel, shouts of pain, and the crash of cannon fire from our own ship. It was a brutal, desperate struggle for survival, but we were still very much controlling the battle.

As I fought on, taking down anyone who came at me with little effort, the Navy soldiers seemed to part to allow someone to pass. That was where I caught sight of a towering figure making his way towards me through the melee – the enemy Captain. His eyes locked onto mine, and I knew that our confrontation had always been inevitable. This was what Captains lived for after all, and this one single battle could determine the outcome of this entire engagement.

We immediately clashed like titans, our blades moving in a deadly ballet of thrusts, parries, and ripostes as members of both crews began to encircle us. They all knew that their own small battles didn't matter anymore; whoever came out victorious in the battle of the two Captains would decide which vessel had won.

I could tell that the Captain was a skilled fighter, but I was determined to bring him down.

"This is my ship, and I must request that you and your crew leave immediately," the Captain said in a gruff yet official tone.

"Afraid I can't do that, Captain," I said. "The Iron Will and her crew have never lost a fight, and we aren't about to start now."

I lunged at my counterpart, but it was a clumsy attack, and he saw it coming. He wasn't quick enough to bring his cutlass back to strike me before I darted back, but it was close.

The Captain, then sensing an edge, struck out with a series of powerful blows, overhead and cross-body. Without a moment's rest in between, I could do nothing other than shift to the defensive. I parried and sidestepped, barely keeping ahead of his relentless assault. My muscles ached with every blow that contacted my sword, and sweat began to bead on my face, but I refused to back down.

Looking up, I managed to catch a glimpse of my crew, their eyes filled with hope and determination. It was that sight that renewed my resolve. I had to win this for myself and for the men who had stood by me through thick and thin. The Iron Will was my heart. My soul.

With a roar, I redoubled my efforts, ducking under a slow but powerful swing. I took the chance I'd been waiting for and struck out straight-armed with my sabre. The tip bit into the Captain's chest, and he leapt backwards but the damage had been done. Red blood spilt from his chest, and he made the last mistake he would ever make: he looked down to assess his injury.

With his eyes off the battle, I took a single step forward and ran the Captain through with my weapon. He barely had the chance to look surprised before he slumped to the deck of his own ship and died right there and then without another sound.

With their Captain defeated, the remaining Royal Navy sailors quickly lost what little of their resolve that still remained and began to surrender in a wave of dropped weapons. My crew cheered victoriously along with my final blow, but there was no time to waste. I gestured for my crew to take the Royal Navy sailors as prisoners while I strode towards the entrance to the Captain's quarters. It was time to claim our spoils.

As I gripped the handle and pulled the door open, I couldn't help but feel a thrill of anticipation. We had won the battle, and now the true prize awaited us inside.

But my jaw dropped.

Not because I was greeted with hundreds upon hundreds of shining treasures, gemstones and gold, but because the room was almost entirely empty, save for a small wooden chest sat right in the centre.

There was nothing else for it. I strode over to the chest and kicked the lid open, which creaked annoyedly. I knew how it felt.

Inside, staring up at me, were three small gold coins, and a handwritten note on a piece of paper sat beneath them. Picking it up and reading it to myself, I felt my blood boil.

You think that you have become the bane of our existence, don't you pirate? But you can see now that the Royal Navy is one step ahead of you. Your resources are limited, and the only way that you survive is by taking what is not rightly yours. Perhaps you will eventually come to see that there is no limit to our power, no end to the sailors willing to give their lives in the hunt for scum like you.

We know that you are a skilled crew and a strong vessel, of that we have no doubt. But with each ship you sink, and with each crew you damn to their watery graves, think on how many men you have lost. How many resources does it cost you to do so? How many families have been separated by your piracy? Now look back in this chest and think to yourself: is it worth it?

In time, your ship will sink, and your crew will die, but the Royal Navy will continue on, forever wiping you from the history books and doing what we can to keep more men like you off the high seas.

So, please. Take these three coins and share them amongst your crew as you see fit. I'm sorry that there isn't more to compensate you for your time and efforts here today. I only hope that you can find some way of making such a measly amount equally shareable between you and your men.

But know this: From this day forward, you will lead a cursed life that you will never be able to escape from, and I will not rest until you, your kin and your friends are either rotting away in a mine or sleeping your final sleep.
I wish you well, pirate. And I hope to never hear from you again.
Goodbye, Marcus Reid.

Yours faithfully
Commodore Henry Atherton

I was no fool. It was clear what the Commodore was trying to do with this note and his handful of coins. I'd been told that the Royal Navy had been trying some new tactics already – trying to sow the seeds of doubt into a crew of free men by making the plunder easily pocketable by the Captain or one of the crew alone. It was odd to see a note along with it though; it was like this Commodore was goading us into further action against them. I didn't care for it in truth. Whatever this man had to say didn't interest me any more than what I was going to eat for breakfast the next day.

Once the entire Naval crew had been dealt with, and by dealt with, I mean that a handful agreed to join my own crew, bartering for their lives with servitude, and the rest had been thrown unceremoniously overboard, my boarding party made our way back to the Iron Will, though empty handed and absent the usual merry cries of victory.

Once we had all made it back aboard our vessel, the enemy ship slowly began to list heavily to the side, its weakened hull unable to continue on after the damage caused by our relentless assault.

Our boarding lines were cut, and with a final, deafening crack, the Royal Navy vessel quickly turned and began to sink beneath the waves, the unforgiving ocean swallowing it whole within a few moments. A cheer then finally erupted from my crew as they witnessed the final moments of the once-proud warship that had been sent to kill them all, and all that was left on the surface of the waters was a littering of bodies, sailors trying their best to escape, and chunks of the ship that once was.

I turned to face my crew, who were still celebrating their victory.

"Men, we have once again shown the Royal Navy that they cannot hope to defeat us!" I shouted, raising my cutlass in triumph. "Our determination and skill have carried the day, and our legend grows ever stronger! Long live the Iron Will and her fearless crew!"

My crew answered with their cheers, and I couldn't help but feel an overwhelming sense of pride. Another enemy vessel now called the ocean floor her home, and hundreds of Navy men had been thwarted.

"Tell us about the loot!" One of my crew called merrily, and others quickly joined him.

"Let's all share in the spoils of the great Royal Navy!" Another gleeful shout came.

I held my arms up in the air but couldn't help the woeful expression that had crept onto my face.

"My friends," I called in a rather melancholy tone. "I am afraid that the Royal Navy has been unkind to us today. Inside the chest was nothing to be found but three small golden coins." I thought it best to be straight with my crew, but the fact that the mood turned instantly sour made me second-guess my decision.

"How are we supposed to share that equally?" One man called.

"I want my share!" Shouted another, and what had been a merry celebration of our victory had quickly turned into an angry mob, all expecting answers from me.

I held my hands up again, urging my crew to calm down. "Lads! I understand your frustration," I said, my voice firm but sympathetic. "But we must remember that our fight is not against each other. Our true enemy is the oppressive Navy that seeks to control us and take away our freedom!"

I took a deep breath and continued, "This is not the first time we've faced adversity, and it won't be the last. We have always stood together as brothers, and we will continue to do so. Let us not be disheartened by the lack of treasure today. Instead, let this fuel our resolve to fight even harder against those who would seek to crush our spirits and take away our liberty!"

The crew, though still visibly upset, seemed to quieten and consider my words. I could see the fire of determination burning in their eyes once more, and I knew that they understood the true value of our bond and our cause.

"We are more than just pirates seeking gold," I declared, my voice full of passion. "We are a family, bound together by our shared love of freedom and our unwavering desire to live life on our own terms. The Royal Navy may have denied us our spoils today, but they cannot take away our spirit or our unity. So long as we stand together, no force on earth can break us!"

My crew, moved by my impassioned speech, erupted into cheers and shouts of agreement. The disappointment of the day's meagre loot was quickly replaced by a renewed sense of camaraderie and purpose.

"Bollocks!" a single shout quietened the entire ship, and I peered out to try to see who had spoken up.

"I say you found your treasure over there, and you're keeping it for yourself!" the same voice continued, and I could now tell that its owner was Anthony Cowley, my first mate and someone who I'd been friends with for almost two decades.

"Listen, I'm not…" I started, but Cowley interrupted me.

"Turn out your pockets!" he shouted, and many of the crew sounded like they agreed with his order. "This's been going on for way too long already, Captain." The way that he said 'Captain' told me in no uncertain terms that the authority given to my position was now very much in jeopardy.

"Men, hold him down and let us all see what our beloved Captain has been keeping from us! It's about time, I say, that we get what we're owed! How many years have we sailed under this one single banner without question? How many men have we killed at the order of this man? Do you not think that we all deserve a little more than, at worst, lies and, at best, a pittance? This is our ship, and it's about time we commandeered what's rightfully ours!"

I had no idea what my first mate was talking about. In all the years that we'd been friends, not once had we had so much as a heated disagreement. Now though, the look in his eyes and the tone of his voice suggested that he hated me with every inch of his being. I just had no idea why.

"There's no need for any of this," I said placatingly, but the crew were already advancing like rabid dogs. In the end, I had no choice but to ready my cutlass and prepare to defend myself. I never thought that I would be crossing swords with my own men, though, and the thought alone made my stomach turn.

As I raised my sabre, I could see the hurt and confusion in the eyes of my crew. These were men I had fought alongside for years, and now they were turning against me. Cowley's words had ignited the fire of doubt within them, and I knew that the only way to extinguish it was to prove my innocence.

"Very well," I said, my voice steady despite the turmoil I felt inside. "If it is proof you seek, then it is proof you shall have." With that, I slowly and deliberately turned out my pockets, relaxing my sword arm so that I didn't seem threatening to anyone. Once my pockets were turned out, all that was there to reveal were the three golden coins, which sat comfortably in the palm of my hand.

The crew stared at the items in my hands, and I could see the confusion that grew in their expressions. Had they honestly been expecting more? After all, what could realistically fit into my pockets anyway?

Then as I looked into the eyes of the man closest to me, I saw the reflection of the gold in his gaze. The way that the shining metal reflected the sunlight, the instant feeling that no matter how little gold there truly was, I knew this man wanted these three coins more than anything else in the world.

"He wants to keep them for himself," the man said slowly as though piecing it all together. "He thinks we don't know what these coins are worth…"

"What they're worth…" I started to ask in a very confused tone.

"Take them from him!" Cowley shouted, and once again, I had no choice but to raise my cutlass back between us.

The situation was spiralling out of control, and if I didn't find a way to defuse it soon, there would be bloodshed among my own crew. I racked my brain for a solution, and then eventually, it hit me.

"Wait!" I shouted, commanding everyone's attention. "I have a proposal. These three coins," I said, holding them up for all to see, "I will divide them among the entire crew. Let this be a symbol of our unity and shared purpose. We are all in this together, my friends. We've weathered hardships before, and we'll do so again. But we must stand united, for only then will we achieve our goals and find the riches we seek."

The crew exchanged glances, their distrust and anger slowly melting away as they considered my words. The promise of gold, however small the amount, seemed to have a soothing effect on them. Even Cowley, my first mate, seemed to be wavering.

And then, a fist collided with my jaw, causing a loud smack and sending me spinning down to the ground. It was only by some divine miracle that I managed to close my fists around the coins before I hit the deck, and my crew of Free Men moved in.

I was back on my feet within a moment. I'd taken a punch or two in my time, and it was going to take more than one to keep me off my feet.

I could see the man who'd punched me – John Dene – standing next to me and smiling as though he'd won the battle already, not knowing that I had managed to rebound so quickly. His two front teeth were missing, the rest blackened and all I wanted to do at that moment was to wipe that cocky smile from his face. So not wanting to waste an opportunity, I kicked out at his leading knee with my booted foot as hard as I could. Dene's knees hit the ground with a loud thud, and he let out a surprised yelp. As soon as I saw him drop, I planted my boot into his face to ensure he wouldn't be standing up again any time soon.

"Come on, the lot of you!" I shouted in my heightened state. Of course, I didn't want to actually fight or kill any of my men, but if they were going to come at me, I was going to defend myself.

As I stood there, my heart pounding and adrenaline coursing through my veins, I could see that my actions had made an impact. My crew hesitated, unsure of what to do next. They knew I could fight just as well, if not better than any of them, and I could see at least a little of the fear in some of their eyes.

But it wasn't fear that I wanted to inspire. I wanted their loyalty and trust, as I had always had it. Taking a deep breath and pushing down on my anger, I lowered my weapon and looked around at the men who had been my brothers-in-arms for years.

"This is not what we are," I said, my voice steady and sincere. "We are not enemies. We are a family, and families stick together. We've been to hell and back, and we've always come out stronger for it. Why this? Why now?"

I let my words sink in, hoping they would reach the hearts of my crew. I continued, "I have never, and will never, betray any of you. We've been through too much together. I understand that times are tough, and the desire for riches can turn even the best of us against one another. But I beg you, let us not turn on each other. Let us focus our energy on finding the true treasure that awaits us. Together, we will overcome any obstacle and achieve our dreams. We will take down ship after ship until there are no trees left for the Royal Navy to build its boats from and kill sailor after sailor until there are none left to enlist!"

The tension in the air slowly dissipated as I spoke, and I could see that my words were reaching them. Some of the crew even looked ashamed for having doubted me. Cowley, my first mate, stepped forward with a sombre expression on his face.

"Captain, I apologise for my actions," he said sincerely. "I... don't know what came over us... you have always been a fair and loyal leader. We will stand with you."

Relief washed over me as the crew echoed Cowley's sentiment, but then

I noticed he wasn't looking directly at me. Following his gaze, I could see that his eyes were fixed on my balled fist, the one that still contained the three golden coins from the chest on board the Royal Navy vessel.

In the blink of an eye, the placid Cowley turned from someone who had been beginning to see sense to a feral beast, entirely focussed on taking from me what I held in my hand.

Cowley drew the flintlock pistol that was attached to his belt, drew back the hammer and aimed it directly at my chest.

"Open your hand, Captain," he growled.

My entire body turned cold.

"I… are you going to use that, or is it just for show?" I asked as calmly as I could, though I knew it wasn't particularly calm.

"Trust me, mate, you don't want to find out the answer to that question," Cowley responded, jerking the gun towards my hand. Either you open your hand right now, or I shoot you, then open your hand for you and take what I find. Either way, the crew and I – as their new Captain – will be taking that gold from you."

I knew that I was completely out of options now. I couldn't fight back against a loaded pistol pointed right at me, but my former best friend and first mate had just made it very clear that whatever happened next, he was taking control of the Iron Will. And that meant that I was surplus to requirements.

"OK, just stop pointing that thing at me," I said, raising my arms in front of myself. "You know there was once a time when you trusted me, Anthony."

Cowley's expression didn't change. He simply watched my hand as it moved and kept the gun pointed directly at me. It was strange, as though he was mesmerised by the coins within, even though he couldn't actually see them within my clenched fist.

I don't know what made me do it, but I made a split-second decision and before anyone could do anything about it, I jerked my arm to the side and launched the three coins into the ocean.

"There you have it, Cowley. Mutineers get nothing because that's all they deserve," I growled.

Cowley, though, seemed like he hadn't heard me at all. Apparently forgetting about the gun in his hand entirely, he lurched in line with my arm and tried unsuccessfully to grab the coins from the air before they were out of reach. As one the entire crew on the ship – myself included – watched the golden coins sail through the air before they plopped loudly into the ocean, disappearing beneath the surface within a second.

The silence that followed was deafening. All eyes were on the spot where the gold had disappeared as if waiting for it to somehow resurface. When it became apparent that it wouldn't, the entire crew collectively drew a shocked breath.

Cowley turned to me, his face a mixture of rage and disbelief. "You... you threw it away. You threw away our treasure..." he snarled.

"That was never our treasure to begin with, Cowley," I replied calmly, trying to keep the anger out of my voice. "It was a symbol of the greed that was tearing us apart. And now that it's gone, maybe we can finally remember what we're fighting for."

The crew looked between Cowley and me, uncertainty and confusion written across their faces. It was clear that they were at a crossroads, unsure of which path to take. I took a deep breath and opened my mouth to address the crew, but before I could say a word, Cowley interrupted me.

"Tie him up!" he ordered. "We'll let fate decide how his life ends, as any Free Man deserves. Prepare a pistol and a single shot; Mr Reid will be left on the next sandbank we find."

The first thing I thought as my former crew approached was the irony that I was being called a 'Free Man' when I was about to be tied up and left to die. What I did know, though, was that there was now absolutely nothing that I could do.

Two men held my arms behind my back while a third bound them tightly with thick rope. I couldn't help but feel like they were being tougher than they needed, but also, I'd just thrown their gold into the ocean, so I could forgive them a little roughhousing.

Mutiny, though, was something that I would never be able to forgive, not that I expected my life to last very long now.

When a Free Man was kicked from his ship, the code that governed us dictated that he could be left on any stretch of sand large enough to stand on with a flintlock pistol and one shot – which could be used to take his own life if he so chose.

I only hoped that wherever I would be left would offer something more than simply sand and sea and the warm embrace of death.

Blindfolded and tied uncomfortably tightly, I waited for a long time before anything happened. I had no idea how far we'd sailed or in what direction, but eventually, I felt myself being picked up and loaded into one of our small wooden lifeboats. I was now being rowed, so I knew there was at least one person along with me for the ride.

"Listen, you don't have to do this; it's not too late," I said pleadingly to whoever was in the boat with me. I only hoped it wasn't Cowley. "We can go back and pretend none of this ever happened."

The man rowing with me didn't reply, and I chose to sit in silence for the rest of the journey. If this person wouldn't respond, then I wouldn't be begging for help; I was better than that.

I felt the boat eventually ground itself on whatever sand we'd found, and my restraints loosened just enough so that with a little time and effort, I'd be able to free myself, which is what I did with my next thirty seconds.

My hands once again free and my blindfold removed, I could now see the small lifeboat rowing away towards my former Iron Will. The pistol with its single shot was lying on the ground before me, and I quickly picked it up, aiming it at the boat that had left me, but I knew it had already gone too far away. Besides, Gideon Blackwell was the man rowing the boat, and if anything, the expression on his face was that of sorrow and regret. I didn't want to kill him, even if I could.

But whatever the reason, whoever was truly to blame, my reality was that I had been stripped of my ship, my crew and left to die on a sandbank that I could see was no larger than a few hundred square metres, with absolutely nothing on it that would ever come in useful. I doubted if the little sandbank would even still exist after the changing of the tides.

Chapter 2 - Marooned

I sat there completely dumbfounded for a long time. I could see the entirety of the desert island that I was on from the shore where I'd been left to die, and knowing that there was little chance of another ship happening past that would rescue me was vanishingly small, I resigned myself to the fact that after a day or two without food or water, that pistol and its single shot was going to start to look mighty appetising.

Time seemed to crawl by as the sun beat down mercilessly on my tiny island. The relentless heat and the salty sea breeze only served to exacerbate my thirst, and I knew that I needed to find a way to survive however slim the chances were.

As I scanned the horizon, hoping for any sign of another ship, my mind raced with thoughts of vengeance against Cowley and the crew that had betrayed me. I promised myself that if I ever made it off this forsaken sandbank, I would hunt them down, one by one, and make them pay for their treachery with their lives. But I still couldn't figure out why they would do this to me, and after so many years, so many adventures.

But first, I needed to focus on staying alive. Even though I could see everything that my island had to offer, I began to explore it, searching for any source of fresh water, perhaps in puddles from previous rainfall or anything at all that I could find useful in my quest for survival. I knew that my chances of finding anything were slim to none, but I couldn't just sit there and wait for death to claim me; it was completely against my nature.

As I wandered the perimeter of the island and my hopes of finding something good faded to nothing, I eventually came across a small outcropping of rocks near the water's edge. To my surprise, I found a shallow pool of water trapped within the rocks, likely from the last high tide. But there was no way to be sure by just looking at it. I scooped up some of the water in my hands and splashed my face with it, letting a tiny amount enter my mouth. The water tasted heavily of salt, and I immediately spat it out. It was no good to drink salt water; every Free Man knew that.

Then something caught my eye. It was something at the bottom of the pool that was reflecting the sunlight back up into my eyes, and as I moved, it shimmered and sparkled as though it wanted me to investigate it further.

Dutifully, I reached into the water, picking up the small round object. When I pulled it free from the small pool, I was utterly shocked to find that this small, golden object was one of the very coins I had thrown from the deck of the Iron Will.

I couldn't believe my eyes. The odds of one of those coins ending up here, on this tiny island, seemed astronomically low. Yet, there it was, sitting in the palm of my hand, shining brilliantly in the sunlight. I couldn't help but laugh at the absurdity of it all. It was as if fate was playing some cruel joke on me, reminding me of the very thing that had led to my current predicament.

As I stared at the coin, a thought began to form in my mind. Perhaps this coin was a sign, a beacon of hope in my darkest hour. Maybe it was meant to guide me, to help me find a way off this island and exact my revenge on the mutinous crew. But maybe it was a different coin after all, and maybe I was already starting to go insane.

I pocketed the coin and lay with my back flat on the warm sand. I couldn't help but laugh at the fact that the crew had mutinied because of these small insignificant coins and the fact that they had thought I looked to steal them from my men, keeping them from myself. Now, not only had the Iron Will lost its captain, but it had also lost those tiny treasures. I wondered if they'd take me back, knowing that fate seemed to conspire that I should own one of these coins.

Eventually, as it always did, night fell. I huddled against the rocks for whatever little shelter they would provide, the pistol clutched tightly in my hand. I managed to close my eyes and eventually fell into slumber.

Sleep was fitful and restless; I was haunted by dreams of revenge and the faces of the men, my friends, who had betrayed me. I didn't sleep through the darkness though, and eventually, I resigned myself to the fact that there was no more sleep to be had for me this night. Opening my eyes annoyedly, I was greeted with the sheer nothingness that my small island provided. I was lucky that the tide hadn't swallowed us entirely.

Sitting upright, I patted myself down in a habit I'd picked up when waking to ensure I still had everything that I'd gone to sleep with. In this case, though, there was little to search for. Save for my pistol and the single gold coin I still had in my pocket that was.

I pulled the coin out of my pocket, curiosity getting the better of me. The moon was high in the sky, casting its pale, silvery light down upon the world below. It was then that I noticed something peculiar about the coin; in the moonlight, it seemed to take on an entirely different appearance.

The once brilliant golden hue had shifted, becoming a mesmerising, iridescent mix of colours that danced and shimmered in the soft lunar glow. It was as if the coin itself had come to life, imbued with an otherworldly power that I couldn't quite comprehend.

I couldn't help but stare, utterly captivated by the beauty of this coin that I had thought nothing of. The intricate details etched into its surface seemed to stand out more prominently in the moonlight, revealing symbols and patterns that I hadn't noticed before. It was almost as if the coin were trying to tell me something, to reveal a hidden secret that would unlock its true potential.

As I looked more closely, I noticed that the symbols seemed to be a blend of various kinds of writing, some of the shapes looked vaguely familiar while others were entirely foreign to me. I had been educated in my youth, and was sure that I'd never seen anything like this before. They all seemed to be arranged in a deliberate pattern, perhaps forming a message of some kind that I couldn't make any sense of. I traced the symbols with my fingertips, following their curves and angles as if doing so would unlock their hidden meaning.

As I did so, the coin began to glow, casting a warm, ethereal light that enveloped me like a protective embrace. I could feel a pulsating energy emanating from the coin, a powerful force that seemed to resonate deep within my very being. It was as if the coin was alive, possessed by some ancient, otherworldly spirit that was now making its presence known.

I couldn't help but wonder if this was a curse or perhaps a blessing in disguise. Was this coin the harbinger of my doom, or the key to my salvation? As I continued to trace the symbols, I felt an inexplicable connection to the coin, as if we were bound together by some unseen force. It was as if the coin had chosen me for reasons that I couldn't quite fathom.

But it had come into my possession at this desperate, seemingly hopeless moment in my life.

I could do nothing.

Closing my hand around the coin again tightly, I shut my eyes as I imagined what possible wonders this trinket would've bestowed upon me had I been anywhere else or at any other point in my life. But now it was useless, so I cocked my arm back and launched it as far away into the calm sea as I could. I would be dead in a few days anyway, so what good was any of this? Opening my eyes again just in time to see the coin plop into the ocean, I stood and watched the place where it had landed, some small part of me waiting for something miraculous to happen. But it didn't. I was left standing in the moonlight, listening to the water lapping lazily at my feet.

Exhausted and disheartened, I eventually lay down on the sand once again, cradling my pistol in my arms like it offered some precious lifeline. Sleep came more easily this time, the combination of physical and emotional fatigue finally taking its toll on me.

When morning came, the sun's rays washed over me, slowly rousing me from my slumber. As I blinked away the sleep from my eyes, I realised that I felt different somehow, as if a weight had been lifted from my shoulders. I knew that I still faced impossible odds, but for some reason, I felt an inexplicable sense of hope and determination.

Stretching my limbs, I decided to take another look into the rock pool where I had found the coin the previous day and I froze in disbelief. There, at the bottom of the pool, was the very same coin I had thrown into the sea the night before looking up at me as though it was smiling.

Had I been dreaming? Was this some cruel trick of the mind, or had the coin somehow found its way back to me? Regardless of the explanation, it was clear that the coin was not ready to be cast aside just yet.

Kneeling down, I hesitantly reached into the water and retrieved the golden trinket. It felt warm to the touch, almost as if it were alive. As I held it in my hand, I couldn't help but feel a renewed sense of purpose and connection to the artefact. It was as if the coin was trying to tell me something, urging me to embrace its power and use it to forge a new path for myself.

This time, instead of rejecting the coin, I chose to embrace its mysterious nature. Whatever force had brought it back to me, it was clear that the coin was meant to be in my possession. Perhaps it truly was a magical talisman imbued with the power to change my fate.

I held the coin in my hand again, again tracing the markings and the etchings with the tip of my finger. I circled the surface of the coin so lightly that it almost vibrated beneath my touch. And then it happened. The most melodic, sweet sound began to arise from the coin itself, filling the air around me with an enchanting tune. It was as if it was singing to me, its mysterious, ancient melody resonating with the very core of my being. The sound was unlike anything I had ever heard before, and it seemed to emanate not only from the coin but also from deep within me as if the two of us were connected on a profound, spiritual level.

As the melody continued, I felt an intense surge of energy coursing through my veins, filling me with a newfound strength and vitality. It was as if the music was unlocking hidden reserves of power within me, invigorating my body and mind like never before.

And then the pain started.

In the beginning, it felt like a gentle warmth starting in my chest and radiating out towards my body, my arms and my legs, but within just a few moments, it started to change into a white-hot searing pain. It was as though my body was being torn apart from within, fire coursing through my veins until I couldn't help but open my mouth to scream.

But instead of a scream, a torrent of musical notes poured forth from my lips, intertwining with the melody of the coin. The harmonious notes seemed to be a language of their own, weaving a story of some ancient power.

As the pain intensified, I fell to my knees, finally managing to grit my teeth and clench my fists. I could feel something happening within me; my body and mind were being reshaped by whatever was happening because of the coin. It was as if the artefact was changing me somehow, reshaping me into something else.

I felt as though my entire body was being compressed. Smaller and smaller until I was tiny enough to fit through the eye of a needle. My bones creaked and cracked, and with each passing moment, I fought the urge to fall into unconsciousness because of the unbelievable pain that I was experiencing.

The symphony of pain and music grew and grew, getting faster and faster until the entire world around me, the music, the pain and the darkness all merged into one and with a loud popping sound, it was all gone.

I was no more.

In fact, nothing was any more.

I was alone. And the world around me was silent and pitch black.

Had I been blinded and deafened? I tried to open my eyes or listen for any faint sounds, the waves curling over the sand even, but I could hear and see nothing.

Panic.

I tried to move, but it was as if I were encased in an invisible, unyielding cocoon. The sense of isolation was overwhelming, and I could feel despair gnawing at the edges of my consciousness.

Slowly, however, the inky blackness began to dissipate. Gradually, my surroundings became more defined, as if the world was being painted back into existence with each passing moment. I could now perceive faint glimmers of light, the first timid rays of dawn after the longest and darkest of nights.

As the shadows receded, I realised that I was no longer on the island that was supposed to be my end. Instead, I found myself lying on the ground in an unfamiliar yet eerily beautiful landscape. I could see from the corner of my eye that the ground beneath me was shimmering with a coating of bright iridescent colours that seemed to defy description. The sky above was a breath-taking canvas of deep purples and blues, studded with stars that twinkled with an ethereal light.

Something wasn't right.

As I looked around myself, there wasn't even the slightest sign of an ocean or even sand. The glowing ground beneath my feet as I raised myself up stretched on for as far as I could see, in what I could only assume was the first morning light in whatever this place was, and trailed off into tall trees all around me, as though I was in some clearing in the middle of a forest made of unfamiliar trees in some unfamiliar place.

My instinct was to reach for my cutlass. Whatever had happened, I certainly didn't feel safe in this new place, but my hand simply clasped fresh air where my sword used to be. I'd momentarily forgotten why I had been on this island in the first place.

Then I laughed. It was the only thing I could do, really, wasn't it? It had only taken a day and a mouthful of salt water, but I had gone entirely insane.

I shook my head, still chuckling at the absurdity of it all. Here I was, in the middle of some strange landscape, seemingly transported from the desolate island where I was supposed to die. Was this all a figment of my fevered imagination? Or perhaps I had, in fact, perished on that forsaken island, and this was the afterlife? Whatever the case, I couldn't deny the beauty and wonder that surrounded me.

As I stood there, taking in the otherworldly scenery, I remembered the coin that had started this entire journey. I reached into my pocket for it, but it was gone. I couldn't even decide if the coin itself had been a part of my imagination or not.

I decided that, for now, my only choice would be to try to make the best of my situation. Whether this place was real or simply a figment of my imagination, I had little choice but to explore it and learn what I could about it. After all, if I truly had gone insane, indulging in my own delusions could hardly make things worse.

Slowly, I began to walk towards the tree line in front of me. The trees were like nothing I had ever seen before, their trunks spiralling upwards like the tendrils of a giant vine, their leaves a riot of vibrant colours that seemed to shimmer and change with every passing breeze.

Then the hairs on the back of my neck began to dance, and I had the distinct feeling that somebody was looking directly at me. I stopped moving and remained completely still for just a moment, and then I heard a rustling sound somewhere ahead.

I paused, waiting to see if I could discern any movement in the trees, but nothing seemed to happen as I watched. I gave it at least a minute, then decided that I must've been imagining things.

I took another step forward; then I definitely heard something. It was like every time I moved, whatever it was took the opportunity to mirror my motion, trying to disguise its own.

I didn't wait for it to happen again.

I took three quick steps forward and to within an arm's length of the tree line, stopping for just a moment to make sure this was definitely what I wanted to do before I moved onward, but as I lifted my foot to take just one more step, a golden beak the size of my little finger popped into existence before me. It parted to allow an ear-piercing screech to leave its tiny mouth and darted towards my face with a cascade of golden silk-like wings behind it.

I stumbled back and fell to the ground at the surprise attack of the creature, but it didn't stop there. The small golden bird floated above my stunned body, and as it did so, I took a moment to take in what I was dealing with.

Two jet-black eyes, a small, sharp beak. Not quite wings, but it had something more akin to the many tails of a fancy goldfish where I would have expected wings to have been. And it didn't seem to be flapping those wings like a bird would. The creature seemed to be able to suspend itself in the air above me, with its flowing appendages moving as though they were silk and it was underwater.

Not knowing quite what to do, I raised myself onto a single forearm and began the process of standing up. The bird-thing, though, had other ideas, and as it let out a second ear-piercing screech it lunged forward and pecked me on my forehead. Hard.

The sudden sting of pain made me instinctively cover my face with my hands, attempting to shield myself from the creature's relentless attack. I couldn't understand why this tiny, beautiful being was so intent on harming me. Was I intruding on its territory? Or was this just its way of communicating?

Despite the pain, I knew I couldn't just lie there, defenceless. I had to try to communicate with the creature to make it understand that I meant it no harm. With my arms still raised in a show of complete non-threat, I slowly stood up and tried to speak.

"Please," I implored, my voice trembling slightly. "I mean you no harm. I don't know where I am or how I got here, and I just want to find my way out of this strange place."

The creature stopped its assault for a moment, cocking its head to one side as if considering my words. It seemed to be studying me intently, its jet-black eyes piercing into my very soul.

Then, as if it had reached a decision, the creature let out a soft, melodic trill, and the tension in the air between us dissipated. It floated closer to me, no longer attacking but still cautious and curious.

"I'm sorry if I frightened you," I said softly, trying to keep my tone gentle and remaining non-threatening. "I just want to understand where I am and what's happening to me."

The creature trilled again, and then, to my surprise, it began to sing. The melody was hauntingly beautiful, and as it sang, a strange calm washed over me. It was like the music was communicating with me on a deeper level, conveying emotions and thoughts that transcended words, just like the coin had. And that made the hairs on the back of my arms stand on end.

As the song continued, I began to understand that the creature was not only intelligent but also empathic. It had sensed my confusion and fear, and it had reacted accordingly, giving me something that would calm me.

Then the bird moved closer to me with a wisdom in its eyes that I hadn't seen before. It floated closer and closer, and just as I felt as though I may have been able to reach out to touch the bird, its flowing wings began to spread out behind it, growing wider and wider and before I knew what was happening, the creature had entirely engulfed me in a warming embrace.

The golden wings had wrapped around me like a silk robe, and for a moment, it made me feel happier than I could ever remember. That was for all of two seconds before the pain began.

Once again it started as a subtle burning sensation on my skin, growing more intense with each passing second. I tried to pull away from the creature's embrace, but its wings clung to me like a second skin, impossible to remove, and whenever I managed to peel the creature's touch from my skin for even a moment, all I could see underneath was my skin being torn away from my body. The burning sensation intensified and quickly turned into pain, becoming unbearable, like acid searing my flesh, and I couldn't help but let out my own pained scream.

As my cries filled the air, the creature's wings then started to dissolve, melting into my skin as if they were being somehow absorbed by my body. The pain was excruciating, and I could feel the bird's essence fusing with mine, but with each small part of the bird that was absorbed, my pain was lessening. I knew I didn't want this creature to do whatever it was doing, but it had already got so far, and it was nearly over. It wasn't going to be a good thing, I knew, but I couldn't stand much more and there was nothing I could do.

Finally, the last remnants of the creature's wings disappeared into my skin, and the pain dissipated to nothing. I was left gasping for breath, my body trembling from the ordeal, and I fell to my knees. For the second time in as many hours, I'd experienced pain beyond anything I had ever experienced before, and if things were going to continue in this manner, it wasn't anything that I wanted to be a part of.

Eventually, my body returned to normal. Though when I say normal, I mean it in the most liberal of senses; I was still in this weird and unfamiliar place, and whatever had happened with the strange bird creature was surely not over yet. I didn't feel like it was within me, devouring me from the inside or anything like that, but there was surely a reason for whatever it had just done to me.

I looked down at my hands and turned them over and over again, trying to discern if there was anything different about my skin, but they looked normal to me. What wasn't normal, though, and something that I almost ignored because it looked so normal and in place, was the new, small tattoo of a bird on my forearm.

I didn't have any tattoos. Well, none that I knew about – one can never be too sure after spending his entire life as a Free Man aboard the Iron Will. Especially when you can't see a good half of your own body.

As I stared at the tattoo on my forearm, it seemed to shimmer slightly, the black ink catching the iridescent light that filtered through the strange forest and flashing a delicate gold. I had a deep, almost instinctual feeling that this bird marking meant something terrible, but I didn't know exactly why.

Then as if on cue, it began to burn.

Again my skin made me feel like the only course of action was for me to tear it from my body and run as far away as I could from it. The difference this time, though, was that the pain only seemed to come from the tattoo itself, not my entire body as before. It was the small things that made life enjoyable.

I forced myself to stand up, and as soon as I did, the pain stopped. It was like some divine miracle – simply standing up; I had never felt such relief in all my life. The pain had completely disappeared, and if anything, I felt, well... great.

Then I moved to sit back down on the ground to take a moment to appreciate how amazing I felt, and all of a sudden, the pain returned.

It was becoming very clear to me that the pain I felt was linked to my position – standing or sitting. I wondered if this was a side effect of the bird's essence merging with mine, or if it was a purposeful manipulation by the creature itself. Regardless, I knew that if I wanted to avoid the pain, I needed to stay on my feet.

But then, after almost a minute of standing still and doing nothing, once again, the pain started to build back up again. No, I didn't know what to think – it hurt to sit, and if I stood still for a while, it hurt again. The pain was almost blinding me by now, though, and If I didn't do something soon, I didn't know if I was even going to be able to do anything.

So I moved my feet and took a single step forward.

The pain lessened.

I took another step, and it lessened some more.

Then I turned to my right, and it was all that I could do to drop to my knees as an all-encompassing pain overwhelmed my entire body. My head felt like it was going to explode, and I felt as though I was going to vomit up the entire contents of my stomach. Which, in truth, wasn't actually that much.

Knowing that walking had helped, I forced my body to respond to my commands, raising myself back to my feet and turning back in the direction I'd been walking before I had decided to take the fateful turn. This time, I turned in the opposite direction, and this time, the pain dissipated entirely. Once again, if anything, I felt amazing.

I took a step forward, and nothing changed.

I gingerly looked to my right again, and I found that the more I turned my head to look, the more I could feel the pain building up inside me again, like it was some warning. I looked back straight ahead, and it disappeared. I looked to my left, and it started to build up again. It was now very clear to me that there was a 'wrong' way and a 'right' way to go. Not that I knew how or why, but when there was an option that involved no pain at all, and perhaps even something slightly better than that, I was going to take it.

So I continued to walk in the direction that seemed to be the 'right' way, carefully avoiding turning too far to the left or right. The tattoo on my forearm seemed to be dictating my path, and I couldn't help but wonder what purpose lay at the end of this journey. The bird creature had chosen me for something, and now I was following a path dictated by this new and mysterious pain.

As I ventured deeper into the strange forest, the environment began to change. The once vibrant, multi-coloured leaves gave way to darker hues, and the trees themselves seemed to grow more gnarled and twisted. Despite the unsettling appearance of the forest, I was compelled to move forward, guided by the pain — or lack thereof — emanating from the tattoo.

After what felt like hours of walking, I finally reached the end of my path. The seemingly dying forest had finally been replaced by a large, flat cliff face made of a bright grey stone, and in the centre, right in front of me, stood an opening. This was clearly some kind of cave, but why I was here was still a mystery to me.

I wondered if this was the bird creature bringing me back to its home so that its family could all peck at me and feast on my flesh, but I just didn't really have any other choice but to follow the path of least resistance.

The cave itself was dark, though I could see from within at least the telltale flickering of lit torches. I presumed that the bird, or even the bird and its family, didn't need torches, so this could only mean one thing: people.

As I stood there, taking in the sight of the cliff face and the mysterious cave, again I began to doubt my sanity. The entire situation seemed beyond surreal — how was it possible that I was following this strange path determined by pain under the control of a mysterious bird creature that had imprinted itself on my very skin? It felt like a nightmare that I couldn't wake up from, and the more I thought about it, the more anxious and uncertain I became.

Was I just a pawn in some twisted game? Was I being led into a trap? I felt overwhelmed by the unknown, and the thought that I might be walking into danger without any way to protect myself or escape was terrifying. It was hard to shake the feeling that this entire ordeal was just an insane delusion, a figment of my overactive or starving mind.

I took a deep breath, trying to gather my thoughts and steady my nerves. Even if this was all just a mad dream, I had no choice but to keep moving forward. Turning back was not an option — the pain that erupted every time I tried to deviate from this predetermined path was all too real, and I wasn't eager to experience that agony again.

I hesitated at the entrance of the cave, peering into the dimly lit darkness. The torchlight inside flickered ominously, casting eerie shadows on the stone walls. I had to assume that there were people inside, but who were they? Were they captives like me, or were they allies of the bird creature, ready to do its bidding?

Despite my fears, I knew that I had no choice but to press on. I cautiously stepped into the cave, each footfall echoing in the hushed darkness. I tried to stay alert, aware of my surroundings and prepared for any surprises waiting for me.

The air inside the cave was cool and damp, and I shivered as I ventured further in. The walls were lined with sparsely placed and lit torches, but I was yet to find any evidence of more life within.

As I walked deeper into the cave, my thoughts raced with wild theories and imagined scenarios. Was this place a lair for the bird creature and its kin? Were they some sort of ancient beings that preyed on humans, using them for their own dark purposes? Or had I stumbled into another hidden world, one that was governed by rules and forces beyond my comprehension?

Despite the terrifying possibilities, I couldn't help but feel a small spark of excitement. This was an adventure, after all — one filled with mystery, danger, and the promise of discovery. As I continued my journey into the unknown, guided by the mysterious pain and the enigmatic bird tattoo, I knew that there was no turning back.

Chapter 3 - Captive

Eventually, I began to feel the pain within me rise again. I hadn't walked too far into the cave, but there didn't seem to be anything out of the ordinary for what I had been accustomed to. There were more lit torches along the walls but no sign of anything else within.

But still, the pain was rising, and I got the impression that without there being any forks in the path or anything of the like, other than turn back entirely - and something told me that wasn't the correct course of action either – I was being told that in a moment or so, I was to come to a stop.

Then I saw the place where I instinctively knew that I had been heading towards. On the ground stood a small, lit torch illuminating a small pile of loose black rock and stones. It was clear that somebody – or something – had pulled these rocks and stones free from the wall, but as they sat in a small pile on the ground, illuminated by dim torchlight, I could see that they were a shade or two darker than the rest of the walls. Whatever this place was, I could only assume that it was a mine of sorts. And that meant I now had a job to do. I did not like the look of any of this.

I didn't even try to walk past the pile; I knew that it was where I was supposed to stop, and dutifully, I did so. Right now, it made no difference to me where I walked or stopped as long as I didn't have to deal with that pain anymore. Plus, if this was indeed some dehydration-induced madness, at least I knew that soon it would pass. The thought brought me back around to the memory of what my crew had done to me and the fascination of them in my place, dealing with this pain.

Standing still, I had no idea what it was that I was supposed to do. I looked down at the pile, but in truth, it looked as though the hard work had already been done. The rocks had been broken free from the wall and lay on the ground as though someone was supposed to come and collect them.

But of course, it wouldn't be as easy as that, would it? After about a minute of standing there trying to think of what it was that I was supposed to be doing, the pain that I felt crawl across my skin began to return to me, handily letting me know that standing still wasn't going to be an option.

Desperate to alleviate the pain before it grew to an unmanageable level, I instinctively reached down and picked up one of the rocks from the pile. To my surprise, the moment I touched the stone, the pain began to subside as though this was exactly what I was supposed to be doing. I grasped it more firmly and tossed it from hand to hand, and the pain continued to ebb away, leaving me feeling that same strange sense of relief I'd experienced before.

As I held the rock, examining it and trying to make sense of my situation, the pain slowly began to creep back, as if my annoying passenger was telling me that simply holding the rock wasn't going to be enough. Frustration welled up inside me as I stared at the stones and rocks scattered on the ground, unsure of what to do with them.

I turned my hand over as though I was about to drop the rock to the ground, but a sharp pang of pain quickly told me that it was definitely the wrong thing to do. So I bent over as though I was going to put the rock back down, and another wave of pain engulfed my entire being for just a second. I had absolutely no idea what it was that I was supposed to be doing with these rocks, and I could only think of one more thing to try; perhaps I was supposed to carry them somewhere. Clearly, standing still wasn't working, and keeping them in my hand seemed like a must.

But what was I doing? I was a Free Man, not some pack mule designed to carry rocks for whatever was truly causing this phantom pain. If it really was the bird doing all of this, then to hell with it. I'd had enough, and I was done with being told what to do and when to do it.

My patience was entirely gone, and with the pain mounting once more, I could no longer contain my anger.

In a fit of rage, I hurled the rock I was holding against the cave wall. The impact shattered the stone, and I didn't even have the wherewithal to notice the fact that the pain had all but disappeared, and now, the rock lay still in two halves on the ground, revealing a gleaming, black flint-like material inside. The moment the rock broke apart, the pain had gone completely. It seemed that the purpose of these rocks was actually hidden within them.

I picked up one of the halves of the rock that had been broken apart and brought it up to my face so that I could examine it more properly. To me, it looked like flint, but the blackness within seemed to shine with a depth that

I had never seen before. It was almost beautiful, mesmerising, and the more I looked at it, the more a new feeling inside of me began to grow: happiness.

It was like a warmth this time; I could tell that it was coming from the same place that the pain had risen from – somewhere beneath my skin in some all-encompassing cocoon of malice – but this time, I embraced the feeling as it spread its comfortable warmth all around me.

But of course, it wouldn't last very long; that'd just be too good, wouldn't it?

The happiness and warmth ebbed back away to where it resided and reminded me that my task here certainly wasn't to simply stand around and waste time. I mean, I still didn't know what it was that I was actually supposed to be doing in any of this, but guided by the pain and surprise when I was doing the things I wasn't supposed to be doing, it was now clear to me that breaking these rocks in half was a good portion of my role.

Puzzled but intrigued, I began to pick up more of the rocks and stones one by one, smashing each one open to reveal the shiny black material hidden inside. The more I shattered, the more the pain stayed at bay and on the occasion that a rock split to reveal that it contained a shiny, flint-like core inside, I even managed to feel the warmth and happiness again. It was like I was now being rewarded for carrying out the correct task, rather than being punished for the opposite.

It became clear that my task here was to break apart these rocks and expose the flint-like substance concealed within. But to my chagrin, only about one in ten of the larger rocks seemed to split neatly into what I had been seeking.

As I continued this process and all thoughts of defiance well and truly quashed, I couldn't help but wonder what purpose these black stones served. Was this some kind of test or trial that the bird creature had devised for me? Was there a deeper meaning to the pain and the path that had led me here? Or were they like coal - fuel for some fire that I couldn't yet see.

Despite the many unanswered questions swirling in my mind, I focused on the task at hand. The rocks, although still a source of confusion and frustration, now provided me with a sense of purpose and, more importantly, a way to escape the torment of the mysterious pain. And there was more. With each hit of the happiness I experienced from finding what I was looking for, it lasted a vanishingly amount of time less and less, leaving me wanting more and more. Each time a rock split and revealed the shiny black perfection beneath, it spurred me on to work faster, harder and do whatever it took to find the next one.

I found solace in the simple act of breaking the rocks; each shattered stone bringing me one step closer to understanding the strange world I now found myself in, but more importantly, it brought me what had quickly become my true reason for being.

Something else occurred to me after a short while: I hadn't felt the pain again for the entire time I had been working. It was like because I was doing exactly what I was supposed to be doing, then there was no need for the punishment. This really reinforced to me, though, that the creature that now somehow resided within me was making me do its bidding. And that wasn't something that I liked at all.

But there I was, completely under its control, compelled to break these rocks and unearth the gleaming black material. As much as I despised being manipulated by this creature, I had no choice but to comply. The alternative was to be subjected to that unbearable pain once more, and I wasn't willing to endure that agony again.

With every rock I shattered, the insatiable desire for that fleeting sensation of happiness and warmth grew stronger. It was becoming clear that the bird creature had not only found a way to control me through pain, but also through this addictive sense of joy it provided as a reward for obedience.

As I laboured away in the dimly lit cave, I began to lose track of time. My world had been reduced to the repetitive act of smashing rocks and the constant pursuit of that elusive happiness. Yet, with every shattered stone, I couldn't help but feel as though I was giving away a piece of myself, slowly losing my identity as a Free Man and being moulded into a mere tool for the whims of this mysterious being.

However, there came a point where I couldn't ignore the gnawing feeling deep within me — the part of me that refused to submit, the part that still clung to the notion of freedom and self-determination. Despite the pain and the lure of happiness, I knew that I couldn't continue down this path forever.

As I raised my arm to break another rock, I paused for a moment, pondering the possibility of escape. Would there be a way to free myself from the bird creature's control? What would happen if I simply refused to continue this task any further and just let the pain to what it would?

Of course, I knew the answer. But what else could I do? I wasn't a puppet; I was a Free Man!

Steeling myself for the inevitable pain, I dropped the rock and let out a defiant cry, challenging the creature's hold on me.

"I don't belong to you!" I shouted as I grit my teeth and clenched my fists, ready for the onslaught of pain. My words echoes along the tunnels and caverns away from me.

To my surprise, the pain didn't come immediately. Instead, there was a momentary silence that seemed itself to echo through the cave as though the very air was holding its breath in anticipation.

Then it hit me.

The pain was far, far worse than anything that I had ever experienced before. If I thought that the last few blasts had been unbearable, this one made me wish I had no teeth in my mouth because I had to clench my jaw so tightly that I was afraid they were breaking in half.

Immediately I fell to the ground, flat on my face, and I didn't even have the energy to arrest my fall. My arms clasped flat down to my sides, the last thing I would see was the ground coming closer and closer to my face, then the cold of the stones on the floor pressing against my cheek. I didn't even have the chance to curse the bird-thing for what it was doing to me.

I didn't know how much time passed.

I didn't know where I was, or even if I was still in the same cave system that I had been digging in.

It certainly looked similar, but where I had been in some narrow tunnel lit by torches, now I was slumped against a hard, cold wall, and it was pitch black.

I blinked a few times. Had I been blinded by the pain?

"Hello?" I called out, and my voice echoed away from me over and over. I must've still been inside the cave.

"Is there anybody there?" I tried.

I knew it probably wasn't a good idea to call out into some unknown darkness, but I wasn't feeling any pain, so that must've meant that I was allowed to do it. Well, that or the bird had finally left my body once I'd been rendered unconscious.

'Wait… allowed?' I heard myself think. 'What do I mean, allowed to do?'

I was right, of course. I had already started to think like a prisoner, and that certainly wasn't going to do.

"If it's all the same to you… if you can hear me… I'm going to be leaving now," I said, the words again echoing over and over into the darkness.

I waited for a long moment to see if anyone would respond to my announcement, but eventually, nothing happened, so I raised myself to my feet and…

That's right: pain.

It surged through my body once more, relentless and unforgiving. My legs buckled beneath me, and I crumpled to the ground, groaning in agony. My mind raced as I tried to come up with any way to escape this torment. I had grown to despise this phantom pain and the creature that had inflicted it upon me with every fibre of my body.

At that moment, I understood the lesson this experience was trying to teach me. I had always been my own master, Captain of my own ship, but now I was at the mercy of a force I couldn't control. My pride and defiance had led me to challenge the creature's authority, and I had paid the price for it.

"Will you please just shut your mouth?" a female voice came from the darkness, sounding terribly annoyed. The accent, too, I couldn't place. It wasn't awful, but I'd been to a lot of places and hadn't ever heard anything like it. "We don't get long to sleep around here, and I'd prefer it if we didn't have to listen to your godforsaken groaning."

"Hello?" I asked again once I realised that not standing, the pain wasn't there.

"I said, shut your mouth," the woman replied.

"But…"

"Shut. Your. Mouth." She said, leaving no room for another response. Though when I did eventually heed her instructions, she followed it up with: "Four hours to sleep, then we will talk. But please, just keep quiet and trust me, you're going to need your sleep."

I hesitated for a moment, unsure of whether or not to trust this stranger. But I knew that I didn't have much choice, and the promise of sleep was too alluring to ignore. I hadn't noticed it so far, but all the work I had done, combined with the fact that my body yearned for food and water, meant that I was incredibly tired. And I ached.

Besides, it seemed that this woman knew more about our predicament than I did, so I followed her instructions, laying my head on the cold stone floor and closing my eyes. As tired as I was, my thoughts kept racing, and it took me a while to drift off into an uneasy sleep filled with troubling dreams and echoes of the pain I had been experiencing.

Four hours passed quickly, and when I awoke, the woman's voice came again from the darkness. "Alright," she said, "it's time to make a move."

As my eyes adjusted to the now dim light – not entirely pitch black - I could just barely make out her figure, a slim silhouette against the cave wall.

I watched as she stood up and began walking away from me, and without missing a beat, I quickly followed suit.

I could tell that I was slightly taller than the woman, but beyond that, there wasn't much to say. As I followed behind her, though, I had the dreadful thought that if this wasn't something that I was supposed to be doing, then I was about to be in a whole world of pain.

But nothing happened. I breathed a sigh of relief as I realised that I wasn't about to be punished for following this person.

"Hey," I called out to remind the woman that I was still there. "Who are you? And where are we going?"

"Just follow," she replied, and again, I tried and failed to place her accent. "You'll see."

I opened my mouth to speak again, but deep down inside, I knew that it wasn't the right thing to do. I needed to be patient… obedient.

'Obedient?' I thought. That didn't sound right at all. I'd have to check up on that later.

As we walked, the light in the tunnel began to grow to a more social degree. Lit torches again began to light the way, and now I could see the woman in front more properly as I tried to keep up in my state of both hunger and thirst. My body felt heavy and weak, but having someone else around could only be a good thing.

But then we rounded a corner, and I found myself at the back of a long line of people.

People! This was definitely a good thing, but as my eyes followed the queue, eventually they reached the front, and I could see what we were queuing up for. There were two stone fonts cut out of the wall itself, the first filled with water and the second some kind of beige porridge. Gruel perhaps? I couldn't tell from this distance, but the sight of it gave me two conflicting feelings. I was so hungry that I was grateful for anything at all that would sustain me, but the look and now the smell?

I'd all but forgotten the queue of people in my search for food and water, though. They all shuffled along in silence, each drinking some of the water and then scooping some of the food up in their bare hands. Twenty-two people, including me, the woman who had yet to tell me her name, and not a single one of them was making even a sound. What was more, as I looked more closely at each of these people, they all seemed to have the same gill things where their noses should've been, just like the woman did after I looked a little closer at her.

Torn rags, tattered robes, blood and dirt were all that the people before me wore on their bodies, and I had just one single thought: These people looked very much like prisoners whose spirits had been broken. Absent the will to fight back, all that was left for them was to continue on as they were told and embrace the warmth of death when it would eventually arrive.

"Can we..." I started to say, but the woman held out an open hand by her side to silence me. I didn't argue. We shuffled along with the rest of the people in the line without speaking.

As we waited in line, the grim reality of our situation became painfully clear to me. It seemed that these people could only have been trapped here just like me; their spirits crushed over time, though I don't know how long it had taken. I couldn't help but wonder how many of them had once been as defiant as I had been, only to be worn down by the unrelenting torment of pain and suffering.

When it was finally my turn, I hesitated before drinking the water and taking a handful of the unappetising gruel. It was far from the feasts I was accustomed to on my ship, but I knew I needed sustenance if I wanted to survive. I hadn't eaten in so long. At least the water was cool, and it made my parched throat feel so much better.

The woman who had guided me here took her share of the meagre provisions as well, and we followed the person in front to a space on the ground just a few steps away. There were no chairs or tables, and everyone had just sat on the ground to slowly eat their food from their hands.

I couldn't help but study the faces of my fellow captives. I saw despair, exhaustion, and defeat in their eyes, and it was difficult not to feel the same emotions washing over me.

"We can't let this be our fate," I whispered to the woman sitting next to me, my voice barely audible over the sound of distant water dripping from the cavern ceiling. "We have to find a way out of here."

The woman had long red hair braided into a single thicket. Her eyes were green, and instead of her nose she had those gills – two on either side of where her nose should've been – that made it look like she was anything but human.

I almost fell over as I tried to move away from the creature. Whoever she was, I was now questioning again what the hell was going on.

"What... are you?" I managed to splutter out. In all my days on the high seas, I'd never seen anyone who looked anything like this woman.

"Don't be an idiot," the woman replied. "You know full well what I am."

I shook my head slowly. "Actually, I don't. I don't know where I am or even how I got here. And I have no idea who, or even what you are."

The woman sighed and rolled her eyes. "Fine. I am a Selari. You know, bred to be the rulers of a kingdom that never came to be, forced into slavery by the Entropics. Ring any bells with you? And as for how you got here, you were the unlucky recipient of the Siren's curse."

"Entropics? Sirens?" were the only two words I could force out in reply. My hands had started shaking, and the gruel had already started to spill out.

"Eat," the woman said. "It'll make it easier, you'll see." Then abruptly, she finished her own handful of gruel and watched, waiting for me to follow suit.

I didn't want to. I wanted to throw it onto the ground and run as far away from this place as I could. But I could feel my chest burning. Really, I wanted to eat the gruel more than anything, and every moment I wasted had begun to feel like an eternity of starvation.

Reluctantly, I brought the gruel to my lips and took a bite. The taste was as bland and unappetising as it looked, but I couldn't deny that my body was thankful for it. I forced myself to swallow, taking another bite and then another until I had consumed the entirety of the meagre portion in my hands.

As I finished eating, I realised that the burning sensation in my chest had subsided, replaced by a strange feeling of clarity. It was as if my mind had been clouded, and the gruel had lifted the fog. Despite its taste, I couldn't deny that it provided some much-needed sustenance.

"So," I said, wiping the remnants of the gruel from my mouth and with a newfound appreciation for the world around me. "You mentioned Entropics, Selari and Sirens. What's the connection? Why are we here? Spill."

The woman, who I now knew was a Selari, sighed. "The Entropics are a powerful, ancient race that once enslaved my people. They are ruthless and cruel, capable of bending the forces of the universe to their will. They are the ones who own this mine and the ones who we will be working for until the day we die."

"I don't understand," I said. "How does something like that happen?"

"The Entropics cause chaos and destruction wherever they go. Wild and unpredictable, they seek both excitement and power. That was why they created the Sirens in the first place."

"Created the sirens? Forgive me, but I don't see how some mythical creatures have anything to do with this."

The woman turned to me and looked straight into my eyes as though searching for something that I didn't know I was hiding.

"Sirens are not..." she started, then stopped herself. "Before you arrived here, did you pick up an object that looked valuable, made the people around you act out of character? Sang to you, perhaps?"

My mind immediately returned to the coin that my crew had stolen from the Royal Navy vessel.

"That... that coin," I stammered, recalling the strange events that unfolded after we had taken it. "It had a strange melody coming from it. I didn't know what it was, but it… and the crew was... different after we took it. More aggressive, paranoid. It was like they were different people…"

The Selari woman nodded solemnly. "That coin was a Siren, crafted by the Entropics. It has the power to lure those who possess it to their doom, and it led you here, to their mine, to work breaking rocks for the rest of your days."

My heart sank as I realised the implications of what she was saying. I had been ensnared by the cursed artefact, and now I was trapped in this godforsaken place, doomed to a life of servitude and suffering.

"But… why would a race of creatures capable of creating something use it to lure just a single Free Man into servitude? It doesn't make sense… and how do you know all of this? Were you ensnared by the Siren too?"

The woman stared at me again for a moment before answering. "I suppose you can be forgiven a little idiocy," she said. "As I said, I am from this place. The Selari were an experiment of the Entropics centuries ago. We were created to work as slaves for the race, carrying out all of the tasks that they found to be beneath them or boring. Once, they ruled all of the eight kingdoms, but now their enemies are too numerous to wage effective war on all fronts. Instead, the Entropics now have to mine, hunt and forage for what they need to survive and grow – but these are not tasks that they enjoy. They enslave any beings they can get their hands on, and that includes pulling in creatures from other worlds, just like you. The problem they face, though, is that it is a costly task to craft a Siren, and as resources grow more limited, fewer are created and sent out into the universe. That's why each Siren they create must have a significant impact," she continued. "Instead of targeting entire groups of people, they focus on individuals who are influential or powerful in their own right – leaders, and those with potential for rebellion. By capturing such individuals, entire crews can be brought to serve the Entropics, giving the best return on their investment."

There was so much information now coming my way that I could barely get my head around it all. If what this woman was saying was true, then my crew should've followed me through to this place, not marooned me to die on some godforsaken island.

"But it was just me," I said slowly. "The coin… uh, siren, brought me through by myself. My crew marooned me to die alone, and I found the coin in a pool. In fact, I tried to throw it away, but it kept coming back."

The Selari then opened her mouth and scratched her chin. She looked pensive for a moment and then finally spoke again.

"How did you come by the Siren?" she finally asked.

"We took it as loot," I said flatly. "It was on board a Royal Navy ship, and I took it when we overpowered them. I showed the Siren to the rest of the crew and offered to share them, but they went mad and tried to take them from me."

"Them?" the woman asked.

"Well, yes," I said. "There were three. Eventually, I threw them all overboard, but one of them seemed to follow me when I was kicked off my ship. Then I ended up here."

The Selari scrunched up her face as though none of this now made any sense to her either.

"H… how could any of this have happened?" she asked.

"That's exactly what I'm asking," I replied with a furrowed brow.

"No, not that…" she said slowly. "I mean, how did you withstand the will to keep the coins for yourself, hiding them from the rest of your people? Is it something to do with whatever this 'ship' of yours is?"

Now these were two questions that I had never been expecting.

"Honestly, I don't know," I said truthfully. "I didn't really have the desire to keep the coins and would've gladly shared them with my men. And what do you mean 'whatever a ship is?'"

"You had no desire…" the woman repeated slowly. A thoughtful expression crossed her face. "That's unusual. Normally, the Siren's call drives people to keep the artefact at any cost. It creates an insatiable desire for possession and power. The fact that you didn't succumb to it entirely… Perhaps there's something different about you, something that makes you more resistant to its influence. And with regards to your 'ship', I've never heard the word before."

"You've never heard the word 'ship' before. Seriously?" I looked at the woman as though she had grown an extra pair of arms. "You know a boat, vessel, something that you use to sail the seven seas on?"

"Seven seas?" she followed. "It doesn't matter. There's plenty of water around here, but you never want to 'sail' on it; why would you?"

I had no idea what to say. How did you describe to someone the inbuilt urge of every single Free Man to sail the seas, conquer the oceans and take from the rich? But beyond that, did these people not have to trade goods across the continents? Did they not want to see the world in more direct routes, faster than any other means?"

I didn't get to ask my question.

"We don't need to travel the waters. The continents of this world are all separated by water, but like I said, it's too dangerous to cross, and the enemies found in each of the eight lands are strong in their own ways. We stay where we are supposed, and that is that."

I took a deep breath, trying to process everything I had learned. The idea that the people of this world did not travel the seas was as strange to me as my own immunity to the Siren's call.

"And trade? Exploration? What about those?" I asked with wide eyes.

"I don't know of these things," the woman said. "But we can either keep talking and await the arrival of the next wave of pain, or we can get to work."

I couldn't help but agree with her. The idea of enduring more pain and suffering was not something I was eager to face, and if we were supposed to get to 'work', then I was all for it. Besides, the gruel that I had eaten had apparently settled in my stomach, and I could feel it giving me a new energy and a desire to work as hard as I had ever done in my life. Again, I didn't know if this was some property of the food, the desire to avoid pain, or the anticipation of the happiness that finding the flint-like rocks would bring. Whatever it was, it didn't really matter; the result was the same in any case.

The Selari then stood, and it was clear that I was supposed to follow. Along with the woman and me, a mass exodus of the cave followed, and everyone within, who had all apparently finished their gruel, slowly trudged into the tunnels beyond.

There were many tunnels and entrances that led away from what I could only assume was the galley, and not everyone took the same paths. The woman who I had decided to follow wasn't joined by anyone else, and if I wanted to keep asking questions, then that was fine by me.

"What's your name?" I realised I hadn't yet asked the question and immediately felt my cheeks redden.

The woman didn't even look over her shoulder at me as she spoke.

"Marina," she said. "And I'm going to tell you what we have to do around here to stay alive."

Chapter 4 – Hard Work

"So, did I die to come here?" I blurted out as I looked at the wall that housed all of the stones I had been breaking, what I could only assume was 'yesterday'. "I mean, it's one thing to suddenly wake up imprisoned in some dark cave, forced to work breaking rocks, but now you're telling me that I have to dig them from the walls with nothing but my fingers and nails?"

Marina nodded with a strange smile on her face.

"We don't have any tools, so unless you're hiding something underneath those strange clothes of yours, then we have no choice but to pull the walls apart with our hands. Don't worry, though; you'll get used to it."

I took a sideways glance at Marina's hands as they moved towards the wall and couldn't help but notice that her fingernails were worn down to stubs and the fingers beneath were black and calloused.

I was about to say that this was the last thing that I was going to do, that digging with my bare hands like an animal was where I drew the line, but before I could even think the words, I felt a helpful twang on the back of my neck. The kind of twang that reminded me of what would happen if I didn't do what I was told.

And so, without any other choice, I took a deep breath and pressed my hands against the rock wall. It was surprisingly softer than I had expected, with the texture resembling rough clay. As I dug my fingers into the material, I started to pull small chunks of it away, leaving tiny indents behind. It was tedious, slow work, but Marina was right – after a while, I began to adapt to the sensation.

I followed Marina's lead by leaving the entire pile of loose wall and stone on the ground where I was working, and if past experiences were anything to go by, this was the pile that I would then be working on, smashing the rocks in half and searching for the magical flint.

But this just wasn't me.

I couldn't just stand there and work, over and over, for no reason other than the fact that I was punished if I didn't. I was a Free Man!

"How do you do this?" I asked aloud, not taking my gaze off the wall.

"You kind of just dig your fingers in and…"

"No, I don't mean like that," I said. "I mean, really, how do you do this, day in and day out, without going absolutely insane?"

Marina stopped what she was doing for a moment and looked down at the ground as she replied.

"It… it's not been very long for me. I was only caught about a year ago, so I can still think for myself… the others… they've been here longer. They don't need to think any more, so they just work, eat and sleep. They don't talk, they don't want or think… that's what awaits all of us in this. We become the perfect workers."

"WHAT?!" I exclaimed, forgetting my task entirely.

Marina also stopped what she was doing to look at me with a quizzical expression on her face, like all of this was entirely normal.

"Yes, it's tragic," she said, her voice barely a whisper. "The Entropics have a way of stripping you of your will, your thoughts, your very essence. The longer you're here, the more you forget who you were. You become a hollow shell of your former self, existing only to serve them. I've seen it happen to many, and I'm afraid it will happen to me too."

My heart pounded in my chest as I absorbed her words. This was worse than any fairy tale I'd heard, more horrifying than any nightmare I'd ever had. I suddenly understood the vacant stares and the mechanical actions of the people around us. They weren't just exhausted or subdued. They were broken.

"No," I muttered, shaking my head. "I refuse to become one of them. I won't let this happen to me."

Marina gave me a sad smile. "That's what they all say in the beginning."

"But there must be a way to fight it," I insisted. "There has to be a way to retain our sanity, our identity."

She shrugged her shoulders. "If there is, I haven't found it yet."

I clenched my jaw, determination flooding through me. If there was a way to resist the Entropics' brainwashing, I was going to find it. I refused to become another mindless drone in this hellish place. I would find a way to escape or die trying.

"The bird…" I said, suddenly remembering how I'd come to be in this mess. "Is that an Entropic? The thing that got into my body somehow? The thing that causes all my pain?"

Marina shook her head, but her attention had already turned back to the wall. I got the feeling that I only had a few seconds before I had to follow suit.

"That's a Sylph," she said nonchalantly. "Beautiful creatures, and at one time, they were revered as gods. But now they've been twisted too, and they do the Entropic's bidding. Trust me, if you saw an Entropic, you'd know about it."

"How?" I asked.

"Just trust me, you'll know," she said. "But don't worry; they never come in here. Probably too boring for them, or they don't like to get their hands dirty. It doesn't matter, I've only ever seen one, and that was when I was captured. He walked into my town, set fire to everything he could lay his eyes upon, took scores of people as captives and killed the rest. We tried to stand up to him, but no matter what we did, whatever we tried, we just simply couldn't hurt the thing. And that was just one."

As I watched Marina's recitation of the destruction of her home, I couldn't help but feel the pang of sympathy, but then it was quickly replaced by the slowly building pressure that told me if I didn't get to work soon, then I was going to be in trouble.

Marina's story ended, and I did the only thing I could think of: I dug my fingers into the soft wall and began to pull the rocks from it, letting them fall to the ground with dull thuds that didn't echo.

I let out a low breath as my attention wandered. The image of an invincible enemy that could bring entire towns to their knees was chilling. I'd faced many a powerful foe in my life, but they had always been mortal, always been vulnerable in some way. The Entropics sounded like nothing short of monsters.

"There must be a way to hurt them," I murmured, more to myself than to Marina. "There's always a way."

Out of the corner of my eye, I saw Marina give me a long, assessing look, her eyes seeming to pierce right through me. For a moment, I thought she was going to scold me, tell me to give up such foolish thoughts. But instead, her lips curled into a small, grim smile.

"That's the spirit," she said, her voice quiet but firm. "Once hope is gone, there's nothing left but..." she trailed off. Then she turned back to the wall, her hands resuming their monotonous task of scraping and digging.

Of course, I had no idea how we were going to defy the Entropics or how we could possibly even escape from this prison. But I knew one thing for certain: I wasn't going to give up. I would fight, resist, and, if necessary, die trying.

We worked in silence for a little while, our movements synchronised, our focus unwavering. As I scraped away at the wall, I couldn't help but let my mind wander again, away into the voyages of my past, my mutinous crew, the golden Siren that had brought me to this place, the beauty of the Sylph who had entrapped me, forcing me to mine the black rocks for as long as I could stand… 'hold on', I thought.

"Marina, what are these rocks, and why do the Entropics want them?" I asked.

"You aren't telling me that you don't know what an Obsidian Core is, are you?" Marina replied, her voice laced with surprise. She paused in her task, turning to face me with her eyebrows raised.

"No," I confessed, shaking my head. "I have no idea, actually." The words sounded alien to me, and I was telling the truth when I told Marina that I had no idea.

Marina sighed, glancing back at the wall. "Obsidian Cores are… special," she began, choosing her words carefully. "They're not just some 'rocks'. They're rare, and they contain a form of energy that is… difficult to explain."

She trailed off, scratching her head as if searching for the right words. "Think of it this way," she finally continued. "You know how some materials can be used as fuel, right? Wood, coal, oil… they can all be burned to release energy. Obsidian Cores are like that but… different. The energy they contain isn't released by burning. It's… more complex than that. But the important thing is, it's a lot of energy. More than you'd get from burning an entire forest. But that's not all," she added, her eyes narrowing. "Obsidian Cores are also… transformative when someone knows how to use them. They can change things in ways that I don't fully understand. I've heard of them used to turn lead into gold, to make plants grow in barren soil, to heal wounds that should have been fatal… and those are just the things I've heard about. I don't know if any of my people ever knew what they could truly do. I've never met anyone who could use them."

Her voice dropped to a whisper. "I've also heard rumours… stories about the Entropics using them for… darker purposes. Warping minds, bending wills, controlling the Sylphs… Who knows what else they could do with them? I think it's a part of how they make the Sirens, but I don't really know."

"So that's why they want them," I mused, looking at the pile of rocks at my feet with a newfound respect – and a healthy dose of fear. These seemingly innocuous stones held a power that I could barely comprehend, a power that the Entropics could use for unimaginable ends. Looking down at them, I somehow now felt more powerful than before – like I had a bargaining chip that I could somehow use to escape this place, or at least barter with for my freedom.

"These Entropics..." I said slowly. "What are they like? Are there loads of them spread out across the lands? Or is it just a handful? Do they have ships? An army? Weapons?" I knew I was never going to fight these things single-handed, but any information I could get about them was only going to help me from my plans in the long run.

"Why do you want to know all of this?" Marina asked. "It's not like you're ever going to be able to do anything about it."

"In my experience," I said. "When the ocean is as vast as it is, there will always be an even bigger fish."

"I have no idea what you're saying..." Marina said. "But I kind of understand. In this case, though, you're wrong. Nobody can stand up against them. In truth, I don't know how many there are. The rumours I've heard are that they hibernate for years and years, and they leave Caretakers out to make sure their captives are carrying out their tasks properly."

I could already see that between Marina and I stood a chasm of unknowns, and I felt like I couldn't even begin to understand how this world worked.

I tried to turn over the facts in my head. The Entropics were a powerful race of beings who seemed to be able to do whatever they wanted, and they used the Sylph to enslave the Selari so that they would mine the Obsidian Cores. Only... I didn't really know what the Cores did. Marina seemed to be a little vague with the details, but I had the feeling that it wasn't because she was hiding them from me.

"Hang on," I said. "Didn't you say that the Entropics were now hunting and foraging because their enemies grew too numerous?"

"Yes, I did," Marina replied slowly, "But there are enemies and there are enemies. The things that the Entropics wage war against are on a completely different level than us and on the other continents. Truth be told, I've never even heard of an Entropic even having something close to a fair fight, no matter how many people stand against it."

"OK then, the Cores," I said slowly. "Have you ever tried to use them or keep them for yourself? I mean, if they're so powerful, they could be used as a weapon, right?"

Marina looked at me again as though I had just asked the stupidest question she'd ever heard.

"Of course not!" she exclaimed. "Don't you know what happens if..." she trailed off and placed her palm against her forehead. "I haven't seen it happen. But if someone tries to call upon the power of an Obsidian Core – someone who isn't an Entropic... they don't last very long."

"They die?"

"Well, yes… but the way I heard it was that they instantly exploded, unable to contain the power of even a single Core."

"But you haven't seen it for yourself?" I asked, deadpan. Marina didn't respond. "So what you're saying is that these stones are really powerful, and you've been told that if you try to use them, you'll die. But you have no evidence of that?" My mind was whirring into life, and I kept pulling on the thread that I was positive was dangling right before me.

Marina shook her head in silence.

I looked down at the small pile of stones and rocks we'd made and thought about how best to continue along this course of action. Bending over, I picked up a handful of the stones and began to smash them together, looking for the black, flint-like stones I'd found before. It only took four stones, but eventually, I found what I was looking for.

Dutifully, my pleasure response kicked in and again, finding this rock was rewarded with the immediate and all-encompassing feeling of joy and accomplishment. When that eventually dissipated, I held the Obsidian Core in my hand and turned to Marina, who had been watching me the entire time.

I could see in her eyes just how much fear the Core instilled within her. She seemed fine with working, digging the stones from the wall, but when it came to actually examining the shiny black object, she seemed almost petrified.

"My guess is that whoever wants these Cores – the Entropics probably – they don't want people to use them for themselves. If that was me, I'd spread a rumour that they cause people who don't know how to use them properly to explode. That way, my treasure would remain safe from thieving hands."

Marina was slowly shaking her head but didn't respond. Her mouth was slightly open as though she wanted to scream at me to stop being such an idiot, but I continued in my goading.

"The thing is, I'm not from this place. I've never heard these stories, and I've never heard of these magic rocks. So with that in mind, I think I might just keep them for myself," I announced.

Then I stopped.

Something wasn't right. If I really could use these rocks for my own good, then surely the bird-thing, uh, Sylph should try to stop me, shouldn't it?

I looked at Marina, not quite so sure of myself anymore. Of course, I didn't know what I was actually planning to do with the rock, but it seemed like just threatening to keep it and use it for myself was enough to petrify the woman.

I held the Obsidian Core out in front of me, biding my time and examining its shiny black surface. It was warm to the touch, and I could feel a faint hum of energy pulsating from within. I had no idea how to unlock its power, but the very idea of being able to use it for my own purposes was tantalising.

Marina watched me with wide, fearful eyes. "What are you doing?" she asked, her voice barely more than a whisper. She looked terrified, her gaze flitting between me and the Obsidian Core.

"I'm going to see if these stories are true," I said simply, meeting her gaze. I could see the alarm in her eyes, but I needed to know, and at that very moment, I made up my mind. I was going to free these people, I was going to overthrow the Sylph, and I was going to do whatever I could to fight back against the Entropics. Being a Free Man was everything. It was my life, and whenever I saw anything – some mythical creature or not – threatening that very belief, I was going to do something about it.

And if I was going to fight the Entropics, then I needed to understand these Cores. I needed whatever power they had, and I didn't have a moment to spare.

I held the Obsidian Core closer to my face, my heart pounding in my chest. The cave was silent, the air thick with anticipation. I could feel Marina's fearful gaze on me, but I didn't look at her. My focus was entirely on the Core in my hand.

I held my breath and pressed the Obsidian Core to my forehead, closing my eyes as I did so. It was warm against my skin, and I could feel a tingling sensation spreading from the point of contact. I waited for something to happen, for some sign that the Core was reacting to me, but there was nothing.

"What are you doing?" Marina asked in a surprised tone, all fear now completely absent.

"What?" I asked, opening my eyes.

Then I watched as her entire face changed, morphing into a wide smile. Then she began to laugh. It was a hearty, warm laugh that told of no malice whatsoever. In fact, the sound made me smile too.

Marina managed to compose herself after a short while. "You seriously thought…" she couldn't help but break out into laughter again. "You thought that you'd just press it against your head? It's like you're a child!"

Her laughter was contagious, and despite my embarrassment, I found myself chuckling along. I lowered the Obsidian Core from my forehead, feeling a blush creeping up my neck. "Well, how was I supposed to know?" I protested, a wry smile on my face. "You did say they were powerful."

Marina wiped a tear from her eye, her laughter subsiding. "Yes, they are, but it's not as simple as just touching it to your forehead! As I said, only the Entropics seem to know how to unlock their power. And they're not exactly handing out lessons."

Despite the lightness of our conversation, a sense of frustration was building within me. These Obsidian Cores were the key to everything - to escaping this place, to fighting the Entropics. And yet, they were useless to me. They were only useful if I could figure out how to unlock their power.

I stared at the Obsidian Core in my hand, its shiny black surface reflecting my determined gaze. "Then I suppose," I said, more to myself than to Marina, "I have some figuring out to do."

With that, I pocketed the Core and turned my attention back to the wall and pile of stones we'd been making. I didn't know why I hadn't felt the rising pain from the Sylph within me again, but I was definitely thankful for it. At least I had something to look forward to now, though: the beautiful feeling of breaking the stones in half to reveal the Obsidian Cores within.

After a long while, I actually found myself wanting to work the rocks. It was a strange sensation, not because I'd never taken pride or pleasure in my work; rather it was because I had quickly forgotten that what I was doing was forced. I didn't choose to be here, and I wasn't being paid – hell, I wasn't even a Free Man anymore! So why was I enjoying it so much? It was because each time I split a rock in half, and it revealed a shiny black Obsidian Core within, I was rewarded with an overwhelming sense of joy and pleasure.

I broke rock after rock, searching for that next hit, and when it came, I could barely remain on my feet because of just how wonderful it made me feel. Plus, as a bonus, I hadn't felt the pain return again for as long as I had been working; as long as I did what I was supposed to do, then I was left pain-free as well!

But that wasn't me, was it? Stopping abruptly, I felt my wits return to me and I assessed my situation. Could it be happening so fast? Was I already being broken by this place?

Marina was staring at me again.

"You felt it, didn't you." It was a statement and not a question. "You felt your sanity slipping away from you for just a moment, the will to work and to get to that next rock, only to be replaced by the realisation that it really isn't something that you want."

I nodded slowly but couldn't manage to push any words out.

"You get used to it. It'll happen quite often in the beginning, then it'll go away. It's when you stop noticing it that it becomes a problem."

The expression on Marina's face told me everything I needed to know about how she was feeling.

"Are you the only one left?" I asked.

She nodded. "There's no way back for the rest, and I'm not far behind. A month maybe before I forget who I am." Her eyes began to well with tears as she spoke. "I guess I'm just grateful that I'll be happy, I suppose, not knowing any better, just like the rest of them."

I honestly didn't know what to say. What could I say? That everything was going to be OK? That I was going to overthrow our oppressive overlords and break free from this place, undoing all of the damage that the Entropics had done? Even I wasn't stupid enough to believe anything like that. So, instead of making empty promises, I sat down next to Marina and put an arm around her. It felt like the right thing to do, to show her some kindness in this unfeeling place. We sat there in silence, the oppressive darkness of the mine pressing in on us from all sides.

"Marina," I finally broke the silence, my voice soft and determined. "I don't know if I can undo all the damage that's been done. But I promise you, I'll try. I'll figure out these Obsidian Cores, and I'll find a way to fight back against the Entropics. I won't let you forget who you are."

Marina looked at me, her eyes bright in the dim light. She didn't say anything, but there was something in her gaze that told me she believed me. Or at least that she wanted to believe me.

I had no idea how long we sat there for, but either it was a designated break time, or the Sylphs within us had decided to afford us a little mercy. Whatever the reason was, the result was the same. The pain didn't return, and in time we both turned back to the wall and resumed our work.

Eventually, a tiny pinprick of pain touched the back of my neck. It wasn't uncomfortable, just noticeable, and it made me start.

"That one means it's time to sleep," Marina said nonchalantly. "Pick up all the Obsidian Cores you can, and we will take them to the tunnel where you first came in."

Nodding and scooping up everything I could carry in both my arms, I dutifully followed Marina in silence until we found ourselves at the back of a queue of Selari workers, each stepping forward and dropping their Cores onto the ground in a pile. I peered forwards to see if anyone was coming to collect them, but by the time Marina and I had made it to the front, nothing new had happened. We added our Cores to the pile and turned to walk away back to the large open cavern that the light from the torches didn't properly reach. It was clear that 'sleeping' was no more than laying on a free patch of ground and doing your best to let your fatigue take you away into slumber. At least it wasn't too cold in the mine, and I still wore my clothes.

Marina told me to find my own place and to make sure it wasn't too close to any of the other workers and I did so. But lying down on the ground, I immediately felt something hard and uncomfortable digging into my leg: the Obsidian Core that I had pocketed earlier.

I checked with my hand in front of my face how well I would be visible in the almost pitch-black cavern and decided that even if the workers around me were conscious, taking the Core out of my pocket would remain unseen by anyone more than about a metre away from me, and that gave me an opportunity.

I pulled the Core out of my pocket and held it in front of my face again, willing it to tell me of its secrets, of its power. But it remained stubborn, simply glinting back at me with no motion to divulge its hidden wonders.

Then when I'd had enough of examining the thing, I was left with a new conundrum: what to do with the Core. My Sylph hadn't made any notion to let me know I shouldn't have it, so I could only assume that I wasn't going to be punished for keeping it. I just didn't know why not.

Chapter 5 – Caretaker

My life had begun to be measured in singles. And by this, I mean that only once did I try to walk away from the caverns and back into the outside world. Only once had I tried to see what would happen if I simply refused to eat or drink – rendering my physical body useless, and only once did I try to remain on the ground where I slept at the end of a long workday.

The Sylph within me let me know in no uncertain terms that there would be no second chances and disobedience was not going to be tolerated.

One day. That's what life felt like in the mine. One. Long. Day. Without seeing the outside world, or the glow or warmth of the sunlight, I had no idea how long I had been inside. The torches that were perpetually lit throughout the mine seemed to serve as a reminder that our servitude was eternal, and there was nothing that any of us could do about it.

I had tried to talk to some of the other Selari workers, but I couldn't get them to even look at me. They moved as though they were undead, slowly marching ever onward until such a time came that they would meet their end. To be honest, they all seemed nonchalant about it.

Marina had spoken to me frequently, though I couldn't say if it was because I was the only person that would answer her, or if she had begun to see me as a friend of sorts. I didn't mind either way. I liked that I had someone to talk to too.

I didn't know if mealtimes were set on a daily basis or not, but my Sylph gave me a handy nudge whenever I was supposed to eat or sleep. To be honest, it was kind of nice not having to make any decisions for myself.

The one act of rebellion that I had been carrying out, though, was one that I was keeping very much to myself. Ever since I had held that first Obsidian Core to my forehead and pocketed it afterwards, I had discovered that it didn't seem to be a punishable offence to keep a little for myself. I still didn't know what I was supposed to do with them or even what I had planned for them, but they were clearly both powerful and valuable, and that meant fair plunder for me. As long as I wasn't being punished for doing it.

I'd managed to collect a little pile that I added to each time I went off to sleep, making sure to hide my stash when nobody was looking. I knew that eventually it would grow too big to hide, but for now, I felt comfortable knowing that I was sitting on my own private treasure.

"What do they do with it all?" I asked as I pulled yet more rocks from the walls. "I mean, there's a lot here, isn't there?"

"What?" Marina asked nonchalantly as she continued her own work. I gestured to the rocks on the ground, not exactly catching what she couldn't understand about the simple question.

"Oh," she said when her eyes met the pile. "They just come and collect it every day."

"No, I mean, then what?" I asked. "And actually, who collects it?"

Marina's expression started off a little sarcastic but quickly relaxed, and I came to the correct conclusion before she had even replied.

"I don't know," she said. "Maybe it's the Caretaker? But no… there would be no way he could collect from all the mines in the area, would there? But then… maybe there's a group that collects? And as for what happens after, I have no idea. I would assume all of the Cores are taken back to wherever it is that the Caretaker spends his time so that he can look after them… or use them?"

I scratched my chin, deep in thought. There was just one thing that caught my attention in Marina's reply.

"So you're saying that there's a huge stockpile of these powerful artefacts out there somewhere, just waiting for someone to come along and take them?"

The Selari shook her head slowly. "No," she said flatly. "I don't know how many times I can tell you just how powerful the Entropics are, and you have a Sylph inside of you now… that's a process that can never be undone."

"Never?" I asked incredulously.

Marina shook her head.

"Once a Sylph binds with another person, they become one. But their fates are truly bound because once the host dies, the Sylph will also be no more." She held her arm out to show me her own little bird tattoo, and it immediately reminded me of all the pain I'd experienced over the last few days.

"The Sylph dies when it enters someone?" I asked in shock.

"No, the Sylph lives until its host dies," Marina clarified as though she was talking to a child again.

"No, I mean," I started to rephrase my question. "They enter a host knowing that it will be the last thing they ever do?"

Marina nodded. "Yes. It's what they are supposed to do, so it's what they do. I don't understand why this is all so difficult for you to comprehend."

I didn't respond to the insult. I knew there was nothing that I could say that would change her mind. Instead, I turned my attention back to the rocks in front of me. I needed to focus on the task at hand, or else I would never be able to escape this place.

We worked for hours in silence as I pondered what I needed to do next, pulling rocks from the walls and adding them to my pile. The work was hard, but I didn't mind. I was determined to get as much as I could before it was too late.

Eventually, the time came again when we were supposed to carry our haul to the tunnel entranceway to leave the Cores for whoever it was that was coming to pick them up.

We carried out the usual routine, and as soon as I returned to my little sleeping area, I uncovered my stash of Cores from beneath their loose dirt covering and added two more to their number.

It didn't take me very long to go to sleep once I had closed my eyes. Working for hours upon hours takes it out of you in ways that can't truly be appreciated without carrying out the task for oneself. But it didn't matter. Something was rousing me from my sleep, and I knew that I hadn't been out for very long.

I groggily opened my eyes, unsure of why I had awoken when my body still craved sleep, but all I was greeted with was the darkness and silence of the cavern around me.

I waited unmoving, staring silently into the darkness.

Then a groan came from not ten metres away from me. It was as though someone was moaning as their life was being slowly sucked from them, like they had nothing left to live for, and the noise was all they could do to convey their pain and suffering.

I tried to see who or what it was that was making the noise, but evidently, it was far too dark to see what was happening, and like the diligent Free Man that I was, I brought myself up to my feet and walked towards the noise that could very well have meant danger.

I only had to take a few steps when I came upon the Selari man who was on the ground, asleep yet groaning and moaning. I wondered why nobody else seemed to be bothered by any of this, but by the fact that I hadn't yet seen any evidence of true consciousness from the Selari in the mine, I wasn't that surprised.

I dropped to my knees beside the man. He looked older than me, some of his black hair was streaked with grey, and his clothes weren't much more than simple rags.

I gently touched his shoulder, trying to shake him awake. "Hey," I whispered. "Are you okay?"

His groaning stopped abruptly, and his eyes fluttered open. They were clouded with pain and confusion, but when he saw me, I was almost certain that a spark of clarity flickered in their depths. But then his eyes rolled back in his head, and he slumped back onto the ground.

In a panic, I checked for a pulse. It was weak and erratic, but it was there. His skin was hot to the touch and slick with sweat, indicating some kind of fever.

Then the Selari opened his mouth and let out a loud, shrill scream that almost caused me to bring my hands up to my ears.

I needed to do something. But I had no idea what.

Then my mind fell back upon the place where I had been sleeping, the place where I had been squirrelling away the magical Obsidian Cores, and I did the only thing I could think of at that moment. I rushed to my secret hiding place, dug up one of the Cores and took it back to the pained Selari, pressing it against his chest. I had thoughts of Marina laughing at me for being so stupid again, but I had to at least try something, and if this man was dying anyway, then what was the harm?

To my surprise, the man's scream abated, fading away to nothing more than a faint whimper, and I was about to become very pleased with myself when I looked up to see the entire complement of miners standing around me as though I was about to be tied up and thrown overboard. 'Why does this all seem so familiar?' I thought.

I didn't know if I was now being surrounded because I had helped the pained Selari in a way in which I shouldn't have, or if it was the manner in which I had helped.

My question was quickly answered, though, because as I stared up at the blank faces surrounding me, as though in the blink of an eye, a new face appeared not three inches from my own.

Whatever the thing was, it could clearly move faster than anything I'd ever encountered before. Its eyes glowed a bright blue which seemed to leak out like some magical mist, and attached to its skin were pieces of metal that looked like they'd been poured onto him, fusing man and metal together. Behind the face, I could see a bright orange glow, like he'd arrived with a trail of fire and as I looked up to assess the creature in its entirety, I could see that his muscular physique was entirely shirtless.

There was no doubt in my mind that this was an Entropic. This was the Caretaker and Marina had been right, there was no mistaking one of these beings. Almost human, but certainly more... Godlike.

If I said I wasn't terrified, then I'd be lying. In my life, I'd fought and killed countless men, suffered terrible wounds, stood face to face with the swirling stormy seas aboard the Iron Will, and walked through cannon, rifle and pistol fire towards enemies who were stronger than me. But this Entropic turned my very soul cold.

The Caretaker wasn't much larger than me, but I could tell that it would stand at an easy seven feet if it straightened itself up, but what was more terrifying was the fact that it seemed to be smiling at me.

"Hello," the Caretaker said in a pleasant, official tone.

I opened my mouth to reply, but the words seemed to be stuck within me somehow. I looked around the mine for help, but the Selari workers just stood there watching. I could see Marina gaping at me and the Entropic wordlessly too.

"What's the matter? Never seen a God before?" the Caretaker asked, still smiling.

"I..." I managed to force it out through sheer determination of willpower. I refused to be pressed into the ground by this creature, and it took almost everything within me to say just that one single word.

"Curious," the Entropic said, his smile shifting for just an instant. "I would like to know what you think that you are doing with my Obsidian Core."

As the Entropic spoke, I felt the weight of his words pushing me down into the ground. In my kneeling position, I knew that I wouldn't be able to stand upright with the force of this presence before me and truth be told, it very much felt like this thing was a God to me.

"I... I was trying to help him," I finally managed to say, my voice barely above a whisper. I pointed towards the Selari man, who seemed to be breathing easier now. The Obsidian Core still lay on his chest, its surface gleaming in the dim torchlight.

The Entropic didn't move. He just kept staring at me, his icy blue eyes glowing in the darkness. I could still feel his gaze on me, like a physical weight, and I had to resist the urge to look away. I had to show him that I wasn't afraid, even though every instinct in me was screaming to run.

"Help him?" The Entropic repeated my words, tilting his head slightly. "That's not your job. Your job is to mine. That's all."

"But he was in pain..." I started to protest, but the Entropic cut me off with a wave of his hand.

"And now he is not. But he will be again tomorrow, and you will not have your secreted Obsidian Core to help him with then, will you, thief?"

"I'm not a thief," I wheezed. "I only wanted… to help."

"I do not like people who want to help in my mines. I do not like people who think in my mines. I think that your time has finally come to an end here, my servant. Your cost has outweighed your worth."

The Entropic then raised a hand as though he was going to do something, and I knew I had just precious seconds left to live.

"Wait!" I shouted, raising my hands.

The Caretaker's own hand stopped mid-action. I didn't know what it was going to do, but I had no doubt that it was going to be something truly powerful.

"I wish to parlay!" I said. It was the only thing that came to mind.

"And what is that?" the Caretaker replied, clearly intrigued by my request.

"Where I come from, if someone invokes parlay, it means that person is allowed to negotiate freely with whoever is in charge. I want to know who your Captain… uh, leader is, and I want to talk to him."

"Fool!" the Caretaker roared. "Your customs mean nothing to me, and there is nobody with higher authority than I!" his words again pushed down on me so hard that this time I felt my knees buckle, and I had no choice but to bow down before the being on all fours.

"I have never witnessed such insolence from a slave, a nothing. Death would be too easy for you. But we will have to make sure that you'll never be able to 'parlay' ever again, won't we?" Even though I couldn't raise my head to see the Caretaker's expression, I could hear the devious smile in his words.

Then I saw his hand reach down and remove the Core from the Selari's chest, who whimpered the moment it was removed, and I felt a large hand on the bottom of my chin, forcing me to look up again.

"Open your mouth," the Caretaker ordered.

I clamped my jaw shut as tightly as I could. Whatever the Entropic had planned for me, I wasn't going to go quietly.

Then he began to squeeze my cheeks, forcing my jaw to separate and my mouth to open. I could now truly see the evil smile on his face as he placed the small Obsidian Core into my mouth and pressed my jaw shut, forcing me to bite down on the rock.

The Obsidian Core was smooth and cold against my tongue, its weight strange and unwelcome. I could feel the power pulsing from it, filling my mouth with a tingling energy that was both invigorating and terrifying. I tried to spit it out, but the Entropic's grip on my jaw was unyielding.

"Learn your place," the Entropic said, his voice echoing through the cavern. "You will feel the power you do not deserve, and it will be the last thing you ever feel before you are torn apart from within."

With a sudden release, he let go of my jaw. I gasped for air, my tongue working frantically to push the Obsidian Core out of my mouth. But it was too late. The Core had already begun to dissolve, its power seeping into my body.

I could feel it spreading, the energy coursing through my veins like wildfire. It was unlike anything I'd ever felt before, filling me with an intense heat that was both painful and exhilarating. My muscles seized and relaxed in rapid succession, my vision blurred, and the world around me began to spin. All I could think about was what Marina had told me about the Cores: nobody could use them except the Entropics. I was going to die, and I only hoped that it was going to happen quickly.

Then, as quickly as it had started, it stopped. The remnants of the Core were gone, dissolved completely, and I was left gasping on the cavern floor. The Entropic was still standing over me, and I drew on every last ounce of strength within me to look up at the creature.

I smiled at him. I *smiled* at him.

"HOW DARE YOU!" the Caretaker roared, and he raised his hand again as though to strike me down.

"How dare YOU!" I shouted back, now completely able to articulate in the way I wanted. "I am a FREE MAN! I've fought enemies with reputations that would make you green with envy, and I've sunk ships that were so large that you'd become lost below deck. I am feared in all the seven seas because I am Marcus Reid, Captain of the unsinkable Iron Will, and you will pay me the respect that I am due!"

I didn't know where it came from, and I certainly didn't know if it was the right thing to do, but the Caretaker stuttered. It was like nobody had ever dared to speak back to him before, and he had no idea what to do.

Eventually, he came to his conclusion. He grabbed me by the shirt, picked me up off the ground and dragged me towards the tunnel entrance, along the torchlit corridors and out into the orange morning sun. It was like I weighed nothing and my heart began to pound at the thought of what was going to happen next. The once vivid and vibrant world was now simply bright, the vivid colours all a distant memory, and I didn't know if this was the way it was or if the perpetual darkness had affected my eyesight.

To my surprise, the mine's entire complement followed us out into the sunlight and formed a large circle around us, like it was some kind of fighting arena.

The Entropic threw me down to the ground with an expression that told me he hated me with all of his being.

"I will show you what it is to be feared. I will show you how a God is supposed to act, and I will show you that you are nothing in this world but a slave. Your life is mine to do with as I wish, and I alone will decide your fate."

The Caretaker then cracked his knuckles and bore down on me slowly. I prepared myself as best I could, jumping up to my feet and raising my fists before my face, ready to fight this creature as best I could.

I didn't even see the first punch coming. It was as though I'd been hit by an iron cannonball fired at me from point-blank range. It had hit the back of my fist where I'd thought to block the strike, but instead of a block, the punch just pushed my own fist against my jaw and sent me spiralling through the air. Before I even hit the ground, the Caretaker appeared next to me and planted a boot into my midriff sending me flying.

I felt all of my ribs break as the wind left my body, and I flew through the air at a speed I hadn't ever experienced before. I was almost grateful when my back impacted the hard stone wall beside the tunnel entrance. I would've been more grateful if it had killed me there and then, though, because as it was, I felt my spine break in two and again the Caretaker was on me in the blink of an eye.

He punched me in the stomach, the chest, my jaw and my temple and with each punch, I both heard and felt my bones break and snap. Then, when my entire world was in pain, and I was seconds away from being conscious no longer, he took hold of my jaw, forcing my gaze to meet his.

"You are nothing," the Caretaker growled. "And I give you the gift of life so that you may remember this lesson and serve me for the rest of your pitiful life."

Chapter 6 – Recovery

I stared at the black ceiling, not knowing if I was going to live or die. My body had been broken to a degree that even I hadn't thought possible. It felt like all of my bones were broken, and I was covered with bruises, blood and cuts. But none of that really mattered, did it? Because I couldn't even look down to appraise the damage if I wanted to. I had been carried back into the cavern and lay on the ground, entirely unable to move for myself.

I had lay on the ground, staring straight upwards for what felt like an eternity. Marina hadn't said a single word to me, though I couldn't be sure if it was because she had been working in the mine all this time or if her Sylph was preventing her from having any contact with me. I could only assume that the rules had been tightened since my very one-sided fight and loss to the Entropic. If you could even call it a fight.

I resigned myself to the fact that I was simply being left here to die alone and in a moderate amount of pain.

But that wasn't right, was it? Surely, I should've been in a severe amount of pain with all the injuries I'd sustained, shouldn't I? And when had it faded from severe to moderate anyway? I began inwardly searching for the answers that I knew weren't going to come to me easily and spent a long time just sending my consciousness to the extremities of my person to try to divine if there was anything telling there.

Of course, there wasn't. I still couldn't actually move my body, but the pain I had been experiencing had certainly fallen to a far more tolerable level.

Sometime later, I heard someone approaching me in the darkness, and I could only assume it was Marina; nobody else would take the time, and I even doubted if the rest of the Selari actually even acknowledged my presence.

It was indeed Marina. The woman shuffled what I would have said was needlessly close to me, and as I was just thinking that there was no need for anyone to invade my personal space in such a way, I felt something hard land on my stomach. I was grateful for the location of the impact because had it been on my broken ribs, the pain might've just sent me over the edge. If it was a little lower, well that didn't even bare thinking about.

I wanted to look down at myself to see what had landed on me, but still, I was unable to move. What I did know, though, was that the thing that had come to rest upon me was giving off a warmth that felt somewhat pleasant. It could only have been one thing, as Marina had passed – and I knew she had moved away now judging by the sound of her delicate footsteps – she'd dropped an Obsidian Core onto me.

The warmth radiating from the Obsidian Core was soothing, immediately easing some of the sharpness of my pain. I could feel a strange tingling sensation spreading from the point of contact, like tiny tendrils reaching out to the damaged parts of my body. It wasn't healing me, I knew that much. But it was dulling the pain, making it bearable, and for that I was grateful.

I wasn't sure how much time had passed since the Entropic had left me broken and battered. Marina had been my only visitor, always under the cover of darkness. She would silently approach me, place an Obsidian Core on my body, and then disappear.

With my assumption of each passing day, I could feel my strength returning, albeit slowly. The dull ache in my ribs had reduced to a tolerable throb, and I could now move my fingers and toes with minimal effort. I was far from healed, but I was no longer at death's door either.

But there was one thing that still bothered me. When the Entropic had forced the Core into my mouth, he had looked so surprised. As though he was expecting it to be my end. Marina had said that nobody but the Entropics could handle their power, so how did I survive such an ordeal?

I wasn't sure if any of the Obsidian Core was still inside my body, but there was nothing that I could do about it if there was. The Obsidian Cores atop me were, in a twisted way, a reminder of my defeat, a symbol of my servitude to the Entropic.

But I knew that it was also a source of strength. With every passing day, the Obsidian Cores seemed to be making me stronger, their energy more potent. I could feel power pulsating within me, like a second heartbeat. It was a strange sensation, but it gave me hope. If the Obsidian Cores could make me stronger, maybe I really could use them to fight back.

Maybe, just maybe, I could find a way to use them to defeat the Entropics. But first, I needed to recover. I needed to regain my strength, to heal my broken body. And for that, I needed more.

"I don't think that's a very good idea, not at all," a very high-pitched, female and anxious-sounding voice reached my ears, and it almost made me jump.

"Oh dear, certainly not something I would do..."

I forced my mouth open slowly, about the say the first words I had uttered in what was certainly days when the voice spoke again.

"He shouldn't be thinking about fighting back, he should just be doing what he's told like a good worker, and nobody would get hurt or upset."

But there was something odd about this voice. It wasn't coming from within the cavern, reaching my ears as I had first supposed. This voice, somehow, in the strangest way I could possibly have ever imagined, was coming from somewhere within my head.

"Hello?" I pointedly thought inwardly.

Silence.

"I can hear you," I thought towards the voice.

"Oh holy crap, is he really talking to me?" the voice said.

"Yes," I thought curtly. "Who are you?"

Silence.

"Who are you?" I repeated. "And what are you doing in my head?"

"You really can hear me, can't you?" she said.

"Yes, I really can hear you, and if you don't start answering questions any time soon, I'll..." I trailed off, knowing full well that I was in no position to make any threats, least of all to a voice that seemed to reside within my head.

"I... I am the Sylph that is bound to you..." the voice replied slowly. "Or, more accurately, what is left of her."

I blinked. "You're the bird who's been causing me all this pain?" I asked incredulously. "The one who's been forcing me to work, digging for rocks with my bare hands?!"

"But I don't understand this," Sylph replied. "You shouldn't be able to talk to me like this. If they find out... If anyone finds out... oh please... I don't want to die. Please!"

I had absolutely no idea what was happening. This creature seemed, for some reason, to be begging me for mercy, as though I had some kind of power over its life.

"I don't want to kill you," I said honestly. "I want you out of my body. I want you out of my head, and I want to go home!" I couldn't help my internal voice from rising again as I spoke. I was upset, and understandably so.

"But... you've been marked," the Sylph said as though that meant something to me. "There is no way for us to part, for we are now one and the same. If you die, then I will die along with you."

I let Sylph's words sink in, struggling to keep up with the creature. If I died, it died. I knew that. But had I been marked? What did any of this mean?

"You're going to need to explain more than that," I thought bitterly. "You're the one who's been controlling me, right? You're the one who made me work in the mine, who made me face the Entropic."

"That wasn't my fault," Sylph's voice returned, sounding distressed. "We have to keep you working. The Entropics, they... they force us to bind to you. They use us to control you, to force you to do their bidding. But it's not our choice; they make us!"

I was silent for a moment, trying to digest this information. "So, you're a prisoner too?" I asked finally, picking up on the distress and hearing the truth in her words.

"Yes," the Sylph answered, her voice filled with relief. "Yes, I am. I was captured, forced to bind to you. I have no control over my own actions, just as you don't."

"But why can I hear you now? Why are you in my head?" I asked, frowning in the darkness. "And what does it mean that I've been marked?"

"The mark... It's a symbol of the bond between us," the Sylph explained. "It's not something that can be removed. It's... permanent. You can see it on your skin. And as for why you can hear me now... it must be because of the Cores. When the Entropic forced it into your mouth, it... it did something. I felt it. It changed the bond between us. It made it stronger."

I was silent for a moment, my mind reeling with the implications of this. If what Sylph was saying was true, then we were stuck together, whether we liked it or not. And if we were to survive, we would have to work together. I remembered the tattoo on my arm, though, and how it had appeared when the Sylph had dissolved into me.

"Can you help me?" I asked finally. "Can you help me get out of here to fight the Entropic?"

"No no no! Nobody can fight the Entropics," the anxious voice replied. "They keep Sylphs locked up to experiment on. Almost every Sylph on this continent is in the hands of the Entropics... my kin... my family... that's how they keep forcing us to do what we do, and if we fight back, they'll all die. Even if there was a way we could stand up to them."

What the Sylph was saying only served to cement my hatred for the Entropics even more. Everything I knew about them told me that they were worse than the worst men I'd ever had the misfortune to know. They were slavers, murderers, and the thought of them made my blood boil.

"Then what use are you to me?" I asked in a low tone. "Why can we talk now? What's changed, and what good is it if you won't help me?"

The Sylph didn't respond again. It seemed like if I pressed too hard or showed a little too much emotion in my words, the bird would shrink back down. It actually made me feel quite bad.

"I can help you understand," the bird offered in a very small voice.

I wanted to say something sarcastic. To tell the creature that I wasn't interested if it had nothing useful to me, but in the end, I could only conclude that information was something that I needed at this point, and getting it without anyone else knowing was at least a little advantageous.

"Do you have a name?" I asked eventually.

"I do, though you would not be able to pronounce it. You would not even be able to think it," Sylph replied.

"Would you mind if I gave you a name?" I asked.

After a short pause, the Sylph told me that it would be acceptable for me to assign her a name; it was the least she could do to actually allow us to be able to communicate properly – especially if this bond was somehow supposed to last for the rest of my life. I still wasn't happy about that, but I thought that maybe it was just that no one had yet figured out how to part once the Sylph had bonded.

"And the real you... you're that golden bird right?"

"I am," the Sylph replied. "I mean... I was."

"Right. When I was sailing near the Caribbean, my crew and I had just docked and had taken our treasure ashore," I explained. "We were quickly surrounded by natives who didn't speak our language. Things could've turned really bad for everyone there. They wanted to know what we carried in our chests. My men didn't want them to see the gold within and were ready to fight to the death to protect what was theirs. Eventually, I made the call to show them the treasure inside. I don't know what made me do it, but I had the feeling they weren't looking for riches or for treasure. When I opened the chest, and all of the gold and treasure inside met their eyes, the natives lowered their weapons and began to sing and dance; it was like they were celebrating the treasure, not wanting to take it for themselves. They chanted one word over and over, the word that to us meant that the gold we carried was there to save our lives. Yari. That's what I'll call you if that's ok?" I quickly added.

"I like it," the Sylph replied quietly. "It makes me feel more... real somehow. And because you shared your story with me, let me share what I can with you. Wait."

Then as soon as Yari finished speaking, my mind was flooded with dark, warped images. It took me a minute to realise what I was seeing and for my brain to process it properly, but in the end it was clear: this was one of Yari's memories.

The images in my mind were fragmented and unsettling. At first, they didn't make sense, a chaotic swirl of colours and shapes, but gradually they began to coalesce into something more understandable.

I saw a family of Sylphs, their luminous golden bodies glowing softly in the darkness. They were in cages, their bright eyes wide with fear and confusion. They were beautiful, ethereal creatures, but their beauty was marred by the cruel iron bars of their cages. An Entropic was standing guard, his hulking forms casting long, menacing shadows.

Among the Sylphs, I saw one that seemed familiar. She was smaller than the others, her glow not as bright, but there was something about her that tugged at my heart. It had to be one of Yari's family. I could feel my companion's fear, her sadness, her longing to help.

Suddenly, the small Sylph took flight, her wings beating furiously against the confines of her cage. She flew against the bars, her body glowing brighter with every beat of her wings. There was a moment of pure, unadulterated hope, and then...

Pain.

As I watched the Sylph trying to escape, I knew that Yari had been caught, her small body writhing in agony as an Entropic grasped her with a cruel, iron grip. Her wings fluttered uselessly, her glow dimming with every passing second. I could feel her pain, her despair, her resignation.

Then, the memory ended abruptly, leaving me with a hollow feeling in my chest. I was back in the cavern, lying on the cold, hard ground. The Obsidian Cores were still atop me, their warmth a stark contrast to the icy chill of the memory.

Yari was silent in my mind, but I could feel her sadness, her pain. It was a part of her, a wound that had never fully healed. It was a reminder of the cruelty of the Entropics. She had been unable to help her family, and she had been caught just as they had. I wondered if the Sylphs I'd seen in the memory were in the mine with us, but I couldn't ask that question right now.

I didn't know what to say, how to comfort Yari. I was still processing what I had seen, the raw emotions that the memory had evoked. I could only lay there, feeling the pain of a creature I barely knew, yet was intimately connected to.

"I'm sorry, Yari," I thought, my mind filled with sorrow. "I'm so sorry."

There was no response, but I didn't expect one. The memory had been a glimpse into Yari's past, a part of her she had chosen to share with me. It was a painful reminder of the reality we were both trapped in.

We didn't speak for a long time. I didn't want to be the one to break the silence, knowing how much hurt Yari was feeling, but eventually I knew I had no choice. Yari needed pulling from this dark place, and there was no one else here but me.

"We'll get them back," I said forcefully. "Whatever it takes to set them free, I promise that until my dying breath, I will fight for the freedoms of the Sylph and of the Selari. No people should live in slavery. That is the creed of the Free Man."

My words echoed back at me, resonating through our shared consciousness. Somehow through our quickly growing link, I felt Yari's pain recede a little, replaced by a flicker of hope, a glimmer of defiance. Her silence remained, but the shared pain within our link began to dissipate, replaced by a mutual understanding of our shared objective.

In the darkness, amidst the oppressive heat and the weight of the Obsidian Cores, we made a pact. It wasn't spoken, but it was felt. A bond between two very different beings, linked together by fate and circumstance.

Together, we would fight. Not just for our own freedom but for the freedom of all those held captive by the Entropics. I felt my resolve harden, my determination growing stronger with every heartbeat.

Yari's memory was a painful one, a definite reminder of the cruelty and injustice we were up against. But it also served as a powerful motivator, a call to arms. We were no longer just a lone human and a Sylph trapped in a strange situation. We were allies in a fight for freedom, for justice.

And in that moment, I knew that I wouldn't back down. I wouldn't allow the Entropics to continue their reign of terror unchecked. I wouldn't let Yari's family remain in those cruel cages any longer than they had to.

I don't know how long we lay there in silence, united in our shared purpose. The time seemed to stretch and warp around us as if the cavern itself was holding its breath, waiting for our next move.

Eventually, our silent stillness was replaced by something new happening, though this time, it was within the real world and not the internal dimension that I shared with the Sylph. It was the sound of footsteps, followed shortly by Marina coming into view above me and kneeling down above my head.

"Are you feeling any better? Are you healing?" Marina asked quickly, with a definite pressured speech.

"What?" I asked. It had been the first word that I had spoken in days. I didn't know when I had actually regained the ability to form words and make sounds, but I replied on instinct, and to my surprise, it worked.

"What?" I said again, though this time it was in somewhat shock that I had managed to speak the first time around.

"Are you better yet?" Marina said slowly, as though she was speaking to a child.

"No?" I said though it sounded more like a question than a statement. It was again an instinctual reply because, in reality, now that she had mentioned it, I was feeling a little better.

"Don't lie to me," Marina said.

"I'm not..." I started.

"Your broken jaw has repaired itself, your bruising is down, and you seem to be able to talk to me now. So I'll ask again, feeling better?" Marina pressed.

I sighed. "I've been able to move my fingers and toes. My ribs ache more than they hurt, and you're right; I can talk again. But... why didn't you help me?" I asked.

"Help you? Marina almost scoffed. "What, you wanted me to get myself killed all because you had sticky fingers? It's a miracle that you're still alive... and I think that... I think that it's because of the Cores..." she trailed off, her anger replaced by something that seemed much more akin to hope.

"I thought you didn't know how to use them," I asked, raising an eyebrow.

"I don't," Marina said slowly. "But I saw that Entropic force one into your mouth... with the power they hold... that should've killed you..."

"She's right," Yari's voice came from inside my head. "I've seen people killed just like that. An Entropic force-fed them a Core, and it made them explode from the inside out!"

"Are you going to tell me why you seem to be able to withstand the power of the Cores?" Marina asked.

At this point, there were already too many voices going on all around me. I couldn't concentrate on my conversation with Marina if the Sylph was going to interrupt like that. I knew that Marina couldn't hear my internal passenger because if she had, she'd have made a big deal about it. In any case, I mentally asked Yari to wait her turn as politely as I could manage.

"Well?" Marina asked, her eyes wide.

"I don't know," I said truthfully.

Marina's eyes narrowed, and she studied me with a fresh intensity. There was an edge to her gaze, sharp and focused. I could tell she was torn between the relief of seeing me alive and the frustration of not understanding why.

"But that makes no sense... you should be..." Marina began, then paused, looking as if she was biting back her words. After a moment, she shook her head, dismissing her own thoughts. "It doesn't matter. You're alive, and that's what counts."

There was a heavy silence between us, filled with unasked questions and unspoken thoughts. I could still feel Yari's presence in my mind, quiet but persistent. It was clear that she wanted to add something, but she respected my earlier request for silence.

"Do you think you can stand?" Marina asked, breaking the silence. Her voice was stern, but there was a concern in her eyes that belied her tough exterior.

"I can try," I replied, shifting slightly. The pain that shot through my body was a clear reminder of the ordeal I had been through. But it was bearable now, less of a sharp, stabbing sensation and more of a dull ache.

"Was that you, Yari," I asked mentally.

"N... no," the Sylph quickly replied. "We only use the pain we cause as indicators for something you do that's not right... now that we can communicate like this, I don't have to steer you in the right direction anymore."

Then I was reminded of something else the bird could do. "And the pleasure when I would find a Core?" I thought.

Yari was silent for a moment before answering. "Yes, that was me... but it is dangerous. If you keep experiencing this response, then eventually, it will break you, like the others. But again, we don't have to work like that anymore. If that's what you want."

"If that's what I want?" I internally questioned. The pleasure response when I'd found a Core had been unlike anything I'd ever experienced before, and even now, I wanted it more than anything. I left the question hanging in the air, though; it was something that we could deal with later.

Turning my attention back to the real world and with Marina's help, I managed to push myself up to a sitting position. My muscles screamed in protest, but I gritted my teeth and pushed through the pain.

Marina offered me a small, grudging smile. "Good. At least you're making progress."

I glanced down at the Obsidian Cores still resting against my skin. I could feel the raw power emanating from them, a steady thrum of energy that pulsed in time with my heartbeat. I knew they held the key to my survival and possibly the survival of Yari's family as well.

"Good. Now tell me what the Cores are for," I said.

"I just had a feeling," Marina said. "The Cores didn't seem to hurt you, and I've never seen someone take a beating like that before… and from an Entropic? It's a miracle, plain and simple. So I thought that perhaps a few of them would help you with your healing, you know if they were touching or near you this whole time. You know it's only been three days, and it looks like all of the bones that were broken have fused back together."

That made me remember my spine and how I was sure that it had broken neatly in two. I'd seen sailors retired by such an injury, never to walk again. If it truly had only been three days, then the miracle was perhaps too light a word for it.

"It has to be the Cores," Yari said in my mind. "You absorbed one because of the Entropic, and that power has to go somewhere… I think that… I think that you have a level of natural resistance to them, and maybe because your body was so broken, the power was used up in repairing you and not in causing you to explode… It's the only thing I can think of."

I relayed the theory to Marina as though it was my own. The last thing I wanted to do right now was tell the woman that I could talk to the bird that lived in my head.

"A natural resistance," she replied slowly, with her eyes wider than ever seen them. "That would be… you can't tell anyone," she added quickly and sternly. "If the Entropics found out that you can use the power of the Cores, even if you don't know how they'll kill you and everyone you ever met. They don't share power, Marcus."

I nodded slowly, understanding the weight of Marina's words. The Entropics were ruthless in their pursuit of power and control. The revelation that I perhaps had a natural resistance to the Cores, that I could potentially use their power without succumbing to its destructive force, would make me a target. I would become something they'd want to eliminate at all costs.

"I understand," I said, my voice barely a whisper. The gravity of the situation was beginning to set in. I was a potential weapon, a ticking time bomb for this 'Caretaker'. And only Marina and Yari knew my secret.

"Good," Marina said, her voice hard. "We'll need to play this smart if we're going to survive. And you... you need to see if you can learn how to control this power. If you can use it without harming yourself or others, it could be our only chance against the Entropics."

I glanced at the Obsidian Cores resting against my skin. The dull hum of their energy was almost comforting now, a constant reminder of the power I held and the danger it posed.

"I'll try," I promised. "But I don't even know where to start."

"We'll figure it out," Marina said with determination. "We have to."

There was now something in Marina's eyes I hadn't seen there before: hope. A hope that there could be a way to fight back against these beings, to bring about a way to free her people from slavery and tyranny.

"Yari, why isn't Marina's Sylph causing her pain? Knowing what she is doing is against the rules of this place?" I asked.

"Because the Sylph that resides within this Selari, like me, can see everything that their host does. The Sylph is also a fourth part of this conversation, even though they are the only member unable to communicate. They can surely see, like me, that there is something different within you, and they will wait to see if there truly is hope in the actions of the Selari before they make a decision whether or not to intervene."

"So you're saying that the Sylph within Marina is deciding if it is going to let her help me fight back?"

"Yes," Yari replied. "It's clear that Selari's Sylph has not yet forced her away from her current actions, but that doesn't mean that it will last forever."

"Then let's convince her," I thought.

"Marina," I said assuredly, doing my best to hide any pain or discomfort from my voice. "I haven't been in this place very long. In fact, I don't even know what or where this place is, but there are a few things that I have learnt so far: The Selari and the Sylphs have been forced into servitude by the Entropics. Yes, the Sylph are victims here, too, we'll come back to that. But for whatever reason, I seem to be able to use the power within these Obsidian Cores. I know it's not perfect yet, but I can use it. I'm sitting here as proof, aren't I?" I waited for my words to begin to sink in, and I looked Marina in her eyes. "But in my life, I have never backed down from a challenge, never sailed away from a larger ship, and I have never stood by and allowed free people to be forced into slavery. And I'm not going to start now. I promise you, I promise you all," I added purposefully, "that I will not allow this to continue. I will fight for the freedoms of the Selari and the Sylph, and I will use every shred of power that I can amass to overthrow the Entropics and make them fear us as we have feared them. We will become the Iron Willed, the feared. We will take their power, I promise you."

I watched as Marina's mouth opened a closed a few times. She had no idea that my words had also been for the benefit of her Sylph, but it wouldn't have hurt for her to hear them too. I waited a few moments before I turned my thoughts inward again.

"Did that work?" I asked.

"We won't know yet," Yari replied in her high-pitched tone. "We'll just have to wait and see."

"You don't have the ability to communicate with each other?" I asked. "So once you take your host, you're alone forever? You can't talk to anyone at all?"

"Yes and no…" Yari replied. "I can talk to you right now, though I think that this has never been done before. But we take our instructions from the Entropics. They have a way to speak directly to us, to give us our orders. But only when they are close by."

"I see," I mused internally, feeling a pang of sympathy for Yari. To be isolated from your own kind, only receiving orders from the very beings that enslaved you, it was a truly tragic existence.

I turned my attention back to Marina. She was quiet; her eyes focused on the Obsidian Cores resting against my skin. I could see a myriad of emotions playing across her face: surprise, hope, fear, determination.

Finally, she nodded. "Alright, Marcus," she said. "We'll fight. We'll do whatever we can to stand against the Entropics. But we'll have to be careful. If they find out about you, about your ability…"

"They won't," I interrupted, hoping my words would bring her some comfort. "We'll be smart about this. We won't give them a reason to suspect anything until the time's right."

Marina gave me a small smile, appreciative of my confidence. "Ok," she said. "For now, we'll focus on getting you back to normal, and then we'll see what we can do to make you stronger. I don't know how we're going to do any of this, especially with the Sylph forcing our hands at every opportunity, but I'm open to trying if you are."

I clicked my tongue and had to force myself not to smile at those words. The control of the Sylph was indeed a big hurdle in being able to leave this place, but I'd already overcome that. I didn't yet want to tell Marina about this particular fact, but when the time was right, it was certainly going to be the edge we needed.

As Marina walked away, I was left alone with my thoughts and the almost humming of the Cores. Yari was a comforting presence in my mind, a companion amidst the loneliness and uncertainty.

"Yari," I began. "Do you think we can really do this? Stand up to the Entropics?"

There was a pause before she replied. "No, Marcus," she confessed. "The Entropics are powerful. But you... you have something they don't and something I've never seen before: A resistance to the Cores. It might not seem like much, but at least it's a start. Besides, if none of this works, we can always go back to mining."

I sighed, leaning back against the cavern wall. It was a lot to take in, a heavy responsibility. But as I closed my eyes, I could almost feel the power of the Cores pulsating within me, a dormant force waiting to be unleashed. And despite my fear, despite the uncertainty, I couldn't help but feel a spark of hope.

"We'll figure it out, Yari," I said, echoing Marina's words. "We have to."

Because it wasn't just about survival anymore, it was about freedom, about standing up against the tyranny of the Entropics. And if there was even a glimmer of hope, a chance to make a difference, then I was willing to take it. No matter the cost.

Chapter 7 – Communication

Two more 'days' passed as my recovery eventually brought me back up onto my own two feet. I'd spoken with Yari briefly about how the world worked, the races that resided within it, how the Entropics had seized power for their own… and I'd taken in very little. There just seemed like so much to learn, and it was immediately clear that this place was very, very different to where I came from.

I knew that days had passed because Marina placed a new Obsidian Core on my body each day. I didn't know how much of a difference the things made, but judging by the speed of my recovery and the waning pain that I felt all over, they were certainly doing something good.

Now though, I could finally stand up, walk around even. The darkness that I'd lived in for what I could only assume was about a week had begun to soften as my eyes had adjusted to it, and it gave me an odd sense of comfort – like this place had somehow become my home.

Walking slowly around the dark cavern, I found myself drawn to the soft dark glow of the Obsidian Cores. The energy they radiated was like a lighthouse beacon in the darkness, both comforting and inspiring. It was a reminder of the power I held and the potential within me.

In the dim light, I could make out the vague shapes of the cavern walls, the jagged stalactites hanging from the ceiling, and the smooth floor beneath my bare feet. Every step I took echoed through the cavern, a testament to the progress I had made.

I felt Yari's presence at the back of my mind, a silent observer of my exploration. I could sense her curiosity, her fascination with the world outside the confines of our shared body.

"Yari," I began, breaking the silence. "Can you... see? Through my eyes, I mean?"

There was a pause before she responded. "I can perceive, yes. It's a bit um, fuzzy, but I can make out shapes, colours, movements. It's... different."

"That's good," I said, a small smile tugging at my lips. I was glad that Yari could share this experience with me and that she wasn't completely confined to the darkness of our shared mind.

I continued to wander around the cavern, taking in my surroundings without Yari's guiding pain keeping me away from places I shouldn't have been going. Despite the darkness, there was a certain beauty to the place. The way I could somehow now sense the Obsidian Cores within the walls, a constant, soothing melody.

And in the midst of it all, I felt a sense of peace. A sense of purpose. I was in a strange, alien world with an even stranger companion in my head. But I wasn't afraid. I felt ready. Ready to learn, to grow, to fight.

"Marina," I said as soon as I had arrived at the place where the Selari was mining. There was a small pile of stones by her feet that let me know she had been working hard without me, a testament to her dedication to carrying on with the status quo.

As soon as Marina heard my voice, she turned to face me with her eyes wide.

"Marcus! Are you walking around already? How can this be?" she asked quickly, her eyes wide with surprise.

"I don't rightly know," I replied. "But I'm willing to be that it has something to do with all the Cores you've been placing on me, right?"

Marina smiled and nodded. She had known what she was doing, and her gamble had paid off.

"How do you feel?" she asked. "Do you feel stronger? Faster? Anything?"

I shook my head slowly. "Actually, I feel just OK. Not as good as I was before, but not hurt any more either. That's impressive, though, isn't it?"

Marina nodded, her eyes reflecting a strange mix of relief and curiosity. "It is. I've never seen anyone recover as quickly as you have, especially given your condition after your beating. It's remarkable."

I frowned at the word 'beating'. But I could only agree that that was what it was.

"But not entirely unexpected, given what we suspect about your ability to handle the Obsidian Cores," she continued, her gaze shifting to the ground. "We're dealing with unknown territory here, Marcus. It's hard to predict what might happen."

I nodded, understanding her concerns. I knew that I was a walking enigma in this world, a puzzle that neither Marina nor Yari had a complete picture of. But it was a puzzle that we needed to solve for the sake of all the Selari and the Sylphs enslaved by the Entropics.

"Have you thought about our next move?" I asked, moving the subject along, away from the past and into the future.

"I don't know if we can really talk about it," Marina replied, her voice lowering to a whisper. "I don't know how much my Sylph can hear or understand, but if we start putting feet wrong, then I don't know what will happen to us."

I didn't know what else I could say at that point. I found myself at a crossroads: tell Marina that I could communicate with Yari or try to convince her that it would all be somehow OK. In the end, I concluded that telling anybody about my link with Yari was most probably a bad thing, so I tried something different.

"Well, it hasn't stopped you yet, has it? Hasn't tried to cause you any pain or tried to steer you away from me? Have you tried asking it?" I said.

"Asking it?" Marina asked with a grimace. "What does that even mean?"

"I mean, why don't you vocalise what you plan on doing and see if you get a response from your Sylph? If it can hear you or even see what you're doing, then surely it will try to stop you if it thinks what you're doing is wrong."

It was then that Yari decided to join the conversation, though, as usual, I was the only one privileged enough to hear her thoughts.

"That's a great idea!" the Sylph said in my mind. "I think that Marina's Sylph is on board, but that would certainly be a good way to find out."

I smiled cockily at Yari's words, and Marina gave me a questioning look, which I ignored.

"OK," Marina announced slowly. "I want to escape from this place. Do you have any objections to that?" She gave me a sarcastic look this time, as though what she was doing was entirely stupid, but I nodded to tell her to keep going.

"I think that Marcus here has some ability that could help us fight back against the Entropics. I think that if we all work together, then we could work to gain our freedom and maybe help others?"

Again, nothing happened.

"OK, Marcus, this is stupid. I don't think that the Sylph can hear… AAH!" she exclaimed as I recognised the look of a wave of pain washing over Marina.

The pain passed just a moment later, and Marina straightened back up, looking at me with a fair amount of annoyance in her expression.

"They can hear you, huh," I said, folding my arms across my chest, a gesture which I regretted once I remembered that I still wasn't really fully healed from my fight with the Entropic.

"But what was it answering?" Marina asked. "It's OK with me trying to escape? That we can help others?" she trailed off and winced, ready for another bout of pain. "You can hear me, can't you." She said. "Give me the tiniest nudge if that's true."

I watched as Marina's face scrunched up. She had her answer, and she'd made it there without me having to divulge my own little secret.

"That's... that's something," Marina said after a moment, her voice filled with astonishment. "I never considered... I mean, I never thought that they could hear us, understand us."

I nodded, a sense of relief washing over me. "Well, it seems they can. And that's a good thing, Marina. It means we can communicate, even if it's in a very limited way. It means we're not entirely alone in this. And I think they're on our side – that is, if they really do believe that we can fight back if we all work together. I think they've had their fair share of enslavement by the Entropics too."

Marina was silent for a moment, her gaze drifting towards the darkness behind me. "I just can't believe they're... aware. That they can understand us. It's not something I ever thought possible."

I could understand her surprise, her confusion. It was a lot to take in, a lot to process. But it was also a step forward, a new weapon in our arsenal that we would eventually be able to use in our fight for freedom.

"There's a lot we don't know, Marina," I said, echoing her earlier words. "But every day, we're learning something new. And we'll keep learning, keep understanding. For ourselves and for everyone the Entropics have enslaved."

Marina nodded, her gaze returning to me. "For the people," she echoed, a newfound determination in her voice.

She looked at me, her eyes filled with a resolve I hadn't seen before. "We're going to figure this out, Marcus. Together, we're going to fight back. For my people, for our freedom."

"And for the Sylph," I added, not wanting the bird creatures to change their mind about any of this.

Yari added her own words to the call to arms for my benefit too. "I believe in you, Marcus Reid."

It was music to my ears. And not that terrible music that the Siren had played that had brought me to this place, but a sound that filled me with hope and joy. I had Marina, Yari, and I assumed Marina's Sylph on my side, and in my mind, that was going to be enough; we would be able to leave this place and start making our plans for the future.

"So what are we going to do?" I asked. "I think we can leave this place now that the Sylph are on board, but we aren't exactly set up with food and shelter when we do. As bad as it sounds, we're safe here. And the food isn't all that bad once you get used to it."

The mention of food reminded me of something else though: in all of this, the fight with the Entropic, the pain, the recovery, through all of it, I hadn't felt hungry, not even once. Even now, with my attention solely focused on my appetite, I didn't feel the need to eat. It wasn't making me feel weak, either. Quite the contrary, actually, I felt like I was OK, not underfed, nor overfed, just kind of, well, OK.

"I can answer that," a tiny voice came from inside my head, and once again, I found Yari to be the font of all knowledge.

"The Obsidian Cores are giving you the energy your body needs. It's been mostly used to help you repair and recover, but a little energy has found its way to help you survive without the need for food."

I clicked my tongue, not wanting to give away the fact that I now knew why I didn't need to find food moving forward, but it didn't change the fact that Marina would need to eat, along with anyone we saved along the way.

"There's plenty to eat out there," Marina said, not noticing my hesitation. "Plants, fruits and things, there's food all around us, not that anyone bothers to collect it for us in here. We get the gruel, and that's about it. You don't want to even know how they make that stuff."

I truly didn't. So I didn't ask.

"And shelter?" I asked. "I know this place isn't perfect, but it's not too cold or hot, it's dry, and now that I say all this out loud, I'm starting to have second thoughts about leaving."

Marina looked at me with disgust written on her face. It was clear that sarcasm wasn't a major structure in her wheelhouse.

"I know a place," she said as though I should've known that fact. "It's not too far from here but far enough that I don't think we'll get into too much trouble if the Caretaker comes back. Why would he care if a couple of workers go missing anyway? He'll probably think you died after your fight and I doubt he'd even give me a second thought."

I scratched my chin. I knew that Marina was trying to say all the right things, but something told me that the Entropic would care very much that a couple of workers were missing. After all, from what I'd been told, just getting me here had been a costly exercise.

"I don't think running and hiding is going to last us very long," I said. "If we want to make a real difference, then the only thing these slavers will understand is a fight. And it isn't going to be easy. But if we do it right, we can cause them a lot of pain, just like they do to everyone they enslave."

Marina nodded in agreement. "I know. They come for everyone in the end," she said quietly. "People try to hide, they really do, but in the end, they all end up in the mines, or anywhere else the Entropics put them."

I didn't ask where else people went. We would tackle the mines first, cutting off the Entropic's power source before moving on to the rest.

"Then I have a plan," I said abruptly. I don't know why I thought of it so quickly or even where it had truly come from, but it was there, and I felt the need to voice it.

"We work all day as normal. We collect the Cores, and at the end of the day, when we're supposed to drop them off at the tunnel, we take everything that we can carry and run. We run to wherever it is you're thinking of, and we make our plans there. Is this place big enough to house more when we rescue them?" I asked, my mind moving forward ten steps at once.

Marina nodded. "But I…"

"Good," I said, interrupting her. "Then we have a plan. Tell me, is my stash of Cores still there, or did it get collected? Actually, It doesn't matter," I interrupted myself this time. My mouth was working faster than my mind at this point, and I simply had to keep going. "There's going to be enough Cores mined by everyone at that point anyway, so I don't need those ones. How many do you think we'll be able to carry anyway?"

My vision began to blur, but I kept on talking, ignoring it.

"And how far do we have to go? Is this place an hour's walk, or are we talking a day?"

Sweat began to bead on my forehead.

"It doesn't matter either. Actually, we'll get there, and then we can start saving people like we're supposed to."

I felt my cheek hit the hard floor as the world around me faded to black.

"Marcus?" Yari's small voice in my head asked nervously.

"Ugh," I replied out loud. It was all I could manage. Suddenly I felt very, very heavy.

I knew some time had passed when I opened my eyes to find that I was still in the place where Marina had been mining, but now I had been propped up against the wall.

"What happened?" I asked groggily, rubbing my jaw and cheek. They hurt, but I was more worried about the fact that I'd just blacked out.

"You kept talking," Marina said. "Really, really fast. I tried to stop you, but you just kept going and going, and then you kind of just shut down."

"It was the Cores," Yari said in my mind. "You took in too much power at once, and you went into overdrive. Please, you have to be more careful…

I know you think that you are immune to their effects, but you aren't. Your body tolerates the Cores more than others, but everyone has their limit."

I snaked my hand around the back of my neck and rubbed it nervously. "Do you think it was the Cores?" I asked. "Like an… overdrive… or something." I really needed to play this off as my own idea, but I also needed to get a second opinion from Marina.

"Maybe?" she said. "It does seem likely. Maybe we'll put that plan of yours into action tomorrow, let you get some rest… or get back to normal or something. I don't want you blacking out on me halfway out the door; I won't be carrying you, you know."

I nodded, looking over her shoulder and not particularly listening to what the Selari was saying; my mind was now focused on something else: the fact that I seemed to have an almost safe way of determining the effects of the Cores on my body. And that was definitely something that I'd make use of later.

We mined for the rest of the day as per the original plan. Well, neither of us put too much effort into it, and I left Marina to finish up before I knew it was time to call it a day; I had something else in mind: I wanted to see if there was any way that I could speak to any of the other Selari in the mines. I knew Marina had said that they were too far gone, and Yari told me the same thing over and over as I made my way through the caverns to the place where the nearest Selari was working, but I just wanted to make sure for myself. After all, neither Marina nor Yari had met someone like me before.

Also, without the pleasure response from finding the Obsidian Cores, I found mining for them a lot less enjoyable. Honestly, I didn't know how Marina was still doing it, unless her Sylph was still giving her the reward, that was.

It didn't take me long to find another Selari. I don't know what made them all go to mine in their separate locations, but the one I found was an elderly looking Selari man wearing tattered rags. I stood and watched him for a moment as he worked, and either he didn't see me standing there, or he simply didn't care. My stomach turned when I saw through his methodical tool-less mining that his fingers were black, worn down to shorter than I guessed they once were, and slightly bleeding. Again, he didn't seem to care.

"Hey," I said, eventually deciding to try to just talk to the worker.

The Selari didn't even flinch. It was like he was deaf.

"HEY!" I tried again. Only much louder, and if the man had heard me, he didn't let on that fact.

So I moved on to the only other thing that I could do; I stepped closer to him and tapped him on the shoulder. His skin was cold through his tattered rags, and it felt fragile. I wondered just how nourishing the gruel in this place really was.

But the Selari didn't respond again. Whatever the Sylph had done to him – or more accurately, the Entropics – it had worked; what stood before me, working his fingers to the bone, was no man.

I placed my hand on the Selari's shoulder tightly and pulled hard to force him to turn to face me. I was ready for his reaction, planting my feet on the ground so that I could jump back out of the way if he attacked me for taking him from his work. But that wasn't what happened. The Selari turned fairly easily once he knew that was what was happening and stood still, facing me. His arms fell down to his sides, and his milky-white gaze fixed over my head. The sight made me feel sick to my stomach.

Then, after a few seconds, the Selari slowly turned back around to face the wall and continued on with his work.

"Are you still in there?" I whispered to the man. I hoped beyond hope that this man was simply in a trance. I'd seen things like it before in Opium users when they'd sampled too much of the poppy, but this seemed like something far worse, something far more permanent.

"He won't come around," Yari's voice filled my head. "The pleasure that the workers feel isn't just something that they experience on a whim; it creates fundamental changes in their minds and bodies… it changes them, and they can never change back."

I stopped watching the Selari, turning my attention inwards to Yari.

"There has to be a way," I thought. "People don't just change because they're chasing the next high."

"It isn't a high," Yari said. "I know it might feel like that at first, but these workers are now entirely dependent on finding the next Core. It is their entire reason for being. I know they may not look like they're well… but truly, they are cared for. But that doesn't change anything; these people now live to work, and they work to live; that is a fact, and it cannot be changed. I have seen it before: if one of these workers is taken from his task and confined, even fed and watered, he will quickly die. Their work sustains them, and the response from the Sylph has become what fuels them."

The very, very short thought that I would've liked workers like that on the Iron Will came and was quickly forced away. Regardless of whether these people were sustained by their work, hell, even if they were enjoying it, I knew it was wrong. I was going to do everything I could to put an end to all of this.

But then, something was nagging at me. If someone enjoyed carrying out their task, was it right to force them not to do it? I turned the thought over and over in my mind, trying to decide how best to proceed, and eventually, Yari's voice returned.

"If they enjoy it, and it gives them safety, food and shelter... is it really that bad?"

I could hear a small amount of hope in her tone, like all that the Sylph wanted was to feel better about what was happening here.

"No," I thought. "These people were taken against their will, from their friends and families and forced to work..." I trailed off as I remembered the crews of the Royal Navy vessels my Iron Will had taken and forced into work. Was I any different? After all, I was pleased when these crews would seem contented, happy even after a while on my ship. Nearly all of the former Navy sailors integrated into my crew, and none of them ever really seemed unhappy...

"As the animals work in the farms," Yari continued. "They are given food and shelter in return for their work; are they slaves?"

I closed my eyes so that I didn't have to watch the Selari man working as I turned all of this over in my mind.

"But that's different," I said. "Animals don't think; they don't have desires..."

"But they know freedom, and it is taken away from them without their choice," Yari replied.

I didn't have an answer. She was right in one way – working animals were treated much like these Selari, but what was troubling me the most was the comparison I'd made with my own crew. How had I been viewed by the rest of the world, taking crews from their ships and forcing them to work? For some, it was more than they deserved, of course, the cost of war for killing many of my men as well as the crews of other free vessels. But some of them had been forced into servitude to the Royal Navy too. And those men I'd taken and held captive. The thought made me feel sick to my stomach, and immediately, I thought of all of the faces of my former crew, each of their smiles slowly dropping into sad frowns.

I couldn't remember which was the truth anymore. Had I been so caught up in revenge against the Royal Navy that I hadn't seen how truly unhappy my men were? Or had something happened to me down in this mine, watching these people forced into slavery? I couldn't decide. But no, my men were happy; I was sure of it. Wasn't I?

"You need to stop second-guessing yourself," Yari said loudly. "It makes me uncomfortable."

I didn't want to say that this line of thinking was making me feel very uncomfortable too, but I got the feeling that the Selari knew that. Besides, there was nothing I could do about any of that right now, so I placed the Iron Will and her crew in a distant corner of my mind; I had more immediate things to worry about right now.

I looked back at the Selari miner, his fingers again slowly and methodically scraping at the cavern wall. I felt a profound sadness, not just for him but for all the Selari in the mine. For all the free will that had been taken away from these people, and for all the lives reduced to this monotonous, mindless existence.

"Yari," I began, my inner voice shaking with uncertainty. "I don't know if I can change anything here. But I have to try. I can't just stand by and let this continue. I'm going to need your help."

There was a pause before Yari answered. "I know," she finally said, her voice sounding slightly surprised. "We can't just stand by and watch. I may not be able to do much, but I will do what I can to assist you."

That was a start, at least.

I looked around the mine and thought of the countless Selari scraping away at the walls, here and in countless more mines, their lives reduced to the simple pursuit of Obsidian Cores. It was a thought that burnt itself into my mind, and one that I would carry with me forever, a reminder of the cost of unchecked power and control. And something more: a subtle reminder of the life I used to lead.

It was clear to me now, more than ever that I needed to do everything in my power to stop the Entropics, to free these people. And in doing so, perhaps I could find some redemption for myself as well.

Chapter 8 – Freedom

I searched for more of the Selari after I'd left the first to get back to his work. It wasn't difficult finding them all, and with each one I found, my hope that I would find even a shred of consciousness in any of them faltered and eventually disappeared. By the time I'd seen every single Selari in the mine and realised that they were all acting in exactly the same way as the first, my heart had sunk about as low as it could go. It was only the fact that Marina was still herself that really kept me going, as well as knowing that we would be leaving this terrible place before long.

Even in the face of the disheartening reality of the Selari's condition, I refused to surrender completely to despair. I had to believe that there was some way, some means of breaking the spell the Sylph had over these people. I needed to believe that for my own sanity, and for the sake of the Selari.

As planned, Marina and I spent another day in the mine to make sure that I wasn't suffering any ill effects of my recovery, and thankfully, I wasn't. I didn't suffer another 'overdrive' episode or another blackout; it was very much all back to normal. Plus, the aches and pains that I had been experiencing were all but a distant memory.

I had mustered the courage to speak with the Selari workers again, but after the first one I found, I knew that trying again was doing nothing other than making me feel worse about their whole situation. I didn't know what I was going to do about them, but it was going to have to be a problem for future me once Marina and I were free and safe. Being stuck in this place wasn't going to help either of us.

The time finally came for us to make our move. We stood in line, watching the Selari drop their Cores in a pile at the entrance to the tunnel that led out of this place from the back. The pile already contained too many Cores for us to carry, but by going last at least, we might not have been watched as we made our escape and anything that gave us a little extra time before discovery was going to be worth its weight in gold.

Marina and I were next in line. I could feel my heart beating out my chest and the vein in my neck pulsating with excitement, fear and anticipation. My legs felt weak underneath me, and it was all that I could hope that my hands weren't too sweaty to pick up as many of the Cores as I would've liked.

"Deep breaths," I whispered to Marina, my gaze never leaving the pile of Cores. Her eyes met mine for a brief second, nodding in understanding before her attention returned to the task at hand. The line moved forward, and it was our turn.

We stood before the pile of Cores, neither wanting to make the first move. Then Marina stooped over and dropped what she had collected in the course of the day, adding it to the pile. I followed suit. Then after a brief pause, Marina used both her arms to scoop up as much as she could carry. I watched as she grimaced, clearly worried that her Sylph was about to stop her from stealing from the pile; then her expression morphed into a smirk, and she stood back up, her arms full. I repeated her actions.

We had each taken a sizable share of the Cores, their strange, cold weight a reminder of the strange reality we found ourselves in. My heart pounded in my chest as we slowly, casually turned to leave, every instinct screaming at me that we were about to be discovered. But no alarm sounded, no shout of discovery echoed through the mines. I wanted to run, but we needed to remain calm.

With each step towards the exit, the oppressive atmosphere of the mine began to recede. The heavy, stale air was gradually replaced by the fresher, cooler air from outside. The constant, low hum of the oppression that had been ever present in the mine became less and less noticeable. The change was subtle, but each shift brought a new wave of hope and once we were finally out of the mine, the sudden absence of the thick air was like night and day. I felt strangely light, my mind clearer than it had been in days. I turned to Marina, her face reflecting the same sense of relief I felt.

Marina and I shared a glance, both knowing we needed to remain quiet for the time being, and we each took a step forward, out of the mine and into the world.

The sun was well and truly setting, and it was casting a dull glow on the world around us. Soon it was clear to me that we were back in the forest where I had arrived in this world, but where once the colours were new and vibrant, purples, reds and yellows, suddenly now everything seemed so... dull. I didn't know if it was because I had become used to this place, if the mine had done something to my vision in the short time I was in there, or what, but something definitely felt much more normal about this place.

"This way," Marina said as she gestured forwards again and again. Not knowing where I was or being able to see the stars in the sky, I wasn't sure which way we were heading, but then again, I didn't even know if this world had stars, let alone if I would recognise them.

"Are there a lot of villages, towns and cities in this world?" I asked as we walked slowly through the forest. I could tell that the forest itself wasn't being used regularly because there was no path, track or evident damage to the trees or vegetation. In fact, I didn't see any signs of life at all, no animals, birds or even insects.

"Sometimes you ask the stupidest questions," Marina said quickly, but then she corrected herself. "Sorry… I forget you aren't from here sometimes. To answer your question: no, there used to be, a long time ago. But it's mostly ruins now. The Entropics don't allow the Selari to gain too much power or grow in too large groups. They didn't have a problem in wiping us out to the point of extinction, but they've made it clear that they don't want to go through the trouble again."

"I still don't get it," I said after thinking about that for a moment. "They destroyed everything of the Selari, and nobody did anything about it? Are there no other nations or powers that the Entropics are afraid of? Or would cause them trouble?"

"Oh, don't misunderstand," Marina said. We did fight back in the beginning. But we found that all that happened was death and destruction. If anyone challenged the Entropics, their entire town was wiped from existence, so in the end, we simply stopped fighting."

"And let them take you?!" I asked incredulously.

"Not… let," Marina said. "We didn't have a choice. The Entropics… they offered us a trade, of sorts."

My blood ran cold. Something was telling me that the fact that Marina had waited this long to tell me about whatever this deal was, it was a very bad sign. I didn't interrupt her, choosing to allow her to tell me about this 'deal' in her own time.

She sighed, letting her shoulders drop in defeat.

"If we agreed to stop fighting back, to stop doing all the things we were doing that made the Entropics' jobs harder… then they said they would leave the children."

"Leave the children?" I heard myself say automatically and in a very high pitch. What does that even mean?"

"It means that anyone of age is taken to work, and the children… the children get left behind to fend for themselves."

I felt my mouth hang open and nearly tripped as my attention fell away from our path.

"Are you insane?" I managed to growl. "How can children possibly survive... this?" I waved an arm about to indicate the entire world. "And you let that happen? What's wrong with you?"

As soon as I said it, I regretted it. It was how I felt about the situation, but my words had sounded far harsher than I'd meant them to.

Marina stopped walking and turned to me, anger clear on her face. "Don't you talk to me about what's right and what isn't," she was pointing an accusing finger at me now, and it made me feel very, very small. "I risked everything to follow you out here, to try to make a difference. Do you know what will happen if we can't fight back? If we lose?" She paused. "No, you don't know because you're an idiot. You aren't even from this place, and I've risked so much," her gaze fell to the ground, and I could feel that she wanted to call this whole thing off and simply head back to the mine.

"I'm sorry," I said calmly. "It was just a shock to me... I didn't mean for it to come out like that. Besides, it doesn't change anything, does it? I mean, if anything, it gives us more of a reason to fight back, to win, right?"

Marina didn't look up from the ground now, and she spoke in a very small voice.

"The children aren't as helpless as you'd think. They've adapted to this world. They forage and gather what they can to survive, and they hide whenever the Entropics search for new recruits. I know how bad it sounds, but it's not all like that."

"But they just wait until they're old enough to work?" I asked, trying to remain placating.

Marina nodded. "It's the only way we can save as many of them as we can. It's better than everyone dying, isn't it?"

I thought about that. Of course, if this truly was the only way that children would survive into adulthood, then it was the best way. But it seemed so terrible to me, like the Selari were cattle born to be slaves for the rest of their lives.

"Why?" I asked eventually. Then clarified: "Why don't they take the children?"

"Because..." Marina replied quickly and then stopped. "... I don't know," she finished. "Maybe they aren't very good as workers when they're small and weak. Whatever the reason, if the children get a decade or two to live, then it doesn't matter. They get to be free for at least a part of their lives, and then once they're broken by the Sylph, it all goes away."

"It's because they can't bind with a Sylph," Yari said in my mind. "They have to be of the right age, or the Sylph can't absorb into their body."

This wasn't particularly useful information to me. It was good to know, but if I told Marina that I knew, then she'd know something was up. But it didn't really make any difference anyway; the children weren't being taken or killed – rather, they were being raised, much like calves, into cattle.

"We have to stop this," I affirmed, keeping the information to myself. "We need to stop the Entropics, save the Selari, and save the children. There's nothing else we can do."

Marina looked worried but slightly placated. I could tell all of this was difficult for her, but I wasn't just going to stand by and let children become slaves.

We walked for a long time. Eventually, the forest thinned into grassland, open fields, hills and areas of dead or dying vegetation. In some areas, it was much like the earth had been scorched, but we kept quiet and walked through the darkness. I still found it odd that we hadn't come across any wildlife at all, but now Marina explained why.

"The animals can sense the Obsidian Cores, so they don't come near. Around the mines, you won't find anything at all, and because we're carrying so many, they won't even come close to us."

"They don't like the Cores?" I asked.

"It isn't that they don't like them," Marina said. "It's more like they know what they mean. Because where there are Cores, there are usually Entropics."

I digested that quietly as we moved through the eerily silent landscape. It made sense. I imagined this world once teeming with creatures, their calls and songs filling the air. But now they were silenced, driven away by the ever-growing presence of the Obsidian Cores and the lurking menace of the Entropics.

The night was truly upon us now, and the darkness had crept across the land, deepening the shadows around us. But, oddly enough, I wasn't worried. The darkness would hide us as much as it would hide any threats that looked to harm us. Plus, if the Cores really did keep animals away, then we surely had enough to make a wide berth all around us.

We took turns carrying extra Cores, switching a small pile between us whenever one of us started to struggle with the weight. The Cores were deceivingly heavy, a testament to the raw power they held. Each shift of weight brought a fresh wave of determination. These were our keys to freedom, our weapons in the fight against the Entropics.

Hours passed in silence as we travelled across the grassland. The twin moons of this strange world hung low in the sky, their pale light casting long, eerie shadows. I hadn't noticed before that there were two of them. It was almost surreal, like walking through a dream. But every step, every laboured breath was a reminder that this was not a dream; this was our grim reality.

"Are we nearly there? I think we should find shelter soon," I suggested, glancing over at Marina. She nodded, her face etched with tiredness.

"Just a little further, you'll see."

But I heard it before I saw it. My heart rose with the familiar sound of an ocean. Waves were lapping against a beach or crashing against rocks. I knew that sound, and now, too, I could smell it in the air. We were heading towards the water, and my heart filled with anticipation I didn't know I could muster. I immediately felt at home.

As we crested a final shallow hill, the sight of the vast ocean stretching out before us took my breath away. The bright moons of this world reflected off the surface, creating a shimmering canvas of silver and blue. It was beautiful, serene even, a true contrast to the harsh reality of the world we were in.

The sight of the ocean brought forth memories of my home, of days spent on the sea, carefree and oblivious to the existence of other worlds and the struggles they endured. A pang of longing hit me, but I pushed it aside. This was not the time for reminiscence.

Because before the ocean, I could see what we had come here for. As my eyes fell downwards and away from the waters, I could see the ruins of an old settlement.

"This is the place," Marina said as she watched my gaze. "It's been abandoned for a long time. The Entropics burnt this place almost to the ground, but there's still some shelter here, and the foundations are stable I think."

What I gathered from this conversation, though, was the fact that Marina and I had very different ideas of what the word 'stable' meant. All I could see of the ruins were the skeletal husks of a handful of timber-framed houses. Two still had parts of roofs, but where they had shelter above, their walls were almost entirely missing and blackened with soot. Beyond the settlement, I could see that there was a small, sharp drop down to the ocean below. Jagged rocks broke the tide and the waves, meaning that there wouldn't be any flooding, but also getting down into the water would be an almost impossibility from here.

"Is this a place where...?" I trailed off, not sure how to ask the question that was nagging at me.

"Yes," Marina replied, not needing me to finish. "This was a village of Selari. A thriving community, once. Now it's a ghost of what it was."

I swallowed hard, the reality of the situation hitting me like a punch to the gut. The Entropics didn't just take the Selari to work in their mines; they destroyed their homes and their communities. They took everything.

We made our way into the ruins, careful to avoid the broken pieces of wood and rubble strewn about the place. Despite the destruction, there was a sense of peace here, a quiet solitude that seemed to have seeped into the very stones of the ruined houses.

We chose one of the houses with a partial roof as our shelter for the night in case it rained, and we placed the Cores in a corner, then set about making the place as comfortable as possible.

Despite the bleak surroundings, I found myself feeling oddly hopeful. It was as if the sight of the ocean had awakened something in me. A determination, a resolve. The Entropics had taken so much from the Selari, but they couldn't take their spirit, their will to survive.

And I was going to help them take back what was theirs.

Once our makeshift camp was set up, Marina and I sat down, leaning against the remnants of a wall. We stared out at the ocean, its vast expanse a silent reminder of the challenges that lay ahead.

"We should rest," Marina said eventually. "Tomorrow, we'll start planning how to use these Cores."

I nodded. "Do you think we should light a fire?" I asked.

"Not tonight," Marina said. "I think it's OK, but when it's light, we'll get a better idea of the surrounding area. Until then, it's best that nobody knows we're here."

"Who would know?" I asked. "Are there people around here?"

"I don't think so, but it's better to be safe, right?" Marina said.

I nodded again.

"Best to try to sleep for now. We don't have the food that the mine provided, so tomorrow, we're going to need all our strength to go out and find some."

"That makes sense," I murmured, suddenly aware of a very slight hunger creeping its way into my stomach. I honestly couldn't remember when the last time I'd eaten was, and I knew Marina hadn't had anything since the morning. The long journey, coupled with the weight of the Cores, had left us both exhausted and in need of a good meal sooner rather than later. I wondered how much the ambient power of the Cores had actually helped us as we had carried them, but it was a metric that I had no idea how to quantify. And I really didn't know if Marina gained anything from them at all.

With the decision made to rest, we settled down for the night, using what was left of our clothing to fashion crude pillows and blankets. The half-wood, the half-dirt floor was cold and hard, but I was so tired that I hardly noticed.

As I lay there, staring up at the broken roof and the empty sky beyond, I felt a wave of mixed emotions wash over me. Fear, uncertainty, but also a strange sense of exhilaration. We were out here, free from the oppressive confines of the mine, free to make our own choices, to determine our own fates. I was a Free Man once more.

I glanced over at Marina, her face barely visible in the dim light. Her eyes were closed, her breathing steady. She looked calm, at peace. The sight reassured me. We were in this together, and together, we would find a way to survive.

With that thought in my mind, I closed my eyes and let the sound of the distant ocean softly lull me to sleep.

"Marcus?" Yari's voice came into my head as I was about to drift off.

I waited to see if the Sylph would continue without my prompting, but it was clear that she was waiting for an answer.

"Yes, Yari?" I asked, doing everything I could to keep any frustration out of my tone.

"What are you planning to do next? This place isn't exactly somewhere that you can launch an attack from… are you going to do something now that you're free… or… um…" the Sylph trailed off. I could see what she was trying to figure out, though.

"You want to know if, now that we are free, are we simply going to try to run, escape and look out for ourselves rather than try to help those in need?" I asked.

"Yes?" Yari replied slowly.

"No, Yari," I replied. "I will not stand by and watch people… and Sylphs… forced into slavery. I will not stand by and watch as the Entropics destroy everything in their path. I will do whatever I can to stop them. But first, we need to be prepared. We need food, we need shelter, we need a plan. And then... then we'll see what we can do. We'll find a way to fight back."

There was a pause before Yari replied, and when she did, her voice was soft. "Thank you, Marcus."

"Don't thank me yet, Yari," I said. "We've got a long road ahead of us. But I promise you, we'll do whatever we can."

I felt Yari withdraw from my mind, leaving me alone with my thoughts.

As I drifted off to sleep, I could only hope that our determination and resolve would be enough.

The next morning, I woke up feeling refreshed and ready for the day ahead. Marina was already up, looking out towards the ocean with a thoughtful expression on her face and I joined her. Together we watched as the tide ebbed and flowed, lapping against the jagged rocks at the end of our new home.

"Food," I said simply. I wanted to say more, but Marina clearly knew what we were going to be doing to get food out here. I hoped it was fishing.

Chapter 9 – Home

It was not fishing.

How I would have loved to have done a bit of fishing. Not only because I really wanted to taste something other than nonspecific gruel, but because fishing was, well… peaceful. And a little bit of peace was something that everybody needed, once in a while.

Fishing would've been lovely, but instead, once Marina and I had both awoken in our makeshift shelter, she took one look at the warm, bright sky and announced that we were going 'foraging'.

Now I don't mind the odd bit of foraging here and there. I don't mind eating what I find or even spending time looking for it, but what Marina had us doing, was looking for any particularly large tree – or indeed anything that would cast a shadow for long periods of daylight – and hunt around the base of it for… that's right, mushrooms. I hated mushrooms. Yes, I ate them when I had to, when supplies had run low, and there was literally nothing else to eat on board the Iron Will, but they sat at the bottom of the food chain for me, with no exceptions.

I had wanted to start making plans for what we were going to do to seek our revenge on the Entropics, how we could save the Selari, the Sylph and now even the children of this world, but Marina had rightly said that we needed to be able to feed ourselves first, then help others, then feed others. I did grumble a little, saying that with enough people, foraging would go faster, but I was soundly ignored.

"Mushrooms?" I echoed, looking sceptically at Marina as she explained our task for the day.

"Yes, mushrooms. They're a good source of food, they grow abundantly around here, and they're easy to gather," she stated matter-of-factly. "And don't make that face, Marcus. We don't have the luxury of pickiness right now. What is it with men and salad anyway?"

I sighed, realising she was right but partly wanting to argue that mushrooms weren't salad. But the struggle for survival didn't come with the convenience of culinary preferences. So, pushing aside my aversion to fungal food, I grudgingly resigned myself to the task at hand.

We spent the morning scouting the surrounding area, searching for patches of shade where mushrooms would likely grow. We found a few patches and carefully harvested the gross little toadstools, placing them in a makeshift bag we'd fashioned from a bit of cloth I'd found.

Despite my dislike for mushrooms, I found the activity oddly calming. There was something peaceful about being in the wild, surrounded by nature, and gathering our own food. It was in contrast to the oppressive atmosphere in the mine, and I found myself appreciating it, despite the circumstances.

By the time the sun was high in the sky, we'd gathered a decent amount of mushrooms, and we decided to head back to the shelter to rest and prepare our very first meal. On the way back, I managed to see more of what our new home had to offer in the bright sunlight.

Broken buildings, ruins, burnt husks, but the backdrop of the calm sea that spanned away as far as the eye could see? I was at home here for sure, no matter how run down the place was. The sunshine made the water shimmer, and the wind carried the salty scent of the sea, reminding me of distant memories of my own world. Despite everything, there was beauty to be found in this desolate place.

Back at our shelter, Marina and I began the task of preparing our meal. We set up a small fire, and soon the smell of cooking mushrooms filled the air. Despite my reservations, I found myself salivating at the scent. Hunger, it seemed, was a powerful persuader.

While our meal was cooked, I found myself lost in thought, gazing out towards the sea. It was peaceful here, despite the ruin and desolation all around us. For the first time since I'd been dragged into this world, I felt a sense of calm. A sense of hope. We were far from safe, and our situation was anything but ideal. But we were free. And we were together.

"Um, are you going to eat that?" Yari's voice made me jump so high that Marina asked what was up. Passing it off as nothing, I turned my thoughts inward.

"Yes… why?" I asked.

"I can feel how much you don't want to," Yari said. "So why are you going to?"

"Survival," I responded simply, keeping my eyes forward so as not to alert Marina to my inner monologue. "We need food to survive, and right now, mushrooms are all that we have."

There was a pause, and I could almost picture the Sylph contemplating my answer. "I understand survival," she eventually said. "But you're not just surviving; you're living. There's a difference."

"Yes, there is," I agreed. "But sometimes, survival comes before everything else. And sometimes, to live, you need to do things you don't particularly enjoy. Like eating disgusting, slimy gross mushrooms."

"I guess," Yari conceded after a moment. "It's just... I can feel your aversion, and it makes me feel bad."

I couldn't help but smile at that. It was a strange thing to hear from a mystical being like Yari. "Well, Yari, welcome to the human experience. It's filled with things we don't particularly enjoy but have to do anyway."

"But you're free now," she pressed. "Isn't freedom about doing what you enjoy and not what you don't?"

"Yes and no," I replied, smiling wryly as I realised I was having a philosophical conversation with a Sylph. "Freedom means having the choice. And right now, I'm choosing to eat mushrooms because that's the best choice available to me. Someday, when we're not just surviving but truly living, I promise I'll avoid mushrooms at all costs."

"I hope so," Yari said, her voice tinged with amusement. "I can feel your strong desire for something better, something like fish."

My gaze fell back onto the calm waters, and it made me wonder.

"Are there actually any edible fish in these waters?" I asked Yari.

"Yes, of course!" Yari replied. "Millions and millions of fish that are all edible!" she sounded excited at the notion that one day we may actually get to fishing, and it made me wonder how much of the Sylph was becoming more and more like myself as time went by.

"I think… I think I really, really want fish," Yari stated.

And with that, I couldn't help but laugh out loud, drawing a puzzled look from Marina. I shook my head and reassured her it was nothing, and then picked up a mushroom and took a bite. It wasn't fish, but it was food, and it was keeping me alive. For now, that was enough.

"Definitely," I agreed with Yari. "When we've got a bit more stability, we'll definitely try fishing. I'm sure it'll taste much better than these mushrooms."

There was a touch of happiness in Yari's mental response, like she was sharing in anticipation of the potential meal. It was strange to think that a Sylph, a being simply a part of me without a physical body of her own, could appreciate the idea of food. But then again, she'd shared my experiences and my memories, so perhaps it was only natural that she'd develop some of my preferences.

As I chewed on the mushroom, I turned my gaze to the sea again. The water was calm, reflecting the bright sky above. There was something soothing about the rhythmic sound of the waves crashing against the shore. It was a reminder that even in the face of ruin and desolation, life went on. Nature went on.

And so would we.

Marina had finished preparing the rest of the mushrooms, and she brought them over to where I was sitting. We ate them in silence, watching the sun slowly make its descent towards the horizon. The fiery ball of light painted the sky in hues of orange and red, creating a beautiful spectacle that was both inspiring and humbling, and after we had finished eating, Marina and I started to discuss our plans.

Of course, It was clear that we needed more than just mushrooms to survive. We needed to find more sustainable food sources, and we needed to start to figure out our surroundings and take stock of what we had and what we needed. Most of all, I needed to understand more about this world and about the Entropics.

With the ocean in front of us and the vast wilderness behind us, we had a lot of exploring to do. But for now, as the day turned into night and the first stars began to appear in the sky, we needed to rest.

"I think we've had a productive first day," Marina said, breaking the silence. She looked at me with a small smile, her eyes reflecting the flickering flames of our small fire.

"Yes, we have," I agreed. "Tomorrow, we start anew. We'll do what we can to start making a difference in this world, no matter what it throws at us."

"Well that sounds like a plan," Marina replied, her eyes twinkling, and she leaned back against the wall of our shelter, closing her eyes.

She awoke a second later when a big, fat droplet of rain landed right on her forehead. I laughed as she stood bolt-upright in shock. Though followed quickly after her when the skies above turned to thick, black clouds and a fork of lightning lit up our world. Then followed the mother of all storms.

Within moments it got so loud that I had to shout to be heard over the sound of the rain pounding the ground.

"We need somewhere with a roof!" I yelled.

Marina nodded back, clearly not wanting to battle the rain for audial superiority. But then it looked like she had another idea; she pointed to the ground where puddles had already formed. Well, puddles may have been a little tame for the lake that had started to appear all around our new home, but this wasn't the time for semantics. Stooping down to the ground, Marina cupped her hands, picked up as much of the water as she could, and drank it.

"Shit," I thought. "I hadn't thought about drinking water." It was strange; when I'd been Captain of the Iron Will, my body had been so good at reminding me to restock our food and water supplies, but here, I didn't feel much hunger or thirst at all. I wondered how much of that was because of the Cores.

It didn't matter. I followed Marina's lead and cupped my hands together to collect some of the water. Not wanting to be a part of any muddy puddle – and without any alcohol to turn the rainwater into much safer and much tastier grog, I scanned our surroundings for something a little cleaner than floor-rain.

My eyes followed the rainwater pounding down onto our small roofless house and cascading to the edges, where it spattered loudly against the former wooden frame. I followed the water's path with my gaze all the way down to the floor, then out to the front of the building. I couldn't help but smirk at my own genius when I found that just outside of our little home was a tiny spout of water, free flowing just an inch or so from the ground. This was more like it for a Captain. Much better than floor-rain.

I stooped down and caught some of the water in my cupped hands, checked it briefly to make sure it at least looked clean, and then drank it. The rainwater was cool, and I felt it travel down my insides into my stomach. It made me feel happy, revitalised even, and I immediately wanted more, so I cupped my hands again and went back in for a second helping.

"No, no, no, no, no!" Yari's terrified shouts filled my mind. "What are you doing?!" she asked. "What is this?"

Frozen in place, I had no idea what the Sylph was talking about.

"Uh… what?" I asked before moving another muscle.

"So much… there's just so… much…" Yari said more to herself than to me. "Can't… what?"

None of this was making any sense to me, but it was worrying me. What had I done that was so wrong? Was Yari dying? It certainly sounded like it. Surely water wasn't that much of an issue, was it?

"Yari talk to me," I pressed. "What's happening?"

"I… I don't know," Yari replied, a little calmer though still evidently distressed. "The water you just drank… there's something in it… I can feel it. I'm trying to help, but please… don't drink anymore."

I had no idea what Yari meant by 'trying to help', and I didn't see how rainwater was causing her so many problems. I didn't feel like anything was wrong with me anyway. But if drinking rainwater was going to be such a huge issue, it was going to cause much bigger problems in the future.

Not realising that I was stood hunched over in place by the small spout of water, I was surprised when Marina arrived and placed a hand on my back.

"Marcus?" she asked. "Is everything all right? Are you hurt?"

I didn't have the wherewithal to deal with two simultaneous conversations at that particular moment, so I ignored Marina and turned my attention to Yari, who I decided was in more danger than Marina, whose red hair I noticed was matted flat against her head with rainwater dripping from her.

"Yari? Talk to me," I pressed. "What's going on?"

But no response came. It was strange; for the first time in as long as I could remember, I felt alone inside my own head. The silence wasn't like it had been when Yari wasn't talking in general – it was like my passenger was gone entirely.

Then the pain hit me like I'd been struck point blank by an iron cannonball fired by an oversized cannon. I felt pain like my ribs were breaking and shattering all at once, and I fell to my knees with a cry that dwarfed the sound of the rain around me.

I couldn't move. I didn't want to.

But I was still conscious of what was happening around me. I could see Marina run up to me, dropping to the ground, her knees splashing in the wet mud. There was something else, though: from my new vantage point on the ground, I could now follow the trail of water that was hitting the structure of our little wooden building. The water was running down the ruined wooden frame, collecting on the floor wherever it met wood, but it was also washing over our pile of Obsidian Cores. Water was filtering through the Cores, then dripping down beneath, onto a smattering of broken planks and floorboards and eventually culminating in the spout from which I'd drank.

'Shit,' I thought.

I didn't black out this time, though. I remembered the last time I'd dealt with too many of the Cores and how it caused me to eventually crash, but this wasn't like that: I felt helpless, unable to move, totally and utterly weakened beyond anything I'd felt before, but I didn't black out. My mind was still working, and that had to mean something, right?

The pain was excruciating, though. It felt like a thousand tiny daggers were cutting into every inch of my insides. I curled up in agony, clutching my knees to my stomach. Through my hazy vision, I saw Marina's face filled with worry and confusion. She was shouting something at me, but her voice seemed distant and muffled through the pounding of rain and my own painful gasps. It was so hard to breathe.

Suddenly, a strange sensation spread through me. It felt like something was shifting inside, moving to combat the pain. The sensation was unfamiliar, yet I instinctively knew what was happening - it was Yari. She was trying to help, just as she had promised.

Through the haze of pain, I tried to speak to Marina to let her know what was happening. "The water," I gasped, "ran over... the... Cores."

Marina's eyes widened as she followed my gaze and immediately realised what had happened to me. She looked horrified. She understood the implications - I'd been poisoned by the residual energy in the Cores, just as I had been back in the mine. She nodded, pulling me closer to shield me from the rain, her eyes darting around as she tried to come up with a plan.

But there was nothing we could do. We had no antidote, no medical supplies, nothing. All I could do was hope that Yari would be able to counteract the poison before it caused any more permanent damage, whatever she was doing in there.

Time seemed to stand still as I lay there, shaking with pain. The world around me was a blur, the sounds of the rain and the crashing waves a distant murmur. All I could focus on was the pain and the fear that this might be the end. Marina held me against her but said and did nothing. I only wished I'd live long enough to repay her kindness.

But then, slowly, thankfully like a gift from the Gods the pain began to lessen. It was a gradual shift, the stabbing pains dulling to a throbbing ache. My breathing began to even out, and I found myself able to focus on my surroundings again.

I carefully uncurled myself to lay in Marina's lap, her hand brushing through my wet hair in a soothing manner. Her eyes were filled with concern but also a touch of relief. She smiled down at me, her lips moving in a silent prayer of thanks.

"We need to be careful," she murmured, her voice barely audible over the sound of the rain. "We can't afford to make mistakes like this. Too many things rely on us now."

I nodded, too weak to speak. We had been lucky this time. But we wouldn't always be so lucky. We needed to be more cautious, more aware.

We also needed to find a way to store the Cores properly or at least find a way to protect ourselves from them. We couldn't keep risking our lives like this. It was clear that the Cores would be a part of our lives for the foreseeable future if we ever planned to figure out how to use them in our fight back against the Entropics, and we needed to learn how to handle them safely.

As I lay there in the rain, my body weak and my mind racing, I made a vow. We would survive this. We would learn, and we would adapt. This was our world now, and we would make it our own.

The sound of the rain falling around us became a comforting lullaby, and despite the pain and exhaustion, I found myself smiling. We were far from safe, and we had a long road ahead of us. But we were free, and we were together.

And that was enough. For now, at least.

But were we?

"Yari?" I asked softly in my mind, trying my best to remain calm and quiet in case I frightened the Sylph, who had no doubt just been through the same hell as I had.

I waited for a moment, but no reply came.

I was about to call again, just a little louder this time, when a very, very tiny voice reached me.

"I'm here," Yari said in almost a whisper. "Please… don't do that again. I don't know how I managed to get through that, but I did my best… I don't know if it will be the same next time or not."

I thought about the Obsidian Cores. They were surely the answer to all of this, but if I couldn't even drink rainwater that had washed over them, just how much was I going to be able to tolerate?

"I'll try not to, Yari," I replied. "But we are going to have to find a way to use the Cores at some point. I know I didn't mean to do it just now, but we're going to have to do a little experimenting… maybe when you're back up to your old self, after a little rest," I added thoughtfully. I didn't add that I needed to get back to my old self, too; this one little mistake had almost killed me.

I managed to prop myself back up into a seated position, and the first thing I noticed was that it was still raining. I had all but forgotten with everything else going on all around me, but helpfully, Marina cupped her hands to catch some of the water straight from the sky and poured it into my mouth. It was cool and pleasant, but it made me cough a little.

"You're alright," Marina said. "Just in a little bit of shock, that's all. Get a little water in you and a few more mushrooms…"

"Please, no," I spat. "No more mushrooms, I beg of you…"

Marina looked at me with an expression that told me she couldn't believe that someone in my position was up to refusing food, whatever it was. But when she saw the weak smile I gave her, she burst out laughing and pulled me into a tight hug.

"If you keep doing stupid things like that, I'll..." Marina said and didn't finish her sentence.

"Please no..." I repeated with mock fear in my eyes. "Anything but that."

"You know, if you keep talking about my cooking like that, I'm going to have to kill you, right?" she said.

I shut my mouth. The joke had run its course, and I was too weak to keep moving around so much right now; I needed rest again more than anything else in the world.

Marina let me sleep.

The next morning, I awoke in a puddle. Not because it had been raining all night but because my clothes had been drenched in the downpour and had slowly released all of the water they'd absorbed underneath me. Standing up, I held my arms out to my sides and watched as the sodden fabric flopped about. I was cold and uncomfortable, but I was upright.

Then my eyes fell on Marina, who looked entirely dry and happy, cooking mushrooms once more over a small fire.

"Good morning!" Marina said as soon as she turned to look at my drowned-rat form. I simply grunted back.

"Some of us got up early, dried our clothes over this fire, then cooked breakfast, so before you go complaining, that's on you, not me. I wasn't sure what you wanted to eat, so..." She gestured to the makeshift grill and the mushrooms with a devilish look in her eyes.

Of course, I knew there was nothing else to eat, but did she really have to be like that?

"We have to do something today," I announced. I hadn't yet had the time to get my thoughts all lined up properly, but what this whole experience had taught me was that if I waited long enough, it could be too long. Everything I had set out to do, all the people who I'd vowed to help... I needed to make my move right now, not wait around and see how it all goes.

"Yari, are you there? Are you OK?" I asked inwardly to see if the rest had given my companion the chance to regain her strength.

"Yes, I'm here," the small voice returned inside my head, though I could tell that Yari was far stronger than she had been the last time we'd spoken.

"How are you?" I asked.

"I'm OK, I guess," Yari replied. "But there's something different; I can feel it. Like the barrier between us has fallen a little more. I thought the same the last time you had taken in some of the Cores... I think it's why we can talk the way that we can, but nobody else is able to."

I scratched my chin. "What do you mean 'different?'" I asked, not fully grasping what Sylph was trying to say.

"I don't know," Yari replied slowly. "Only, I feel a little more connected with you now, but also a little more in control… somehow. Do you feel any different?"

I mentally checked all the extremities of my physical body, but the only thing I could come up with was that I was fine.

But before I finished my check and replied to Yari, she spoke again.

"Let me just try something," she said.

A moment passed, and nothing happened, and then as though I had been touched by a red-hot poker, my forearm felt like it had lit on fire. I looked down at the tattoo of the bird that the Sylph had left there when it had entered my body, and my eyes widened as it began to glow with a bright golden light.

"Y… Yari?" I thought, not sure if this was something that she was trying to do or not, but no reply came, just more pain, though it was centred around my forearm still, so while it was uncomfortable, it wasn't unbearable.

The pain pulsed rhythmically, in sync with my heartbeat, and then began to ease, replaced by a strange warmth that radiated from my forearm. Then, to my astonishment, the glowing tattoo of the bird detached from my skin and rose into the air, gradually transforming into a familiar and very tangible form.

The golden bird shimmered, ethereal and beautiful, its light piercing the morning fog. Its flowing wings beating in a graceful rhythm, projecting tiny sparkles like fireflies. The bird, however, wasn't just an ordinary bird; it was a perfect replica of Yari, with her long, elegant tail and the delicate golden feathers and even her sharp black eyes.

"I did it!" Yari's voice echoed in my head, filled with excitement and a sense of achievement.

"Yari, is that... you?" I stammered, surprised by the sight in front of me. All thoughts of keeping this from Marina were now long gone, and I briefly saw the Selari's mouth drop open though she didn't make a single sound.

"Yes! Yes, it's me!" Yari replied, still inside my head and sounding a little breathless. "I am not sure how it works exactly, but I think I can... sort of project myself beyond our body. This is a physical manifestation of my energy. But I believe I can still feel your sensations and your thoughts."

I didn't miss the fact that Yari had called it our body, but I could let it go for now; this was just so much more interesting.

As the Sylph spoke, I noticed that the glowing bird seemed tethered to me somehow, as though an invisible string connected us. She fluttered around, stretching her wings and exploring the space around us within a very specific but very small radius. Yari could only venture a certain distance from me, yet she was clearly relishing her newfound freedom.

"I... this is amazing, Yari," I said, my voice filled with awe. I reached out to touch her shimmering form, and to my surprise, my hand passed right through her. It was like touching a warm breeze, comforting yet insubstantial.

Yari fluttered back toward me and settled on my shoulder, her ethereal form casting a soft glow against my skin. A strange calm washed over me, a reassuring sense of companionship. I realised that this was another dimension to our bond, something that made us even closer.

"I think with practice, I'll be able to control it better," Yari said, her voice echoing in my mind. "But I think I can help us this way. I can be your eyes from a distance; scout ahead and see things you might miss."

"How far can you go?" I asked aloud in hope.

Yari paused for a second, then said: "Just a little way, the length of your arm or two at the moment, but I feel like we can make it better. I know it can be better. Oh, Marcus! This is more than I ever thought possible!"

I couldn't help but smile. The emotions that the Sylph was sending into our shared connection were simply too overpowering, too positive, and I loved every second of it.

The possibilities that this development presented were extraordinary. If Yari could extend her range, we could gain a significant advantage in exploring this new world and dealing with any potential threats. It also meant that we were becoming even more inextricably linked, a realisation that made me feel both awed and a little apprehensive.

"Yari, this is… this is incredible. I don't know what to say," I admitted. I looked over at Marina, who was staring at the glowing bird with wide eyes, but was still yet to utter a word.

"What in the actual fuck is happening?" Marina asked, her voice barely more than a whisper.

"I think…" I started, trying to find the words to explain, "I think this is Yari."

"And what is a Yari?" Marina asked incredulously, and I realised the mistake that I'd made. I'd kept all of this a secret from Marina, and now I knew I had to come clean.

I turned to face her, taking a deep breath, my fingers mindlessly tracing the spot where Yari's symbol was. The golden bird on my shoulder trilled softly, a comforting presence as I struggled to find the right words.

"Yari… is my Sylph," I began slowly. "She… we… are bonded. I have been able to communicate with her for a little while now, and she told me how the Entropics enslaved her race to force the Selari into their work. She's just as much a victim in any of this as we are, Marina." I gestured to the shimmering bird form. "She's been with me since we arrived in this world, and I thought that she was the reason I was imprisoned. This, this projection thing, it's new... we haven't quite figured it out yet."

Marina blinked, her gaze flitting between me and the glowing bird. There was a long moment of silence, the crackle of the fire the only sound permeating the morning air. "So, you've been talking all this time?" she finally asked, her tone a mixture of disbelief and annoyance. "Why didn't you tell me?"

Her question stung, and I felt the twinge of guilt. I had been secretive, yes, but it was to protect both her and Yari. It was a defensive mechanism I had picked up from the old world, and it seemed I had not yet shaken it off.

"I... I wasn't sure how you'd react," I confessed truthfully, my eyes meeting hers. "And Yari, she wanted to remain hidden; she was afraid. She's just like us: forced into working for the Entropics, making us do their work, but she didn't have a choice; the Entropics have all of them, their friends and families... Yari and the Sylph are no different to the Selari in this world."

Marina's eyes softened, and she gave me a small, understanding nod. "Well," she said after a moment, "this is a lot to take in. I'm going to need some time to process all of this."

I nodded back, acknowledging her need for space, but I could tell that she wasn't entirely sold. Honestly though, she'd taken all of this quite well.

With a sigh, I turned my attention back to Yari. The golden bird was still perched comfortably on my shoulder, her presence a reassuring reminder of the bond we shared.

"I think we have a lot to learn about each other, Yari," I said quietly.

The golden bird on my shoulder ruffled her feathers, a soft glowing light sparkling from her form. "I look forward to it, Marcus," she replied. Her voice echoed in my mind, a soft melody that made me feel hopeful and excited for the days to come. It was clear that although we could speak normally inside my mind, the bird projection was unable to talk.

I could feel a stronger connection with her now, a bond that transcended the physical. Despite the uncertainty that loomed ahead of us, I couldn't help but feel a surge of optimism.

"OK, so let's say this is a thing that you can do now... how does that help us exactly?" Marina asked with an expression that I couldn't quite place. It looked somewhere between hope and anger. Both perhaps?

"Well, I can..." I started, then realised that being able to do this didn't actually seem to give us any new options or opportunities.

Before I could answer, Marina spoke again.

"And can I do this? Can I talk to the Sylph inside of me?"

"She mustn't try!" I heard Yari's voice inside my head. "I don't know why you can withstand the power of the Obsidian Cores, but I've never seen or heard of a Selari survive when trying to use them to gain their power. They cooked them into their food, crumbled them to dust to sprinkle on other foods, and even used them to grease cooking pots and pans. Nothing has ever worked to my knowledge and it always ended the same way!"

As Yari spoke, I was watching the small golden bird as though it was the one talking to me. It actually made things a little easier having something to focus my attention on.

Turning my attention back to Marina, I slowly shook my head and relayed to her what Yari had told me. She seemed a little upset, but I figured that she hadn't held much hope for it anyway.

"I think if we work on getting more Cores into you without killing you, then my range will increase," Yari said.

Thinking about how I'd basically nearly died both times I'd had dealings with the Cores on a personal level, that was something that made me wince. Though had I nearly died? The first time I'd blacked out and eventually levelled out, and this time, although painful and uncomfortable, I'd managed to pull through it with Yari's help. I was going to point this out, but Yari must've known the risks to her if she was the one suggesting it.

I didn't have a chance to respond; I was sidetracked by Marina closing in on me and slowly holding her hand out to the Sylph sat on my shoulder. I didn't move away, and Yari certainly didn't seem to mind Selari reaching out to her. I held my breath as Marina hesitated, then moved into touching distance. I felt nothing as Marina's hand passed unchallenged through the projection of my companion, and I didn't feel or hear any objections from Yari either.

"It's... I don't even know what to say," Marina said slowly. "It's like there's nothing there at all, but I can see it."

"Her," I corrected.

"Her," Marina repeated, though I couldn't tell if she was being sarcastic or not. "And you can talk to her like she's a person?" she asked.

I could tell now that Marina was asking these things not to be sarcastic; rather, she was simply so shocked that she had so many things to ask that she was saying the first things that came to her mind. With that being said, I then told Marina everything. When I had first spoken to Yari, how I was the one to name her, the visions of Yari's family taken by the Entropics, how we could speak, understand and feel each other, everything right down to the latest bout of pain brought on by the Core-soaked water that seemed to have given Yari and me this new ability.

"And as you might've guessed," I finished, "I kept this from you because… well, I don't know what any of this means yet. I don't know if it'll go away tomorrow or if I'm going to turn into a bird and fly away into the sunset."

Marina stared at me with her mouth open wide. I couldn't tell if she was going to hit me or tell me that this was the most wonderful thing she'd ever heard. In the end, she closed her mouth, looked at Yari and spoke directly to the projection of my internal friend.

"My name's Marina," she said softly. "I know how you must feel, having your family taken away from you, but we're going to do everything we can to put things right. I don't know if you can understand me or not, but I hope you can find it within yourself to see me not as a threat but as a friend."

I looked at the Yari sitting on my shoulder, and her voice came inside my head. "It means a lot," Yari said, which I relayed to Marina.

"Your Sylph too…" I said. "You may not be able to communicate with it like Yari and me, but you should name it, let it know what your plans are. We think that it agrees with what we are doing, but it could be comforting for it to have a better understanding of what we have planned."

Chapter 10 – Children

"Just drink it!" Marina stamped her foot on the ground, and it made me smile. The rain had all dried up, and the bright sunshine was doing its bit in drying everything out to a far more comfortable degree, but Marina had decided that it was time to start forcing the issue. She'd collected some Core-soaked water in a makeshift wooden bowl made from some old scraps that she had found lying around and was trying to get me to drink it. Her theory was that with each ingestion of the Cores, I was getting a better bond with Yari, so she wanted to see what would happen if we simply kept going.

"You don't know how it feels!" I protested loudly. "And what if it kills me… or Yari? You think you could live with yourself after that?"

Yes, it may have sounded like a cheap way out of doing something, and I was supposed to be a fearsome Free Man and all that, but Marina had no idea of the pain that the Cores had caused me. Plus, what I was asking were genuine questions. We had no idea what would happen if I ingested more of the Cores too soon or in too high of a quantity.

"This is too important!" Marina replied, pushing the liquid towards me again.

"Marcus… it might be the only way," Yari's voice filled my mind. "Marina's right: you could be the key to stopping the oppression we all face in this world, and we both owe it to everyone who the Entropics have enslaved to do whatever we can to become stronger, to increase our chances of survival."

I'm not going to lie; I felt ambushed.

But if Yari was on board and Marina seemed as though she couldn't care less about my well-being, then I guess I was outnumbered. This was something that I simply had to do.

I closed my eyes, mentally preparing myself for the wave of discomfort that was likely to follow. I reached out and grabbed the bowl, my fingers brushing against Marina's in the process. Her hand was cool in contrast to the growing warmth inside me.

"It's OK," Marina said softly, almost in a whisper. "I just showed them the water, this shouldn't be anything like the last time."

Somehow, the words didn't comfort me, but it didn't really make any difference.

Taking a deep breath, I raised the bowl to my lips. The Core-soaked water smelled faintly metallic, with a strange, underlying sweetness that I somehow associated with the Cores. For a moment, I hesitated, the potential consequences of my action weighing heavily on my mind. But then I remembered Yari's words and the conviction in her voice. I was doing this for her, for us, and for everyone else the Entropics had wronged.

I tipped the bowl back, the liquid sliding down my throat. Almost instantly I felt the familiar sharp pain blossom within my body, radiating out as though I had been stabbed in the stomach, and the force of the wound was sending tendrils of pain to all of my extremities. But this time, it was different; it was accompanied by a warmth, a warmth that radiated from the mark on my forearm and spread throughout my body. It was as if Yari was already doing what she could to fight the pain away, to shield me from the power of the Cores, absorbing it as best she could.

"Marcus," Yari's voice echoed in my mind, calm amidst the storm of sensations. "Hold on. I'm here with you."

It felt like an eternity before the pain finally started to subside, replaced by an incredible sense of connectedness. I could feel Yari, stronger and more present than before, her essence intertwining with mine in ways I still could not comprehend. And then, almost as if a switch had been flicked, I could feel Yari's happiness within me and it made me smile. We had intentionally tried to take in the power of the Cores for the first time, and it had worked.

Gasping, I opened my eyes. Marina was staring at me, wide-eyed. "Did it work?" she asked, her voice filled with a mixture of concern and curiosity.

"Yes," I replied, my voice barely above a whisper. "I think it did."

I could feel Yari, her joy and excitement radiating through our bond. This was a whole new level of connection, one that was both exhilarating and terrifying. But as I looked at Marina, her eyes wide and hopeful, and felt Yari's reassuring presence, I knew we had taken the right step.

"What's different?" Marina asked in anticipation. "Can you separate completely, or something like that?"

It was strange; hearing Marina say those words was the first time that I'd even thought of separating from Yari. The more we walked our path and the tighter our bond became, the more it simply felt normal. I didn't want to separate from Yari any more than I wanted to turn my back on Marina and walk away. We were part of a whole, and that was the way I hoped it was going to stay.

With those words, though, Yari showed us exactly what had changed. She emerged from within me, though this time from my chest and the tiny projection soared up into the air and began to spiral upwards in circles above our heads. It was as though Yari had been caged for her entire life and had just been set free. She listed side to side, swooped, and flew in loops, moving faster and faster until it was difficult to keep track of her.

"Yari!" I gasped, my eyes following the glowing figure as it soared high above us, her golden form radiant in the sunlight. It was as if a small sun had been released into the sky, and the sight was breath-taking. I couldn't help but feel a sense of awe, along with a feeling that I presumed was at least partly Yari's: pure delight.

"Is this... is this what you meant?" I asked aloud, forgetting for a moment that Yari could hear my thoughts. "Can you go further now?"

"Yes," Yari's voice echoed in my mind, brimming with joy. "It feels... liberating. I can see so much more from here, Marcus! I don't know how far I can go, but it's amazing. So… amazing."

Marina was staring at the glowing figure in the sky, her mouth hanging open in astonishment. "Marcus," she breathed, turning to me, her eyes wide with awe and disbelief. "This is... This is amazing!"

I nodded, unable to tear my gaze away from the spectacle above us and smiling at the phrase that Yari had used and that had been repeated by Marina. Yari's form shone brightly against the clear blue sky, her radiance shining down on us. The small golden bird hovered in the air for a moment longer before swiftly descending and settling back onto my shoulder. The feeling of her presence re-entering our shared space was comforting, like a piece of me that had been missing had returned.

"Yari," I said softly, a smile playing on my lips. "You are truly extraordinary. Now, how far can you go?"

Yari didn't need to be asked twice. Jumping from my shoulder again, she darted away from me in a straight line. A few moments passed, and the bird had grown so tiny that I had to squint to follow her. Then her thought sounded in my mind.

"I can't go any further," She said. "It's like I'm still tethered to you somehow, and I can feel the rope around my body. The further I go, the tighter the rope gets… but do you think with more Cores…?"

I didn't answer. Right now, I could see that Yari's range was about five hundred metres or so, and that was quite an improvement over the first version of her projection.

Yari then flew in an arc to make sure that the range of her newest ability was circular around me as a central point and then returned to my shoulder. The sheer happiness reaching me through our shared link forced me into a wide smile. One that Marina was about to ruin.

"You think you can drink more?" she said, holding out another bowl of water for me to take. I didn't know where she had pulled it from, but looking at the liquid made my stomach turn.

I closed my eyes and sighed. The way that the Cores had just given Yari and me something so special, I couldn't refuse to try for more.

I didn't say a word. I took the bowl and once again drank the cool liquid within without any hesitation, not even taking a moment to take in its metallic aroma. This time though, it didn't feel pleasant as the liquid entered my throat; it burnt. It burnt with such intensity that my entire body seemed to reject the idea of even keeping this within me, and I couldn't help but bend over, open my mouth and vomit the water straight onto the ground.

"Marcus!" Marina's voice broke through the pain, a touch of panic lacing her tone. She was at my side in an instant, her hands gripping my shoulders to steady me. The world spun around me, a nauseating whirlwind of colours and sensations that threatened to pull me under. I could see stars.

"Marcus, are you alright?" she asked, worry creeping into her voice.

"I'm fine," I lied, swallowing back the bile that had risen in my throat. I could still taste the metallic tang of the Core-soaked water on my tongue, my stomach churning at the memory. I knew Marina was right that the Cores were our best chance at enhancing our abilities and fighting back against the Entropics, but this was simply too much to bear.

"Maybe we should take it slow," Yari's voice echoed in my mind, a soothing balm amidst the storm of discomfort. Her worry seeped into our bond, tinged with a hint of guilt. "I'm sorry, Marcus. I didn't think it would be this painful."

I shook my head, trying to clear it of the dizzying vertigo. "It's not your fault, Yari," I replied aloud, my voice coming out hoarser than I intended. "We need to do this for all of us."

I could feel Yari's hesitation, her fear and worry curling around me like a protective shroud. But she didn't protest. She knew, just like I did that we needed to push through this if we had any hope of challenging the Entropics.

Gritting my teeth, I pushed away from Marina and stood up straight, wiping the back of my hand across my mouth. My head hurt with a dull ache, and my stomach protested at the sudden movement, but I forced myself to stay upright.

"Alright," I said, turning to Marina. "Let's try again. But let's do this slowly, one sip at a time." I held up a single finger as though to punctuate my point. Marina looked uncertain but nodded, handing me another bowl of the Core-soaked water. I had no idea where she was getting them from.

She watched me closely, ready to intervene at the slightest sign of distress.

I raised the bowl to my lips, hesitated for a moment, then took a small sip. The liquid burned its way down my throat, a fiery trail of discomfort that settled in my stomach. But I kept my eyes closed, focused on the sensations flooding our shared bond. The power. The connection. The potential.

But it was no use. Once again, my body rejected the liquid inside me, and for the second time in as many minutes, I emptied the contents of my stomach onto the ground before me.

This time Marina didn't need to steady me; I'd braced myself for the inevitable reaction. But the repeated experience of the Core-soaked water was nothing short of excruciating. I crumpled onto my hands and knees, coughing and gasping for breath. My entire body felt as though it was rejecting not just the Core water but everything inside me.

I felt Marina's hand on my back again, rubbing soothing circles in an attempt to offer some comfort. It was a futile gesture, but I appreciated it nonetheless. My stomach ached with a dull and persistent throb that permeated through my whole body.

"No more," I rasped, pressing a hand to my belly. "I can't... I just can't."

"Marcus," Yari's voice floated into my thoughts; her presence tinged with worry and remorse. "I'm so sorry. I didn't think it would hurt you this much. Maybe we should stop."

"I think maybe we should stop," Marina once again echoed Yari's sentiment, her hand stilling on my back. "Maybe we should take a break. You look like you've had enough."

It was true. I felt utterly spent, physically and emotionally. My body had reached its limits, and it was begging for respite. I couldn't help but wonder if we were doing more harm than good.

"You're right," I finally admitted, the taste of defeat bitter in my mouth. "Let's take a break. We'll figure something out. Maybe it just takes time or something? Maybe try again tomorrow?"

I forced myself to sit back on my heels, my muscles protesting with fatigue. Marina moved to sit beside me, her concern evident in her eyes.

"I'm sorry, Marcus," she said quietly, reaching out to squeeze my hand.

"We'll take it slow, and we've already come so far."

I nodded feebly. "I think I just need to rest," I said. "Tomorrow, we can do better," then I added thoughtfully: "Have you thought about drinking it?"

"I... I can't. We can't."

"But is that the truth?" I asked, a questioning look on my face. Marina had always been braver than me, always ready to leap into the unknown for the sake of our cause. This sudden reticence was unlike her.

"If we... if any of the Selari people ingest the Cores or any part of them... we die," Marina said, her voice barely a whisper. "Straight away. The Cores tear us apart as soon as they enter our bodies, and within a moment, we're gone. It's the truth Marcus and I don't want to risk..."

I stared at Marina with wide eyes. "AND YOU KEEP MAKING ME DRINK THEM?" I shouted.

"Yes, but… you already had… I mean you…" Marina struggled to find the right words but simply stopped speaking.

I lay down on the warm, dry ground and let my muscles relax, trying to forget the fact that Marina had been gambling with my life. I had to admit, though, it felt good to let everything go, and I watched as Yari's projection leapt high up into the sky above us and began to circle us overhead.

I had just started getting comfortable, not thinking about Marina's actions or anything else for that matter, when a few moments later, Yari's voice arrived in my head.

"Smoke! I see smoke!" she announced loudly.

"What?" I asked aloud, not exactly sure if I'd heard her correctly.

"Smoke!" She repeated, not adding anything more, and I couldn't help but realise that she was telling me that this could only mean one thing: that there were people nearby. Did this mean that our task was about to begin? Were we about to encounter some people in need of help?

"Marina," I called, "Yari can see smoke not too far away. Do you know if there are any settlements near here?"

"No," Marina replied, but I haven't been to this place for a long time. I don't remember there being any settlements near to this one; that's why I chose it; I thought we would be safe here. We should be able to learn and grow without other people interfering… but I guess… settlements come and go as people move… otherwise the Entropics…."

I tried to steer the conversation away and to a more positive end and replied: "Where there's smoke, there's fire in my experience."

Marina nodded. "Yes, it's certainly something we need to have a look at, especially if there are people there. Perhaps they need our help. But even if they don't, maybe they can share some of their mushrooms with us?"

I scowled at Marina, but I could see that she was trying to be light-hearted. I could see she still felt bad about the situation with the Cores, but honestly, we had bigger fish to fry right now.

"Who do you think they could be?" I asked. "I don't want to walk into a camp full of Entropics."

"No, it won't be them," Marina said. "I've never heard of more than one being in the same place at one time. They're more likely to be children, or less likely it could be a handful of Selari who have managed to hide from the Entropics… but they're becoming rarer and rarer as time goes by. Our race is on the brink of extinction. I'm sure that if nothing changes soon, all hope will be lost for us as a people."

I thought about what Marina was saying and I wondered how I was going to feel if we did indeed find a camp full of children; what could I do with children in a world that I knew nothing about? What would I teach them? Would they even accept me? But I'd made a promise to Marina, to Yari, and to myself. No, I'd do anything I could to help these people whoever they were, and if this truly was going to be the first camp that we found in this place, then we were going to help them.

"Yari, can you see anything else? Can you see who they are," I asked.

"No," Yari replied straight away. "It's too far past the end of my range to see anything more; I can't even see if there's anything more than smoke. It's maybe two hours to walk, but quicker if you can run."

"In that case, we're going to have to go and have a look for ourselves, aren't we," I replied, "but when we get close, I want you to fly high into the air and see if you can look for any dangers before we arrive. I don't want any surprises when we get there. And I don't think we'll be running."

I saw Marina watching me as I gave my orders and couldn't decide if the uneasy expression on her face was because the fact that we were about to do something potentially dangerous that could put a lot of people in danger was dawning on her, or if she was simply worried about her people.

But if we wanted to help these people, possibly these children, we would have to do things that were going to be dangerous, not just for us, but for everyone involved.

Getting to my feet and brushing myself off, my mind switched to the task ahead; any thoughts of lazing around all but gone, and I had a new task to focus my attention on. I could tell that Marina had come to a similar conclusion by the way that she now looked less apprehensive and surer of herself. I didn't need to check on Yari; I could feel through our shared link that she knew this was the right course of action, and it made me feel good that all three of us were on the same page, working towards the same goal.

It was like I had my crew back again.

We didn't have to prepare anything for the short journey away from our makeshift home – not that we had yet done anything to make it a home. Instead, we simply began walking in the direction that Yari had indicated, and all the while, she flew high overhead at the extremity of her boundaries, searching in the ground before us for any signs of anything that would wish us any harm.

It seemed as though the rain had caused small patches of grass to grow over the mostly flat terrain between us and where the smoke was coming from, and it made me feel like I was at home again. The ground was soft and warm, and instead of a thick forest of unfamiliar trees, we walked across rolling fields, through small bushes, and over small patches of undergrowth that were easy to traverse. I barely had to think about where to put my next step, which in my mind was much better than when we were in the forest.

Eventually, we could see the smoke for ourselves rising above the landscape, and it made my heart leap.

My steps quickened with anticipation as we neared the source of the smoke. A sense of urgency filled my veins, wiping away the lingering weariness. As we got closer, I asked Yari to fly high and scope out the surroundings for any sign of danger.

As Yari soared overhead, the bond between us surged with power and I felt her focus, sharp and clear. Something was certainly different now, and as I felt Yari's effort being pushed into our bond, her vision became mine, and through her eyes, I saw the lay of the land stretch out before us. There was a small, wooden-built settlement hidden amongst a sparse grove of trees and the smoke Yari had spotted was rising from the centre.

There was no sign of immediate danger anywhere around, and if these people thought that it was safe to allow smoke to rise from their settlement, then I could only think that there was a reason for that: They felt safe.

As I focussed through Yair's vision, I could now just about see figures moving about - small, quick, and busy. Children.

"We're here," I announced to Marina, my voice betraying a small amount of concern.

Marina nodded, her face apprehensive too.

We approached the settlement slowly, Yari continuing to monitor the area from her high vantage point and I told her mentally to keep me up to date of any changes as we approached; it was too difficult paying attention to the images she sent and also walking in a straight line without falling over so I returned my attention to my own senses. As we neared, the sounds of the settlement reached our ears - the crackling of the fire, the rustling of leaves, and above all, the soft, high-pitched laughter of children.

But then abruptly, it stopped.

"Wait," Yari instructed through our bond and I dutifully came to a halt, placing a silent hand on Marina to relay the message. She looked at me quizzically, but kept quiet. Then I turned my attention back to Yari.

"Look at this," Yari said through our link and I dutifully returned my attention to her.

What I saw was truly awe-inspiring. I didn't know how the children had managed it, but they knew we were approaching and all of a sudden, their settlement, filled with excited laughter, general chit-chat and the noise of joyful playing in their carefree ways, vanished.

The once lively settlement was now eerily silent, the sounds of laughter replaced by a pressing quiet. The children had disappeared from view, hiding behind the worn-out wooden buildings and underbrush. The fire that had once risen, cheerily sending up tendrils of smoke into the sky, had been almost immediately doused, the plume of smoke thinning and dissipating into the air. Even the air around us felt heavy, filled with a palpable tension that hung like a thick fog.

It was as if the settlement had been swallowed by the grove, vanishing without a trace, leaving behind only a ghost of what once was. From Yari's vantage point, I could see the settlement transformed into an empty, abandoned ghost town, devoid of any life.

Incredible. The children had created a system, a well-rehearsed plan of action for when strangers approached. In an instant, they had made themselves invisible, a testament to their survival skills and their resilience in the face of adversity.

Marina, sensing the change, looked at me with wide eyes. "What's happening, Marcus?" She whispered, her voice barely audible against the backdrop of the silent grove.

"They've hidden themselves," I murmured back, my eyes refocusing on the desolate scene before us.

A sudden movement through the sparse trees then caught my attention. It had been hard to see from where we stood before, but the movement gave it away. My heart thudded against my chest as I watched the entrance gate to the settlement, clearly previously open and inviting, shut closed with a resonating thud, effectively sealing the settlement from the outside world. There were also walls surrounding the place, seemingly innocuous and harmless at a glance, almost not there at all. But now I really looked, they appeared impenetrable, a fortress against the unknown.

It dawned on me then; these children weren't just survivors. They were warriors, survivors trained in the art of evasion and deception. In a world that was ruthless and unforgiving, they had found a way to protect themselves, a way to persist. They were the future of the Selari people, embodying the spirit of their race in their innocence and bravery.

"We can't just barge in now," Marina observed, her voice filled with both awe and concern. "We need to show them we're not a threat."

"Yes, you're right," I agreed, a plan slowly forming in my mind. "Yari, land and stay with us. They might be less scared if they see we have a friendly bird with us."

Yari sent a slight feeling of confusion back down our link, but I didn't have to waste time in explaining what I actually meant. As Yari descended, landing gently on my shoulder, I looked at the sealed settlement. "We'll sit here, in clear view, but at a safe distance. We'll show them we mean no harm."

It wasn't the most active or perfect of plans, but I knew that this would either work, or it wouldn't. And so, we sat, Marina and I, under the watchful eyes of hidden children, on the edge of a vanishing settlement, our actions speaking louder than words. We were not invaders or threats. We were friends, offering our help and protection. The question was, would they accept it? Time would tell.

It didn't take long for something to happen.

I had noticed a slight shuffling in the trees around us, but had never been able to manage to catch a glimpse of what was up there because of how the thick tree trunks winded and twisted in all directions, and the low-hanging branches obscured most of what was happening above. But I somehow sensed that this was how their early warning system had worked – they must've had lookouts – but they were just so well hidden.

After about five minutes, a young boy who could have only just been ten or twelve at the most jumped down from a tall tree, which I thought was way too high for such a manoeuvre, and stared at us. He was clearly Selari with the gill-like ridges on his face. I tried not to stare.

"What're you doing here?" he asked. It sounded to my ear as if the boy had been poorly educated, but I guessed that was just part and parcel of his upbringing.

"And don't try anything," he added. "Got archers aimed at you all over this place. One wrong move and you're done."

I held my hands up placatingly.

"Hello," I said, careful to keep my voice soft and non-threatening. The boy looked at me, his eyes wide and wary.

Tattered rags for clothes, an unkempt blond mop atop his head and dirt covering a good portion of his skin. Yes, this was most certainly a young lad that had been left to fend for himself in a world that simply didn't care.

"We mean no harm," Marina added quickly, her voice also soothing. "We're here to help."

"We're here to protect you," I said simply, "And to make sure you and your friends can live without fear. Can you show us around? We'd like to understand better how you've managed so far."

"I said what're you doing here?" the boy repeated, seemingly not hearing our explanation. "You come to take us away? To feed us to the monsters? We ain't coming with you, we don't care what you have to say."

"Take you away? No," I responded, maintaining my gentle tone. I glanced at Marina who was tensely observing our exchange. "We are not here to harm or frighten you. As I said, we're here to help. We have no intention of forcing you to do anything you don't want to do. We're not like the others."

As he stood defiantly, I noticed the boy clutch a small stone tightly in his hand, ready to throw it at any sign of threat. "We've heard of the dangers you've faced. The monsters... the Entropics," I said the name softly, testing the waters. I saw his eyes widen slightly but he maintained his defensive stance. "We're here to protect you from them. Not feed you to them."

I gave him a reassuring smile. "We have food, we're pretty good at finding mushrooms," I offered, sending a sarcastic smile to Marina. "We just want to help, you know. It's safer if we all stick together, right?"

"Ha!" the boy laughed. "Mushrooms? We get our own food around here mister. And we all know what happens when adults start turning up in settlements like ours, don't we? They get burnt down," he answered his own question. "We stay alive 'cos we're all alone out here, and that's the way we like it."

"They get burnt down when adults..." I started then trailed off, remembering what I'd already been told. The Entropics left the children alone because they couldn't control them yet for whatever reason, but any Selari adults out there, they were not to be tolerated.

"They get burnt down when the Entropics find adults in the settlements, don't they?" I finished my sentence, my eyes meeting Marina's. We both knew the gravity of what the boy was hinting at. We were the adults in this scenario.

A heavy silence fell over us as the boy nodded slowly, his eyes wary but not unkind. "And you'd be bringing them right here to us."

"We wouldn't..." Marina began, but the boy cut her off with a sharp look.

"It's not about what you would do, ma'am. It's about what they would do," he said, his voice hardened by the cruel truths he had to live with. "You could be the nicest people in the world, but your presence would still bring those things down on us."

I nodded slowly, understanding the depth of his fear and the strength of his resolve. We had come to help, but our mere presence could bring about the destruction of this fragile sanctuary.

"You're right," I said, my voice barely above a whisper. "We didn't think about that." My mind raced.

The boy looked at me, seeming taken aback by my admission. Perhaps he had expected denial or anger, but not agreement.

"We won't risk your safety," I continued, my gaze steady. "We'll leave, but only after we've had a look around your settlement and made sure you're all safe here. If anyone needs help or anything like that, we'll do what we can, and then leave, we promise. Just please, let us in so our minds can be at ease."

The boy looked at us suspiciously for a moment, but then he seemed to soften. "Alright," he said grudgingly. "But remember, one wrong move and our archers won't hesitate."

Marina and I nodded, understanding his caution. With a wave of his hand, he signalled us to follow him. As we approached the gate to the settlement, I felt a renewed surge of awe at how quickly the place had gone from a bustling village to an eerily quiet ghost town at the first hint of a potential threat. Then I wondered where the archers were hiding.

Chapter 11 – A Huge Mistake

Just as the gates began to creak open, there was a sudden rustle from the trees above and my question was answered. Two small figures dropped down from the branches, landing gracefully on the ground before us. Both were armed with small bows, arrows strung and ready but not drawn.

The first was a girl, perhaps a few years younger than the boy who was leading us. Her hair was a wild mane of fiery red, and her eyes were a piercing blue that matched the intensity of her scowl. Her clothes, though ragged and dirt-stained, hung on her small frame with a sense of pride and defiance. The second figure was another boy, his skin deeply tanned from the sun, and his brown hair fell in unkempt waves. His face was smudged with dirt, and his clothes were as ragged as the others, but his posture exuded a calm assurance. Both were dishevelled, their appearances reflecting the hard life they led.

These were clearly the archers we had been warned about, their wary eyes never straying from us. Despite their young age, they had the hardened look of warriors. The sight of these children, armed and ready to defend their home against us, was a reminder of the harsh realities of this world. And it made my heart hurt.

As the gates swung open, the sight that greeted us was both admirable and astonishing. Of course, I'd already seen the settlement from above through Yari's eyes who was incidentally back within our shared body, but up close it really was something to behold.

Within the fortified walls of the settlement, life seemed to thrive against all odds. The settlement was a hive of activity - children were again bustling about, some carrying bundles of firewood, others tending to a variety of chores. Every pair of eyes that met ours held the same wary curiosity, a testament to their shared hardship and resilience.

Huts constructed from wood and leaves dotted the landscape, each one expertly built and looked like they'd stand the test of time. The heart of the settlement was marked by a large communal area, where a fire pit sat at its centre, surrounded by log benches. Smoke again rose from various points, indicating the presence of hearths where meals were being prepared. From the edges of the settlement, the tops of trees could be seen, the walls hiding the forest beyond - likely the source of their sustenance and materials.

Despite their obvious hardships, there was an overwhelming sense of unity and determination within the settlement. The Selari children had created a society of their own, a haven against the dystopian world outside their gates. Their resilience and adaptability were truly a testament to the enduring spirit of their race.

As we stepped inside, under the watchful eyes of the archers, we knew that we were entering a world where children were warriors, survivors, and protectors of their own future.

"What's your name?" Marina asked as we walked.

"Guy," the boy said, and he gave some hand gesture to the trees around us, which I could only assume meant that he was telling someone, somewhere to get back to their watch.

"Welcome to our home," Guy said, his voice hard but not without a hint of pride. His gesture encompassed the entirety of the busy settlement, children darting in and out of the huts, laughter and shouts echoing off the walls. It was a vibrant, living community, held together by the sheer determination and tenacity of these children who had been forced to grow up too quickly.

We walked through the settlement in awe, flanked by Guy and the two archers, their bows still at the ready, their eyes alert and watchful. Every so often, we'd catch a snippet of conversation, a burst of laughter, or the whispering rustle of someone running past. Life here was clearly rough and unrefined, but also full of a strange kind of vitality, a testament to the indomitable spirit of these young souls.

It was like we didn't even exist to the Selari kids around us as we walked. None of the children stopped and stared, all of them lost in their own little worlds, or the tasks they had to carry out.

"You'll have to excuse the mess," Guy said, though there was a slight twitch at the corner of his mouth that suggested he found our wide-eyed wonder amusing. "We do our best with what we have."

"We've seen worse," Marina said, her voice gentle. She looked at the huts, the children, the archers guarding us - a motley crew of survivors, each one a small miracle in their own right. "You've all done an incredible job here."

"We had to," Guy replied, his voice hard. "There's no one else to do it for us." He looked a little saddened at his own words and again I couldn't help but feel this young boy, this child seemed all so, well, adult.

"So you've seen what you need to, and you'll be leaving then?" Guy said in a questioning tone that could well have been a statement. "We're looking after ourselves pretty well if I do say so myself."

I didn't know what to say. It was clear that the children here had so much more than us, were safer, able to fend for themselves... yet I still had that overwhelming urge to try to protect them. It was just in my nature I supposed.

"Well..." I said slowly, trying to think on my feet. "Do you have any food? Any food that isn't mushrooms I mean," I added quickly and didn't look at Marina because I knew she would be staring daggers at me.

"We do..." Guy said, "But I don't know what that... uh, bird thing eats. I don't know where it is right now, but it's yours, right?"

I smiled. "You don't have to worry about Yari. But I suppose we should all introduce ourselves, right?"

Guy's eyes flicked between us, something unreadable in his gaze. Then he sighed, his shoulders relaxing just slightly, "Alright. Introduce yourselves."

"My name is Marcus Reid," I began, then gesturing to Marina, "and this is Marina. We are... friends. We escaped from the clutches of the Entropics holding us captive in the mines and have started our own settlement, not too far from here actually."

I then called Yari forth and after a second or two, she slowly appeared from my chest and floated up to my shoulder. "And this is Yari. She's the Sylph that I'm bonded to me, but that's just her... projection? I guess. Anyway, she doesn't need to eat or anything so you don't need to worry about her."

Marina added, "We're not here to harm you or bring any danger to your home. We were hoping to maybe... collaborate. Exchange knowledge, resources? See if we can't all help each other out, you know?"

She glanced at me, her eyes speaking volumes. We knew it was a long shot, but the children seemed more than capable. If they were open to the idea, we could learn so much from them, and hopefully offer them at least something in return. What that might have been, we were yet to discover.

"But," I quickly added, seeing the wary look return to Guy's face, "if you're not comfortable with that, we understand. We'll trade for some food, if that's alright with you, and then we'll be on our way."

Guy seemed to ponder this for a moment. "Trade, huh? What have you got?"

"Well, uh..." I started, but Marina interrupted me.

"We can get you all the mushrooms you can eat?" she offered.

A soft snort came from one of the archer children, the girl with fiery red hair, before she quickly covered her mouth with her hand. Her bright eyes twinkled with amusement, suggesting she found Marina's offer humorously absurd.

Guy's face, however, remained impassive, albeit there was a flicker of amusement in his eyes too.

"We've got enough mushrooms around here, thank you very much," he replied, though there was a hint of a smile tugging at his lips.

"Listen," Guy said flatly. "I don't think there's anything you got that we need, and I think you can see that too. So how about we just give you some food – not mushrooms," he added for my benefit, "then you be on your way. You know where we are when you get something we might want, right?"

"Fair enough," I responded, the corners of my mouth turning upward in appreciation of Guy's forthrightness. Despite the tough exterior, the boy had a fair heart.

"We appreciate that," Marina added. She cast a grateful look at Guy, then towards the other children, nodding her acknowledgement. "We'll remember this. And you're right, we'll come back when we have something worthwhile."

Guy nodded, signalling to one of the children nearby, a smaller girl with mousy brown hair who seemed to have been waiting for his orders. She scampered off, presumably to gather the food they were offering.

We waited in silence, the other children returning to their tasks or simply watching us but now with curious eyes. After a few moments, the girl returned, holding a small sack made from some sort of plant material.

"Here," Guy said, passing the sack to me. It felt warm in my hands, and through the material, I could tell it was full of something grainy - not a mushroom in sight. It was surprisingly heavy for its size. "It's not much, but it should last you a couple of days."

I could tell from Marina's silent gasp next to me that she too was touched by the children's generosity. They must've had so little, and yet they were willing to share with us.

"Thank you, Guy," I said sincerely, "and thank you all," I added, raising my voice a bit to address the entire settlement.

Guy merely nodded, his gaze shifting back to the archers who had been silent throughout our exchange.

And that was it, our welcome had expired. As we turned to leave, I cast one last glance over my shoulder at the children's settlement. It was a small sanctuary in an otherwise unforgiving world - a beacon of hope and resilience. Their existence alone was a testament to the indomitable spirit of the Selari, a spirit that could not be extinguished by the likes of the Entropics.

But then, my attention turning back to the gate that still stood open ready to allow us our exit from the settlement, my blood turned cold.

Three figures stood at the entrance of the settlement, their presence casting an ominous shadow across the bustling sanctuary.

The children fell into a hush, their eyes wide with new wonder at the arrival of these people. The figures were men, their large, imposing builds towering over the children who quickly moved to surround them. Their clothes were ragged, much like the children's, but there was a dangerous air about them, a palpable malice that turned the air ice-cold.

My heart pounded in my chest as I recognised the men. Andrew Swift, Nicholas Crowe, and Samuel Drake - crew members from the Iron Will. The same crew members who had mutinied on board my ship. The same crew members who had tossed me aside and left me to die. But here, now? There was no way this was going to be anything good.

They hadn't seen us yet, their attention solely on the children who'd now instinctively started backing away from them. Guy was beside me in an instant, his voice low and urgent. "We need to go, and hide, quickly." He didn't say anything, just turned and beckoned for us to follow him towards one of the wooden huts nearby. Marina and I exchanged a quick glance before we followed him, my heart hammering in my chest.

We managed to slip inside the hut unnoticed, just as one of the children, a boy no older than ten, stepped forward to the new arrivals, pointing in our direction and saying something we couldn't quite hear to the men. Swift, the one leading the group, nodded slowly before walking forward and raising his voice.

"We know you're here," he called out, his voice echoing deviously throughout the settlement. "Come out, come out, wherever you are. We just want to talk, old friend!"

We remained hidden, peering through a small crack in the wooden walls of the hut. The men slowly made it to the centre of the settlement, still calling out various cliched phrases, Swift's gaze sweeping across the crowd of children and wooden buildings as they walked. I could see the malice in his eyes.

Suddenly, Drake stepped forward, pulling one of the smaller children from the crowd that followed them and holding him by the shoulder. Panic erupted inside of me as he held the boy by, a nasty grin on his face as he pressed the barrel of his flintlock pistol against his captive's head. Then his two companions followed suit, each taking a hostage of their own before the kids could make their escapes.

The children's archers moved in swiftly though, surrounding the men, their arrows drawn and ready. But Swift merely laughed, raising his hands in a mock surrender. "You really think those little toys of yours can stop us?"

I could see the gears turning in the children's minds. I knew they were well-organised, and this situation would have been considered in their planning. But they were just kids still, and these were hardened men, armed and willing to harm them. Even if the archers were to let loose their arrows, the men's flintlocks would have already done their deadly work.

I had no choice. I couldn't bear to see innocent children hurt, not on my account. It was me they wanted, after all. I stepped out from our hiding place, my heart pounding in my chest.

"I'm here," I called out, raising my hands. My voice echoed around the silent settlement. All eyes were on me. I could feel Marina's gaze, a mix of surprise and worry. But I couldn't afford to look back. "Let the children go. It's me you want."

Swift's wicked grin widened at the sight of me, while Drake and Crowe seemed taken aback, evidently not expecting me to come forward. "Ah, there he is. The runaway Captain." Swift's voice dripped with malicious satisfaction.

They released the children, who quickly scampered away, and I felt a small bit of relief wash over me. At least they were safe. For now.

"Look at you, playing the hero," Swift sneered, his eyes raking over me. The other two, Drake and Crowe, had a hard look in their eyes but said nothing. They simply observed, their fingers drumming rhythmically against their flintlocks.

"We've come a long way, haven't we boys?" I tried to keep my voice steady. It was just like facing down any other adversary. Only this time, it was not on the open seas, but a foreign land, and the stakes were higher than ever.

"I don't recall you being quite so altruistic when you were in command," Swift said, amusement touching his voice. "Things change, I suppose."

"What do you want?" I asked, cutting straight to the chase. I didn't have time for a war of words. Not with the children's lives at risk.

Swift's grin faded as he got down to business. "We want to explain, don't we lads?" he said sarcastically. This surprised me. I had expected threats, demands. Not an offer for explanation. But I gestured for him to continue.

"You remember the Sirens, don't you?" Swift asked, his tone almost casual, as if we were discussing the weather. But I caught the look of glee in his eyes. He was eager to tell this tale. "Those shiny gold coins you were so fond of?"

The Siren... the gold coin. It had been the last loot I had ever plundered as a Free Man – and by all accounts, the very reason I was stuck here in this strange, foreign place. My heart clenched at the memory of it, and it kind of made me angry.

"After you..." Swift paused, seemingly searching for the right word, "... left, one of the Sirens found its way back to us. We thought about throwing it overboard like you did, but we decided you were an idiot, I guess you could say that greed got the better of us."

He shrugged, the casual nature of his confession making me grit my teeth. But I kept silent, waiting for him to continue.

"And then the storm hit," Swift went on. "We were sure we were going to perish. But then, the Siren, it... well it glowed, then sang. And then, we were here. In this place. What a rush, let me tell you. But I guess you know that already, right Captain?"

I blinked. Just like it had done to me, the Siren had brought my former crew through into this world. A shiver ran down my spine. The golden coins were so powerful. It made me baulk at the thought of the true power the Entropics held, if this was merely a trinket to them.

"Once we were here, we stumbled upon a thing calling himself the Caretaker," Drake chimed in, a malicious glint in his eyes. "You know him, right?" he smiled. "He got us to join with these golden bird things, and told us about you and how you escaped from his care. So you know what we did?" a malicious grin crossed his face. "We promised to round you up with the rest of the, the, um..."

"Selari," Crowe helped.

"Yeah, Selari," Drake took back over. "We said we'd round you lot up in return for freedom and power we never thought entirely possible where we come from... and here we are. And all we had to do was leave the mines with some of those new recruits, you know, those pricks from the Royal Navy ship, you know the one? You were there, right?"

"And you expect me to just... what, go quietly?" I asked, incredulity creeping into my voice. They had not only mutinied but had also sold their souls to the Caretaker, to the enemy. I also spared a moment to think about those sailors who the crew had apparently sold into slavery - just another casualty in this new war we faced.

Swift's grin returned, chilling me to the bone. "Oh yes Captain, we do indeed expect you to surrender. You're outnumbered, after all."

For a moment, silence fell upon us, each man gauging the other, an unspoken understanding passing between us. We couldn't fight them.

This was far from over. They had their demands, and I had my own resolve. A rush of determination filled me. I was not about to surrender without a fight.

"Even if I am outnumbered," I said, my voice strong, "I won't be surrendering. Not to you, not to the Caretaker. I'm not giving up on these kids." I gestured toward the children, huddled around us at what they'd deemed a safe distance, watching us with wide and fearful eyes. "They're better than you, than us. They deserve more than the lives they've been handed."

Crowe and Drake exchanged glances, but Swift just laughed, the sound echoing off the walls of the huts. "You always were sentimental, weren't you, Captain?" He shook his head, his smile turning into a snarl. "That sentimentality won't save you here."

"Maybe," I shrugged, keeping my gaze steady, but the way he kept saying the word 'Captain' was really grating on me. "But it will keep me fighting. That's more than what your greed will do for you."

Swift scowled, the levity in his demeanour evaporating. "You're playing a dangerous game, Captain. But let me make this easier for you. The Caretaker don't want the children. Just you. So why don't you come along with us and we'll leave this place right alone, right lads?"

The other two crewmembers nodded, each grinning sarcastically. I doubted that there was much truth in Swift's words.

At his words, a chill ran down my spine. My life, for the safety of the children? It was a trade that made sickening sense, one that would give Swift and his companions exactly what they wanted. It was the kind of deal a Captain would make, a true Captain willing to sacrifice everything for his crew.

But the Selari... they weren't my crew. They were innocent children, pulled into this madness by no fault of their own. To give myself over would guarantee their immediate safety, but what about the long term? Without me, they would be vulnerable to other threats, to the ever-expanding reach of the Entropics. But they were safe right now.

"No," I said, my voice resolute. "That's not going to happen."

Swift's eyes flashed with surprise, then anger. "Are you willing to risk their lives for your pride?"

"It's not about pride," I snapped back. "It's about them. They're not bargaining chips in whatever game you're playing with the Caretaker. And I won't let them become that. I'll fight you, Swift. I'll fight the Caretaker, the

Entropics, and whatever else this world throws at us. But I won't leave them alone to have their lives dictated by the likes of you."

For a moment, the world around us held its breath. Then Swift laughed, a harsh, ugly sound that echoed off the trees and huts around us. "Then you're a fool," he spat, "and you'll die a fool's death."

"Perhaps," I retorted, "but at least I'll die knowing I did everything I could for them."

Swift's snarl was the only answer I got before the entire settlement seemed to shake, the ground vibrating beneath our feet. Some of the children's eyes widened, and even Swift's scowl faltered as he glanced around, searching for the source of the commotion.

Then, out of nowhere, a massive arrow, more of a ballista bolt shot from the top of one of the walls, straight into the centre of the settlement, narrowly missing the men from the Iron Will by just feet. A clear warning shot. I glanced up at the wall and caught sight of the enormous ballista the children had set up, a feat of engineering that was truly impressive, especially for a settlement of such tiny individuals.

The men from the Iron Will were stunned, their grins well and truly wiped off their faces. They quickly retreated, Swift shooting me one last venomous look before they bolted for the gates. But the gates were already being closed by a group of children. The crew of the Iron Will were about to be trapped if they didn't pick up the pace.

Suddenly with a loud squark, Yari appeared from our previous hiding place, her wings flapping anxiously. Her projection flew up and over the wall above Swift and co., and I could see through her eyes, sharing her bird's-eye view. My blood ran cold at the sight.

But the gates didn't get the chance to close fully, and the kids pushing them scattered in the face of what I also saw through Yari's eyes. Six more men were just outside the gate, pushing a massive cannon towards us. The sight of it turned my sweat cold. The children could not fight against that kind of firepower. We needed to run.

"Everyone, listen!" I shouted, gaining the attention of the children and Marina. "There's a cannon outside. We need to get out of here, now!"

I could see the fear in their eyes, but also calm acceptance. They were ready to fight. But this wasn't a fight they could win. Thankfully, it seemed like Guy understood that, even if he probably didn't know what a cannon was. He stepped forward, nodding at me. His voice was steady, determined, belying his young age.

For the second time that day, I was in awe of the bravery and resilience of these Selari children. This was their home, and yet they were willing to abandon it to ensure their safety. They were more than capable; they were survivors.

And together, we would flee.

"Alright!" Guy commanded, his voice resonating through the settlement. "Everyone follow me, now! We're leaving!"

But by the time the message had spread to all of the residents of the settlement, the cannon had been rolled fully into view and the gates had been left only partially closed. I could see the fuse being lit on the weapon and I had to make an announcement of my own.

"DOWN!" I screamed, but as I did so the cannon released an ear-shattering boom and the huge round form of a deadly iron cannonball belched from its muzzle. Thankfully the cannon was yet to be sighted and the shot didn't hit anyone directly, but as the iron ball sailed into the settlement, it careened into a wooden building with a loud crash. Splinters flew up into the air as the building was severely damaged and a large round hole was all that was left as evidence of the first strike of the battle. I could already see the cannon being reloaded for a second strike, though this time I could see that the two cannonballs being fed into the muzzle of the weapon were linked by a long, thin chain.

"Chain shots," I muttered under my breath, racking my brain for any strategy I could remember from my old life that would help us now.

"What is it?" Marina asked from beside me, following my gaze to the cannon.

"Chain shots," I replied loudly, "They're used to destroy masts and rigging on ships. Against buildings... they'll be devastating. But against people..." I trailed off, feeling a sick dread in the pit of my stomach. A cannonball alone could cause immense damage, but two attached by a chain could effectively act as a massive flail, wreaking havoc on anything - or anyone - in its path.

Without another word, I raised my voice again. "Everyone! Move! Now!" My order was met with a surge of activity as the residents of the settlement heeded my warning and scattered again. Children ran in every direction, their faces marked with a fear that made my heart heavy.

Once the next shot from the cannon had caused its devastation, levelling one of the wooden huts but thankfully not causing any casualties, the children then entered and exited other huts quickly, packing armfuls of their belongings, and whatever else they could carry while all the time keeping an eye on where the cannon was pointing.

Yari squawked again, flying up into the sky as she shared her vision with me. The men from the Iron Will were lighting the fuse again.

I couldn't see how many cannonballs they had with them, but they also had their pistols at their sides, which I was thankful they hadn't yet started using. I wondered if their ammunition was limited. I hoped so.

At least the children were fast. Guy motioned for us all to follow his tiny frame darting between the houses with incredible speed. Marina was right behind him, her arms full of supplies that some of the kids had loaded onto her. Everyone was now running toward the back of the settlement, where high above the thick wooden wall I could see the dense foliage of the forest beyond.

BOOM.

The next chain shot tore through the air, ripping apart another building on its path. But we were now so far out of the way that we were safe from the shot. The structure of the settlement was not so lucky though. Just this one chain shot caused a cascading failure as buildings creaked, splintered and ultimately failed. I felt so bad for all the kids' hard work in the place being cut down to nothing, but I was reminded of the danger of our situation when I heard the first flintlock pistol fire and echo in the settlement behind us.

Only slightly above our heads I heard the small iron ball impact the wall and then followed the laughter of my former crew as they all began to fire at will in our direction.

I would never be able to forgive myself if any of the children were hurt.

But then somehow, as if by some divine miracle, Guy pulled a part of the wall open and we all managed to creep through one by one. A few more pistol shots rang out but by the time I was to go through – and I was the last – they had all but stopped, replaced by the taunting of my former men.

"Enjoy your time in the wilderness, Captain!" Swift's voice rang out, dripping with cruel amusement. "Don't worry, we'll take good care of your little fort!"

His laughter followed us into the forest, a bitter reminder of the home that had been lost. But as I glanced back at the settlement one last time, I saw that it was already being consumed by flames. The men from the Iron Will were setting fire to the buildings, the bright orange flames dancing against the blackening smoke-filled sky.

A part of me wanted to charge back in, to fight them off and reclaim what the kids had built. But I knew that wasn't an option. Not against a cannon and a group of armed men. My former men, who I knew to be both skilled and fearless.

I took one last look at the burning settlement, then turned my back on it, pushing through the dense foliage and into the forest.

The children and Marina were already waiting for me, their faces pale in the dim light filtering through the trees. Their eyes held fear and confusion. But they were survivors. And though they had lost their homes, they hadn't lost their will to fight.

As I caught up with them, Guy handed me a heavy sack filled with supplies. "We managed to save some food and water," he said, his voice barely above a whisper. "We can get by for a few days… but you said you had somewhere to go?"

I nodded, patting his shoulder in gratitude. "Good work, Guy. And we do, but we don't want to go straight there in case we're followed. We need to put some distance between us and them. And then we'll circle back around, OK?"

Guy nodded solemnly.

As we ventured deeper into the forest, I couldn't help but feel a sense of dread hanging over us. We were on the run, the kids were effectively homeless, with an enemy hot on our heels. But we were also together, united in our determination to survive.

We had escaped, but this was just the beginning. Now, we were truly in a battle against the Iron Will, and I was determined to do whatever it took to protect these children. And then I wondered too, if my former ship had made it through to this world intact, and what that could mean for the safety of all of us.

Chapter 12 – A New Home

We wasted no more time than necessary in circling back around in the forest to start making our way back towards our own settlement without the threat of being immediately followed. I didn't know if that was a part of their plan or not, but it was always better to be safe than sorry.

Our settlement. A place where the children would no doubt be far less safe than they had been, given the fact we had no protective walls, no forest nearby to keep ourselves hidden and no actual honest to God complete houses, but honestly we had no choice. Deep down I couldn't help but feel responsible for what had happened to the kids, for losing them their home, but I was glad that none of them had been hurt.

That was something, at least.

As we moved silently through the undergrowth, I couldn't help but remember my own childhood. Born and raised in a small coastal town, I was no stranger to hardship, but if anything like this had ever happened to me... But the pain and fear etched onto the faces of the children that surrounded me now was a far cry from the wide-eyed fascination of change I remembered from my own youth.

Truth be told, I didn't have a rough upbringing. I wasn't orphaned and destined to sail the seas a captive on some pirate ship. No, I was well-educated, mostly respected as I grew through my first few years in the family estate. I chose the life of a Free Man. I Watched the fat cats and landowners getting wealthier and fatter day by day whilst the people around them starved. But that's a story for another day.

As we walked, Yari flew on ahead, her sharp eyes scanning the terrain for any signs of danger. She'd been quiet for a long time and I could tell through our link that it was because seeing the kids like this took her right back to a place where she didn't want to be.

She had quickly become an important asset to me, perhaps even more than that. As she swooped back down to me, landing lightly on my shoulder, I felt a strange sense of peace wash over me. Despite everything, we still had each other. And as long as that remained true, I knew we would find a way through this.

"Talk to me, Yari," I said to my companion inside my mind. "Tell me what you see."

She turned her golden eyes on me, her gaze filled with an emotion that was all too human. "I see pain, Marcus," she said softly. "I see fear. But I also see hope. The children, they remind me of my own family. The ones that the Entropics took from me. The ones I'll never see again."

My heart clenched at her words. I didn't know how long it'd been since Yari had been with her own family. I didn't have to know; I could feel her pain through our link. And though I knew it pained her to do so, I couldn't help but be grateful for her willingness to share her experience with me again.

"I'm sorry, Yari," I replied earnestly, reaching up to gently stroke her feathers, forgetting that my hand would pass right through her golden projection. "I know this isn't easy for you."

"It's not about me," she said, her voice steady despite the emotion in her eyes. "It's about them. They need us, Marcus. Everyone in this world needs us and I don't know what we're going to do about it. But we're going to do everything we can to keep them safe."

I nodded, feeling a renewed sense of purpose surge within me. We had our mission. Our goal. And though with each passing day the odds against us seemed to grow and grow, I knew we wouldn't back down. Not now, not ever.

As we emerged from the forest and onto the open grassland between the children's old settlement and the home that Marina and I had forged, we quickly made our way onwards once we were sure that my former crew – or anyone else for that matter – were nowhere to be seen and we weren't being watched or followed.

After a few hours travel, we had arrived at our new home at the edge of the sea and as it had before, the sight that greeted us was one of desolation. What must've once been a thriving, bustling settlement was nothing more than a ruin, burnt and broken old wooden buildings overlooking the ocean, jagged rocks protruding from the waters below. But amidst the wreckage, I could still see the remnants of what once was. The places where people had lived, had laughed, had loved. And I knew that, with time, we could rebuild.

"This is it," I said, my voice echoing across the abandoned landscape. "This is where we'll make our home."

As the children looked out at the ruins, I saw a mix of emotions cross their faces. Fear, yes. But also determination. Resolve. They had already lost one home. They wouldn't lose another. And I was going to do everything I could to make sure of that.

"We'll rebuild," I said, meeting each of their gazes in turn. "And we'll make this place better than it was before. We'll make it a home."

"You call this a settlement?" Guy said after a short pause in what I could almost call disgust. "What have you been doing all this time? Sitting about on your arses watching the sea?"

I let out a small chuckle at his frankness. It was just like him to cut through the silence with a sharp-edged comment and I wouldn't have expected any of the other children to make a statement like that.

"You've got it all wrong, Guy," I said, gesturing towards the remnants of the settlement. "We've been working hard, haven't we, Marina?"

Marina, who had been standing silently with the rest of the children, gave a small nod. "We managed to create a guttering system that nearly killed Marcus here, and we moved some of the debris from over here to… well over there. Honestly I don't think there's much left to do."

Her sarcastic response made me snort. I don't know what I'd been expecting in terms of agreement from her, but she was right; we'd basically done nothing other than sleep, eat mushrooms, drink rainwater and nearly die. The settlement was in as poor shape as we had found it.

"See?" I said, turning back to Guy in contrast to Marina's words. "We've just started. And with you lot here, I'm sure we can make it into something even better than it already is."

"Are we going to fix these old buildings or start from scratch?" asked one of the older girls of the group, though she was certainly only ten at the most.

"It's going to be a mix of both, I think," I answered. "Some of these structures still look good. We can patch them up, reinforce the weak spots. Others will probably need to be torn down and rebuilt. It's going to be a lot of work, but if we all pitch in, we can get it done."

I knocked on the closest wall that was still standing as though to prove my point, but when I did so, the entire structure creaked as though it was about to topple over.

"Uh… why don't you leave the building work to us," Guy said. "We're used to this kinda stuff anyway and I don't think you uh… well never mind, just leave it to us, right?"

As the children all nodded in collective agreement that they were far more skilled at construction work than I seemed to be, I knew that I had been soundly outnumbered. Not that I actually minded; the settlement the kids had come from was wonderous and if they had built that on their own, then they could have free reign in this place for all I cared.

Over the course of the next few hours, the children made it very clear that the remnants of this settlement were not going to be up to their standard and so I watched as they began to systematically dismantle everything they could get their tiny little hands on. It was amazing to watch actually, because what they lacked in strength and size, they made up for in ingenuity in their use of tools. If they needed to lift something heavy, they worked together or made a lop-sided see-saw. If they needed to pry something apart, they made a lever of a length that would allow them to complete their task with what looked like relative ease.

And as the children worked, I took the opportunity to bring Marina up to speed on what had happened. She'd been there with me of course, but so many things had happened that needed explaining.

"Marina I…" I searched for the right words. "I'm sorry that I got the kids' settlement destroyed. I feel so responsible."

Marina watched me for a long moment before responding. "Marcus," she began softly, "you can't shoulder all of that guilt. We went to save those children, to offer them a home... It isn't your fault those people turned up."

"But they were looking for us," I replied almost in a hiss. "Those men, my old crew… the Iron Will… it's all my fault, isn't it? If I hadn't come here, if we hadn't gone out looking for those kids… they'd still be back there in their settlement, wouldn't they?"

"And what?" Marina replied, speaking so fast that she almost interrupted me. "Just waiting for the day they're old enough for the Entropics to come for them, bind them with a Sylph and send them to work in the mines? However you look at it, Marcus, someone was going to come for these children eventually, and I say they're better off here and now."

I stroked my chin in thought, and eventually Marina's words sank in. It made me feel a little better, but not totally without blame.

"Those men, they were my crew back in my old life… before the Siren. They'd do anything for me and we were like a family. Now, I hardly recognise them."

"Power does terrible things to people," Marina said.

"Yes, but if they truly are terrible people now, then I don't know what we are going to do to stand against them," I said. "Those weapons they had, and I don't just mean the cannon. The pistols they carried… they're tools of war and death, you have no idea… and that cannon. It was from the Iron Will and if the entire ship has made it through to this place…" I trailed off, not wanting to admit the trouble my old ship could cause for the Selari people.

Marina sighed, a grim understanding etching lines onto her youthful face. "I don't suppose we can just... talk to them? Reason with them?"

"I don't know, Marina," I confessed, rubbing my eyes. "Once upon a time, maybe. But those men... I didn't recognise them. They've changed. The moment they saw those Sirens... and not for the better."

"But they were your friends once. Surely, there's still some good left in them?" she persisted, a hopeful glint in her eyes.

"They were more than friends, they were my brothers. But the men I saw today... they were monsters," I said, my voice low and pained.

A quiet moment passed between us as the gravity of the situation sunk in. The laughter and chatter of the children, busy at work rebuilding, formed a clear contrast to the grim conversation we were having. It was heart-warming to see that they could adapt to their situation so quickly.

"What about the Iron Will? Could it really be here?" Marina asked, breaking the silence. Her voice was barely more than a whisper, as if speaking it aloud could make it true.

"I don't know," I replied, my heart heavy. "But if it is, we're in more trouble than I can rightly say."

"Then we'll face it, like we've faced everything else," she said firmly. "We've got the kids, we've got each other, and we've got a home to protect."

Her words, filled with a determination that far outweighed our grim situation, stoked a flame of resolve within me. "You're right, Marina," I said, looking at her with newfound conviction. "We've faced harsh odds before. We'll face them again. And we'll win. But I think the kids might be the answer to all of this; did you see the ballista they made? The contraption that fired the huge arrows?" Marina nodded. "That's the kind of thing we're going to need if we want to fight back against the Iron Will. I know how they work, and If we have to cut them down before going after the Entropics, then so be it, it'll just be good practice."

Marina looked at me, a bit of surprise flickering in her eyes. "You're talking about teaching the children warfare? To fight?"

I took a moment before responding. "Not warfare, Marina. Defence. There's a difference. They need to learn how to protect themselves and the people they care about."

She still looked uneasy, but she didn't argue further. After a moment, she sighed. "We don't have many options, do we?"

I shook my head. "I'm afraid not. If my old crew comes back, and if they bring the Iron Will... we need to be prepared."

A brief silence settled between us, filled only by the sounds of the children working and laughing in our settlement. I looked out towards the sea, my mind heavy with thoughts of the challenges that lay ahead.

Eventually, Marina spoke again. "Alright. If it comes to that, we'll do it. We'll teach them. But let's make sure they understand the gravity of it all, Marcus. This isn't a game."

"I know, Marina. I know," I reassured her, my voice filled with an unwelcome gravity. "But I think they understand that better than we think. They've already seen too much in their short lives, haven't they?"

She nodded, a resigned look on her face. "We'll do what we have to do."

"Yes, we will," I agreed. "Together."

It was a heavy promise, laden with the weight of the unknown. But it was a promise we made to each other, to the children, and to this new home we were building together. No matter what came, we would stand strong. We would protect our home and each other. We would face any threat, any storm. Together.

And as I looked out over the now bustling settlement, the children working hard and filled with a resilience that defied their age, I couldn't help but feel a sense of pride and determination. They were strong. We were strong. And we would protect them.

"Excuse me," Yari's small voice entered my head and I gave her my attention. "What were those things? You said cannons, and guns? I've never seen anything like them before."

"Yes, Yari," I answered, "those are the weapons that people use where I come from. The cannon is a large gun that fires heavy metal balls with explosive force. The guns that the men held are called pistols, smaller versions that can be carried and used by one person."

"And they... they can hurt people?"

I nodded solemnly, not wanting to hide the harsh reality from her. "Yes, Yari. They can cause great harm. That's why we must learn to defend ourselves against them, it's what we're dealing with here... I just wanted you to know how difficult this is all going to be."

Yari was silent for a moment. "So, we are going to build our own cannons and guns?"

"Not exactly," I replied, "I used to use these weapons and I know how to and all that... but we didn't exactly uh... make our own... and even if we knew how to, then I don't know if this place has all the materials we would need. But we can build defences, strong, thick walls and learn to use what we have effectively. Like the ballista the kids built, It's a powerful tool if used correctly. These are the things that will give us the edge here; let's say the Iron Will has come through. Suppose they run out of cannonballs, or ammunition for their pistols, will they know how to make more? Will this place even have the materials they'd need to do it? I think by adapting to this world, we have the advantage – and they won't even know what hit them."

"Okay," Yari replied quietly, "You know I'll help however I can."

"I know you will, Yari," I said, sending as much warmth as I could through our link. "We're all going to do this together. We're a family, and families protect each other."

"And if those men come back... we'll be ready," Yari said, her small voice carrying a surprising amount of resolve for something that always seemed so anxious.

"Yes, Yari. We will be," I assured her, feeling a swell of pride at her bravery. Despite the daunting challenges we were facing, in that moment, I couldn't help but believe that we could overcome anything.

"OK," Marina said, figuring out for herself that my internal conversation with Yari was over. "So what happens when we build a wall, and those men come back with that cannon and just destroy it?"

"Well," I replied, again scratching my chin. "Some of the best defences I ever came across in my time on board the Iron Will weren't just walls. We need to take more of a multi-layered approach to this. The Iron Will will come from the sea, so we need to focus all of our attention…"

Then Marina cut me off with a relieved laugh. It took her a moment to stop but when she did, I looked at her with a raised eyebrow.

"The Iron Will is a ship!" she said, almost like that fact should have told me everything I wanted to know. I didn't reply.

"I told you already," she continued. "Nobody goes out into the oceans here. When I told you that, I meant nobody. The creatures that reside out there… the monsters that call the oceans their home… there's never been a ship built that would stand up to those things. Eventually people just stopped trying. And that was centuries ago."

I stared at her, letting the words sink in. She was right. I had been so focused on what I knew from my world that I had forgotten how different things could be in this new reality. And then it hit me. I laughed too. A hearty, relieved laugh that echoed through our settlement and out across the water.

"That's... that's good news, Marina," I managed to get out, catching my breath. "Better than good. If the Iron Will can't survive the oceans, then we don't need to worry about it at all."

Marina's smile was bright, her laughter infectious. But she quickly sobered. "We still have those men to worry about, though. And they did manage to reach us once."

"Yes, and they will likely try again," I acknowledged. "But that just means we focus our defences on the land. We've got the kids, and with their innovation, I think we'll manage. We need to prepare them, train them. We need to keep watch, always be ready. And with the ocean on our side, maybe we have a fighting chance after all."

"Plus we have our little secret, right?" Marina cooed. I cocked an eyebrow at her, entirely unsure of what it was she was trying to say.

"Your ability to ingest Obsidian Cores," she said in a monotonous drawl.

Of course, how could I have forgotten? We still needed to figure out how that was going to actually help us in the long run, but for now at least it meant we had an early warning system by way of Yari.

"I suppose you're right," I agreed, letting a small smile creep onto my face. "That could indeed be a game changer."

Marina looked out into the distance, a thoughtful expression on her face. "We should think about trying that again soon really," she said almost to herself. "Who knows what'll happen next time you…"

"Maybe I'll be so sick that I'll actually cough up one of my lungs," I interrupted her. She might not remember what had happened the last time I'd tried to drink some of the Core-infused water but I sure as hell did. I could still practically taste the vomit.

Marina didn't respond. I knew that she was going to get me to do it one way or another and honestly, I was OK with that. It was going to either work, or kill me.

After a while, the silence was too heavy, too full of the questions we both didn't want to ask so I broke it with a weak attempt at humour.

"If I vomit a lung, Marina, you'll have to fetch it for me. You're the one pushing this experiment, after all."

She looked back at me, a small smile playing at the corners of her lips. "I think I can handle that," she said, and I could hear the unspoken promise in her words. No matter what, we would face the challenges ahead together.

I tried to help the children with their work, I really, really did. But every time I tried to do something, I was either in the way, or messing with the delicate equilibrium of their skilled work. If I said I was amazed by them, it was an understatement. It was only when I realised that I was being given menial tasks like 'carry that plank over there', and that each time the distance seemed to grow, did I realise that they were simply giving me busy work to keep me out of the way. I couldn't blame them really.

Resigned to my fate as the glorified errand-runner, I did my best to be helpful where I could, fetching supplies, moving materials, and offering encouraging words. It was a humbling experience, to be sure. I was used to being the one giving orders, making strategic decisions. But here, in this place, these children, who had been forced to grow up far too quickly, were the experts.

The day rolled on and we carried out our task of disassembling the entire settlement and taking stock of what we had to work with. Thankfully, the children had created some small makeshift shelters that looked far more watertight than anything that had been in the place previously, and that's where we would all spend the night, taking turns keeping watch.

Later, as I sat with Marina out of earshot of our little workers and with the stars twinkling overhead, I confessed my feelings to her.

"I feel like a fifth wheel," I admitted. "The kids are so capable, so skilled. They don't need me getting in their way."

Marina turned to me, her eyes soft in the moonlight. "They may be skilled, but they're still children," she said gently. "They look up to you. You give them hope. And that, my dear, is far more valuable than any physical skill you could contribute."

I looked at her, surprised by her words. But then I thought about Yari, about her fierce determination when I had reassured her earlier. Maybe Marina was right. Maybe what I offered was not in the realm of construction or strategic planning, but something else, something intangible.

Resolved, I decided to focus on the contribution I could make. It wasn't the role I had envisioned for myself, but it was a role that was needed nonetheless. As I looked up at the stars, I promised myself that I would do everything in my power to protect these children, to give them the hope they needed to face whatever challenges lay ahead. And for the first time in a long time, I felt a sense of purpose, and maybe something more: the promise of peace.

Chapter 13 – We Will Rebuild

The next morning I was surprised to wake up to find all of the kids already out and about in the settlement working. The piles of materials had been sorted and stacked already, and the settlement seemed to be bare apart from our little shelter. Now that I could stop and take stock of our situation, I counted thirty children with us working already, and I could see more further away, obviously gathering food from whatever they could find all around the settlement.

I smiled at first, but then it hit me.

"Nooooo!" I moaned aloud. "Not mushrooms, please. Anything but that!"

Marina then appeared beside me and placed her hand on my back.

"Oh don't worry," she smiled. "I have something else, just for you." And she handed me a bowl of water that I knew must've been the remainder of the Core-soaked water that'd made me so sick before. Or perhaps it was a new batch, I really didn't care which it was.

"Listen, I know what you're going to say," Marina said before I could object. "But if you really can get those Cores inside you and they give you any advantage at all, then it's worth it, right?"

I couldn't argue. Drinking the Core-water was the reason that we had Yari as our little sentry, and that was a bonus that I couldn't even apportion a value to.

"I suppose you're right," I conceded, eyeing the bowl of water warily. The memory of the last time I'd tried this still lingered, a nauseating shadow that threatened to overpower me. I took a deep breath, steadying myself. The health of the children and Marina, the safety of our home... everything was riding on this. But still, I didn't want it.

With an unhappy nod, I picked up the bowl, my hand slightly trembling. The water was clear, but I knew it was laced with the powerful essence of the Obsidian Cores. I closed my eyes, took a deep breath, and downed most of the contents of the bowl in one gulp.

The effect was immediate, the taste so intense and foreign that it was almost overwhelming. My head spun, my stomach clenched, and for a moment I was sure I was going to lose consciousness. But then, just as suddenly as it had come, the wave of nausea passed. I was left panting, my heart pounding, but I was still on my feet. I felt... different. Stronger, somehow, and more aware. I could feel the power of the Cores within me starting to do their work.

"What... what now?" I asked, looking at Marina with wide eyes.

She shrugged. "You want more?"

I looked down at the bowl and the sight of the water made me feel so sick that I had to hand it back to Marina. This time I just knew that drinking more of the concoction wasn't going to do me any good.

"No, no more," I replied, shaking my head vehemently. "That was... more than enough."

Marina gave me a knowing smile, a spark of sympathy in her eyes. "Alright, but if you're not going to finish that," she said, pointing at the bowl I'd handed back to her, "You better get back to work. We have a wall to build and defences to plan."

I nodded, my thoughts spinning almost as much as my stomach. "Right, let's get back to work." Then I added: "Have you seen Guy around anywhere?"

Marina frowned, glancing around the bustling settlement. "Now that you mention it... I haven't. That's unusual, he's usually quite chatty."

I felt a small pang of worry. Guy was an important character for the kids, his presence always a comfort for them – exactly how a good leader should be. We set off to look for him, my concern growing with each passing minute. If anything had happened to him, I didn't know how I was going to react.

Thankfully, it wasn't long before we found him at the edge of the settlement, standing facing the sea, his small frame silhouetted against the horizon.

"Guy!" I called out, rushing over. "What are you doing?"

Without responding, Guy then released armfuls of rocks over the edge of the sea wall and into the rocks jagged rocks and waters below.

I didn't know what he had done at first, but Marina shrieked.

"No!" She exclaimed, rushing towards him. But it was too late. The rocks Guy had been throwing were not just rocks. They were the Obsidian Cores we had carefully stashed away.

I felt my heart drop as I watched the Cores disappear over the edge, lost forever to the sea. I reached out to try to grab any of them before they disappeared, but they were gone and there was nothing I could do.

"These things," he said, turning to me with a grave expression. "They're too dangerous. Too powerful. We shouldn't have them."

"But we need them, Guy!" I protested. But Guy simply stepped back and looked at me as though I'd grown two heads.

"You don't understand them," he said, his voice steely. "You don't know what they can do, or how dangerous they are. I..." he trailed off.

In a way he was right. We didn't fully understand the Obsidian Cores, the powers they held, or the effects they had on us. But despite all that, they were the best shot we had at defending ourselves.

"You don't know what they've done for us, and the trouble we had to go through to get them!" I almost shouted, unable to keep it in. While I was there I ordered Yari to project herself over the edge of the settlement to see if there were any Cores visible that we might have been able to retrieve.

"No you listen to me," Guy growled back. "Those rocks are nothing but trouble and when they turn up, people die. You think you're too big or too smart to get hurt, but you ain't. I've seen bigger and smarter people than you killed by those things and we're better off without them."

His words hit me like a wave, leaving me momentarily speechless. I stared at him, my anger and frustration slowly giving way to a numb understanding. He was right. I didn't know everything about the Cores, and I didn't fully comprehend the danger they represented.

The silence stretched between us, broken only by the crash of the waves against the jagged rocks below. The wind swept through the settlement, carrying with it the faint echoes of our struggle. Despite the blow Guy had dealt us, I couldn't help but feel a certain relief at his words. We were free of the Obsidian Cores, free of the unknown risks they posed. I was free of being sick every time I had to deal with them.

Guy's face softened, his anger dissolving as he looked at me. "We can survive without the Cores," he said quietly. "We have each other, and that's more important."

His words echoed in my mind, a sobering reminder of our reality. We didn't have the luxury of relying on unpredictable powers for our survival. We had to depend on each other, on our resilience and resourcefulness.

But his words reminded me of something. I'd sent Yari to look for the Cores but she hadn't acknowledged my request and when I called out to her, I received no response.

Fear and panic filled my entire being and goosebumps covered my arms. I knew drinking that water had been too easy this time and finally the warnings everyone had given me had come true. I felt alone.

The world seemed to come to a standstill.

"Yari?" I called out again, my voice echoing into the silence. The phantom presence I had come to rely on was gone, leaving me feeling more alone than I could ever remember feeling.

I felt my heart pound in my chest as I looked at the place where Yari usually projected herself on my shoulder. Empty. Desolate. I looked down at the black tattoo on my forearm and it was still there. Somehow I knew that she was still with me, even if I couldn't talk to her. I could only wait and hope. But that didn't stop my eyes from welling up at the thought that perhaps I could never speak with Yari again.

Marina rushed to my side, her face paling once she saw my expression. "What is it?" she asked, her voice filled with concern.

"Yari... she's gone." I managed to choke out, my voice barely above a whisper.

Guy's expression turned from anger to surprise, then to guilt. "I... I... what?" he said, his voice hoarse as he tried to put what had happened together in his mind.

There was no sense in keeping the truth from our young foreman, so I told him.

"We found out," I said slowly, "that I can ingest a little of the Cores. Only a little," I reinforced, "but that's how I've been strengthening my bond with the Sylph inside me, Yari. She wouldn't be here without the Cores and by all accounts, Marina and I would still be back in the mine if we hadn't found this out. I don't know why I seem to be able to do it, and I don't know what'll happen each time I do… but…"

Guy's face had already turned pale, but at my last statement he interrupted me with a confused look.

"You don't know what they'll do and you do it anyway? What kind of sick experiment is that? And with the Cores? What's wrong with you?"

It took me a second to realise that it was actually a question and not a statement.

"Guy," I began, my voice steady despite the tight knot of fear still twisting my stomach. "I didn't do it for kicks. I did it because I had to. Because we all had to."

Marina had been silent so far, watching our exchange with a tight, grim expression. Now, she stepped forward and placed a hand on Guy's shoulder.

"Listen to him, Guy," she urged. "We didn't take this lightly. We did what we had to do, and we paid the price. Trust me, I know how dangerous those things are."

I met Guy's gaze, seeing the confusion, the anger, the hurt swirling in his eyes. It wasn't easy for him, for any of us.

"You're right, Guy," I said quietly. "We don't fully understand the Cores. We don't know their potential, or their dangers. But we did what we did because we had no other choice. We were desperate, cornered, with no other options. And now..."

I let my voice trail off, gesturing towards the empty space where Yari had always been. "Now, I don't know what's going to happen. Yari is gone and I don't know how else to get her back. With her, we've lost our biggest advantage. But that doesn't mean we're done. We'll find another way, we'll rebuild, and we'll defend ourselves, with or without the Cores. We have to, for the sake of you kids, for all of us."

There was a long silence. I could see Guy wrestling with my words, with the bitter reality that we had all been forced to swallow. I hoped that he could see past his anger, his fear, and understand why we had done what we did.

Finally, Guy looked up. His eyes were hard, but I saw no more anger in them, only a determined resolve.

"Okay," he said, his voice quiet but strong. "We'll figure this out. Together. But if you keep anything like this from us again…"

I nodded before he could complete his threat. I had no doubt that the kids would move along if they thought it was a good idea. After all, what I'd seen from them so far led me to believe they had no trouble surviving out here.

"OK," Guy said, his tone now merry. "Marina here said you like yourself some mushrooms, so make your way back to the centre of the settlement and we've got a nice surprise for you there."

I groaned.

But then I felt a faint smile tug at the corners of my mouth despite the situation. "You know, most people consider a surprise to be something pleasant," I said.

Guy laughed, a childish sound that defied the heavy mood that had just passed. "You should try them before you knock them. We've got some great cooks among us."

Of that, I had no doubt.

As I moved back towards the centre of the settlement, I could only hope that the flavour of these wild mushrooms would be better than the taste of the Core-infused water. I didn't want another surprise.

Still, the earlier confrontation left me with a lot to think about. The decision to ingest the Obsidian Cores hadn't been made lightly, but now I had to face the possibility that we may have lost our only advantage. The absence of Yari was like a missing limb, a constant reminder of what we'd risked and what we'd lost. But we were still here, still standing. We had each other and a determination to survive that was stronger than any Core.

The problem was that each time I had ingested the Cores, I'd gained some benefit from it and this time it just seemed to undo everything. That couldn't be right, could it?

As I approached the centre of the settlement, the smells of food cooking and the sound of laughter filled the air again. Despite everything, life was continuing. Our spirit was not broken and I knew that I couldn't wallow over things I couldn't change.

"Alright, let's see about these mushrooms then," I murmured to myself, heading for the very small fire, clearly kept small to keep our presence hidden from undesirables. The kids must've learnt from how we'd managed to find them.

Stepping into the circle of warm, flickering light, I was met with a number of curious gazes from the kids who were gathered around the fire. The atmosphere was casual, almost familial. It was an unexpected but welcome contrast to the tense, heavy air that had settled over us earlier.

A young boy, probably no more than eight years old, with dirt streaked over his face and a wide grin, stepped forward. In his hand, he held a wooden plate with a steaming mound of something that looked... surprisingly appetising.

"Try this, sir!" he said, holding out the plate to me with an expectant look. The aroma wafting from the food hit my nose - earthy, savoury, definitely mushroomy, but also something else. Something... sweet?

I took the plate and thanked the kid with a nod, setting myself down on a vacant log next to the fire. With the eyes of the entire group on me, I took my first bite.

The texture was tender, almost buttery, and the taste... the taste was not at all what I expected. The mushrooms were rich, flavourful, and that sweet note – it was something familiar, something that reminded me of home. They were incredible. I was so impressed that I almost forgot about Yari's disappearance, almost forgot about the Obsidian Cores.

The taste of the mushrooms, the warmth of the fire, the sound of laughter and conversation - for a moment, it felt like a slice of normalcy in our otherwise chaotic existence. It gave me a glimmer of hope that maybe, just maybe, we could survive this after all.

But the moment was brief. As I finished my plate, the weight of our situation came crashing back down on me. The fact was, Yari was still gone, and with her, our main advantage. The Obsidian Cores were lost to us, and even though they had brought their share of troubles along with them, I couldn't help but feel a sense of loss.

Looking around at the group, I saw faces filled with hope. We were a team, a family, even. We had faced hardship and survived. We would continue to do so, with or without the Cores. And with that thought in my mind, I joined in their laughter, the bitterness of our situation forcibly forgotten.

"So what do you want us to make first, and where?" A small girl asked and the question made me start. I hadn't realised it until now, but after the settlement had been deconstructed, the kids had been awaiting an instruction to continue.

I looked around the settlement, now flat and barren and tried to visualise where things were supposed to go.

"A dry place to store things, and shelter to sleep in," one boy said through mouthfuls of his own food.

"And walls to keep things out in the night," a girl added, wrapping her arms around herself, shuddering as she spoke.

So I guessed my own suggestion of 'a house' probably wasn't needed, but I kept my mouth shut so as to not make a fool of myself. I started making a mental list.

More suggestions came.

"A place to prepare and cook food," chimed in another boy. His eyes were bright with the reflected firelight, his face smeared with dirt and mushroom sauce.

"Storage for weapons and tools," added a sturdy-looking girl.

"And a spot for a garden. For vegetables and herbs," added a smaller girl, her voice barely a whisper among the louder ones. But her words caught my attention instantly. Growing their own food was a sign of them thinking long term, of a determination to stay put and defend their home.

"We also need a safe space for the little ones," an older girl suggested, ruffling the hair of the youngest among them.

"Maybe some watchtowers?" proposed one of the boys, his eyes alight with excitement at the idea.

Each suggestion was practical and well-thought-out. It was clear that the kids had thought a lot about this, possibly had lengthy discussions on how to construct their settlement for the best possible living and defensive conditions. I was both amazed and humbled by their maturity.

"Those are all excellent ideas," I acknowledged. "But I have to admit – all of this is kind of new to me, so I'm going to need all of your help to get this right. From what I've seen, you all really seem to know what you're doing..." I peered pleadingly at Guy who had entered himself into the conversation.

It took him a minute to realise that I was asking for help, and eventually he gave it.

"If you really want to make a home here," he peered around the place with one eye half closed, "then shelter is the most important thing. Then food, then defences."

That made sense to me, and I would've probably concluded the same thing anyway.

"So… start there?" I asked more than I commanded. I knew that the kids were awaiting instructions from me, but even though they were still kids in my eyes, it seemed to me like they knew what they were doing to such a high level, that my input was probably not necessary. After all, they'd done all this before, hadn't they?

The group nodded and by all accounts they looked pretty nonchalant about the whole thing. They started to break into their respective teams, each one a mix of older and younger kids. It was clear that they had done this before and had a system. I was relieved that they seemed to have things under control.

"Um…" a small girl said. "Where do you want things to go?"

That was another thing I hadn't thought about, but I should've guessed. The settlement had been entirely cleared and although a part of me had expected the kids to just repair or rebuild things where they'd found them, I could see now how that approach didn't make very much sense.

I had to go with my instincts on this, and perhaps with a little guidance of what I was used to in the past.

"Well," I said confidently. "Trace out a wall around the perimeter of the settlement first. We don't have to build it yet, but it'll be nice to know the space we've got to deal with. After that," I continued, "we can start placing the shelters. I suggest we keep them close to the centre of our designated area, leaving space on the outskirts for things like the garden, the tool and weapon storage, and of course the watchtowers."

The girl nodded, her eyes wide with understanding and I could tell that everyone else understood me too. I hoped I was making the right call. It seemed logical, a centralised hub of shelters would make it easier for us to stay close and defend ourselves if needed.

"But remember," I added almost as an afterthought as the idea came to me, "keep enough space between the shelters to prevent the spread of fire. We wouldn't want a small accident to turn into a disaster."

The girl nodded again. Then, with all of the others moving simultaneously, the kids began to filter away from me and started carrying planks and other materials to the general locations of where they were needed. I smiled too when I saw that not just a few of the kids had brought tools along with them to make the work a little easier.

I was about to turn to speak to Marina when a sudden wave of dizziness hit me. The taste of mushrooms in my mouth now sour, and I had to put a hand on the log to steady myself. The world around me seemed to spin, the fire flickering and dancing in my vision.

My heart pounded in my chest, a familiar fear gripped me. Was this another side effect of the Cores? Or was it something else? I barely had time to ponder the question when my vision started to blur. The last thing I remember was the sound of Marina's panicked voice calling my name as I succumbed to the darkness.

Chapter 14 – Yari

"Marcus! Marcus! Are you there? Can you hear me? Oh no, oh no no no no no," Yari's voice echoed in my head. I tried to respond before she threw herself into a tizz, but realised that through the pain that I was experiencing well, everywhere, I had no choice but to grunt. I couldn't even open my eyes.

"What have I done? What have I done?" my small Sylph companion repeated, beside herself with panic, fear and sorrow.

I grunted again, only louder this time. I had tried to open my eyes too, but if I had actually managed to, all that I could see what blackness.

"I've hurt him so bad," Yari was saying to herself. "And if he dies then… oh no, oh no no no no no!"

"Yari!" I managed to force myself to say aloud. "Its… OK. I'm... OK."

But it wasn't OK. Every millimetre of my body was in complete agony and I had no idea why. I could only assume that my blindness was a side-effect of how much my head was pounding.

"Marcus! Oh, Marcus! You're alive," Yari's voice echoed, filled with relief, but also a profound sorrow. "I'm so sorry, Marcus. I didn't mean to... I didn't mean for this to happen."

"I know, Yari... I know," I murmured through the pain, my words sounding muffled and distant. But then, what did she mean?

"You didn't… mean…" I trailed off and from the pause I received in response, I could tell that Yari understood what I was asking.

"I, I tried to help, when you drank the water again," Yari stuttered. "I thought that if I took all of the bad effects away from you, shielding you from the Cores… but it didn't really work. I think it delayed it for you but in the end it just overcame me. I don't know if it would've been so bad if we had just dealt with it all together in the first place."

I knew that Yari had tried to help the last time, but this time she had gone way overboard, and the pain had been so much worse.

"It's OK, Yari," I said softly. "You meant well and I'm OK now, right?"

Yari didn't respond and suddenly I became aware of the strangeness of the darkness around me. It was not the absence of light that one would typically associate with blindness, but rather, a velvet, engulfing darkness that seemed almost tangible, as if I could reach out and touch it.

What was this? Where was I?

"Yari... where am I?" I asked, my voice barely above a whisper.

"You're... well, you're inside your mind, Marcus," Yari responded, her voice trembling. "In the space where I spend most of my time – well that's before I could fly out in my projection form, at least."

"In... my mind?" I echoed, confused.

"Yes, the Obsidian Cores... they seem to have placed you in here. You've retreated inside your own mind, into your subconscious. I can see that time is standing still in the physical world right now."

Something new from the Cores? Inside my own mind? This was beyond anything I could comprehend. But each time the Cores had affected me in the past, I'd gained something useful, an ability to heal myself from mortal wounds, being able to talk to Yari, but this? This was just strange.

I tried to move, to explore this new space, but found I couldn't. I was merely a consciousness floating in an endless expanse of blackness.

I felt a wave of panic surge through me. If I was stuck in here, inside my own mind, was there a way out? I didn't know how to navigate this new landscape, this new reality of mine. And would I be stuck here forever? Until my physical body died out in the real world?

"Yari," I called out, my voice echoing in the emptiness. "Yari, how do I get out?"

For a moment, there was only silence. Then, her voice came through, clearer now, but still laced with worry.

"I... I don't know, Marcus. You'll have to figure it out. But remember, it's your mind. You're in control."

Taking deep, steadying breaths, I willed myself to calm down. My heart was racing, my thoughts a whirlwind of fear and confusion. But Yari was right. This was my mind. I was in control.

I focused on that thought, on the feeling of control. Slowly, the darkness began to recede, replaced by a wide-open space and as I forced my eyes to work properly once more, finally I could see the bright golden form of Yari, floating mid-air not far from where I now stood.

"I... I can see you," I said slowly. Then after looking around at the nothingness that was the inside of my own mind added: "You live here?"

Yari looked around and gave a small, melancholy chirp. "I do, or at least,

I used to. This was my reality for a long time before the Obsidian Cores gave me the ability to project myself into the physical world. But it's not usually this... barren. The mindscape usually reflects the mental state of its inhabitant."

She gestured around at the void surrounding us. "Yours is empty because you're new to this, you haven't learned to control it yet. When you do, it could be anything you want. It could be a replica of the physical world, it could be an idealised place, a sanctuary... anything."

The idea that this emptiness could be filled with anything my mind conjured up was both exciting and daunting. A sanctuary, a haven from the real world where time stood still? The possibilities were endless. But first, I needed to figure out how to leave.

"Yari," I asked, looking around at the vast expanse of my own subconscious. "Do you have any idea how to get out?"

Her golden form flickered a little before she responded, her voice uncertain. "Not really, Marcus. For me, the Cores just suddenly gave me the ability to project myself out. I never really had to consciously leave. But, if I were to guess, I'd say it should be something like to... well, waking up. You'd need to have a strong desire to return, a sense of urgency perhaps. An emotional response might be a trigger."

I nodded, taking in her words. My initial panic had receded, replaced now by a quiet determination. I looked around again, at the vast, formless expanse that was my mind. Then I closed my eyes, took a deep breath, and tried to evoke a sense of urgency, a desperate need to return to my physical body.

With a jolt, I was suddenly back in the real world. My eyes blinked open to the familiar sight of the settlement, the kids all standing around me, their faces a mix of relief and worry. They had no idea how much time had passed, but to them, according to Yari, it seemed like I had just blinked.

I took a moment to reassure myself that I was indeed back, feeling the rough ground beneath me, the cool air on my skin. But I knew in the back of my mind, that a new door had been opened. And while it may be a bit daunting to explore, the possibilities it offered were intriguing.

"I'm okay," I said, not just to the kids but to myself. Then turning to Yari's projection who had arrived out in the real world with me, I added: "Thanks, Yari. You've shown me something... new."

"And next time, maybe we can try to make the place a little more comfortable," Yari added in my mind. I smiled at her words but then after a moment realised that she wasn't being sarcastic.

"Are you OK?" Marina asked as the children filtered away from me again. I could tell that she was genuinely concerned, and I told her what had happened right away.

"I'm alright, Marina," I assured her, sitting up and letting out a slow breath. I looked around at the familiar faces of the children, their relief palpable in the air. I then glanced back at Marina, her eyes wide with worry but also curiosity.

"It's... a little hard to explain," I started. "I think I was inside my own mind. Like where Yari is usually, except, well, the opposite."

Marina's brows furrowed in confusion. "Inside your own mind? That sounds scary."

"It was, at first," I admitted. "But Yari was there, and she helped me understand what was happening. It's... like a new ability the Obsidian Cores have given me."

Marina nodded slowly, absorbing the information. After a moment of silence, she asked, "And you're okay now? No more pain?"

I stretched my arms, flexing my fingers. "Yes, I feel much better now. No pain. Just a little tired, maybe. But I'm okay."

She looked relieved, the tension around her eyes smoothing away. "Well, that's good. I'm glad you're alright, Marcus."

I smiled at her. "Thanks, Marina. But there's something else." I paused, gathering my thoughts. "Yari said time stood still when I was... in there. It was like a personal sanctuary, a place outside the usual flow of time."

Marina blinked at me, her eyes wide. "That... that's amazing, Marcus. It sounds... it sounds like a gift."

I nodded, but thinking about the real potential of this new ability, I simply couldn't come up with anything. "How though? I mean, what can I do with it if anything that happens to me in there has no effect on the real world?"

"Well what if you can go in there if you're hurt, and wait for your real body to heal up?" she asked.

I shook my head. "If time doesn't pass when I'm in there, then I don't think that's going to happen."

"Well what if..." Marina furrowed her brow, clearly trying to think of something amazing.

I waited, and the longer Marina went without coming up with anything amazing, the larger the smile in my face grew. Eventually I had to put her out of her mystery.

"It doesn't matter, anyway," I said. "I'm sure it'll all become clear at some point."

"Well, as long as you're okay, that's what matters," she said, the worry finally easing from her eyes. "You're full of surprises, Marcus."

I chuckled at that, shaking my head lightly. "Believe me, Marina, I'm just as surprised as you are. And that's not the first time you've said that."

"And hopefully not the last," she punctuated.

That reminded me. "The Cores!" I practically shouted, and then remembered my audience. The last thing I wanted was for Guy to think that I was going to give him a good telling off for disposing of our most precious resource. "Without them… do you think we can go and find them? Make our way down the edge of the settlement and see if we can fish any of them out? And the ocean, the water… will they kill everything in there?"

"You're lucky, but not that lucky," Marina said. "If it was as easy as that to kill all the things that live in the water, then it would've been done a long time ago. I can't remember exactly what the deal was, but basically I don't think the Cores will actually do anything in the sea – other than get lost forever that is. And I already told you, you don't want to go into the water. There's a reason you don't see any of those 'ships' you're so fond of around here."

"But why?" I pressed. "What is it in the ocean that's so bad around here? I mean, are they worse than the Entropics."

"Not worse, just different," Marina said thoughtfully. "Around here, they'll probably be…"

"Sand worms," Yari's voice echoed through my mind.

"Sand worms," Marina said a second later.

"Sand worms." I said flatly. "We're not going into the ocean because of… sand worms?"

"Yes of course that's the reason!" Marina said sternly. "Unless you enjoy creatures that will attack you on sight and have the ability to bore a hole straight through you in less than a second?"

"Wait… what?" I asked. "That's not…"

"Sand worms aren't exactly worms," Yari explained. "More like eels. Light brownish things that have rows of sharp rotating teeth that they use to bore into rock to make their nests. About the size of one of those children, actually."

"Do I have to explain everything to you like you're a…" Marina started to say, then stopped as her gaze fell on the children working hard in our settlement. "Actually it's worse than that. I have to explain everything to you like you're a baby! Children actually know better!"

Well I couldn't argue with that; I actually knew almost nothing about this world, and truth be told I did seem to throw up a lot. Like a baby.

"Well, I can't exactly say that I'm an expert in marine biology," I retorted, trying to mask my embarrassment with a hint of humour.

"That's for sure," Marina shot back, though I could see a smile tugging at the corners of her mouth.

"But I'll have you know that back where I come from, I could gut a fish in less than ten seconds, fight off a handful of sharks and all the while sword fight against the best men the Royal Navy had to offer."

Marina peered at me. "You know you sound crazy, right?"

I hung my head in annoyance.

"But, back to the matter at hand," Marina said, turning serious again. "As far as the Cores go, they're probably lost. The currents would've taken them by now."

I nodded, accepting the harsh truth. It was a significant setback, but at the back of my mind, something was itching me: the knowledge of where we could get more of the magical artefacts, if we were so brave.

The thought led me down a strange trail, and to something I hadn't thought about for a while: the Selari workers. They were still back there in the mine, hooked on a drug that kept them working, but had also turned them into the zombies that they were. I wanted to help them, I still needed to do something.

"Marina I…" I started to say, but she interrupted me.

"They can't be helped," she said, somehow knowing exactly where my mind had gone. "The Selari workers are too far gone, I already told you."

"But that doesn't mean we can't set them free, does it?" I asked. Just like Yari and your own Sylph… by the way did you ever give it a name?"

Marina shook her head.

"Anyway," I continued. "We can let all the Sylph in that place know that we can do better for them, that we can fight back against the Entropics and they don't need to keep on working."

"No, you don't get it," Marina said. "The Sylphs and the Selari working in the mine, they don't do it by choice anymore, neither of them. It's what they know and so it's what they do. You won't be able to convince them of anything."

I didn't let Marina's words deter me from my plan to save everyone, but I could sense that she didn't want to talk about it anymore.

"Well either way," I said. "If we want more Cores, we know where to go to get them, right?"

Marina nodded slowly, but I could see that she absolutely didn't want to go back to that place.

"We'll have to be careful, Marcus," she warned, her voice barely more than a whisper. "The mine is a dangerous place, even more so now that the

Caretaker knows what we've done."

"We can't let fear hold us back, Marina," I said, feeling a rush of adrenaline at the prospect of our impending mission. "The Cores could be crucial for our survival. Without them, I don't know how we're ever going to win a fight against those monsters."

I watched Marina's face as I said those words. I'd forgotten that the Cores were only useful to me in all of this, no one else could use them the way I had already, and it made me feel a little guilty.

"I understand," she replied, a determined gleam in her eyes. "But if we're going to do this, we need to plan carefully. We can't afford any mistakes."

"I completely agree," I said, nodding. "We'll take our time and come up with a strategy. We'll need to think of everything to make sure we don't get caught with our pants down. "

Marina stared at me, but didn't comment.

"I never thought I'd be going back to that place…" she muttered almost to herself.

"We've managed to do the impossible before, Marina. We'll do it again."

Marina gave me a tight smile. "You're right. We've come this far, haven't we? Alright, let's do it. Let's get our Cores, and see if we can't force feed you them until you're sick."

I smiled, but the sentiment did not reach my stomach, which growled angrily at the thought.

I watched the children working for a little while. It was odd, like watching a skilled team of workers erecting buildings from the ground up – the footprint first followed by plank upon plank as the buildings slowly grew all in tandem, but eventually the whole thing began to bore me, and I turned my attention inwards and back to my new ability.

I closed my eyes and imagined the place inside my mind where Yari lived.

As I drifted inward, I focused on the sense of calm that enveloped me. It felt as though I was crossing a threshold into a different realm, a world entirely separate from the physical one around me. The noise and activity of the settlement, the children at work, Marina's concerned face, all faded away as I delved deeper.

I saw it then, a space of infinite dimensions and yet, simultaneously confined within the realm of my mind. It was a place of indigo and obsidian, the colours intertwining like a beautiful cosmic dance. The nebulous mist was thick with starlight, casting an ethereal glow across the expanse.

At the centre of it all was Yari. Floating like a beautiful golden bird in the darkness.

I took a second to make sure I was safely within the space, and then decided to try what Yari had told me already. I began to use my memories, my imagination to restructure the place.

I knew what I wanted my internal space to look like, there was only one choice after all: the place I'd called my own for as long as I could remember: the Captain's quarters aboard the Iron Will.

Slowly, I began to construct the scene. The first thing to materialise was the scent, that mixture of salty air and polished wood that always reminded me of home. Then, the textures came into existence – the smooth, cool touch of brass fixtures, the rough grit of the wood-panelled floors, the plushness of the burgundy velvet coverings of my four-poster bed.

The cabin was spacious, its central feature a hefty oak desk scattered with ancient charts, maps, and an old-fashioned, rusty brass telescope - a relic from times past but a piece that held sentimental value. Above the desk hung an aged, oil-painted portrait of the Iron Will in full sail against a stormy sea, its hull defiant against the thrashing waves.

On one side of the room was a small bookshelf, worn and weathered but filled to the brim with scrolls and old leather-bound books. The books were a collection of stories from the seven seas, tales of old voyages, and some handwritten journals, rich with notes and thoughts about the voyages the Iron Will had undertaken under my command.

Against the opposite wall stood a drinks cabinet, a dark cherry wood piece containing a variety of liquors from every corner of the world we had visited. Above the cabinet, hanging on a hook, was my tricorn hat and cutlass - symbols of the Captain of the Iron Will.

Beside the window, a large, burgundy armchair sat invitingly, its worn surface telling stories of countless nights spent reading, planning, or merely staring out into the vastness of the ocean. The window itself was a large, circular porthole that let in the starlight, its glass subtly distorting the cosmos outside, making it seem even more mystical than it already was.

The ambiance of the room was further enhanced by soft lantern light, casting a warm, flickering glow that danced on the wooden walls, making the shadows play hide and seek in the corners of the room.

As the final details of the room fell and faded into place, a sense of peace washed over me. This was my sanctuary within the sanctuary, my haven in the heart of the cosmos. Here, within the imagined confines of the Iron Will, I could think, plan, and prepare for the battles ahead. It was a reminder of the journey, of the purpose, and of the home I carried within me wherever I went.

"This... what is this place?" Yari asked as her small golden form buzzed around the room, seemingly captivated by everything.

"This is the Captain's quarters aboard the Iron Will," I replied, an affectionate smile spreading across my face as I watched Yari's bright form flitting around the room. "It's a place that was... is very important to me."

Yari zipped towards the desk, her golden light reflecting off the worn maps and brass telescope. She paused, hovering over a worn parchment, the contours of an island sketched upon it. "You miss it," she stated, not as a question but an understanding. The subtle shift in her light told me she could sense the nostalgia, the longing in my voice.

"I do," I admitted, my gaze drifting to the oil painting of the Iron Will in full sail. The painting served as a constant reminder of the life I had led, the freedom of the sea, the camaraderie of my crew, and the exhilaration of exploration. "It was home."

"But now you're here," Yari said, leaving the desk and coming to hover in front of me. Her light pulsed, gentle waves of warm, comforting energy radiating off her. "And we're here with you."

"Yes," I said, my heart swelling with a complex mix of sorrow and gratitude. Yari, Marina, and the others - they had all become my family in this strange, new world. "And for that, I am incredibly thankful."

"Good," Yari said, her light brightening as if she was pleased with my answer. "Now, let's get to work on this plan of yours."

With that, she zoomed over to the desk, hovering above the blank parchment I'd unravelled there. I followed suit, letting the comfort of the familiar surroundings ground me, prepare me for the daunting task that lay ahead.

"What will you do if the Caretaker comes?" Yari asked in a small voice, like she didn't really want me to hear the question.

But what could I do if I once again came face to face with the Entropic? I couldn't match the creature in speed or strength and by all means, I knew that he wouldn't allow me to go free for a second time. No, if the Caretaker caught us, it would mean our end.

"It's not the Caretaker that worries me," I said, trying to shift Yari's focus. "It's leaving the kids behind with the Iron Will out there looking for us. I can't be in two places at once but I won't take the kids to the mine."

"You're right," Yari agreed, her light dimming slightly at the mention of the Iron Will. "The children... they've been through so much already. They don't deserve to be put in harm's way again."

I nodded, feeling a knot in my stomach at the thought. "We need to find a solution, a way to protect them while we're gone."

We sat in silence for a while, the weight of our situation pressing on us.

It was a delicate balancing act, and the stakes couldn't be higher.

"There's just no way around it," I said eventually. "The best I can think of is to leave Marina here with the children, and I go and collect as many Cores as I can. Plus that way at least if I get caught, it's just me."

Yari's light dimmed noticeably, casting long shadows across the desk. "That's... a significant risk, Marcus. And what if something happens to you? Who will use the Cores then?"

I rubbed my temples, feeling a headache coming on. "I know it's risky, Yari, but do we really have another choice? If we leave the children unprotected and something happens..."

I slammed a fist on the table and it returned a satisfying wooden thud.

"There's just so much risk here damn it!" I exclaimed.

Silence hung in the air for a long moment before Yari spoke again.

"But why do we need the Cores right now?" she asked in a small voice.

"Because I need them to be able to fight back!" I replied angrily.

"But do you need them to fight the Iron Will, or its crew?" she asked, her voice getting smaller by the second.

"I... what?" I asked, my mind catching up with my mouth. That was actually a fair point.

"I mean... couldn't we deal with the crew of the Iron Will first, then we know the children will be safe if we leave them behind to go and get more of the Cores?"

My mind reeled as I processed her words. It was so simple, so straightforward. We didn't necessarily need the Cores to deal with the crew of the Iron Will. Yes, they were formidable and they had pistols and cannons, but they were still human. Vulnerable in their own way.

"That... that could work," I admitted, leaning back in my chair. "We focus on neutralising the immediate threat first. The crew of the Iron Will. If we can do that, we buy ourselves time. Time to retrieve the Cores without leaving the children unprotected."

Yari's light brightened, pulsating with what seemed like excitement. "Yes, and if we plan it right, we could possibly even capture the Iron Will, if it's still out there somewhere. If we have their ship, we have their resources. Guns and cannons. It could make the retrieval of the Cores much easier."

"I like the way you think, Yari," I said, feeling the knot of tension in my stomach loosening. This plan wasn't without its risks, of course, but it felt more manageable. More within our control. And it took into consideration the safety of the children, which was paramount.

There was much to do. Planning, training, preparing. But for the first time in a long while, I felt a spark of hope. A glimmer of a chance that we might actually pull this off.

"Alright," I said, determination creeping into my voice. "Let's get to work."

Chapter 15 – Children's Brigade

"If they come by water," I said.

"Which they won't," Marina replied.

"I said if."

"I know," Marina said. "And I said they won't."

"Well anyway," I continued. "If the Iron Will is still sailing."

"Which it won't be, not if it's out there on the sea with all the terrible monsters about."

"You know they have cannons right? And pistols?" I asked. "Those weapons you saw? They can kill things from pretty far away and by the sounds of those sand worm things you told me about, they'll be pretty easy to spot coming at them."

"And then they'll have to deal with everything else out there, creatures so terrible you couldn't even imagine," Marina said.

"Why must everything around here be terrible beyond my imagination?" I asked. "You know I've seen some pretty bad things, and I have a good imagination. You have no idea how imaginative I can get."

Marina rolled her eyes but there was a hint of a smile on her lips. "Oh, I've seen your 'imagination' in action. That's why I have to keep reminding you to be realistic."

"I am being realistic!" I protested, "We can't just dismiss the possibility that they might come by water. We need to prepare for all eventualities. Land, sea, even air."

"Oh so does the Iron Will suddenly have wings too, Marcus," Marina asked in a very sarcastic tone.

"Well no, but it has cannons, and they fire cannonballs through the air. Besides, I don't know everything about this world yet. There could be creatures they could harness, or strange new technology they could employ. The point is, we need to be prepared for the unlikely, even if it probably won't happen."

Marina sighed but she didn't argue any further. "Fine, we plan for all possible approaches. Happy?"

I shrugged, "As happy as one can be while planning for an invasion."

"Then let's talk about how your former crew like to fight. Presumably they know more than just pointing those guns and cannons at things, right?"

"Indeed, they do," I admitted, running a hand over my weary face. "They're pirates, through and through. Skilled fighters, both on land and sea. They're not just good with cannons and guns, but also cutlasses, knives, and their bare hands if need be. Uh a cutlass is a kind of sword, but designed to slash more than stab."

Marina nodded, absorbing the information. "And how about you, Captain? How do you like to fight?" She emphasised the last word, a playful glint in her eyes.

"Well," I chuckled, despite the grim topic. "I don't like to toot my own trumpet, but if I have to, I'm more of a cutlass and dagger man myself. There's something about the feel of a blade in my hand that gives me a sense of control."

"I see," she said. "Do your old crew have any... quirks? Anything that might give us an advantage?"

I thought for a moment, trying to recall any relevant details. "They always fought like they were in a rush, impatient. They don't like to wait around for the enemy to organise themselves properly – they like the element of surprise. It means that they often rush into situations, not that it's actually been an issue, mind. If we can bait them into action somehow, they're likely to move before they think."

"And are they all loyal to their new Captain?" Marina asked, her gaze steady on me.

I didn't say a word in response. In truth I hadn't thought about my former first mate Anthony Cowley in a very long time and now, I realised just how hurt I'd been by the whole situation.

"That's a little harder to answer," I admitted. "They probably fear him, it's how most Captains work. And fear can be a powerful motivator. But I don't know if that translates into unshakeable loyalty. They might be swayed if the odds are stacked heavily against them."

Marina hummed thoughtfully. "A trap and the promise of riches then? Maybe we have something to work with."

We kept talking, brainstorming, and working on our plan. And even though the day was rolling by, for the first time in a while, I felt a sense of true purpose. It was a small thing, a tiny flame in the midst of a storm, but it was there, and it was enough to keep me going.

"So, we have a foundation for a plan," I concluded, leaning back a little on my log before remembering it didn't have a back to it. "A trap to lure them in, something to make them think they're getting the upper hand. And if that doesn't work, a promise of riches to sway those on the fence."

Marina nodded. "It's a good start. But we still need to think about the specifics. How do we set the trap? How do we make the promise believable?"

I frowned, contemplating something that would be feasible. "I'm sure I'll come up with something. As for the promise... I'm not sure. They know I've been stranded here, why would they believe I suddenly found a treasure?"

"Because they want to believe," Marina said, her gaze distant as if she was seeing something beyond the horizon. "People believe what they want to believe. And greed... Greed can blind even the most sceptical."

I nodded, acknowledging the truth in her words. "True, but we still need to make it convincing."

"But all of that can come later," Marina said. "We need to get this place built up and prepared to take an onslaught."

I nodded. "And… I hate to say it, but I think we're going to have to teach the kids to look out for themselves. Not to be fighters," I added quickly, raising my hands at Marina's surprised gaze. "Just in case they get caught or find themselves one to one with one of the crew. I hate to think of them having to fight, but at the same time it'd be worse if they found themselves in a fight, and didn't know what to do."

Marina was silent for a long moment, staring at the ground, her expression unreadable. Finally, she sighed, looking back up at me. "I don't like it," she said slowly. "I don't like it at all. But you're right. They need to know how to defend themselves."

She frowned, rubbing her temples. "But how do we teach them? I know how to fight, but they're just kids."

"I'll teach them," I said resolutely. "I'll start with the basics. I'll make sure they understand that it's a last resort, only to be used if they're in immediate danger. And it will be more about avoiding harm and getting away safely rather than engaging in a fight."

I could see Marina's mind working, her brow furrowing in thought. "I don't want to scare them, Marcus. The world is already a terrifying place for them. But you're right. We need to prepare them."

"Believe me, Marina," I said, "I wish there was another way. But in a world filled with the likes of the crew of the Iron Will, we have to make sure they know how to protect themselves."

After a long silence, Marina finally nodded, determination steeling her features. "Alright, let's do this. Let's prepare them, prepare ourselves. We'll make this settlement a fortress they won't dare to invade."

"We can do this," I added, reaching out to squeeze her shoulder. "For the kids, for our future. We have no other choice."

I sent Yari up as high and as far as she could travel with our current link and although it seemed slightly further than before, it still wasn't anything ground-breaking. At least with her high up in the sky though, we could see for miles all around, including out to sea, so if anyone did approach our growing little home, we'd know about it.

I decided not to interfere with the kids' work for the rest of the day. As I watched them, I knew that they didn't need someone like me sticking their oar in, and by all accounts by the time they stopped in search of an evening meal when the sun began to set, the five buildings they'd started were more than halfway complete, and looked like very, very good examples of wooden buildings from back in my own world. They all formed a perfectly straight line and looked big enough to be comfortable for five people in each, or ten if the situation so required it. But regardless of that, I knew that they could expand to more shelter as time passed and the settlement grew.

The next morning after the entire settlement had awoken – and I made sure I wasn't one of the last this time – I called a meeting. As we all sat around the fire, eating a mixture of what the kids had brought with them from their last settlement, and the mushrooms and various other bits and pieces we'd managed to forage so far, I explained my plan.

"I know it might sound difficult, daunting even… but you know those men… they're probably going to come back, right?" I said to the kids, doing my best to ease them into the idea that they should be trained to fight. "So with that being said… I think it's going to be best if you learn how to defend yourselves. Not fight..." I added quickly with my hands raised. "I mean, if the situation calls for it, or you get into trouble."

There was a hush among the young ones, their eyes going wide as the weight of my words sank in. I looked to Marina, hoping she could help them understand, help them feel less frightened.

She nodded, leaning forward and catching the gaze of every child. "Marcus is right," she said, her voice firm but gentle. "We're not trying to scare you or turn you into soldiers. But this world, as beautiful as it can be, can also be dangerous. And sometimes, the danger doesn't come from the monsters in the forest or the creatures in the sea."

She paused for a moment, letting her words sink in before continuing. "We just want to make sure that if you're ever in a situation where you're in danger, you know how to protect yourselves, how to get away safely. We hope that day never comes, but it's always better to be prepared, believe me."

There were a few nods, a few uncertain glances exchanged, but overall, the response was much more positive than I had expected. Then again, these kids had seen their fair share of danger already. They understood the need for survival better than anyone else.

Then, unexpectedly, it was Guy who broke the silence. "So what do you want to do? Make a circle in the ground and have each of us fight each other? Or should we all fight against you for practice?"

"I… what?" I asked with my mouth hanging open. That was certainly not the response that I'd expected.

"Guy, that's not quite what we had in mind," I said, trying to regain my composure. I looked at Marina who was doing a poor job of hiding her amusement. "This isn't about fighting each other, and I'm certainly not looking for a fight. We're all on the same side here."

"Then what do you suggest?" Guy challenged, leaning back with a nonchalant shrug. His grin didn't falter, but there was a curious glint in his eyes, and if I wasn't mistaken, a challenge.

I leaned back, crossing my arms and considering my words. "The goal here is to learn how to defend yourself, and how to disarm an opponent if need be. It's about quickness, and agility, and thinking on your feet. It's not about strength or brawling."

Seeing a few puzzled faces, I sighed, running a hand over my face. "OK, think of it this way. If I were to attack you," I looked at the nearest child, a tiny girl who I was almost positive was named Bella, who couldn't have been older than seven. "What would you do?"

Ria, wide-eyed, shook her head and said with a slight lisp: "I... I don't know. Run?" her response almost made me want to cancel this whole idea. These were kids for Christ's sake! But then I remembered why I was doing all of this.

"That's a good start," I managed to reply with an encouraging nod. "Running is always a good option when you're facing an opponent who is bigger or stronger than you. But what if you can't run? What then?"

Guy sat up straight, interest sparking in his eyes. "Then you fight."

I nodded, "Then you use whatever you have at your disposal to protect yourself, yes. And that's what I want to teach you - some basic self-defence moves, ways to get out of a dangerous situation if you can't avoid it. No brawling, no sparring. Just survival."

Guy seemed to mull over my words, then finally he responded. "But if we practise, then we'll know what it's really like, right?" he asked. "Like if you tell us all the easy stuff, the stuff you think's going to scare us, then if it happens for real, we won't be best prepared."

I rubbed the back of my head. Guy was right, I knew he was and he was simply saying exactly what I was thinking. But I was stuck. Could I really try to enact a terrible situation just to show these kids how to deal with it?

"Actually, you know what," Guy said suddenly, "It doesn't matter anyway, let's just forget about this whole training idea, OK?"

"What?" I asked, still not completely up to date with the conversation. "Doesn't matter? Why?"

"Because I doubt that there's anything you have to teach us anyway," Guy replied with a smile.

I looked at Marina and as she saw my expression of sheer confusion, she had to put her hand in front of her mouth so that the kids couldn't see her laughing.

"Why do you say that, Guy?" I asked, arching an eyebrow at him.

He shrugged, trying to act nonchalant. "I mean, no offence, but you're not exactly a warrior. We all saw you when then Iron Will's men came. You were hiding just like the rest of us."

Marina, no longer able to contain herself, let out a loud, ringing laugh. "Oh, Guy, you have no idea. I'm sure Marcus could give those brutes a run for their money if he wanted to." Something about her tone sounded very sarcastic though, and I had to fight the urge to protest.

My expression turned stern and I took a deep breath, realising this was probably a pivotal moment. I could take offence at Guy's words, I could laugh them off, or I could use them as an opportunity. As a teaching moment.

"You're right, Guy," I said. "I'm no warrior. But that's the point. You don't have to be a warrior to defend yourself. In fact, it's better if you're not."

I paused for effect, letting my gaze sweep over each child in turn. "Being a warrior means looking for fights, seeking out conflicts. That's not what we want to be. We want to be survivors. We want to be able to stand our ground when we have to, to protect ourselves and each other. But most importantly," I continued, "we want to avoid fights whenever we can. It's always better to escape a dangerous situation than to engage in it. That's the first rule of self-defence."

I saw comprehension dawn on Guy's face, and a new kind of respect in his eyes. "Alright," he said slowly. "I think I understand. So, when do we start training?"

I couldn't help but smile at his enthusiasm. "How about now?" I said.

"And remember, we're learning how to defend ourselves. Not how to fight."

It wasn't that I wanted to prove to the kids and Marina that I was a more than capable fighter – as Captain of the Iron Will I had fought in more battles than I could count – but it was just something about the nonchalance with which Guy had spoken that caught me off guard. He wasn't being sarcastic or abrasive, he was simply stating a fact. A fact that I knew to be untrue.

A short while later, I found myself facing Guy in a wide-open patch of grass, the children forming a circle around us. Their wide, expectant eyes watching our every move. Guy, for his part, looked surprisingly focused, a far cry from the carefree character I'd seen just moments earlier.

"All right, Guy," I began, my tone serious. "The first thing I'm going to do is show you a move that's meant to disarm your opponent and give you a chance to run away. I call it the 'Hit and Run'. Now, it's not the most honourable of moves, but if you're cornered and it's a matter of survival... Well, sometimes you have to do what you have to do."

He nodded, a determined expression on his face. "Got it," he said.

"Good," I continued, "Now, pay attention. One of the most vulnerable areas on anyone, male or female, is the… the… um…" I struggled to say the words aloud to the young man, so just generally gestured to my groin area. "It's not a pretty move, but it is effective. If you aim your knee, elbow or foot there with enough force, it'll give you a few seconds to get away."

I proceeded to demonstrate the move slowly, carefully explaining that finesse wasn't particularly the main driving force here and I showed him how to use his body weight to deliver the blow. Then, it was his turn.

He mirrored my movements, albeit a bit awkwardly at first. However, when he went to deliver the blow, he pulled it at the last second, causing me to flinch, "Hey, watch it!" I chided.

"Sorry," Guy said, barely hiding a grin. "I guess I don't know my own strength, if you're worried little old me can hurt you so easy that is."

I gave him a disapproving look, "This is serious, Guy. These moves could save your life one day."

But then I looked at Marina, who had a hand in front of her mouth as though she was once again stifling a laugh.

Don't ask me why I did it, but I simply felt the need to prove myself in that moment.

"Listen Guy, I'm going to hold you like the crew of the Iron Will did the other day. I want you to try and escape my grip and I'll do what I can to cling on. Be warned though, I'm not just going to stand there and let you hit me.

"Yeah, yeah," Guy replied, waving his hand dismissively. "I've got some moves of my own I can show you... and ones that don't involve hitting the groin as hard as I can."

Marina laughed.

We set our position up, with me holding onto Guy and standing behind him, just like what had happened in their settlement.

"Alright," I said. "Go!"

Guy moved swiftly, quicker than I anticipated and spun within my grasp. Before I had a chance to react and follow along with his movement, Guy pushed back to break my grip around him, gripped my wrist, and twisted. The unexpected pain shot up my arm, causing me to gasp and pull back instinctively. The kids watching let out a collective gasp, their eyes wide with surprise.

"Guy!" I shouted, clutching my wrist. "What was that?"

He shrugged, his grin spreading wider, "Just a simple joint lock. If you can control your opponent's arm, you can control their whole body. Plus, it doesn't require much strength, just technique."

Marina howled with laughter. I looked over in her direction but the sight of me holding my wrist in pain with an annoyed look on my face must've been too much for her; she fell back onto the ground and her body convulsed with silent laughter. I'd have to remember to get her back for this.

Rubbing my sore wrist, I turned back to Guy with a newfound respect. The kid had some moves. "Alright, now that you've shown us that, I suppose it's only fair if I try it on you, yes?"

He laughed and held out his arm, clearly expecting me to decline. To his surprise, I took him up on the offer. With him guiding me through the steps, I found my grip on his wrist and twisted. His smile vanished as he grunted in pain, "OK, OK. You can let go now." It had taken far, far more effort than I'd expected to hurt the boy though.

There was a pause as I let go and Guy massaged his wrist. He looked at me and for the first time, I saw a grudging respect in his eyes. "You're stronger than you look yourself," he said.

"Self-defence isn't about being strong, it's about knowing how to use your body and mind to your advantage," I replied. "Just remember, these moves are meant for defence, not aggression. You use them when you have no other choice."

Guy nodded, his grin returning. "Got it. Hit the groin and twist the wrist, when there's no other choice. But then… you know what, why don't we just have a fight, and we'll see if there's anything we can learn from each other, right?"

I stared at Guy. There was no way I was going to fight a child, and even less so one about one-third my size.

"Unless you're worried you might lose in front of your girlfriend there?" he goaded.

"Girlfr… Marina isn't my girlfriend," I replied on instinct.

I looked at Marina who was now sat up and staring at me.

"No it's OK," she said. "We should all get to see what you're made of if we're going to follow you around like lost puppies right? If that's all we are?"

"I… what?" I replied. I had no idea where that had come from.

"So what do you think? A fight until one of us surrenders?" Guy asked and a few cheers erupted from the other children watching.

"I'm not fighting you, Guy," I replied sternly. "But if you really want, why don't you attack me and I'll just defend myself. I don't want to hurt you."

Guy smirked, crossing his arms over his chest. "Yeah, we'll see about that."

Before I could even react, he lunged at me with an unexpected quickness. I was taken aback by his speed, but was just about able to sidestep his charge and use his momentum against him to gently toss him aside. He quickly got up, shaking his head to clear it, then charged again. This time I managed to catch his wrist and redirected him, once again using his own momentum to unbalance him.

This went on for a few more exchanges, with Guy attacking and me simply defending and redirecting. His movements were becoming more and more erratic, fuelled by frustration. I could see him becoming winded, but his determination didn't seem to waver.

Suddenly, Guy came at me with a wild swing of his arm. I instinctively blocked it, redirecting his momentum and pulling him slightly off balance. In the next moment, Guy used this to his advantage, using the momentum of my redirection to spin and land a solid kick to my side.

I stumbled back, caught off guard, and a cheer erupted from the kids around us. Marina had a hand over her mouth, but she was grinning. I took a second to catch my breath, rubbing the sore spot on my side where Guy had landed his kick. I had to admit, it was a good move.

He stood panting, his eyes flashing with excitement. "I told you I had some moves."

"You're right," I said, "You're more capable than I initially thought. But, I also want to remind you, and all of you," I said, turning to the rest of the kids, "that this was a demonstration. In a real fight, I wouldn't be holding back. But the goal here is not to hurt each other. It's to learn how to defend ourselves."

I could see a mixture of reactions from the children. Some nodded in understanding while others looked a bit disappointed at the end of the spectacle. Guy, on the other hand, was still catching his breath, but his grin remained intact.

"You're right, Captain," he said, a little breathlessly, "I have been going easy, haven't I?"

Then he leapt at me again and I pulled an arm up to block the same kick he'd already hit me with once. I stepped back and Guy kicked out at my trailing shin, causing me to howl and drop to one knee in pain.

Then it hit me. Guy used my bent knee as a springboard, using the full momentum of his body to punch me in the side of my face with a loud crack.

My world turned to black, and the soft ground caressed my face as I lost all consciousness.

I woke up with a groan, my head pounding and my body feeling like I had been trampled by a herd of wild beasts. Slowly, I pushed myself up onto my elbows, my vision swimming. I was vaguely aware of a crowd around me. Children were staring with wide, anxious eyes, and Marina was kneeling next to me, her face a picture of concern.

"You OK?" she asked, her voice echoing in my ears as though she was speaking from a long distance away.

I tried to sit up but my head swam, and I fell back onto the ground. I groaned again, putting a hand to my aching head.

"I told you, Captain," Guy's voice floated to me from somewhere nearby. It sounded uncharacteristically apologetic. "I have a few moves of my own."

I turned my head to where his voice had come from, squinting through the light. He was standing a little ways off, his arms crossed over his chest, his gaze fixed on me.

"I..." I began, but my voice came out as a weak croak. I cleared my throat and tried again. "I can see that."

"I'm sorry," Guy said, and he actually sounded like he meant it. "I didn't mean to hurt you that badly. But you did say I should attack and you would defend. I didn't think you were going easy on me."

"I wasn't," I admitted. I pushed myself up again, this time managing to sit upright. Marina was right there, her hand on my shoulder to steady me. "You're good, Guy. You're very good. You've clearly had some training."

A smirk slowly spread across Guy's face. "Nope, just gifted I guess."

I didn't believe him, but if he didn't want to tell me about it, I didn't want to press.

I sighed, looking up at him. "Well, if anything, this has been a good lesson for all of us. Not just in self-defence, but also in humility."

There was silence for a moment, then Guy extended a hand to help me up. I took it, letting him pull me to my feet. I swayed for a moment, but Marina was right there, her arm still around my waist to steady me.

"That was a good fight," Guy said. He seemed to have lost his earlier bravado, replaced with something resembling respect. "You're not so bad yourself, Captain."

I couldn't help but laugh, despite the pounding in my head. "Thanks, Guy. I'll take that as a compliment."

As Marina helped me walk away from the crowd, I glanced back at Guy and the other children. They were watching me as I walked and I couldn't tell if they were worried or thought that I was now somehow much weaker than they'd once assumed. They were still kids, and if the rest of them could fight like Guy I wondered how much I actually had to teach them.

I turned my attention back to Marina, her worried gaze fixed on me. "I'm OK," I reassured her. "Just a bit shaken up."

She gave me a small smile, her eyes softening. "I know. But maybe next time, don't be so quick to underestimate your opponent, especially when they're half your size."

I chuckled weakly. "Lesson learned," I admitted. I glanced over at her, noticing the gentle concern in her gaze. "And Marina," I added, "Thank you."

"For what?" she asked, raising an eyebrow at me.

"For being there. For all of this. I couldn't do it without you."

Her eyes softened even more, and for a moment, she looked like she might say something. But then she just smiled, giving my waist a reassuring squeeze.

"We're a team," she said simply. "That's what we do."

"Right," I replied, then quickly changed the subject. "Are all Selari kids like that? Strong, and fast, and know how to fight I mean?"

Marina furrowed her brow. "I don't think so. I mean it's been a while since I've been around any kids… and I guess I don't really have anything to compare them to… but I'd say these ones are a bit different. As for fighting, I've never seen a kid fight, so I can't really answer that."

"I can sense something different about them," Yari spoke up in my mind. It made me jump as she'd been quiet for a long time. I hadn't called out to her as I thought after the last time we'd taken in some of the Cores, she needed some rest.

"Different? How?" I asked internally.

"I don't know," Yari said. "Like they have a small amount of power within them, or on them maybe? It's hard to say and it's more of a feeling than anything I can quantify."

"Like he had a Core on him, or he'd swallowed one?" I asked quickly, my mind racing with worry at the thought that perhaps Guy had seen how the Cores had helped me, and wanted to try it out for himself.

"No…" Yari replied slowly. "Not like that… just… something. I'll try to find out more if you would be able to teach him some more self-defence?"

I internally scanned Yari's question for sarcasm, but didn't detect any.

"Are you suggesting I should spar with Guy again?" I asked Yari internally, the idea making my head pound a bit more.

"Not necessarily," she replied. "But the closer you are to him, the more I can try to figure out what's different. And when he's moving about, using whatever he is to do whatever he does, it'll become a bit clearer."

I sighed, rubbing my temples. "We'll see, Yari. I just need some time to recover first."

Marina glanced at me, clearly hearing my sigh. "You really do need to rest," she said, looking at me with concern.

"You're right," I agreed. "I think I might have underestimated the kids… and overestimated myself."

She laughed lightly. "Well, that's one way to learn a lesson. I'm glad you're able to see your own shortcomings though."

It was a humbling experience to be sure. In my previous world, I had always been the stronger one. The leader. The mentor. Here, I was forced to re-evaluate my abilities and my role. But perhaps that was a good thing. If nothing else, it was a reminder to never underestimate my opponent, no matter their size or age. It was a lesson I would keep in mind moving forward. And it was a lesson that might just make me a better leader for these kids. Plus, it reminded me that I was still a stranger in this new world, and the rules I'd always lived by didn't necessarily wash here.

"We'll get through this," I said quietly, more to myself than to Marina. "We have to."

She simply squeezed my shoulder in response, a silent promise that we would indeed get through this, one way or another.

And in the end, wasn't that what it was all about? Not about being the strongest or the fastest, but about being able to protect yourself and those you cared about. It was a lesson I had learned the hard way, and one I hoped these kids wouldn't have to.

But for now, I needed to rest. To recover and reflect on what had happened. Because no matter how much I wished otherwise, I knew that this was only the beginning. There would be more challenges ahead, more battles to fight. And I would need to be ready.

After all, I was their leader. Their teacher. Their protector.

And I wouldn't let them down.

"I wish we had a Core, or some of the infused water left," Marina said as I sat on one of the logs we used as our meal-time benches.

The thought of the stuff made me groan.

"What with the last time, I'd bet it'd heal you back up to perfect in a few sips and in a matter of seconds!"

I couldn't argue with that. But it did occur to me that Marina always seemed to want to get more of the Cores in me. I guessed that with this world the way it was, we needed to do whatever we could to get as strong as possible, as fast as possible.

Chapter 16 – A Ship out of Water

"There's something I've been meaning to ask you," I said to Marina once the kids had all separated and returned to their work the day following my beat-down by Guy. Today though, I'd been clever enough to have the kids spar lightly with each other, so that I could assess their competencies on a level playing field.

Marina stopped sorting through the supplies she had been working with and looked at me as though to tell me to carry on.

"How did you end up in the mine?" I asked.

Marina paused at my question. She looked at me, her usually bright eyes clouded with mixed emotions. She took a deep breath and put down the bundle.

"It's a long story," she said, her voice quiet, almost a whisper.

I moved to sit down on a nearby rock, indicating for her to join me. "We have time," I reassured her, "if you're ready to talk about it."

She looked at me for a long moment, her gaze searching. After which, she nodded and sat down beside me, her posture stiff.

"Alright," she said finally, her voice just barely above a whisper. "I'll tell you."

She paused for a moment, gathering her thoughts, then began speaking slowly. "I was part of a hidden settlement of adult Selari, not far from here. The children... we had left them a long time ago to fend for themselves because they were safe, we thought. We'd managed to avoid the Entropics, but... but that changed."

Her voice cracked a little, and she paused to take a deep, shaky breath. "One day, one of them arrived. Just one. But it was enough. The Entropic came with an army of Sylphs, enough to bind our entire settlement. We... we didn't stand a chance."

Her voice became quiet, almost lost against the faint sound of the waves crashing against the sea wall leading up to our settlement. "It attacked us. Killed anyone who tried to run or fight back. It was... it was a massacre."

Tears welled up in her eyes, and she quickly wiped them away. She took another deep breath, her chest rising and falling heavily. "I ran. I ran and hid for weeks. I barely ate, barely slept. I was terrified. Every noise, every rustle of the leaves... I thought it was them. I don't know how I managed to escape. But eventually I was found," she continued, her voice growing stronger. "I don't know how. Perhaps they had been tracking me, or perhaps it was just bad luck. But they found me. I was captured, bound to a Sylph and taken to the mine. When I arrived... none of my settlement was there. Just a few other Selari I didn't know. I didn't know if they'd been taken somewhere else or even how many mines there were..." Her voice broke again, and she paused, taking a moment to compose herself. "The Entropic... it kept us in check with the Sylphs. We worked in the mine, day in and day out, our bodies aching, our spirits broken. I held on but the rest had been there too long and... you know what happened to them. We were nothing more than slaves," she finished, her voice almost a whisper. "I lived in constant fear, constant despair. Every day was a fight for survival. Every day was a nightmare."

She fell silent, her gaze far away. I watched her, feeling a heaviness in my chest. Her story... it was heart-breaking. And to think that she had lived through all that... it was almost too much to hear.

I reached out, placing a comforting hand on her shoulder. "I'm so sorry, Marina," I said, my own voice barely above a whisper. "I can't even begin to imagine what you've been through."

She looked at me, her eyes filled with a sorrow that made my heart ache. "It was... it was hard," she admitted. "But I survived. I'm here now, and that's what matters. And we'll do what we can to make sure nobody has to go through any of that ever again, right?"

I nodded, squeezing her shoulder gently. "You're incredibly strong, Marina. And I'm grateful that you're here. That you're part of this team. And that you're my friend."

She managed a small smile, her eyes wet with unshed tears. "Thank you, Captain," she said. "I'm... I'm glad to be here. To be part of this."

We sat in silence for a few moments, the air heavy with the weight of her story. But despite the sorrow, there was a sense of resilience. Of strength.

And as I looked at Marina, I couldn't help but feel a newfound respect for her. She had faced unspeakable horrors and came out the other side. She was a survivor. And she was a crucial part of our new home.

Her story was a reminder of the reality of our situation. Of the danger the Entropics posed and the lives they had destroyed. But it was also a reminder of the resilience of the Selari. Of their determination to survive, to fight, and to keep going.

I wanted to do more, to say more and to promise that things would be better in this world. I knew I wasn't the strongest or even the most intelligent person this place had ever seen, but I knew with the Obsidian Cores and whatever they were doing to my body, that I could make a difference. One day. One day soon.

Slowly, I moved my arm to pull Marina in close to me, but as I did so, she leapt up, peering out towards the ocean.

"What's that?!" she cried, pointing towards the horizon.

It took me a minute for my eyes to focus with the bright sunlight reflecting off of the ocean waters, but then it became all too clear.

Large, billowing black sails. A huge wooden frame, dozens of oars repeatedly breaking into and out of the calm waters below. And the scores and scores of hidden hatches that housed a myriad of heavy, black, devastating iron cannons.

The Iron Will had finally found us.

I was on my feet in an instant. The others now seeing what we were seeing and all work immediately abandoned. Faces paled as they took in the sight of the incoming ship.

"Prepare to evacuate!" I shouted, my heart pounding against my ribs. "We're not ready for a fight. Not yet." I looked around the settlement, the shelters all but completed but nothing more. We had no defences to speak of, not even any walls. This was it, this was the end of our new home.

"Not going to come from the sea..."

The words were barely out of my mouth when a shriek echoed through the settlement. It was an inhuman sound, full of wrath and desperation, a sound that froze the marrow in your bones.

I turned to the source, squinting against the glaring sunlight reflecting off the ocean, and what I saw made my breath hitch in my chest. The Iron Will wasn't sailing towards us. No, it was fleeing. Fleeing from some monstrosity rising from the depths of the sea. I doubted they'd even seen us.

It was enormous, a creature of nightmares, a beast from the darkest corners of folklore and tales of Free Men. I didn't need to be told what that creature was. It was without a doubt, the Kraken.

Its body was a titanic mass, dwarfing even the large ship it was pursuing. The Kraken's skin was an impenetrable cloak of inky blackness, shining slick with the cold embrace of the ocean. It was adorned with jagged scars and deep crevices, testament to a life spent in brutal fights in the depths of the sea.

Its tentacles were monstrous appendages, each one taller than even the tallest mast, and lined with suckers as large as a man's head. Each sucker was armed with rows of sharp, curved teeth. The arms moved in a sinuous dance of power and agility, reaching out with terrifying speed to swat at the Iron Will like a bothersome fly.

The Kraken's head rose high above the water, resembling a grotesque blend of a squid and an octopus, crowned by two colossal eyes. They were a maddening abyss of black, rimmed with an eerie bioluminescent glow that seemed to pulsate with the creature's heartbeat.

Its mouth opened to reveal a maw of jagged teeth, each one as long as a man, set in a circular pattern around a beak as big as the ship's hull. Every time the Kraken shrieked, a spray of fetid sea water and half-eaten carcasses cascaded from its mouth, painting a dark picture against the backdrop of the bright blue sky.

I couldn't do anything. But I couldn't look away.

It was a horrifying spectacle. The Iron Will, the terror of the seven seas was being pursued by a creature far more dangerous and fearsome than I imagined I would ever see. A creature from the darkest recesses of the ocean, a creature I had, until now, assumed was nothing more than a myth.

"We need to leave. Now!" I ordered, tearing my eyes away from the spectacle. The kids were rooted to the spot, eyes wide with terror.

Marina was the first to react, her face pale but determined. "You heard the Captain," she called out, turning to gather the children. "Let's move. don't stop to pack, just move move move!" She ushered the kids along as she spoke and they obeyed dutifully, scurrying around away from their work.

Then I felt the pull from inside me as Yari's projection floated away and high into the sky, towards the Iron Will and the terrible sea beast.

"Yari! What are you doing?" I thought frantically through our link but before the Sylph could even respond, she was high above the ocean and hurtling towards the Iron Will and its pursuer.

The sheer abruptness of Yari's departure sent a shock through my system. I could feel the rush of adrenaline surging through my veins as she rapidly ascended, the horizon shrinking below her as the vast expanse of the sky expanded in her sight. Through our connection, I could sense her determination, her resolve... and something else. Fear? No, not fear; It was anticipation.

A part of me protested, wanting to call her back, but it was silenced by an overpowering sense of curiosity. I found myself standing still amidst the chaos, my attention completely captured by the unfolding scene above.

As Yari neared the ship, I could feel the panic emanating from the Iron Will. The crewmen were scrambling, their movements haphazard, as they tried to row faster, evade the reaching tentacles of the Kraken. It was a futile effort. The creature was too fast, too big and too powerful.

Yari halted in mid-air, hovering high above the chaos. Her attention was fixated on the Kraken. The enormity of the creature was even more apparent from this perspective. Its tentacles were flailing, now crashing into the water, sending massive waves rolling out in all directions. The ship was thrown off balance, its wooden structure creaking ominously as it was tossed around like a toy in a bathtub.

Suddenly, Yari darted forward, descending towards the Kraken with breath-taking speed. She circled the creature, speeding around its flailing tentacles with an agility that was beyond what I'd seen of her before. Her small size and speed seemed to render her invisible to the massive beast, but I could still see the images she was sending back to me through our shared link.

"Yari," I reached out through our link, my voice taut with worry, "what are you…"

Before I could finish my sentence, she answered. Her voice resonated in my mind, a soothing whisper against the cacophony of the scene unfolding around her. "Trust me, Marcus. There's something we need to know."

And then, in an action that took me by surprise, Yari plunged into the sea, vanishing beneath the thrashing waves and the monstrous form of the Kraken.

My breath caught and my heart pounded painfully against my chest. The world around me seemed to blur. The sounds of the kids running, Marina's urgent instructions, the distant cries of Kraken all faded away into insignificance like I was the one who had dove into the frigid ocean water. All I could focus on was Yari, and the cold, dark depths into which she had disappeared.

Time seemed to stretch into infinity as I waited, my connection to Yari feeling as though it was stretching thin. I stood there, frozen in place, my eyes locked on the spot where Yari had vanished, my mind consumed by worry, dread and anticipation.

After what seemed like an eternity, a faint glow emerged from the depths. A beacon of hope in the abyss. Yari was ascending, and in her wake, a trail of luminous bubbles rose to the surface, their light shimmering in the oceanic gloom.

She broke the surface, shaking off droplets of sea water, her form glowing with an ethereal light. Her projection turned towards me, the distance closing rapidly, and with a jolt, I was back in my body, my surroundings snapping back into focus with startling clarity.

"Marcus…" her voice resonated within me, laced with a sense of urgency, "we have a bigger problem than the Iron Will."

"What do you mean?" I demanded, my eyes still locked onto the distant spectacle of the monstrous Kraken bearing down on the Iron Will. "Is it coming here? Is it coming for us?"

"No," Yari responded. Her voice seemed calm, but there was an underlying tension that did not escape me. "It's not just the Kraken. There's something more… something beneath the sea."

The implication of her words took a moment to sink in, and when it did, a chill swept over me. My gaze slipped from the distant conflict, falling instead upon the gentle ebb and flow of the waves lapping at the shore before us. Suddenly, the sea no longer looked inviting or beautiful. Instead, it looked mysterious and ominous, a vast expanse of unknowable dangers lurking beneath the surface.

"Beneath the sea?" I echoed, frowning deeply. "What do you mean?"

"It doesn't always happen, but the ocean is full of scavengers, and they often follow around the larger beasts like the Kraken. The Kraken… she isn't really a threat to us because once she's done, she'll just go back to where she came from… but the scavengers… if they find out there's more prey here for them…"

Yari trailed off, her words echoing ominously in my mind. I understood what she was trying to say. The Kraken, as terrifying as it was, was a known entity. An apex predator, the terror of the sea, but it had its habits, its territory. But scavengers, they were unpredictable. They followed where the food was, where the opportunity presented itself. And if they discovered our location...

"What are they? Can we fight them? Will they come onto land?" I asked all of the questions at once without waiting for an answer.

"The ones I could see were Skimmers," Yari said. "They have hard shells and pincers…"

"Like crabs? We can deal with crabs," I replied assuredly.

"I don't know what that is," Yari replied. "But if they're shelled creatures about the size of… well one of the small children actually, with ten eyes, four pincers and an appetite for anything that moves… then yes that's what they are."

I swallowed hard at her words, picturing the creatures she described. Not crabs, then. Nothing like the small, harmless crustaceans I'd known back in my world. These sounded more like monsters. The sort of creatures you'd expect to find in a nightmare, not in the real world.

I relayed the information Yari had sent me over to Marina. It was annoying; as much as having Yari to help with early warning of threats just like this, she didn't give us any ability to actually do anything about them.

"Can we fight them?" I asked again, trying to keep my voice steady.

"Perhaps," Yari responded, "But they tend to swarm, and once they get the scent of food, they won't stop until it's all gone."

"We need to leave," Marina stated flatly. Her face was drawn and tense. "The kids... they can't defend against that. We need to find a safer place."

I turned to look at her, the gravity of our situation sinking in. Marina was right. As much as I wanted to stand our ground, to protect what we'd built, we couldn't risk the lives of the children. Not when we were up against a threat like this. We were survivors, yes, but we were also protectors. It was our duty to ensure the safety of these kids, and if that meant relocating, then that's what we'd do.

"We can't just abandon our home," Guy protested. "We've worked so hard on this place. We can't just let those things take it from us."

"I know it's hard, Guy," I said, looking at him. "But we're not equipped to handle this. Not yet. And we can't risk your lives, or the lives of the others. And remember what I said: sometimes it's better to run and survive than it is to stand and fight – especially when the enemy is much stronger than you are. It's not about being brave, it's about being smart."

"You heard the Captain," Marina called out, turning to gather the children. "Let's get out of here, move move move!"

Most of the children were standing ready to go, but they wouldn't leave until we gave them a direction to run in. I cast one last look at the sea. It had always provided me with food, adventure, and a sense of peace in a world full of chaos. But now, it was the source of our greatest threat. The Kraken still loomed in the distance, its massive form dominating the horizon. But now, its presence felt like a warning. A sign of the dangers that lurked beneath the surface, and of the challenges that we were yet to face.

"We will rebuild," I whispered to myself, more a vow than anything else. We were survivors. We'd faced hardships before, and we would do so again. No matter what lay ahead, we would overcome it. Together.

"We're too late!" Yari suddenly shouted. Whilst I had been relaying the new situation to my friends, Yari had dove back underwater. The Iron Will had completely disappeared but even from where I stood I could see the ripples in the calm ocean waters heading straight towards us faster than any crabs I'd ever seen moving. Even if we turned and ran right now, I doubted if we would even make it a hundred metres before the Skimmers made it to the sea wall, and then, to us.

I looked between Marina, the kids, the settlement and the ocean and let my shoulders drop. We needed to do something to protect ourselves.

"Climb up onto the shelters!" I shouted. "Forget running, we're going to get out of the way and just hope this all passes!"

I had no other options really. We couldn't run and we couldn't hide, so our best bet was to simply hope that these terrible creatures couldn't climb.

Chapter 17 – Out of Reach

We all managed to climb onto the shelters that were all but complete and had separated evenly between them. To my delight, most of the kids had brought bows and arrows from their old settlement, and the ones who didn't – including me and Marina – had managed to grab thick wooden sticks just to make us feel a little better about the whole situation. I didn't know what the Skimmers would do to the makeshift spears with their powerful looking pincers, but rather a stick than my arm.

The first of the Skimmers emerged from the water, their chitinous bodies gleaming in the sun, pincers clacking ominously. One by one, they crawled onto the shore, their many eyes scanning the surroundings, searching for their next meal.

We watched from above, holding our breaths as we huddled in the safety of the shelters. Their tall, wooden roofs provided us with an overhead vantage point and a certain amount of camouflage, but it was only a matter of time before the Skimmers noticed us. I wondered how the crew of the Iron Will had felt when they had succumbed to the creatures because I know out there between the Kraken and the scavengers under the surface, they would've had no chance. Still now though, I couldn't see any sign of my former ship, not even a single plank of wood floating atop the water's surface.

I could see the fear in the kids' eyes as they clutched their makeshift weapons, their small bodies trembling despite their brave fronts. Marina, with a reassuring arm around one of the younger children, was giving them quiet words of encouragement and promises that we would make it through this.

The Skimmers though, had made it into our camp and were walking about as though they owned the place. I held my breath.

Just when I thought the tension couldn't get any worse, a shuffling noise echoed through the shelter. My heart dropped as I turned to see the source - one of the younger kids trying to adjust her position. A murmur of protest went through the group, but it was too late. The roof then creaked loudly under her movement, the sound echoing eerily in the near silence.

Immediately, a Skimmer's attention snapped up towards us, its multifaceted eyes reflecting an eerie, otherworldly glow. Fear gripped me as I realised we'd been found, but before I could react, a sharp whistling sound tore through the air.

An arrow, sleek and deadly, shot from the edge of the roof and found its mark in the Skimmer's eye. It let out a horrendous noise and thrashed around for a moment, but the damage was done. The creature fell to the ground, its many legs twitching in its death throes.

The silence that followed was deafening. For a moment, it was as if time stood still. But then the real chaos began. With a chilling war cry, the Skimmers rushed towards our shelters, their pincers snapping and their beady eyes full of predatory intent.

"We need to defend the shelters!" I called out, my voice resounding through the structure. "Hold your ground and don't let them get too close!"

As the Skimmers began to claw their way up the shelters, the kids opened fire, their arrows raining down on the creatures. I, too, lunged forward with my stick, hitting any Skimmer that came too close as, to my horror, they began to pull themselves slowly up the wooden walls. Beside me, Marina was doing the same, her face set in a determined grimace.

We fought hard, but the Skimmers were relentless.

"Keep fighting!" I yelled over the chaos as I batted another skimmer back down to the ground. "We can do this!"

The skimmers moved with an eerie synchronicity, a wave of glistening carapaces and snapping pincers, their compound eyes reflecting the desperation and fear in ours. Their low, chittering calls echoed around us, creating a macabre symphony that resonated through our once peaceful settlement.

The battle seemed to stretch on for hours, each passing minute a test of our endurance and willpower. The kids, young as they were, displayed an impressive level of courage and determination, their little faces grim but resolute as they continued to let arrows fly from their bows. Each shot was met with a sickening thud, as the pointed tip found purchase in a Skimmer's hard shell. But there were just too many of them.

Marina was a whirlwind beside me, her makeshift staff spinning and cracking against the hard exoskeletons of the Skimmers. She moved with a dancer's grace, each attack precise and calculated, her eyes never leaving the onslaught of creatures. Her courage was infectious, and I found myself pressing forward with renewed vigour, fighting off the wave of exhaustion threatening to overtake me.

"No!" I heard a cry from behind me, a young voice filled with fear. I turned to see that the young girl who had accidentally alerted the Skimmers was cornered against the wall by one of the creatures. Her bow lay discarded at her feet, an arrow notched but never released.

Without thinking, I threw my staff at the Skimmer. It hit the creature square in its head, startling it enough to give little Bella the time she needed to scramble away. I ran to her side, picking up the fallen bow and handing it back to her. "You're doing great, Bella," I assured her, trying to instil some confidence in her. "Just keep shooting, okay?"

With a nod, she took the bow and began to fire again, her aim a little shaky but still deadly when her arrows found their targets. I turned back to the fight, looking for my discarded staff, but instead found myself face-to-face with another huge Skimmer.

Its numerous eyes glowed in the darkness, an alien intelligence studying me with chilling indifference. Its pincers clacked ominously, and for a moment, I froze, realising that I had nothing to defend myself with. Just as the Skimmer lunged, an arrow pierced straight through its eye, and it fell to the ground, convulsing.

Looking up, I met Guy's gaze. Without uttering a word, he turned back towards the enemy and returned to his task.

I could see that the arrows that the kids had brought up with them were starting to dwindle though, and if this went on for too much longer, we were going to be overrun.

"Yari!" I shouted mentally to the Sylph who had retreated back inside me. "I need you to try to draw them away!"

For a moment, there was only silence. Then, Yari's voice echoed in my mind, quiet but resolute. "I will do my best, Captain. But remember, their numbers are many... and I'm just a projection..."

With that, I felt her energy surge within me, and she was gone. Seconds later, the little golden bird emerged from me, her form glowing brightly. She was a captivating sight, a beacon of light and to my relief, the Skimmers noticed too, their multifaceted eyes tracking her movements with predatory interest. She was smaller than the rest of us, so perhaps the creatures would see her as an easier target.

Yari floated slowly towards the edge of our shelter, her form shimmering with ethereal light. Then, with a flourish of her wings, she created a dazzling display of glowing orbs and sparkling lights that danced above her. The

Skimmers were momentarily captivated, their attacks faltering as they gazed upon the spectacle.

Seeing our chance, I yelled out to the others. "While they're distracted, conserve your arrows! Only take the shots you can't miss!"

With renewed vigour, we all pulled back from the edges of the shelters, drawing breaths that we didn't realise we'd been holding. For the first time since the Skimmers had arrived, I felt a glimmer of hope.

The eerie light that Yari emanated only grew brighter, and she began to move further away from us and closer to the ocean. The Skimmers, entranced by her display, began to detach from the shelters and followed her, their claws clicking rhythmically against the rocks as they scuttled after her.

I mentally urged Yari to be careful, to not push the link between us too far. But the Sylph, ever brave, only continued her mission, leading the horde of Skimmers away from our settlement and back towards the sea.

There was an edge of desperation in our fight now, a sense of urgency that hadn't been there before. We had a chance. Yari was giving us a chance.

But as the distance between us and Yari increased, I could feel our mental connection straining. Yari's thoughts were becoming faint, like whispers on the edge of my hearing. I had to fight to keep my focus on both fronts, to not let the link snap while still coordinating the defensive efforts.

Suddenly, the distant sound of waves crashing became louder, and I realised that Yari had successfully led the Skimmers to the edge of the ocean. With one last dazzling display of light, Yari dove into the water, the Skimmers plunging in after her, their forms disappearing beneath the waves.

Exhausted but victorious, I watched as the last of the Skimmers retreated from our settlement and back into the sea. We had survived. We were safe, for now. And it was all thanks to Yari.

As the adrenaline wore off and the reality of what had just happened sunk in, I couldn't help but feel a surge of pride. We had once again faced an unimaginable threat and come out on top. We were survivors, fighters, and protectors. We were a family. And together, we could face anything.

"And that, is how you fight off an invasion of skimmers," Guy announced triumphantly, holding his bow and arrows aloft. I didn't correct him. It didn't really matter though did it? We'd survived, and that was more than what could be said for the Iron Will.

I looked down at the ground at the remnants of the enemy horde that sought to turn us into its dinner and wondered if it would be too ironic to return the favour. After all, could they be any worse than mushrooms?

"I wouldn't recommend it," Yari's voice echoed in my mind, amusement tinged her mental tone, "Skimmers aren't exactly known for their pleasant taste."

"I'll keep that in mind," I thought back, grinning. I was relieved to hear Yari's voice so clear in my mind again, signalling that our link was stable. "But they're safe to eat?" I asked.

"Well… Yes," Yari replied. "But…"

"Never mind," I thought.

"All right, everyone," I called out, looking at the group of weary but determined faces. "We've fought hard today, and I couldn't be prouder. But we can't rest yet. Let's clean up and re-arm ourselves. Make sure to collect all the arrows, we're going to need them."

Of course, I didn't know if we really were going to need them. It seemed to me like the threat from the Iron Will had been quashed, the Kraken was all but gone and the Skimmers had scurried away to find their next adventure. Truth be told, it seemed like we were safer now than we had been in a long time.

But life never truly hands you something so peaceful, does it?

"There!" Yari shouted in my mind. I hadn't realised but after she'd led the skimmers away, she'd taken back to the sky to keep lookout once more.

I tried to peer in the direction that Yari had indicated, but after failing to do so, she began to send me images through our link. It was unmistakable. The human figure that now walked towards us from the coastline a short way away, was my former first mate and mutineer, Anthony Cowley.

He looked hurt as he hobbled in our general direction, his clothes were tattered and he was covered in cuts, scrapes and both fresh and dry blood.

"Everyone, hold!" I commanded, my voice echoing away into the settlement. The image of Anthony Cowley stumbling towards us was burned in my mind, thanks to Yari's vigilant lookout. It had been a long time since I'd last seen him, on that fateful day when he'd instigated the mutiny. And he looked worse for wear now.

"But… that's one of the crew, Captain," Guy stated when Cowley stumbled a little closer, his face a mix of surprise and resentment. "He would have killed us!"

I held up a hand, quelling any further protest. "I know who it is," I said, my voice steady. "And I'm well aware of what they did. But right now, he is not a threat. He's hurt and possibly in need of our help."

"But Captain, he…"

"Guy, we have been through a lot. I don't need reminding," I cut him off gently. "But let's not forget one thing: we are not them. We help those in need, no matter who they are or what they've done to us."

I walked towards the edge of our makeshift camp, my eyes fixed on the slowly approaching figure of Cowley. His eyes met mine, and I could see a flicker of surprise, then recognition, and finally, what seemed like relief.

"I didn't expect to find you here, Marcus," he rasped as he got closer. His gaze swept over the others, lingering on each face before returning to me. "I... I need your help."

"You can call me Captain," I replied curtly. What he'd done to me still hurt, but before that, our years of friendship at least still held some weight.

For a moment, none of us moved or spoke. My camp simply stared at the man who had once been part of my crew, the man who had betrayed me and left me to die. Perhaps the person that was the reason for my presence in this world.

I broke the silence, "Let's get him something to eat and drink, he's already been through enough."

"I don't know if that's wise, Captain," Guy said, crossing his arms over his chest. "He's dangerous. And give him half the chance I'll bet he'd kill us in our sleep!"

I turned to face my crew, all of them visibly tense, and I couldn't blame them. After all, Cowley had betrayed me and his men had already threatened the kids.

"I know what he did," I said, my voice calm and steady. "But right now, he's just a man, broken and alone. We won't turn our backs on him." I paused, meeting each of their gazes in turn. "Not because of who he is, but because of who we are."

Little Bella was the first to move, disappearing into the shelter before returning with a flask of water and a bowl of what was left of our last meal. She hesitated, looking at me for reassurance, and I nodded encouragingly. She approached Cowley, offering him the food and drink. He took them with a nod of thanks, not meeting anyone's eyes.

"Everyone else, get back to work," I instructed, my gaze lingering on Cowley who was now sitting on the ground, quietly eating and drinking. "Tomorrow, we'll need to be ready for anything, but right now, we've got repairs to make, a settlement to build and dead crabs to barbeque."

That last statement garnered me some sideways glances from the kids, but they seemed to get the gist of what I was saying and within a few moments, they had all disappeared to their tasks.

I stayed behind as the others slowly dispersed, leaving me alone with Cowley.

"Anthony," I said softly, breaking the silence that had settled between us,

"I don't know why you're here or what you've done. But you owe me an explanation, and if you want sanctuary here, you're going to give it to me."

He swallowed, finally meeting my gaze, and nodded. "I owe you a lot more than that, Marcus," he said, his voice a whisper. "But I promise, I'll explain everything."

"And it better be good," I added, settling down on the ground facing him, crossing my arms over my chest. "Starting from the very beginning. How the hell did the Iron Will end up in this place?"

Cowley seemed to take a moment to gather his thoughts, then began to speak. "It all started with the gold coins, the Sirens. After you uh… well anyway, we had one return to us. Don't ask me how it happened but it just did. It found its way back to us and it started singing. None of us knew what it was at the time, of course, so we just put it away with the rest of the loot. It was just another shiny coin." He took a deep breath, and was clearly still in quite some pain. "We were anchored in calm waters that night," he continued, his gaze distant. "That's when it happened... a light burst from the coin and the next thing we knew, we were here. The Iron Will had been dragged into this world, grounded on some weird beach."

I nodded, urging him to go on. He hesitated for a moment before continuing. "There was this... entity. It called itself the Caretaker. I don't know where he came from or how he knew we were there, but he promised us power beyond anything we could imagine. We just had to do its bidding."

I frowned, my mind racing. The Caretaker, the being that controlled all the Selari, the workers. The being that was responsible for pulling people into this world. And Cowley and his crew had been talked into working for it.

"We were told to hunt for the Caretaker, tracking down runaway workers, collect the Selari... and there was one person he wanted more than anyone else. You, Marcus."

He glanced at me, uncertainty in his eyes and added quickly. "He always specified that the children were to be left alone. If we found any, we were instructed to let them be. I swear, we didn't harm them."

I felt a cold chill run down my spine at his words.

"Wait... you found other children out there?" I asked.

"Well, yeah," Cowley replied. "We came across five other settlements out there already." He held his hands up in surrender. "We didn't touch them, I swear... but they're resourceful little bastards let me tell you. They look like they're doing just fine out there on their own. Can I ask though, why does the Caretaker want you specifically?"

I thought about lying, then I thought about saying that I didn't know, but in the end, I just plumbed for the truth.

"Because he had me. I was sent to one of his mines and I found a way to escape. I don't think it's been done before and I think it scares him… But now you tell me, Cowley. Why would the Caretaker just let you go? Why would he trust you to set you free?"

Cowley's face fell into an expression that seemed like genuine remorse. "He didn't let us all go," he said quietly. "We had to give him some of the crew to work the mines. The new crew members, those sailors from the Royal Navy, I sent them to work the mines so that the Caretaker knew we were genuine. Then, we relaunched the Iron Will into the open waters, as a base for our operations," Cowley said, his voice becoming shaky. "But it wasn't like back home, not at all."

A million questions swirled in my mind, but I knew better than to voice them all. Not yet. First, we had to figure out our next step. Cowley had a lot to answer for, but right now, we needed all the information we could get.

"Tell me more about these other settlements," I prodded, pressing for more details. If there were indeed more children out there, we needed to know, maybe we could help each other or pool our resources.

"Well, they were scattered all around," Cowley began. "One is in a dense forest, another is situated in a place with strange, tall structures, almost like pillars of stone. They were different from anything I've seen before, Captain. I… I believe one of the settlements was built in the ruins of some great city, much older than anything I've ever seen before."

"And the children, they were…?" I trailed off, not sure what I wanted to know, just hoping he'd give me some assurance that they were okay.

"Mostly around the same age as yours, a few older ones too," Cowley said. "Looked like they were managing alright. Built themselves some kind of shelters, had food and all. Seemed like they'd figured out the basics."

There was something reassuring about knowing we weren't alone in this, that there were others out there in the same predicament as us, that they were surviving, just like us.

"Why didn't you interfere with them? The Caretaker never gave a specific reason, did he?" I asked, unable to shake off my suspicion of Cowley's actions.

He shook his head, looking almost guilty. "No, he never said why, just that they were to be left alone."

"So you just left them be? You didn't touch them or hurt them?" I asked, wanting more than anything to believe his words.

He looked me in the eye, a sincerity I hadn't seen in him for years. "I swear, Marcus. We never laid a hand on any of them."

I studied him for a long moment, then finally nodded. "Alright, I believe you. Now tell me, Cowley, how do we find these settlements?"

"I... I can show you," he offered, and I was taken aback by the earnestness in his voice. He was still the same Anthony Cowley who had betrayed me, but there was something different about him now. A desperation, a need to atone.

"I don't think you're in any fit state to travel, Cowley," I replied. But I felt the need to gain contacts out there, to perhaps save more of the children of this world before it was too late.

"Oh, don't worry about that," Cowley said. "All I need is a bit of food and drink, a long night's rest and in the morning I'll be good to go."

I eyed the man suspiciously. There was only one way someone in his state would heal that fast, but I didn't want to reveal my hand just yet. We would have to wait and see what the morning would bring.

Chapter 18 – Searching for Something

When the next morning brought the soft new dawn along with it, I awoke after Marina and the kids had already started on their breakfast. Cursing myself for my laziness, I quickly moved to join them.

"Cowley not up yet?" I asked with a half grin. It was nice to know I wasn't dead last to rise.

"No, he's still sleeping," little Bella responded quickly, her voice filled with concern. She'd been one of the first to show kindness to Cowley, and I wondered if she saw something in him that I didn't.

"You're up late, Captain," Marina said, handing me a bowl of something that smelled surprisingly appetising. "But don't worry, I managed to save you a good helping of mushrooms."

Frowning, I looked down at the bowl and indeed it was filled with the slimy brown bastards. But there was something else, too. White flakes that I immediately recognised.

"You cooked the crabs?" I asked with wide eyes. "How are they?"

"Disgusting," Guy interrupted. "But it's what you wanted, right? Don't worry, no one else will eat them so there's a whole mountain for you to work through! Well at least until they go off. I reckon you've got a day or two at the most."

I pulled a handful of the mixture up to my mouth and let the mushroom and fake crab meat sit on my tongue before biting down.

It was wonderful.

Never before had I tasted such a rich combination of foods, and I couldn't help but let out a little moan of delight.

"Terrible, right?" Marina asked. "You can just spit it out onto the floor if you want to…"

Before she finished speaking, I shovelled another handful into my face.

"Mmhmm, delicious," I declared, grinning at her shocked expression.

"You've outdone yourselves."

Marina looked both pleased and surprised. "Well, I'm glad you like it. Just don't expect it every day."

"I think I could eat this every day," I replied before munching on another mouthful. "

Around me, the kids were staring with wide eyes and disgusted expressions on their faces, none of them seeming willing to try my dish.

"Try some, Bella," I offered, handing her my bowl. She hesitated, then took a small bite.

Her face screwed up a moment and she spat the food on the ground. "That's actually... awful! So bad, so bad!" She tried to scrape the taste from her tongue and I just laughed.

And just like that, my bizarre breakfast became my new favourite food.

But all good things would have to come to an end. As we finished up our meals, Cowley emerged from his own shelter, looking surprisingly refreshed and decidedly less injured than yesterday.

I rose from my spot, breakfast forgotten, and walked over to him. His wounds were healing fast, unnaturally so. In fact, if there wasn't as much dried blood on his skin as there was, I doubted that he'd had any wounds at all.

"Morning, Captain," he greeted, his voice steady and strong. "Ready to get started on that tour?"

I glanced at him suspiciously. There was no way he could be healed already, not unless he had discovered one of the secrets of the Cores, as I had.

"Are you?" I asked.

Cowley nodded, pulling his shirt up to reveal a chest that was unmarked, as if he had never been wounded in the first place.

A that moment I was left with a choice. Seem surprised and ask how he had managed to heal so fast, or seem nonchalant and let on that I knew about the Cores.

In the end, I chose the former.

"But... how?" I asked. "You were hurt, and badly... but now..."

"Aye, Captain. The Caretaker has given us this power, but I don't know how long it's going to last me, not now I'm so far away from him and as you say, out of his good books."

"Right..." I said. "And you have no plans to simply take me back to his lair today and claim your reward?"

"Listen Marcus... Captain," Cowley said. "The Iron Will's gone. My crew is all dead. If that's not a wake-up call to do the right thing, then I don't know what is."

At least that was something that I could understand.

"A wake-up call, huh?" I asked, folding my arms and studying him. His features were open, honest, but after all that had transpired, could I trust this man again? "Then let's hope this call has come in time."

Cowley didn't respond, just nodded, his gaze focused on something beyond my shoulder.

"Alright, Cowley. We'll do this together. Show me these other settlements," I said, turning to gather some necessary supplies for the trip. Maybe some crab meat. Our journey would likely take us far, and preparation was key.

"You cannot be serious," Marina's voice came from behind me.

I turned to face her, meeting her worried gaze with a reassuring one of my own. "I know it sounds risky," I began, "But it's something we need to do, Marina."

"But to trust him, Marcus? After everything he's done?" She gestured to Cowley, her face contorted in disbelief and concern.

"I know, I know..." I rubbed at my temples, understanding her fears. "But we need to know what's out there. We need to understand the world we're in now. We can't just hide in our little camp forever."

Marina's eyes brimmed with tears. She understood. She did. But the fear of losing me to another adventure, another risk, held her back. "And what if you don't come back, Marcus?" she whispered, her voice choked with fear.

"I'll come back, Marina," I said, my voice firm and steady. "I promise."

I saw her swallow hard, a tear rolling down her cheek. But she nodded, accepting my decision even though it scared her. "Be safe, Marcus. Please."

"I will," I said, pulling her into a quick, tight hug.

When I pulled away, I found Cowley waiting patiently by the entrance of the camp, his gaze lost in the wilderness. "Let's get going, Captain," he said, his voice carrying both weight and strength. He seemed different, changed. Whether that was due to the events of the past or his newfound 'awakening', I wasn't sure.

As we stepped out towards the unknown, I cast a final glance back at our little camp. Marina was watching us, her silhouette illuminated by the rising sun. I raised a hand in a final farewell, then turned away, our adventure looming ahead.

Of course, Marina had been right. Cowley was probably the last person in this world who I should be trusting, but I didn't want to build my own slice of this place like that. I didn't want to assume people were inherently bad. Yes the opposite would be difficult to swallow, but if we never gave forgiveness or the benefit of the doubt, building our settlement was going to be so much more difficult.

I looked back at the kids and Marina. I didn't want to leave them to fend for themselves, but the threats in this world meant that the kids would be safer staying put – especially if the Caretaker had given standing orders to leave them be. I'd thought about bringing Marina along too, but leaving the kids alone to fend for themselves didn't seem right either.

Marina then quickly ran up beside me and I stopped to turn to her.

"Look, Marina," I started, meeting her eyes with a firm determination and speaking before she had the chance to, "The kids will need you here. They trust you, and they will listen to you."

Marina nodded, pulling herself together. She was strong, one of the strongest people I had ever met. "I'll protect them, Marcus. With everything I have."

"I know you will," I assured her, giving her arm a supportive squeeze. "And that's why I can do this. Because I know you've got things covered here."

Marina gave a small smile at that, wiping her tears away. "You better come back, Marcus. Or else I'll come find you and drag you back here myself."

I laughed at that, a genuine laugh that echoed away towards our little camp. "I don't doubt that for a second."

With a final goodbye, Cowley and I set off, the unknown stretching out before us. As I glanced back one last time, I saw Marina standing tall, the sun shining brightly behind her. She gave us a small wave, her face set with purpose. I waved back, my heart filled with a renewed sense of wonder.

I only hoped that when we returned, Marina and the kids would still be there, waiting for us.

Our journey began in silence, the only sounds being our footsteps and the occasional calls of unseen creatures. The world around us was vast and uncharted, filled with things that I didn't fully understand. But I knew we were on the right path. We had to discover what was out there, for the safety and future of our settlement and everyone else that the Entropics, and the Caretaker controlled. That was why we were doing all of this; not for ourselves, but for this world as a whole.

Cowley broke the silence first, his voice rough yet strangely soothing. "We have a long journey ahead, Captain. Best keep your wits about you."

"I plan to, Cowley," I replied, my tone just as serious. "And remember, we're in this together. If we're to survive, we need to trust each other... but I don't think we'll run into anything too terrible. I was told that creatures in this place steer well clear of wherever the Cores are – you know, the things the Caretaker has his people mining." I wanted to again see if Cowley would show any hint of knowing more about the Cores, of their power, but if he knew something, he still didn't show it.

"You stay inside, Yari," I sent mentally to my Sylph companion. "I don't want to let on more than what's necessary to our friend Cowley here."

As I spoke to Yari, Cowley glanced at me, an eyebrow raised. "Thinking you made a mistake now, Captain?"

"I might be," I replied with a small sarcastic smile, not giving anything away. "Or I might just be going mad. Either way, it's nothing you need to concern yourself with."

"Fair enough," Cowley grumbled, his gaze returning to the path ahead.

We continued our journey, the terrain around us gradually shifting. We passed through fields of tall, rustling grasses and ventured into dense forests, where shafts of sunlight struggled to filter through the canopy above. There were mountains in the distance, their peaks shrouded in clouds, and valleys carved by winding rivers. Despite the uncertainty of our mission, the beauty of this world was undeniable.

As we trekked, we saw signs of settlements that had once been — abandoned campsites, deep footprints in the dirt, remnants of buildings long since collapsed. But there were no people, no communities like the one we had left behind. Cowley seemed unconcerned, leading us forward with unwavering confidence.

Even with the uncertain elements of our journey, the mission gave me a sense of purpose I hadn't felt in a long time. I had promised to do what I could to make this world a better place, and finally that's what I had started doing. Only, I needed those Cores to get better, stronger, and see what I could really do with a little more power. That was a mission for another day, though.

Throughout the journey, I kept an eye on Cowley, observing him, trying to glean any possible clues about his knowledge of the Cores. But he remained guarded, never letting on more than he had to.

Night fell before we had reached anything significant, and we set up a temporary camp. As we sat by the fire, I turned to Cowley, my gaze stern as I came to my decision to confront him.

"You're keeping something from me, Cowley. About the Cores. Now's the time to spill it. We're in this together, remember?"

Cowley studied me for a moment before answering. "The Cores... they're powerful, Captain. They have the ability to change things, to heal. But the Caretaker, he hoards that power. He keeps it for himself and his closest followers."

"And you?" I asked, my tone steady.

"I've... benefited from their power. But only because I was in the Caretaker's good graces. Now? Who knows..." Cowley shrugged, his gaze lost in the fire. "But what matters now is what we do with that knowledge. How we use it to help our people."

And with that, it seemed the veil of secrecy between us had finally lifted. It was the truth, or at least, a version of it. A shared understanding that would carry us forward into the unknown.

"Why didn't you tell me until now?" I asked.

"I didn't think you'd believe me," Cowley said, his gaze not leaving the fire. "And then, after all that happened... I wasn't sure I could trust you with that knowledge either. The Cores, they can be... addictive. They can change a man, make him greedy for more. And I know what we did… I did to you. I wouldn't blame you if you never trusted another word that came out of my mouth… but here we are, comrades again."

"And yet you thought it was wise to lead me out of my settlement alone, while you're potentially still not at full health? You trust me not to hurt you? To get my revenge for what you did?" I pointed out. His hypocrisy was glaring.

Cowley turned to look at me, his eyes glinting in the firelight. "A man can change, Captain. I've seen it in you. Your priority isn't power. It's your people. Looking back, it's always been your people, hasn't it? When you were the Captain back on the Iron Will, you always took the smaller share, always gave what you could for the men... I never saw it back then; I was filled with greed…"

"You're right about that," I admitted, my thoughts drifting back to Marina and the kids. "But we're not just talking about me here. We're talking about the survival of our settlement. You know that if the Cores can give us an advantage, then I'm going to use them. Responsibly, of course."

Cowley nodded, looking thoughtful. "I suppose we'll have to trust each other, then. I know what power does to a man, trust me."

"For now, we need to focus on the journey ahead," I replied. "Honestly, we don't have any Cores to see what they can do for us, so it doesn't really matter. But if all goes to plan, then we'll have a supply larger than anything we'd probably ever need. We'll take what the Caretaker has for ourselves, like the good old days."

"We'll cross that bridge when we come to it, then," Cowley agreed, pulling his tattered coat closer around him as a gust of wind swept through the camp. "For now, we focus on survival. On the journey. And, Captain," he added, looking me straight in the eye, "on getting to those settlements. We'll need allies if we're going to stand against the Caretaker."

I nodded. "One settlement at a time." Then quickly added: "Do you have any idea how many there are?"

Crowley shook his head. "I think there are more than a handful, but I couldn't be sure. The Caretaker didn't tell us everything, but it sounded like this was a big operation; he was talking about the mines as though they number in the hundreds, maybe even thousands."

"What?" I announced. "If that's true... then there could be tens of thousands of slaves out there with no hope of escape!" My eyes had grown wide at the thought of the sheer scale of the Entropic's operation. And just like that, once again I felt insignificant.

"It might not be as bad as that," Yari interrupted through our mental link. "The Caretaker could just be boasting, or making out like he has more than he does…"

"Does that sound like something the Entropics would do?" I asked back mentally.

"No, perhaps not," Yari admitted. "But it is still possible. What I'm saying is, we shouldn't lose hope. I knew the Caretaker has so many slaves to his operation believe me, but does that really matter?"

"Right. Hope," I muttered, glancing over at Cowley who was eyeing me curiously. I cleared my throat and shifted my gaze back to the fire. "Well, if there really are that many settlements... we're going to need more than just hope."

Cowley nodded, his eyes heavy with shared concern. "I agree, Captain. That's why we're out here, after all. To find allies, to rally against the Caretaker and his regime. And if we succeed, if we can free those people... they'll need a place to go. A place they can call home."

I fell silent then, my mind racing with the magnitude of what lay ahead. The task seemed almost insurmountable. But Cowley was right. We needed to succeed. Not just for us, for Marina and the kids back at the camp, but for all those people suffering under the Caretaker's rule.

After a while, I got to my feet, stretching my aching muscles. "We should get some rest," I suggested. "We have a big day ahead."

Cowley nodded, laying down on the ground with his coat serving as a makeshift blanket. "Goodnight, Captain," he said, closing his eyes.

I nodded, my mind still whirling with thoughts and fears. "Goodnight, Cowley."

I laid back as well, the stars above serving as our ceiling.

As I drifted off to sleep, I thought about the journey ahead, the settlements we needed to find, the people we needed to save. It was a monumental task, but I was resolved. We had to succeed. For the sake of those enslaved, for Marina and the kids back at camp, for the world that we were trying to build.

Tomorrow was another day, and it would bring with it new challenges. But for now, under the vast, star-filled sky, there was a moment of peace. A moment to gather our strength and prepare for the trials to come. And as I fell into the grasp of sleep, I held onto that moment, that feeling of quiet determination. It would have to be enough. For now.

"What the hell is that, Cowley!?" I awoke with a start due to the intense heat that was searing my face and unbeknownst to me, had been making me sweat buckets for only God knew how long.

But when I opened my eyes, I was not greeted with Cowley looking sheepish like I'd seen on so many previous occasions; instead he was nowhere to be found, and the small fire that I had left when I'd fallen asleep, was now a towering inferno, billowing black smoke high into the sky.

I shot up, my heart pounding in my chest as the heat rolled off the blazing fire, dancing in the otherwise pitch-black night. I coughed as smoke filled my lungs and I quickly covered my mouth and nose with my sleeve.

"Cowley? Cowley!" I called out, trying to make my voice heard over the crackling flames. But there was no response. Cowley was gone.

Swiftly, I moved to douse the fire, grabbing handfuls of dirt and throwing them into the flames. It took several minutes of frantic work before the fire was reduced to a more manageable level. I looked around, squinting through the smoke for any sign of Cowley.

But before I could dwell on Cowley's absence, the fire, which was now at a bearable level, seemed to bend into a shape, a large, humanoid silhouette. I watched, heart pounding, as a figure stepped through the fire and out the other side, untouched by the flames.

My breath caught in my chest when I realised who this was. It was the Caretaker.

His cold eyes were fixed on me, glowing ominously in the firelight. His voice when he spoke was low and powerful, echoing through the quiet night.

"Human," he greeted, his voice carrying an eerie calmness. "I've been looking forward to this."

The sense of unease I felt was immeasurable. I couldn't understand how Cowley could have disappeared, or how the Caretaker had managed to find us. But one thing was clear: We were in trouble. I hoped Cowley was safe, wherever he was.

"What do you want?" I demanded, trying to keep my voice steady. "Going to send me back to the mines? Get me to work until I turn into a zombie like the Selari workers back there? Because let me tell you something: you may think you're all powerful, untouchable, but you'll never break the spirit of a true Free Man."

The Caretaker smiled, a chilling sight. "You took something from me. You wronged me. And to say that you 'Free Men' can't be broken… well I've already disproven that fact, haven't I?"

"I have nothing of yours," I shot back, answering his first statement.

His smile widened. "We'll see about that, Captain." And with that, he took a step forward, his intentions now clear.

The Caretaker was here, right now. And he wasn't leaving without a fight.

"Wait," I said quickly. "What do you mean, you've proven it?"

The Caretaker paused, his gaze never leaving me. His lips twisted into a smirk. "Isn't it obvious, Captain? You were once a proud, Free Man, were you not? Yet, here you are, having toiled away in my mines, your spirit reduced to a desperate flicker in the grand scheme of things. If that isn't a broken man, then I don't know what is."

His words were like daggers, meant to provoke and disorient. But I couldn't let him see that they had hit their mark.

"I'm still standing," I retorted, my voice resolute. "And I'm not alone. There are more of us out there. Free Men who won't be controlled or manipulated by the likes of you."

For a moment, his cold eyes seemed to flicker with a hint of uncertainty. But it was gone just as quickly as it came.

"Is that so?" he said, his voice laced with derision. "Then tell me, Captain, where are these Free Men now? And where is this comrade of yours... this Cowley?"

And then it hit me. The Caretaker had called me 'Captain', and that meant he knew more than he was letting on.

A knot formed in my stomach. I didn't know where Cowley was, but I couldn't let the Caretaker see my worry. I forced a false but confident smirk onto my face.

"I guess you're not as all-knowing as you think, Caretaker," I said, mustering as much bravado as I could. "As for Cowley, he's out there. And trust me, he's not alone."

"Is that so?" The Caretaker's gaze didn't waver, his voice still cool and composed. "You know what?" the Caretaker asked. "I was going to keep this secret from you a little longer, but since you brought it up…"

My stomach dropped.

"Yes, you know already, don't you? Cowley belongs to me… and he always has. He was the one who lured you out here and he was the one that alerted me to your presence with this fire."

I had been so naïve. Betrayed again by the very same person. Shame on me.

I laughed, a bitter, humourless sound that echoed through the night. "Really, Caretaker?" I said, my voice tight. "You expect me to believe that?" It was the only thing I could think to say. Perhaps if it was true then the Caretaker would bring Cowley back out into the open so that I could see the look on his face for myself.

But the Caretaker merely shrugged, a smug grin playing on his lips. "Believe what you will, Captain. The truth remains.

I felt a surge of anger build up within me. How dare he stand there, with that smug grin. But beneath my anger, I felt a twinge of doubt. What if he was telling the truth? What if Cowley had betrayed me again?

No, I shook the thought away. I refused to believe that. Cowley had changed, hadn't he? And the Iron Will and the crew had been lost to the ocean… so he wouldn't betray his only chance at a home, would he?

"I don't believe you," I said, my voice steady. "Cowley's out there, and any minute he'll…"

"Ah, the blind faith of friendship," the Caretaker sighed theatrically. "So touching, yet so foolish."

I gritted my teeth, but didn't rise to his bait. The Caretaker was trying to throw me off, to plant seeds of doubt in my mind. I wouldn't let him.

"Is this why you're here?" I challenged. "To play mind games? Because if you're looking for a fight, you'll find I'm not as easily beaten as you might think."

The Caretaker's grin faded, his gaze turning icy. "A fight? No, Captain. I'm not here to fight you. I'm here to bring you back home."

And with that, the Caretaker appeared just an inch from my face, wrapped a large, strong hand around my throat and lifted me clear off the ground.

The last thing I saw, was his grinning mouth and straight, white teeth.

Chapter 19 – Experimentations

My head pounded as consciousness slowly returned, a heavy fog clouding my mind. I was no longer outside, that much was clear. The smell of sterility filled the air, laced with an underlying metallic tang that reminded me of blood and fear. My back felt cold and rigid, and when I tried to move, I found my wrists and ankles strapped to a cold, upright metal table.

I blinked, trying to clear my vision, and looked around. I was in some sort of laboratory, filled with cold, gleaming equipment that I didn't recognise. Against one wall were large vats filled with a clear liquid. And floating in each one, a foetus. Selari, by the looks of it by the gills on the face.

My heart pounded in my chest as the pieces fell into place. I remembered the kids back at the settlement, how strong they'd been, how they were able to build the settlement without so much as a word of guidance.

The sound of footsteps drew my attention. The Caretaker entered the room, his cold eyes taking in my expression with a cruel satisfaction.

"Ah, Captain, you're awake," he said, his voice echoing in the silence. "Have you figured it out yet?"

I looked at him, at the vats, then back at him. His eyes held a twisted delight, a perverse satisfaction at my inevitable realisation.

"They're clones," I said, my voice a husky whisper, barely audible. "The children... they're clones."

The Caretaker chuckled, a cold, harsh sound that bounced off the walls of the sterile room. "Very good, Captain. And not just any clones. These are engineered Selari, genetically enhanced to be stronger, faster and more obedient."

I swallowed hard, feeling the anger bubble up inside me. "You're playing God," I spat out, "building an army of slaves."

He didn't even flinch at my words. Instead, he strolled over to one of the vats, looking fondly at the foetus within.

"Why rely on unreliable, free-willed beings when I can create perfection? They're designed for the mines, Captain. A perfect balance of strength and endurance, with an innate obedience to their creator."

I was speechless. This was monstrous. Unforgivable. But even in my anger, I couldn't help but think of the implications of what he'd said.

"It's not true," Yari's voice echoed in my mind. "If they were obedient then we wouldn't have a settlement full of children right now, would we?"

That made sense. The Caretaker was either lying, the children weren't all clones, or some had managed to escape his control. I didn't want to let on about our kids though; if he knew they were poised to rebel then he might simply destroy them all.

"Why?" I demanded, the word tasting bitter on my tongue. "Why do this? Why play God?"

The Caretaker merely shrugged. "Why not?" he responded, his gaze flitting back to the vats. "These clones are mine. They work without question, they're strong, resilient. And with a few genetic tweaks, they're the perfect miners."

I strained against the bonds holding me, the cold metal biting into my skin. But I was stuck fast.

"What I can't seem to figure out," the Caretaker continued, pacing slowly, "is how you managed to convince the Sylph within you to break free. I can suppress the Sylph in the Selari, give them orders they can't refuse. But with you..."

He paused, staring intently at me, as if trying to unlock a puzzle. "You're different," he finally said, an air of fascination in his voice. "I find that... intriguing."

My blood ran cold at his words. I was at his mercy, trapped and powerless. Yet, there was a part of me that refused to give in, a part that was still very much a Free Man.

"I won't be your lab rat," I growled, meeting his gaze with all the defiance I could muster.

"Unfortunately for you, Captain," the Caretaker replied, his voice dropping to a chilling whisper, "you don't really have a choice."

As fear turned to dread, the Caretaker continued to speak, outlining his grand plan. His aim was to have the clones bind with a Sylph upon birth, to come out obeying his orders, saving him the trouble of having to wait for them to mature. It was a horrific plan, and one I was determined to stop. No matter what it took. But the one shining beacon of hope, was evidently that this monster hadn't managed to figure it all out yet. The Selari clones still had to grow into their teenage years before he could bind a Sylph to them.

"So you still need the Sylph?" was the first thing that I could think of saying. "You can't figure out how to bypass the kids' requirement to hit their teenage years… and you think I somehow have the answer to that?"

The Caretaker smiled, but there was no warmth in his expression. "I don't just think you have the answer, Captain," he said, his voice icy. "I know you do. Somehow, you and your Sylph share a bond that's different from the others. Stronger. And it's that strength that allowed you to break free from my control. To resist my influence."

His words rang with a certain kind of truth. I thought back to the time when Yari and I had first spoken. The fear, the confusion, and then... the connection. Something deep, powerful. Unbreakable.

"But I didn't do anything special," I admitted, my voice barely more than a whisper. "I... I didn't even know what I was doing."

The Caretaker shook his head, a glimmer of frustration in his eyes. "You may not think so, but I've seen enough to know otherwise. There's something unique about your relationship with that Sylph," he pointed at my chest menacingly. "Something that I simply can't put my finger on."

I shook my head, disbelief bubbling up inside me. "And what if you're wrong? What if there's nothing special about me or Yari? What if you've just been underestimating the power of free will?" I cursed myself for using Yari's name, but I doubted it would make much difference at this point.

The Caretaker didn't reply immediately, his gaze fixed on me as he considered my words. "Then it would be a monumental waste of time," he finally said. "But I'm willing to bet that's not the case."

His eyes bore into mine, a challenge burning in their depths. "I can't deny that there's a chance I might be wrong," he conceded, a flicker of something akin to respect passing across his features. "But if I'm right... well, you would become a cornerstone in the creation of a new order. Millions of beings across thousands of dimensions, all ready and willing to serve…"

A chill ran down my spine at his words. A new order. His order. Full of obedient, controlled individuals devoid of the freedom to choose, to think, to feel. I looked at the vats again, at the innocent foetuses floating aimlessly, oblivious to the world they were being born into.

The Caretaker leaned in closer, his cold eyes boring into mine. "You see, Captain, I have all the time in the world. You are simply a variable in my equation, perhaps even the one piece of the puzzle that's missing. I have the resources, the knowledge, and the determination. And now... I have you."

His words echoed in the silent lab, the threat implicit. The room felt colder, the air thicker. He straightened up, his hands clasped behind his back as he turned to look at the vats.

"I'll figure it out, one way or another," he said, his voice carrying a note of finality. "You, your Sylph, all of you... will serve me in the end."

I gritted my teeth, rage and fear swirling inside me. But I would not let his vision of the future become reality. I was a Free Man. I always had been, and I always would be. Even if it was the last thing I did, I would fight. For myself, for Yari, for every sentient being he planned to enslave.

Then a thought occurred to me.

"And what about the other Entropics? You think they'll just stand around and let you get away with this?"

Of course I had no idea what the rest of the Caretaker's race thought of his plan, but I had to at least try something.

The Caretaker turned back to look at me, confused for a second, and then laughed a booming, echoing laugh.

"You know nothing of my brothers and sisters," he announced confidently. "When I was chosen as this cycle's Caretaker, it was because of my ideals, my ability to put this plan into action so that when the rest awaken, there is a universe ready for them to inherit. A world where the Entropics are treated as they should be: as Gods."

I was struck speechless at his audacity, his blatant disregard for the freedom and autonomy of sentient beings. His conviction was unsettling, a chilling reminder of the lengths some beings would go for power. Yet, in his delusion, he had revealed something I hadn't considered before.

"So, the rest of your kind... they're in hibernation?" I asked, my mind racing. If that was true, then there might be hope yet. I had to keep him talking, get as much information as possible.

"Very perceptive, Captain," the Caretaker said, an edge of amusement in his voice. "Yes, we Entropics are a long-lived species. To conserve our energy and to prevent a certain amount of posturing, many of us enter a hibernation cycle every few millennia. During that time, in each of our worlds, one of us is chosen to act as the Caretaker to ensure the continuity of our grand plan."

"And you were chosen because of this... this vision of yours?" I said, disgust creeping into my voice. I clenched my fists, the metal cuffs digging into my skin. "What about the others? Did they share your plan?"

The Caretaker shrugged, seemingly unperturbed. "Not all of them. Some were resistant, yes. But the majority saw the potential in my plan. They understood the need for worlds that would be ready for us when we awaken."

But there was something in what he had said. 'Worlds'. Just how many of these being were out there, enslaving races of people that I'd never even heard of?

His words sent a shiver down my spine. The thought of an entire race of beings like the Caretaker, ruling over the universe was horrifying. But his revelation also filled me with a newfound determination. If some of the Entropics were against the Caretaker's plan, maybe they could be persuaded to help us. Or at least, they could be a possible ally in the fight against the Caretaker. It didn't give me much hope, but at least it was something.

"They're all the same," Yari's small voice filled my mind. "They only want power and domination and even the ones who he says were against his plan would've just had a different one… but the result would've been the same."

"Yari," I said softly, my mind welcoming her voice like a beacon in the darkness. "I know it seems hopeless. I know it feels like we're up against an impossible enemy. But we can't give up. We have to believe there's a way to fight back." Then thoughtfully I added: "They're not all the same. Just as we humans are diverse in our beliefs and actions, so must they be. We have to believe that. Otherwise, we've already lost."

I could almost feel her hesitation, the fear and uncertainty she must have been experiencing. "We have each other, Yari. We have our bond. And we have our will. He may underestimate it, but that is his mistake, not ours."

Her voice was weak when she finally replied, "I'm scared, Captain."

"And so am I, Yari," I admitted, my voice breaking slightly. "But we've faced fear before. We've stared it in the face and pushed through. We can do it again. Together."

The Caretaker's cold laughter echoed through the room, his amusement evident. "Such sentimental nonsense," he sneered. "Do you really believe that will be enough to stop me?"

My mouth fell open. The Caretaker had been able to hear our internal conversation.

"Yes, I can hear your thoughts," the Caretaker announced with a devilish smile.

The realisation sent a wave of panic coursing through me. The one place I thought we had some privacy, some sanctuary, was now exposed. The Caretaker had access to our internal conversations, our shared fears and strategies.

"How…" I began, but my voice trailed off, the question hanging in the air.

"Your bond with the Sylph is fascinating," the Caretaker said, his eyes gleaming with a perverse curiosity. "It's more than just a mental connection. It's a complete merging of consciousness. That's what makes it so unique, so… useful."

His words felt like a blow, sapping away the last shred of hope I'd been holding onto. If he could hear our thoughts, what chance did we have? Our every plan, our every strategy would be laid bare before him.

But then, a spark of defiance flickered within me, refusing to be extinguished.

"Then you know," I said, my voice steady despite the turmoil raging inside me. "You know that we won't give in. You can hear our thoughts, our fears, but you can also hear our resolve. We will fight you, Caretaker. Until our last breath."

The Caretaker studied me for a moment, his expression unreadable. Then, he smiled. It wasn't a pleasant smile. It was cold, detached, a predator playing with its prey.

"Good," he said, his voice dripping with anticipation. "I do so love a challenge." He moved closer to me, his eyes never leaving mine. "But know this, Captain: The harder you fight, the more satisfying it will be when you finally break."

Then he whirled around on the spot and looked about the room as though he was looking for something.

"I think we should begin with our experimentations then, no?" he announced.

Fear coiled in my stomach as he announced his intentions, but I suppressed it, fixing the Caretaker with a determined stare. "You may hear our thoughts, but you'll never understand them," I said. "Our resilience, our ability to hope and fight... they're as alien to you as you are to us. You'll never break us, Caretaker!" my last words came as a shout. I couldn't help it; this was going to be my end, I was sure of it.

His unsettling smile widened, and he started walking towards some kind of console by the wall, his fingers dancing over something attached to it. A whirring noise echoed around the room, and suddenly a wave of vertigo swept over me. I could feel something tugging at my consciousness, a mental probe of some sort.

But it wasn't just mental. There was something physical happening too, I just couldn't see what it was.

As the Caretaker's fingers flew across the thing, a strange device slowly descended from the ceiling. It was a large helmet-like contraption, rigged with wires and tubes, all leading back to where the Caretaker stood. It hummed with energy, and a cold shiver ran down my spine as I realised its purpose. It could only be some kind of mind-probing device.

My heart pounded as the Caretaker turned back towards me, the eerie smile still etched onto his face. He gestured towards the device with an unsettling casualness.

"Don't worry, Captain," he said, his voice cold as ice. "This will stop hurting once you stop trying to resist it."

I glanced between the Caretaker and the device, my mind racing. I knew I had no way to escape, and I was just a man. But mentally? I had spent years resisting the oppressive influence of the Royal Navy, surely this would be something I could handle, no?

Maybe, just maybe, I could resist his probing, shield my thoughts, buy myself some time to figure a way out of this. I wasn't going down without a fight.

"Fine," I said, my voice steady despite the fear coiling in my gut. "But if you see something you don't like in there… then I can't be blamed."

The Caretaker didn't respond and started to manipulate the machine again, and I could feel the device powering up again, the low hum now vibrating through my skull. In a moment, the world around me seemed to blur, but what was worse was the pain that came along with it.

I felt a sharp, intrusive presence trying to worm its way into my thoughts, into my memories. But I was ready. I fortified my mental barriers, reinforcing them with every ounce of my willpower. I would not be broken.

But the pain… it was clear that it was more than I was sure I could bare.

But I still willed my entire being to resist whatever this was. I didn't know what the thing was looking for, but it was sure as hell not going to find it without a fight.

"I'm telling you Captain, don't fight this," the Caretaker said.

"I'm scared, Marcus," Yari's voice came to me, though it sounded faint. I didn't want to lose my focus to respond to my friend though; the pain was starting to spread and if it kept getting worse, I didn't know if I could cope with it for much longer.

"You won't break me," I growled through gritted teeth.

But then a piercing sensation at the back of my skull forced me to shut my eyes tightly. The Caretaker didn't respond.

I started to feel like images of my past were beginning to rise to the surface now. I was still trying to resist of course, but the images floated up towards the surface of my consciousness without my influence and I tried to bat them back down again before they could form properly.

"Hmmm," I heard the Caretaker say to himself quietly.

Then a fresh wave of pain engulfed my being. It was like a red-hot poker had been inserted into my skull and was being forced down my spine.

"You will not break me," I thought and wilfully pressed down on anything that started bubbling up within my mind.

"You will not break me."

"It is futile, Captain," the Caretaker reminded me. "If you continue to fight this, it will only worsen for you. Now why don't you start by telling me who all your friends are?"

I didn't open my eyes and I didn't unclench my jaw. In fact, I didn't even know if I could do either if I wanted to.

Then more pain. If it had been like a red-hot poker before, now it was as though that same person had reached inside of my chest and held my heart in their bare hand. I could feel each beat it struggled through, begging for the power to survive.

Then I became aware of a loud, shrill noise filling the room. Louder than the Caretaker, drowning out his warnings and after a moment or two I realised that the noise was coming from me. My mouth had opened and I was screaming. Not screaming in defiance. No. I was screaming in agony. A pure, unfiltered pain that I had never experienced before. It was from within, and I knew that I couldn't stand against it.

"Marcus!" Yari cried in my mind. "He's going to kill you!"

And then it all stopped.

I had remembered something.

The pain had gone, the noises, even the screaming had gone.

And I sat there, in the Captain's quarters of the Iron Will, in my comfortable chair with everything I owned in the world all around me.

Of course, this was all in my mind, but the respite it afforded was complete and unyielding. I had retreated into my own personal space, and it existed outside of the real world. Outside of the pain I was truly experiencing.

"Yari," I said aloud. "Are you here?"

"I am here, Marcus," Yari said. She was sat on my shoulder, her small golden form glowing as brightly as the first day I saw her.

"Do you think this is it? Is he going to kill me?" My voice was quiet, soft. Accepting.

Yari looked at me, her black eyes shimmering. "I don't know, Marcus," she admitted, her voice filled with sorrow. "The Caretaker's powers are far beyond anything I've ever encountered. But we must not lose hope. We've come this far, faced so many challenges... we can't give up now."

I sighed, sinking back into my chair. The reality of my situation weighed heavily on me, but I found a small comfort in Yari's words. "You're right," I said finally, my voice resolute. "We've survived worse. We will survive this too."

"That's the spirit, Marcus," she said. "Now, let's figure out a way to get out of this."

"I just don't know what to do," I said. "If we leave this place and return to the real world, the pain will still be there waiting for me. But time doesn't pass in this place, does it? We can't stay here forever."

"No, but we can make a plan, or just use this time to compose ourselves, can't we?" Yari said.

I nodded at the Sylph. She was right; just being here for these short few moments had made me feel better by some orders of magnitude already.

And then it hit me.

"What if we..." I began, a plan starting to form in my mind.

"Yes?" Yari prompted.

"What if we use our connection to our advantage?" I continued, my mind racing. "Assuming that the Caretaker can see our thoughts... what if we feed him misinformation? We could create a distraction, make him believe that something that isn't true… do you think that maybe… maybe its normal for people to fight against whatever it is he's doing until they break and let go… but what if we actively tried to lie, to generate falsehoods?"

Yari looked at me, her eyes wide. "That could work," she said slowly. "It's risky, but it could work."

We didn't have any other options. It was a long shot, but it was a shot nonetheless. And I was willing to take it. If it meant saving my friends, I was willing to do anything.

I steeled myself, ready to face the pain again, ready to face the Caretaker. "Let's do this, Yari," I said, my voice filled with determination. "We have a fight to win."

With that, I closed my eyes, took a deep breath, and plunged back into reality, back into the pain. The screaming, the agony, it was all still there, waiting for me. But I was ready. I started to think, to imagine, to create a vivid, convincing picture in my mind. I focused on the deception, on the distraction, feeding the Caretaker with a mix of false information and genuine emotions. I did everything that I could to believe what I was creating was the absolute truth.

All the while, I kept repeating a single thought, a single mantra, over and over again.

"You will not break me. You will not break me."

I was a Free Man, and no one, not even the Caretaker, could ever change that.

"What is this?" the Caretaker asked in wonder at what I was creating. I wouldn't have heard him if he hadn't left his workstation and placed his face to within an inch of my own, as though he was trying to see what I was envisioning through my own eyes.

I focussed on my fabrication as hard as I could manage. Images of the Iron Will surfacing and I gave a half-hearted attempt to try to keep them tamped down, like I didn't want the Caretaker to see what I was seeing. Then I let the images flood in.

I imagined standing on the edge of the Iron Will, looking down into the waters below, and then a terrible beast, at least twice the size of the Kraken I had seen destroy the Iron Will in reality rolled into view.

I let slip the words: 'King of the Ocean' and then quickly pulled them back again like bait on a line.

"King of…" I heard the Caretaker mutter, then catch himself.

Then in my false memory, I heard myself shout: "Bring around the destroyer!" I didn't have much time to think up a name, and it was the best I could do.

"Right away, Captain!" I envisioned my first mate, Cowley, responding from somewhere within the ship. I could almost feel the ship's wheel under my hands, sense the determination in my posture. The memory felt so real, the echo of my words still lingered in my ears.

I imagined the massive form of the Destroyer. It was a huge cannon with rugged, weathered features, and a maw large enough to swallow a smaller ship whole. I imagined it to be constructed from the finest and most resilient alloys known to our civilisation, an intimidating presence. Its form was round and bloated, tapering at the ends to form a perfect cylindrical shape. Its surface was scarred with the markings of countless battles, each dent a testament to the titanic clashes it had been through.

Mounted on a massive turret, the cannon was designed for omni-directional movement, allowing it to target and fire at enemies from any angle. Its barrel was wide and long, capable of launching a payload so enormous it could annihilate the largest of adversaries with a single shot. The 'Destroyer,' as we'd so fittingly named it, was the epitome of raw, uncontrolled power. But it was entirely made up.

I could almost hear the hum of the fire in its belly, a low, constant drone that echoed throughout the Iron Will, a reminder of the destructive potential we held within our grasp. The Destroyer was a work of science and engineering, harnessing a power source so potent, so volatile, it made the weapon practically unstoppable.

The sight of the Destroyer would instil fear into the hearts of even the most hardened warriors. It was a symbol of our strength, our will to fight, and our resolve to protect what was ours. It was our hope against the terror that lurked beneath the waves, the King of the Ocean.

"Steady on the helm, Cowley!" I shouted, my voice echoing across the deck. "Ready the Destroyer. We've got a King to dethrone!"

A low murmur rippled through the ship as the crew sprang into action. The hum of the Destroyer being prepared grew louder, a crescendo that signalled the impending chaos. We were ready to face the beast with the Destroyer at our side.

"Load the canon!" I ordered, my voice rising above the clamour of the crew.

A humongous cannonball, the size of a small house, was hoisted into the maw of the Destroyer with a series of winches and pullies. It didn't matter that there was no way in reality the Iron Will would have been able to remain afloat with this thing on board, but it didn't matter right now.

It was an explosive projectile of unprecedented scale, engineered to deliver a devastating impact. Its polished surface gleamed menacingly, a clear threat to any who dared to challenge us.

Once loaded, the great cannon turned slowly, a behemoth aligning its gaze towards the King of the Ocean. An eerie hush fell over the crew, a collective breath held as the moment of confrontation neared.

"Fire!" I commanded, my voice echoing in the sudden silence.

In response, the Destroyer roared to life. It belched out a wall of fire and smoke, the explosive force of the launch shaking the ship to its very core. The cannonball erupted from the barrel, blazing a path of destruction through the air, heading unerringly towards the monstrous beast below.

The King of the Ocean, sensing the impending threat, attempted to evade. But it was too slow, too cumbersome, the enormous projectile was upon it too swiftly. The cannonball struck it dead centre, a terrifying spectacle of force meeting unstoppable creature. A massive explosion followed, the concussive wave radiating outwards, stirring the ocean into a frothing, churning maelstrom.

The King of the Ocean let out a terrible shriek, a sound so horrifying it seemed to echo through the very fabric of reality. It thrashed wildly, struggling against the force of the blast, but to no avail. Its colossal body began to disintegrate, dissolving into the depths from whence it came within just a few short moments.

The sight was terrifying yet awe-inspiring. A testament to the power of human ingenuity, the Destroyer had ended the reign of the King of the Ocean in one, single, devastating shot.

"Such power…" The Entropic muttered. "But there was no sign…"

I redoubled my effort to tamp down on the obtrusiveness of the Caretaker's machines and hung my head like what I had just done was a pure betrayal to my people and my former ship.

"So there is something about you," the Caretaker sneered. "I trust that you know how to build this weapon of yours, this... Destroyer?"

"I'll never tell you..." I groaned.

"But you already have," the Caretaker replied, a malicious grin spreading across his face. "You've shown me everything, Marcus. Your mind, your memories, they've laid the blueprint of the Destroyer bare. And with this power, this technology... Imagine the destruction I could wreak."

"I won't let you," I growled, struggling against the pain that was trying to consume me. "I won't let you use the Destroyer for your wicked schemes."

His laughter echoed through the chamber, a chilling sound that sent shivers down my spine. "And how will you stop me, Marcus? You're helpless, at my mercy. You're broken, and you can't fight back."

"No," I said, my voice barely a whisper but filled with steely determination. "I am not broken."

A sudden surge of energy filled me, a wave of determination so strong it pushed back the pain, pushed back the Caretaker's influence. I was a Free Man, and no one, not even the Caretaker, could ever take that from me.

"I will not let you win," I said, my voice rising, echoing through the chamber. "I will not let you destroy everything I've fought for... but it doesn't matter... you'll never be able to figure out how the pieces of eight fit together..."

I had to admit, I felt very clever. I had goaded the Caretaker into desiring something that didn't exist, and I had also just managed to give him a reason to keep me alive.

"Pieces of..." the Caretaker said, his grin faltering for the first time "...But, Marcus, don't you see? You've already lost. And no matter what secrets you possess, they will all belong to me, eventually."

"No," I said. "I'll never tell you. You can throw me into the mines for fifty years, keep me locked up without food or water and I'll never break."

"YOU WILL TELL ME YOUR SECRETS!" The Caretaker bellowed, appearing in front of my face again, his terrible eyes glowing a deep, angry red now. "But maybe you're right. Maybe you should spend a little time locked away, to really think about what the next words out of your mouth are going to be."

I shut my mouth animatedly and closed my eyes.

I could sense his fury, a palpable force of rage and desperation. But I was resolute, undeterred by his threats. I was playing a dangerous game, but it was my only chance. I needed to buy time, not just for myself, but for my friends, for everyone who was still out there, fighting.

Suddenly, the world around me shifted, the machines and the eerie glow of the Caretaker's eyes fading away. I quickly found myself being deposited in a dark cell, a far cry from the techy torture chamber I was previously held in. The cold, damp stone walls of my prison were an unwelcome reminder of the reality of my situation. I didn't know how the being had managed to transport me into this new place so quickly or easily… but I didn't have the energy to think about it properly.

"I'll see you soon, Marcus," the Caretaker's voice echoed in the darkness. "And you will tell me. Whether it takes days or decades, you will tell me."

As the echoes of his words faded away, I found myself alone in the oppressive silence of my cell. I propped myself up against the cold stone wall as best I could, my mind racing, planning, strategising.

Chapter 20 – Family

The darkness in the cell was oppressive, but it wasn't the physical confinement that scared me. It was the threat that lurked beyond those stone walls, the Caretaker's intent to pry my secrets from me and turn them against everything I had fought for. I could tell from the moment I'd thought up the Destroyer, the Caretaker had wanted that power so wholly. I had simply made the whole thing up to keep myself from thinking about the kids we'd helped, or Marina. From what she'd said, if the Caretaker discovered the beginnings of a revolt, it would be quickly extinguished. And it didn't matter; I'd thought about a terrible, powerful weapon, and just like that it was something the being wanted.

I had bought my friends some time, but I still had no idea how I was going to make it out of this place.

"What do we do now?" Yari asked me in my mind. I wondered if she would project herself out and sit on my shoulder to give me some comfort, but then I guessed that it probably wasn't the best idea, especially if the Caretaker could've been watching us.

"I'm not sure," I admitted, speaking internally. "We need to find a way out of here, but if the Caretaker can hear our thoughts, our plans... then I think this might be the end for us. I just wish we had met someone along the way that could've helped us..."

I let the sentence hang, and hopefully my hidden meaning clear. We were walking a dangerous line, trapped between the need for action and the risk of discovery. Every move we made, every plan we hatched, had to be devised in such a way that the Caretaker wouldn't figure out what we really meant.

"But how?" Yari's voice echoed in my mind, full of worry. "The Caretaker has us locked away in here, isolated. How would we meet anyone, and how would we send them a message?"

I leaned back against the cold, damp stone wall, my mind whirling with possibilities, discarding one plan after another. We needed a way to communicate, a way to reach the outside world and tell Marina what had happened to us.

"There's always a way to escape these kinds of situations," I finally said, more to reassure myself than Yari. "We have to." And besides, I'd always found a way before. When I was Captain of the Iron Will, I'd found myself in situations just like this all the time… well maybe not just like this, but I'd usually find myself in places where the odds of victory were almost nil, and I'd always found my way out… somehow.

I closed my eyes, shutting out the oppressive darkness, and focused on the problem at hand. There had to be a solution, a way out of this predicament. I just had to find it.

As the hours slipped by, a single thought kept looping in my mind, over and over again, like a mantra. We would not be defeated. We would find a way. We had to.

"Yari," I said after what felt like hours. "I can't think of anything."

"I knew it," Yari replied, clearly almost in tears. "I knew there would be no way out of this as soon as the Caretaker…"

"Wait," I abruptly stopped Yari in her moaning. "The Caretaker… he's the only thing in control around here, right?"

"Yes, but that's the problem…" Yari began, but I interrupted her again.

"So if we want to escape, we're going to have to use him, right"

"But it's too dangerous…"

"But once you remove all impossibilities from a situation, all you're left with is the possible, Yari. The Caretaker is the only thing… the only variable…"

"But that cannon… I don't think it's…"

"Don't worry, Yari, I think I have something better to tell him about. Something he'd be very interested to see."

"Really?" Yari's voice filled with curiosity and a hint of hope. "What is it?"

"Us," I said, my voice brimming with newfound confidence. "Our bond, Yari. The Caretaker is fascinated by power, especially one he doesn't understand. He wants to control the Sylphs and the kids, but he can't quite get it to work the way he wants. But what if we showed him a different way? A way that's not about control but about cooperation, about choice. A symbiotic relationship that could potentially unlock even greater power for him. It's what he wants, right?"

I could almost feel Yari processing my words, contemplating the implications of what I was suggesting. I hoped the Caretaker was listening in too.

"But how?" she finally asked. "How do we convince him?"

"We have to show him," I replied. "We have to show him what we've achieved. Yari, I need you to do your thing. We need to demonstrate our bond, prove to him it's real and not something we made up..."

"But Marcus, if we reveal ourselves... What if he decides to experiment on us? What if..."

"He already has us, Yari," I interrupted. "We're already prisoners. And right now, our only chance to get out of here, and stop his plans, is to give him exactly what he wants. Something he could never achieve through force or manipulation. Something only possible through mutual trust and respect."

Silence filled my mind as Yari digested my words. Finally, she said, "Alright, Marcus. We'll do it. Let's just hope this works."

Taking a deep breath, I called out, "Caretaker!" I had a feeling that he either wouldn't be too far away, or he would be listening to our internal conversation. I was not mistaken.

For a moment, there was only silence. Then, just as abruptly as he'd disappeared, the Caretaker manifested himself before me. His gaze was sharp, his eyes glowed an eerie red that contrasted heavily against the darkness of the cell.

"I must be honest, I didn't think that you would break so quickly Captain. I understand you have something for me?"

I felt Yari stir, her energy rising, thrumming with anticipation. She was just a small ball of light at first, but as she concentrated her power, she started to take form.

Her projection materialised into the usual small golden bird, with intricate feathers that flowed with an otherworldly elegance. She unfurled her wings between me and the Caretaker, and in the dim light of the cell, they shimmered as if made of liquid gold, casting long, dancing shadows against the cold stone walls and flowing behind her like she was suspended underwater.

The Caretaker watched, his gaze fixated on the spectacle before him. His eyes widened as Yari, in all her spectral glory, circled around the cell before returning and landing gracefully on my shoulder without making a sound.

"I believe introductions are in order," I said, a sardonic smile playing on my lips. "Caretaker, meet Yari. She's my Sylph, my partner."

The Caretaker's red eyes flickered, then turned blue, which I took as a sign of his astonishment. As I had suspected, he had never seen a Sylph able to leave its host before, nor had he even thought it was possible. Our bond was what he wanted, and we were going to show him what we could do.

"And as you already know, we can communicate," I added for maximum effect.

The Caretaker took a step back, his ever-present grin fading, replaced with a look of genuine curiosity and, dare I say, respect. We had his attention. Now it was time to use it to our advantage.

"How have you achieved this?" The Caretaker asked once he had recomposed himself.

"It's about trust, not control," I replied, echoing my earlier words. "Yari and I aren't master and servant. We're partners. Equals. It's a mutual relationship. Even though it didn't start off that way, we've become friends. That's how this all works."

The Caretaker studied us, his intense gaze flicking between me and the golden bird on my shoulder. His lips were pressed into a thin line, his usual smirk replaced with a thoughtful expression.

"This is possible with all the Sylphs?" he asked, his tone more curious than dismissive. It seemed as though he was already considering the possibilities, the potential this revelation could hold for his ambitions.

"With the right approach, I would say yes," I confirmed, keeping my tone steady. I was threading a delicate line, but I had no other choice. "Every Sylph is different, every Selari, every human is different. They need to understand each other, learn about each other. A bond like this... it can't be forced. That's why you haven't managed anything like this yet with all your experiments."

"And the children," he mused, his gaze not leaving Yari. "They could do this too?"

I knew this was what the Caretaker wanted to hear and in truth, I had no answer to this question.

Yari quickly answered in my mind on my behalf. "With time, with patience. They could form a bond just like Marcus and I have. They could become partners with the Sylphs. But for that to happen, they need to be treated with respect, not as tools. This is why you have so much trouble with my kind."

The Caretaker was silent for a moment, his blue eyes reflecting the golden light from Yari's form. "I see," he finally said, his voice barely above a whisper.

We had presented him with an entirely new concept, a different approach. It was a long shot, but it was the only shot we had. For the moment, it seemed like we had given him something to think about. But whether he would take our words to heart or disregard them altogether was yet to be seen.

"We can show you how to do it, Caretaker," I offered, making sure to maintain eye contact. "You don't have to do this alone. We're here to help. If it means a better world for everyone in it... then I don't think we have any choice but to help you."

The Caretaker looked at me, and for the first time since we met, there was a spark of something else in his gaze. Was it hope? Understanding? Respect? It was hard to tell. But it was a start, a small step in the right direction.

I wanted to press the issue, but I could hear Yari already sending me the feeling to remain quiet, to let the Entropic come to his own decisions.

"But you have to promise that you won't hurt the Selari kids... or the Sylph," I added quickly after Yari's prompting. "If this makes life better for everyone... then I think it's the right thing to do."

A moment of silence followed and again I wondered if there was anything else I should say to fill it.

"Come with me," the Caretaker abruptly said, coming to some internal decision.

He turned, gesturing for us to follow. I felt Yari's projection shudder, her energy pulsing in apprehension as we trailed behind the Caretaker. He led us through the dark labyrinth of the cavern, the glow of his form casting long shadows in the twists and turns.

Eventually, we reached an enormous cave entrance, a yawning gap that opened into a massive expanse of darkness. As the Caretaker led us inside, my heart pounded with anticipation.

The sight that met our eyes was beyond breath-taking. It was a cavernous space, vast and echoing, filled with tens of thousands of Sylphs. They were everywhere, floating like incandescent dandelions, each one of them shimmering with an ethereal light, illuminating the darkness with a beautiful, otherworldly radiance.

There were all sorts of colours. Some were the colour of sunrise, soft pinks and golds blending together, while others sparkled with the hues of deep-sea blues and emerald greens. Each Sylph radiated a unique light, creating a kaleidoscopic spectacle that left me in awe.

"These are the Sylphs," the Caretaker began, his voice echoing in the vastness of the chamber. "Waiting for their bonds with the Selari children, waiting to be awakened."

I looked at the sea of Sylphs, each one of them floating aimlessly. Their lights, although beautiful, seemed... empty. Listless. They were like Yari had once been: without direction. I could feel the pain and despair in the room as well as through my link with Yari and it almost brought a tear to my eye.

"Yari," I whispered mentally, my gaze not leaving the spectacle before me. "Look at them. They're slaves."

"I can feel them, Marcus," Yari responded.

"They will be slaves, but they aren't quite there yet," the Caretaker said aloud, reminding us of his ability to hear our conversations.

I turned my attention back to the Caretaker, determination welling up within me. "We can help them, Caretaker. Show them how to bond with the Selari children. It won't be quick or easy, but if they make the choice, they can form bonds like Yari and I have, and it could change everything."

The Caretaker didn't respond immediately. He was watching the sea of Sylphs, his eyes flickering with an array of colours, reflecting the lights around him. Then, slowly, he nodded.

"Very well, let us try it your way," he said, his voice echoing in the cavernous space. "How long will this take?"

I internally smiled. It wasn't much of a step up, but we had a new hope now.

"Just leave us to try to talk to them for a while. You'll know when they're ready. Just... try not to scare them."

The Caretaker nodded again, this time more thoughtfully, and took a step back. He faded into the background, his form melding with the shadows, but I knew he was still watching. This was his domain, and he would not leave it entirely to us.

Turning back to the Sylphs, I felt Yari's energy pulsing in synchronisation with my own heartbeat. It was a strange sensation, but comforting in its familiarity. I drew a deep breath, focusing on Yari and the bond we shared, then sent out a gentle nudge to her. A feeling of hope.

Yari fluttered off my shoulder, her golden form radiating warmth and encouragement. She circled around me, glowing brighter with each pass, before shooting off towards the sea of Sylphs.

They watched her, thousands of tiny eyes focused on her golden form. She moved among them, her light touching each one she passed, sharing a spark of the bond we shared. A subtle wave rippled through the vast cavern as the Sylphs responded positively, their colours subtly shifting, reacting to Yari's presence.

Gradually, a hush fell over the cavern, the Sylphs' lights dimming as they turned their attention to us. It was as if they were waiting, expecting something. That was when I reached out again, projecting my thoughts, our bond, towards them.

Yari acted as a conduit, amplifying my message. She flew over the sea of Sylphs, projecting to them images of our shared experiences, our struggles and victories, and the bond we shared. The message was simple: we were not masters and servants, but partners. And we were going to do everything we could to destroy this world that the Entropics had enslaved, to set free every slave we encountered and to bring peace to a place where it had been forcibly removed. I only hoped that the method of communication that Yari and her kin used was one that the Caretaker could not listen in on. But he didn't reappear, so we continued.

The response was immediate. The Sylphs stirred, their lights flickering as they absorbed the information, and processed it. It was like watching a wave of understanding ripple through them.

And then, something incredible happened. A few of the Sylphs began to glow brighter, their colours shifting in response to our message. It was a slow process, but the change was undeniable.

I felt a surge of elation as more and more Sylphs started to react. It was working. They were understanding.

"Yari," I whispered, my voice echoing in the cavernous space. "They're responding. We're getting through."

"I can feel it, Marcus," Yari replied, her voice filled with wonder and hope. "They're starting to understand."

It was going to take time. Time to reach all of them, time to help them understand. But we had taken the first step. The first step towards freedom for the Sylphs, for the Selari, and for us. And with each passing moment, that step seemed a little less daunting.

But something more was happening. Something that I hadn't expected. The Sylphs were sending back a desire to help, to break free from their chains and to join our fight. It was more than I had expected, but even with our shared desire, I didn't know how we were going to escape from this place.

Immediately, I closed my eyes and pulled myself back into that place within. That place where time stood still and in that moment I realised, was the only place that the Caretaker couldn't listen to our mental conversations.

"Marcus, we need a plan," Yari chirped, joining me in the Captain's quarters aboard the Iron Will.

"I know," I responded. "But what can we do? How can we get them to help us?"

We were surrounded, deep within an underground fortress guarded by a powerful entity. We had no weapons, no resources, and were heavily outnumbered. It seemed like an impossible situation. But then Yari spoke again.

"We may not have weapons, but we have something far more powerful," she said.

"What?" I asked curiously.

"All these Sylphs. Imagine if they could work together. They've never had a real purpose before – if they'd escaped, then they'd just be sent right back here, or their families killed. They can see what I saw in you, Marcus, what I still see: hope. A hope for a better future."

I knew that the Sylphs were powerful beings, but the fact that their entire race had been enslaved by the Entropics, and that the Caretaker alone seemed to keep this flock in check all by himself, told me that they weren't that powerful. Still though, it gave us a new advantage in both power and numbers.

"What can they do?" I asked, watching Yari as she landed on my shoulder.

"They are capable of more than you know," Yari answered, her voice filled with conviction. "Their energy, when combined and focused, can have a significant effect. Think of them as a collection of small power sources. On their own, they may not be very strong, but together... their light is magnified."

I thought back to when she had floated among the Sylphs, her presence comforting to them. Their lights seeming to glow a bit brighter, and their movements becoming more purposeful. It was as if Yari's hope was infectious, spreading through them like a beacon of hope in the darkness.

"How bright of a light are we talking about?" I asked, cottoning on to what Yari was saying.

Yari's response was almost reverent. "As bright as a new dawn, Marcus. If they all channel their energy in unison, the light they could emit would be staggering."

"Incredibly bright light," I mused aloud, my thoughts returning to the cavern filled with thousands upon thousands of Sylphs. "Could that be used as... a weapon?"

"In a way," Yari agreed, her tone suggesting she had already considered this. "Light can blind, can disorient. It might not cause physical harm, but in a crucial moment, it can provide an invaluable advantage."

"Enough to blind the Caretaker," I said, understanding dawning on me. The Caretaker, from what I had seen had mostly moved around in the darkness, and in caves. It stood to reason that he was a creature of night, a shadow being of sorts. Bright light would surely affect him, perhaps even cripple him temporarily. "We could use that moment to escape."

"It's a possibility," Yari confirmed. "But it would require incredible precision and timing. Every Sylph must emit their light at the same time to achieve the desired effect."

"It might be hard," I conceded. "But it's a chance we must take. Yari, we have to try this. Can you talk to the Sylph and see if they'll join us. It seems the Caretaker can listen in on us, but not your communications with the other Sylphs."

"Of course," Yari agreed, her mental voice full of resolve. "We're all in this together. Let's make them understand."

And all it took this time was for me to blink, and I was right back in the cave, not a single second having passed.

I watched as Yari darted off into the throng of Sylphs, her light blending in with the others. The cavern seemed to shimmer as she moved among them, whispering words of encouragement and explaining our plan to them. Slowly, the Sylphs began to respond again. Their lights starting to glow a little brighter once more, a sign that they understood and were willing to participate.

Time seemed to pass in a blur as Yari worked tirelessly, moving from one Sylph to another, her soft communications echoing through the cavern in a way that neither I nor the Caretaker could understand. I watched in awe as the Sylphs began to come together, their lights merging into a single, brilliant glow.

Finally, Yari returned to my side. She looked exhausted but satisfied.

"They're ready, Marcus," she whispered. "They understand. They'll do what they need to do."

I felt a surge of gratitude towards Yari, and to the Sylphs for their bravery. It was a risky plan, but it was the only one we had.

"Alright," I said, determination welling up within me. "It's time. Let's call the Caretaker back here and get started on what needs to happen to make a change in this world."

I knew that Yari had completed her task before she had announced it, mainly because where the birds were all separate, sitting on their lone little perches and exuding sadness and sorrow, their lights now glowed with something much more hopeful. And I could feel it too. The atmosphere inside this makeshift cage was softer, happier somehow. It was like the Sylphs were happy, or hopeful for the first time in a very, very long time.

But before I could make any motion to call him back out into the open, the Caretaker reappeared from the shadows and stood by my side, watching the Sylph as they pulsated.

"Yes, I can feel it," he practically hissed. "They are better now, more open to the path that lay ahead of them. And it is all because of you, Captain. You have changed the lives of millions, billions even. So many wasted years of mining waiting for the children to grow, but now… now we can bind them sooner! Yes, now Captain, now I will have an army of children working my mines and the Cores they will bring will cement the power of the Entropics for millennia to come!"

Then he turned to me with a wicked look in his eyes. "You have shown me that force is not always the way to get what you want… but in doing so, you have also shown me that your usefulness has finally come to an end. I am sorry Captain, but you escaped from my mines. And that is something that cannot go unpunished."

The Caretaker then, quicker than I imagined possible, clasped a single hand around my neck and lifted me clear from the ground. I tried to fight him off, to prize open his fingers, but his grip was as strong as iron.

"But… the… Destroyer…" I tried to force the words out. It was the only thing I had left to bargain with.

The Caretaker simply laughed. "Do you really think that I bought that story? Do you not think I know when I am being lied to you foolish human!"

"Marcus!" Yari called and spun around the Caretaker, trying to do anything she could to distract him, to give me precious few more seconds of consciousness. It didn't work.

"All I wanted you for, was to show me how you have made your link with this Sylph, and what the pair of you can do. And now that I have that information…"

Yari suddenly burst into a brightness that I'd never before witnessed. She was like a miniature sun and even with my eyes closed, I could see her brightness through my eyelids.

The brightness began to fade a second later and when I opened my eyes again, I could see that the Caretaker was still in a fair amount of pain. His eyes were tightly shut and his grip around my throat had decidedly weakened.

"More Yari, now's the time!" I shouted at my companion aloud.

With a mental affirmation, Yari's light intensified once more, this time with a pulsating rhythm that seemed to resonate with the swarm of Sylphs around us. Their individual lights started to glow brighter and brighter, their power magnified by their unison. The entire cavern was filled with an astonishing, blinding brilliance that again even I had to shield my eyes from.

The Caretaker let out a roar of surprise and pain, his grip around my throat finally loosening. I dropped to the ground, gasping for breath as I rubbed my sore neck. But there was no time to waste.

"Come on, Yari! Lead the way!" I urged her.

The brightness in the cavern pulsed, leaving the Caretaker disoriented and shielding his eyes from the blinding attack. The Sylphs, led by Yari, burst into motion. They swarmed around the Caretaker, their lights forming an unending stream of illumination that kept him disoriented and unable to move.

"Marcus, now!" Yari's mental voice echoed in my mind, clear and urgent.

I saw the Caretaker trying to swat away the glowing Sylphs around him, but there were simply too many.

"Which way, Yari," I asked quickly. "Lead the way out!"

"We need to keep him occupied!" Yari announced, and then my heart sank. Finally, I could see the flaw in our plan: in order for us to make our mistake, some of the Sylph would have to stay behind to stop the Caretaker from simply recapturing us.

"We can't just leave them," I said, looking back at the Sylphs who were still blinding the Caretaker. "There has to be another way."

"I know, Marcus," Yari responded, her mental voice tinged with sorrow. "But this is our only chance. We need to get as many out as we can."

I clenched my jaw, my heart aching at the thought of leaving some of the Sylphs behind. But Yari was right. We needed to make the most of this opportunity, to save as many as we could.

"I won't forget them," I promised. "Once we're out, we'll find a way to come back for them."

"Agreed," Yari replied flatly.

We turned our attention to what I assumed was the exit, a narrow tunnel that looked like it led up to the surface. Yari darted forward, her light illuminating the way as the Sylphs followed behind. I ran after them, my lungs burning and adrenaline surging within me as I pushed myself to keep pace.

I could hear the Caretaker roaring behind us, but I didn't dare look back.

The tunnel seemed to go on forever, but finally, I could see the light of the surface ahead. We emerged into the open air, the night sky above us filled with stars. The sight was so beautiful, so far removed from the dark, oppressive caverns we'd been within that it took my breath away.

But there was no time to rest. We had to keep moving, to get as far away from this place as possible.

Yari led the stream of Sylphs into the sky, their lights mingling with the stars. I watched them for a moment, feeling a pang of loss for those we'd left behind.

"We'll come back for them," I vowed, echoing my earlier promise. "I won't rest until every Sylph in this world is set free from the grasp of these monsters."

I felt a wave of agreement from Yari, her mental presence warm and supportive. Together, we'd already made a difference. We'd freed these Sylphs, given them a chance at a better life. But our work was far from over.

As I watched the Sylphs disappear into the night, I knew that this was just the beginning.

"Let's go, Yari," I said. "We have a lot of work to do."

With a burst of determination, we set back off into the night, ready to finally return home and put this place behind us for as long as we could manage.

Chapter 21 – Our Home

It took a long time for my heart rate to return to normal, and thank God Yari was with me because without her, I would've had no idea which direction to go in. The stars above us were different here, but thankfully Yari knew exactly which way to go.

As we travelled, some of the Sylphs that had escaped had caught up with us. They couldn't communicate with me or Yari in the more traditional way, but the general consensus that we shared, was that some of the Sylphs had decided to join us, some had gone out on their own to look for their own families and kin, and some had been recaptured by the Caretaker. I didn't want to think about how difficult their lives were about to become.

Eventually and after we'd managed to travel quite some distance from the cave, the sun had begun to rise and the world around me started to feel a little more familiar.

As dawn started to break, the world started to change. The unfamiliar, jagged landscape slowly gave way to more recognisable terrains and as the sky turned from black to shades of orange and pink, I could finally make out the familiar silhouette of our small but growing settlement, placed against the backdrop of the vast ocean beyond.

The last hundred metres or so I ran, with Yari flying overhead. I could see Marina standing at the entrance to the settlement and more than anything, my friend made me feel like I was truly home.

Marina was standing there, watching us approach with an expression of surprise and relief on her face.

I couldn't stop myself. I ran into her arms and hugged her tightly. I didn't realise how tightly exactly until she prized me off her. I could see though, that she'd been crying. Her eyes were red and bloodshot.

"I… I thought you were dead…" she said quietly.

"What? Why?" I asked, but she wasn't listening. As we both watched, an entire flock of multicoloured Sylphs flew above us and into the settlement. There were dozens of the beings and seeing so many together for the first time again, I felt a warmth in my heart.

Then as Marina looked upwards, I noticed that she held something in her hand. When I looked closer, I recognised it as an Obsidian Core. I stared at it, not entirely sure what to make of it.

"Marcus," she said, realising where I was looking and stepping forward to offer the Core to me. "I... I found these. Lots of them."

She looked sheepish as she gestured behind her to where I assumed there were more. I knew these Cores could change the tide of our struggle. But I began to panic at where she might've got them from.

"I went to the mine," she continued, her eyes flickering with a fierce determination but also a fair amount of guilt. "I was just going to take a few, you know? So we could see how much more growing you could do... but when I was there, sneaking through the mine... a Sylph arrived and the workers just... followed her. After a while, they all left the mine, all of them. I didn't know what caused it... well until now I guess." She gestured to the flock of Sylphs that had quickly dispersed amongst the settlement and had happily made perches for themselves.

I was stunned. The implications of her words sank in slowly. Not only had she managed to secure some Cores, but the Selari in the mine had now gained their freedom. The Entropics' manpower had been significantly reduced in one fell swoop. And it was all thanks to Yari.

"And what about the workers?" I asked with wide eyes. "Are they OK?"

"Well... not really," Marina replied, kicking the ground. Then gestured to the settlement behind her again.

This time I really looked.

The settlement was bustling with its usual activity. Several wooden buildings now dotted the landscape, testament to the hard work and dedication that had been poured into this place during my absence. The structures were beautiful, and they added a sense of permanence to our humble abode. I noted a few new homes, a storehouse, what seemed to be a makeshift meeting place or perhaps even a school, and even what had the look of a medical facility.

However, it wasn't just the buildings that caught my attention. There were Selari everywhere. Dozens of them seemingly moving around with a purpose, helping to construct and maintain the settlement. Their movements were slow, almost robotic, as they were when they worked in the mines. I knew they weren't entirely conscious, but it was still heartening to see so many of them together, working side by side with the children of our settlement.

The sight was surreal, filling me with a sense of glee that tugged at my heart. The children were now working together with their zombified adult kin to build a home. Their combined efforts were slowly transforming our settlement into a real community, a beacon of hope amidst the bleakness of this world.

My gaze returned to Marina as she shifted uncomfortably under my scrutiny. She was looking up at the Sylphs that now dotted our skies, their bright forms casting a gentle light over our settlement.

Before I could say anything else, a familiar figure emerged from the settlement and my smile dropped.

Cowley was here, looking more ragged and wearier than I had ever seen him. His surprise upon seeing me was evident.

"Marcus... You're alive," he muttered, sounding genuinely taken aback. "We thought..."

His words trailed off as he took in the sight of the Sylphs all around the settlement, their lights glimmering like stars in the daytime. His eyes widened and he took a step back, his gaze flickering between me and the Sylphs.

"I... I don't understand..." He muttered, looking utterly lost. But his confusion didn't last long. The realisation of what had transpired dawned on him slowly, his eyes widening in disbelief and fear. "You... escaped?"

His face paled at my words, and he took a few more steps back. There was fear in his eyes. The question now was, what was Cowley going to do? He had been found out.

"You led the Caretaker to me, and you left me there to die!" I accused bearing down on the man who had now betrayed me not once, but twice.

His lips parted as if to argue, to defend himself, but no words came out. The truth of my accusation hung heavily in the air between us. The initial surprise of seeing me alive had faded from Cowley's face, replaced with an expression of apprehension.

"Yes," he finally managed to admit, his voice a mere whisper. "Yes, I did."

A tense silence descended upon us, the enormity of his betrayal sinking in. I could feel a surge of anger welling up inside me. I felt betrayed, deceived. I had trusted him, relied on him, and he had sold me out.

But despite my anger, I knew I had to keep my cool. Now was not the time to let emotions cloud my judgment. We were in a delicate situation, and any wrong move could jeopardise everything we had achieved so far.

"So what now, Cowley?" I asked, my voice steady, my eyes never leaving his. "You've been found out. You led the Caretaker to me, you left me to die.

What's your next move?"

He flinched at the venom in my voice, his gaze dropping to the ground. I saw a flicker of something in his eyes - fear, maybe, or regret - but it was quickly replaced by a hard, defensive look.

"I... I don't know, Marcus," he admitted after a long moment of silence, his voice barely audible. "I... I didn't think... I didn't think you'd make it out."

"Well, I did," I snapped, my anger bubbling up again. "And now you're going to answer for what you did."

The Sylph, the children, the Selari, they were all watching us now, a silent audience to our confrontation. Cowley looked around at them, panic flickering in his eyes.

"I... I'm sorry, Marcus," he said at last, his voice barely a whisper. "I... I was just... I was scared. The Caretaker... you have no idea…"

"I HAVE EVERY IDEA!" I shouted back at my former first mate… but more than that, he was my friend. "Then you came back here and told everyone I was dead, right?"

Crowley nodded slowly, his expression unchanged.

"But don't worry, the Caretaker told us how you're still working for him. How he promised you Cores if you brought back anyone opposed to him."

Marina gasped.

Then Cowley's expression finally darkened and his mouth twisted into a devious grin.

"Yes, Captain," he practically spat the title. "And what's more is that there's nothing you can do to stop me. You and your…" he gestured about the settlement nonchalantly, "…kids, zombie workers and your little girlfriend here… you have nothing. So I think I'll be leaving now, and you can expect to see me again very soon."

My mouth fell open. How could I have been such an idiot.

I wanted to stop Cowley, to stand in his way, but he was right in a way. We didn't have weapons and really, I didn't want to kill anyone. Not right now at least.

Cowley took a single step forward, then the tip of a cutlass burst from his stomach.

His eyes widened in shock, his mouth opening and closing as he tried to form whatever words he was trying to say. He looked down at the blade protruding from his stomach, his hands reaching out to touch it. But his movements were slow, sluggish.

Behind him, Guy stood, his face pale but determined. His small hands gripped the cutlass's hilt, his knuckles white from the effort. He was shaking, but he didn't let go. He didn't back down.

"Guy..." I started, but he cut me off.

"He was going to hurt you," he said, his voice trembling. "He was going to hurt all of us."

Cowley's knees buckled, and he fell to the ground, the cutlass still embedded in his stomach. He gasped for breath, his eyes wide with shock and pain.

"I... I didn't..." he started, but his voice trailed off. His eyes rolled back in his head, and he slumped to the ground, motionless. Dead.

For a moment, we all just stood there, staring at Cowley's lifeless body. Then, slowly, Guy let go of the cutlass, his hands shaking.

"I... I didn't mean to..." he started, but I cut him off.

"You did what you had to do, Guy," I said, my voice steady. "You protected us."

"But I... I killed him," Guy said, his voice barely a whisper.

"Yes," I said, my gaze meeting his. "And you saved us."

For a moment, Guy was silent. Then, slowly, he nodded. "OK," he said, his voice filled with newfound resolve. "OK."

And with Cowley falling, the last member of the Iron Will was no more. A distant memory, a legend on the high seas. But in truth, the Iron Will had already been gone for quite some time. Ever since I'd been replaced.

"Where did you get that cutlass?" I asked Guy, turning my attention away from the still form of Cowley.

Guy swallowed hard before answering, his gaze dropping to the cutlass in his hand. "It washed up on the shore," he finally managed to mutter, his eyes darting around to gauge the reactions of the onlooking settlers. "It must've been washed up from the Iron Will. Here," he held it out towards me, "you can have it."

I looked at the cutlass before taking it, but when I did, I could tell it was nothing out of the ordinary. Indeed it was probably from the Iron Will, and I was sure that it would come in handy.

"Keep it," I told Guy, pushing the cutlass back towards him. "You've proven that you can handle it."

"But... but I..." he stammered, looking aghast.

"I know," I said, "it's a heavy thing to bear. Taking a life is never easy, and it never should be. But Guy, sometimes we're faced with choices where there's no easy path. You made a hard choice today, but it was the right one. This cutlass," I pointed at the weapon in his hand, "it's a tool. And now it's your responsibility. Use it to protect, not to harm."

He stared at the cutlass for a long moment, his eyes reflecting a myriad of emotions - fear, uncertainty, resolve. Then he nodded. "I understand,

Marcus," he said, his voice firmer now.

Turning back to the crowd, I raised my voice, "Let this be a lesson to us all. In this world, we stand together. Against the Caretaker, against the Entropics, and against any who would do us harm. Cowley chose his path, and it led him here. Let his fate serve as a reminder. We are strong when we stand together, weak when we betray our own."

I let my gaze sweep over the assembled crowd, over the children and the Selari, over Marina, and finally back to Guy. He was standing a little taller, the cutlass now gripped firmly in his hand.

"I know we've all suffered losses, but we must carry on. With the Obsidian Cores Marina found and the Selari now free from the mines, we have a chance. A chance to fight back, to build something here. We are not alone. We have each other, and we have the Sylphs. And as long as we stand together, we can face anything that comes our way." Then I had a brilliant idea. I turned to Marina and gestured for her to pass me one of the Obsidian Cores. Taking it, I held it up high for all to see.

"And this, this Core is what's going to unlock the power that we can wield. I may be the only one able to harness their power, but I swear to you all right now that I will use this power for good, to help others, and to allow everyone to lead the life of a Free Man!"

Then I brought the Core down to my mouth, and bit into it like it was an apple.

I heard the crowd inhale as they watched me. But at least I had made my point.

"WHAT ARE YOU DOING?" I heard Yari scream in my mind.

"It's OK Yari, we have the Cores back and… you know… I don't actually feel too good. Do you think it was the mush…"

Biting into the Core was clearly a very big mistake.

The world spun around me and I could hear Yari shouting in my mind, but her words were a distant echo. My knees buckled and I crashed to the ground, dropping the other half of the Obsidian Core. Darkness crept in from the edges of my vision, and I felt my body growing numb.

"Marcus! What in the Core's name have you done?" I heard Marina's voice asking, somewhere near, filled with terror.

Footsteps rushed towards me, a flurry of voices shouting, calling my name. But it all felt far away, as if I was sinking into a deep abyss of nothingness.

"I thought…" I managed to mumble, the world spinning violently around me. "I thought it would…"

"You thought what? That you'd ingest the Core and gain its powers?" I heard Marina's voice ask, even as I felt my consciousness slipping. "Marcus, you're a damned idiot! You can't just eat the Core, it's too much! I know you did it once before but your body was broken and you were close to death – the power had somewhere to go!"

And then everything went black.

I don't know how long I was out for. When I woke up, it was to a dull throbbing pain in my head and the taste of something bitter in my mouth. I blinked up at the wooden ceiling, trying to gather my thoughts. Then memories of what had happened flooded back and I sat up with a gasp.

The room was quiet and dimly lit. I was lying on a bed, with Marina sitting by my side. Her face was pale, her eyes wide with relief as she saw me awake.

"Marcus, you gave us quite a scare," she said, her voice trembling. "Don't you ever do anything like that again."

I nodded, feeling a wave of guilt wash over me. "I... I'm sorry, Marina. It was a stupid idea."

"That's an understatement," she said, but there was a hint of a smile on her face. "You're lucky Yari was able to get rid of some of that excess power.... We had no idea what was happening, but I think Yari has the hang of it. You should have seen how brightly she was glowing. I thought she was going to explode!"

Yari. I turned to where the small Sylph hovered nearby. "Thank you, Yari," I said, offering her a weak smile.

"Just don't do it again, alright?" She replied mentally, her tone soft but stern. "Obsidian Cores are not for biting into. They're to be used more sparingly, in a way that your body can handle. You should know these things by now."

"I understand," I said, nodding. "I promise, no more Core tasting." I remembered the Core-soaked water though, and next time, I was sure that I was going to do it that way. The right way.

Marina let out a relieved sigh, running a hand through her hair. "Just rest, alright?" she said, standing up. "You've been out for a day. We'll need you to be strong for what's ahead."

I nodded and lay back down, feeling the exhaustion tugging at me. "Just one thing," I said, stopping her. "What happened to Cowley?"

"Guy dealt with it," Marina replied. "He and the others buried him outside the settlement. Despite everything, Cowley was part of the Iron Will once... it seemed like the right thing to do."

A silence fell between us as we both thought back to those earlier times. Times that seemed so distant now.

"Go rest, Marina," I said softly, feeling a wave of exhaustion wash over me. "I'll be alright."

She nodded, giving me a small smile before leaving the room. Alone, I stared up at the ceiling, my thoughts a whirlwind. Everything that had happened, everything that was still to come. It was a lot to take in.

And then there was Yari. I turned to the little Sylph, her form glimmering in the dim light. I realised that despite the intense situation, I felt different. More attuned, more aware. And Yari, her glow seemed more vibrant, her presence stronger.

"Yari," I said, "Do you feel that too?"

She looked at me, tilting her head slightly. "Feel what, Marcus?"

"I... I feel different," I confessed. "Like... like we're more connected. Stronger."

Yari seemed to ponder this for a moment before replying. "I do feel a stronger link, Marcus. It's as if your sudden and uncontrolled ingestion of the Core reinforced our bond. Maybe it's like... like a muscle. You stressed it, and it's come back stronger."

I nodded, considering that. "That's good, right? It means we're getting stronger again?"

"In theory, yes," Yari responded. "But remember, Marcus, it's still a balance. You can't just gulp down Cores. It's dangerous. We were lucky this time. But next time we might not be."

"You're right," I agreed. "I'll be more careful in the future. We have a lot of work ahead of us and the last thing we need is for me to do something stupid."

Truth be told, I once again had the feeling that taking in more of the Cores wasn't going to do me any good yet. It was like a sixth sense – my body had to use up the power of whatever it had taken in before I could try again – else I'd be violently sick. And nobody wanted that.

"Tomorrow, we'll go out and see if we can figure out what's changed," I announced with a yawn. It seemed that getting knocked out was extremely tiring.

Chapter 22 – An Old Friend

The very next morning I strode outside with Yari on my shoulder and a determined glint in my eye. I didn't feel the need to eat or drink anything – a handy side-effect of the power of the Cores, and I walked to the edge of the settlement. I could see that the walls were next on the agenda to be built, and the Selari workers and kids were already starting their work for the day. I had to give them credit; what they were doing with the place was nothing short of miraculous.

Looking up at the sky, I let out a breath. "Ready, Yari?" I asked, my voice barely above a whisper.

Yari turned to look at me, her eyes gleaming with anticipation. She fluttered her wings, a nod of assent. Taking a step back, I extended my arm, providing her with a launching pad. Then, with a single powerful beat of her wings, she took to the air.

I closed my eyes, focusing on the bond that connected us. It was obviously much stronger now, more vibrant, almost like a pulsing, living pathway between us. I could sense her soaring higher even when I could no longer physically see her, and I could feel her joy radiating through our bond. It was such an alien sensation, the feeling of the wind rushing through her feathers, the buoyancy of the air beneath her as she climbed higher and higher.

Opening my eyes, I could see through hers as though they were my own. I could see the world far, far down below. From up high, the settlement seemed much smaller, but I could also see just how far we had come. The ocean glowed in the morning light, and our campsite bustled with activity, a testament to our resilience. The houses, arranged in neat rows, and the people moving around, starting their day brought a smile to my lips.

Yari soared higher still, leaving the boundaries of our settlement behind. From this height, the world started to look entirely different. The lush green forest that spanned off into the distance seemed endless, a sea of verdant green. To the west, the high cliffs where the Caretaker had carried out his experiments. To the east, the vast, sparkling expanse of the ocean, its surface dancing with myriad shades of blue.

A rush of exhilaration washed over me. This was freedom. Through Yari's eyes, I could see the world from a perspective I never thought possible. I could feel the cold rush of the wind, see the world in all its magnificence, and even smell the salty tang of the sea and the earthy scent of the forest down below. I felt as though I was there with her, flying high above the world.

Our bond was more than just a connection; it was a link that allowed us to share our senses, our experiences. It was both intimate and empowering. Yari was not just a companion, she was a part of me, just as I was a part of her.

But even as I was lost in the beauty of the world, I couldn't ignore the practical benefits of our enhanced bond. The range of our connection had significantly increased, giving us a massive advantage. We could scout for miles around, detect potential threats long before they became dangerous.

We could coordinate better, react faster. In short, we had become a more effective team, a testament to the adage that the whole was indeed greater than the sum of its parts.

As Yari finally began to descend, I closed my eyes, the sudden shift in perspective causing a momentary bout of vertigo. When I opened them again, Yari was landing on my outstretched arm, her eyes gleaming with satisfaction.

"That was amazing," I told her, my voice filled with awe. "Thank you, Yari."

"You're welcome, Marcus," she responded. "It was quite the experience, wasn't it?"

"That it was," I said, looking out over the settlement with a wide smile. "And I think today, we'll take the time to do some exploring."

I could tell that Yari was intrigued by the idea, so instead of waiting around, I sent her high up into the air again.

"Go as high and as far as you can, Yari, I want to see how good this can get!"

And with that, Yari launched herself into the sky again, her wings slicing through the cool morning air. I closed my eyes, letting myself feel the sensation of flight through our bond. It was thrilling, invigorating.

Her ascent was rapid, her effortless flight carrying her higher and higher. She dove and twisted, testing the limits of our connection. Every beat of her wings sent a shiver down my spine. It was a feeling of freedom, a sensation I'd never experienced before, and it was intoxicating.

Then, something on the horizon caught Yari's attention. Something familiar, yet unexpected. Without me having to even tell her to, she dove towards it, her speed making my heart race.

And there it was, as clear as day. My ship. It was the Iron Will. And my chest tightened.

Seeing it again brought with it a rush of memories. The battles we'd fought, the storms we'd weathered, the camaraderie. But also the mutiny that had led Cowley and the rest of my crew to leave me abandoned on a deserted island, only to end up in this godforsaken place. But thinking about it, was it godforsaken? I'd made this more of a home than I'd ever had back in my old life. I had friends in Marina and the kids. And a purpose.

But still, there she was, washed ashore like a relic of a forgotten era.

I could tell from this distance that most of the ship was intact. Her hull was damaged, a testament to the Kraken's immense strength. The masts were broken, the sails tattered and torn. Yet, despite the damage, there was something defiant about her, something indomitable.

Yari swooped closer, giving me a better view now. The deck was deserted, devoid of the laughter and banter that once filled it. But underneath the wear and tear, I could still see the traces of our old life.

Feeling a sudden surge of nostalgia, I whispered to Yari, "Can you get inside, see if anything's still intact?"

With a mental nod, she descended down onto the wooden deck, her tiny talons making no noise against the worn-out wooden deck as she landed. She moved with caution, her senses heightened and ready for anything that may be hiding within. The ship creaked and groaned, as though protesting the intrusion, even if she was just a weightless projection.

Through her eyes, I saw the familiar sights of the deck, the doors to the Captain's quarters, the galley. Everything was covered in a thick layer of grime. It was as if the ship had been frozen in time, waiting for its crew to return.

"There," I said as Yari approached my old cabin. "Can you get inside?"

She fluttered up to the window, peering inside. My cabin was just as I remembered it, the familiar sight of my old desk, the bunk, the faded maps on the wall... it was exactly as it was when Yari and I retreated into my mental personal space.

A pang of longing washed over me, and I blinked away the memory. "Thank you, Yari," I whispered, my voice choked with emotion.

"You're welcome, Marcus," she responded, her tone soft. "It must be hard, seeing your old life like this."

But as I watched through Yari's eyes, I couldn't help but feel a sense of gratitude. The Iron Will was a part of my past, a part of me. And now, it felt like a piece of my old life had finally returned. And I wanted to experience it for myself.

"Marina, Guy," I called. "I have something to show you," I announced.

Intrigued, Marina and Guy walked over, their expressions curious.

"What is it?" Marina asked, her eyes following my gaze towards where Yari had flown.

I cleared my throat, bracing myself. "Yari found the Iron Will," I said, my voice thick with emotion.

For a moment, there was silence. Then, Marina gasped, her eyes wide. "You're not serious."

"I am." I nodded, taking a step towards her. "She's washed ashore. Damaged, but mostly intact."

"But... that's..." Marina stammered, "That's incredible, Marcus. But how? The Kraken...?"

"I don't know," I said honestly, "but it doesn't matter. "She's here. And I think... I think we should try and get her back."

"You mean..." Guy started.

"I mean," I interrupted, meeting Guy's gaze, "rebuild her. Repair the damage. She was once the scourge of the seas, the bane of the Royal Navy. A symbol of freedom. We have the manpower now, and the resources. We can do this."

"But..." Marina started, then her gaze softened. "I already told you, Marcus. We don't go out onto the waters here. You saw the Kraken... and the Skimmers... and don't even think for a second that they're the worst of what's out there."

"I know," I replied, looking back towards where the Iron Will remained. "But... we don't have to sail her... I just... I just want her back. We can rebuild her on land and she can be used as a defensive fortification."

There was silence as the two of them absorbed the enormity of what I was suggesting. Guy was the first to respond.

"Marcus, I can't pretend to understand what the ship means to you, or what it was like to live the life you did. But I do understand the power of symbols. The Iron Will, in your hands, could be a beacon of hope for our settlement, a fortress against any threats, or at least anyone who wants to do us harm. I'm all for it."

He paused, considering. "It'll be a monumental task. And it won't be without risk. But if you're sure about this..."

"I am," I said firmly, meeting his gaze.

"Then count me in," he said, offering a hand. I took it, shaking it firmly.

Next was Marina. She was quiet, thoughtful. Then she nodded, a slow, determined nod. "It's a lot to ask. But the benefits... they could be worth it. And you're right, we have the manpower, the resources. We can make this work."

I felt a surge of relief, gratitude. We were in this together. "Thank you," I said quietly.

Marina smiled, her eyes bright. "Don't thank me yet, Marcus. We've got a lot of work ahead of us."

She was right, of course. There would be challenges in returning the ship to the settlement, but I firmly believed that having the Iron Will back under my control was going to be a huge benefit to everyone. I didn't know why, but deep down I could just feel it.

The ensuing days became a flurry of activity. The Selari, despite being new to the art of ship recovery, took to the task with unflinching determination. They repurposed the ship's own long ropes and salvaged timber to devise a system of pulleys and levers, displaying a surprising ingenuity that made me appreciate them all the more.

Every day, I watched as a team of workers and older children hauled the Iron Will across the land using rolling logs. It was a slow, laborious process, but the sight of that once-majestic ship inching closer to our settlement, our home each day was heartening., even if it was a husk of what it once was.

I made a point not to help in the recovery effort. Not because I was an ass, but I wanted to wait until the ship had reached its new home before I went poking around in her. Plus I didn't want to see what was left of the interior of the ship for myself until I had the opportunity to do something about it.

There was an undeniable rhythm to the workers' efforts, an intricate dance born of collaboration and shared purpose. The Selari and the children all worked side by side without even a hint of annoyance. The ship creaked and groaned as it moved, but beneath the hull, there was a sense of harmony, of collective triumph.

Meanwhile, I put my effort to good use elsewhere. The rest of the settlement was undergoing its own transformation. Although the work had slowed due to the workforce being split, tall wooden walls began to take shape, enclosing the settlement in a protective embrace. The Selari workers, guided by me on the rare occasion, but more efficiently by the designs and directions provided by Guy and Marina, worked tirelessly, their hands moving with practised efficiency.

Each log was hewn from the surrounding forest, its bark stripped and its surface smoothed until it fit snugly into place. The walls rose high above the ground, punctuated by strategically placed watchtowers. Every log was notched and locked into its neighbour, forming a robust barricade against potential threats. It was much, much more than I could've ever been able to achieve on my own.

The gate was a masterpiece. Constructed of the sturdiest logs, bound together with thick, iron bands they'd salvaged from the Iron Will, it was both imposing and inviting. I watched as the workers painstakingly carved intricate designs into its surface, adding a touch of beauty to the otherwise formidable structure.

I joined in where I could, lending my strength to the collective effort. The Selari kids seemed to appreciate it, welcoming my assistance with good-natured laughter and the occasional teasing. The older workers from the mine seemed unable to focus on anything apart from their work. I just hoped that their Sylphs were still giving them the rewards they craved. They deserved at least that much.

As we worked, I told my stories of the sea and my former life as a ship's Captain, and having never set sail on open waters, the Selari, and not least of all, Marina, found the stories fascinating.

As I worked alongside the kids, I couldn't help but be amazed by their sense of community, their inherent camaraderie. These were a people who had been uprooted, their homes destroyed, and yet, their spirit remained unbroken. They worked together, lived together, and laughed together, sharing their joys and burdens alike.

Evenings were a time for rest, for sharing food and tales around the fire. Marina would always join us, her laughter ringing out as the children vied for her attention, their innocent faces glowing in the flickering firelight. Guy, ever the stoic, would sit a little apart, his gaze often straying to the ever-growing walls, a thoughtful look on his face. I wondered how such a young boy could be so thoughtful, so wise, and often I would have to hold back a tear at the thought that his entire childhood, and the childhoods of all the Selari children, had been robbed from them.

And always, looming in the background, was the Iron Will. A silent reminder of what was, and what could be. Every day, she inched closer to the settlement, her battered form a testament to our collective determination.

The days rolled into weeks, and before I knew it, the settlement had transformed. Where there was once open land, there now stood high walls and watchtowers. Where there was once uncertainty, there was now a sense of security, of belonging. And where there was once a shipwreck, there was now a symbol of resilience, of indomitable spirit. The Iron Will had made it home.

But we would always live in fear, because the Caretaker would never let us remain free in this world, I was sure of it.

"She's home. She's finally home!" I cried as the first sunlight shone on the Iron Will. It was clear how much damage the Kraken had actually done to her hull now though.

The first rays of sunlight streamed down onto the ship, illuminating her battered exterior. A collective gasp rose from the Selari. It was the first time many of them had seen the Iron Will in the daylight, her dilapidated condition fully exposed.

"She's... she's seen better days," Guy remarked, breaking the silence. His voice was filled with a mix of awe and regret.

"Indeed, she has," I replied, my eyes never leaving the ship. Despite the visible damage, there was a strange sort of beauty to her. A weathered elegance that spoke of countless battles endured and victories won.

"We'll make her better, Marcus," Marina said. Her hand found mine and gave it a reassuring squeeze. "We'll make her better than she was."

The damage was extensive. Parts of her hull had been completely crushed under the might of the Kraken's grasp. Her sails were shredded, barely more than ragged strips of cloth flapping in the wind. The Iron Will was a skeleton of her former self, stripped of her strength and her majesty.

I felt a lump in my throat as I studied her. Memories of storms weathered, battles fought, and victories celebrated on her deck rushed back to me. She was more than just a ship. The Iron Will was a symbol of resistance, of defiance. She had been my home. My fortress. My refuge.

But as I looked at her now, I saw not just the ship that had been, but the ship that could be. With the combined effort of the Selari, Guy, Marina, and myself, we could breathe new life into her. Make her a beacon of hope for this new settlement, a symbol of our determination to survive and thrive in this world.

"Let's get to work," I declared, turning to face the crowd. "She may be broken, but we can mend her. We will restore the Iron Will to more than she was. She will be our fortress, our beacon of hope. A symbol of our strength and resilience." And then a thought occurred to me. "The Iron Will was known by name across all the seas. She was formidable, and her name alone was enough to send fear into the hearts of the Royal Navy Captains. I propose now that our settlement has grown, to name her as well, so that our friends have a place to believe in, and our enemies know the name of the place that will take everything from them!"

A loud roar erupted from the kids and Marina, but the Selari workers, predictably just stood there, listening, with their milky-white eyes unfocused.

"Selari world!" one of the kids shouted.

"Amazing Free Land!" Another chimed in.

"Marcus's Place!" Marina shouted, then snorted out a laugh.

"I have something much better," I announced with a smile. "How about: Atlantis."

There was a short silence as my words sank in.

"That's rubbish!" One of the kids eventually replied.

"What does it even mean?" Marina asked.

"Listen," I said, with my hands up before me. I couldn't help but remember making this exact gesture just before the Iron Will had mutinied. "I brought us all here together, so I'm naming the place Atlantis, alright?"

A few murmurs rippled throughout the crowd, but eventually a few agreeing nods followed.

"Right," I said. "So let this world know that Atlantis…" I peered about in case anyone else had anything to say, "… and the Iron Will, are here to stay, and we welcome any man, woman or child who wants freedom, and to stand against slavery and oppression!"

To be honest, I had been hoping for cheers, but it was a half-hearted response at best.

"To the ship!" I announced, pointing to the Iron Will. It was about time she started undergoing her repairs.

We broke up into teams. Some of the workers began assessing the damage, sketching plans for repairs. Others scoured the ship for usable material and parts. Marina and Guy took charge of organising resources and manpower, ensuring that every task was manned and every worker was well-equipped.

I watched them all, feeling a swell of pride. We were a motley crew, a blend of backgrounds and experiences. But we shared a common purpose. We were united by the will to survive, to build something meaningful from the wreckage of our pasts.

And so, we began. Each day, we toiled under the sun, our bodies slick with sweat and grime. The work was hard, often backbreaking, but no one complained. Every evening, we'd gather around the fire, sharing stories of the day's progress and challenges.

Despite the hard work, the mood was upbeat, hopeful. We were creating something together. We were not just rebuilding a ship. We were creating a symbol, a testament to our collective strength and resilience.

As the days turned into weeks, the Iron Will began to take shape again. The hull was repaired, the crushed parts replaced with strong, new timber. The shredded sails were replaced with fresh ones, crafted from the robust fibres of the local flora. Bit by bit, piece by piece, the Iron Will was reborn.

On the day that the last plank was nailed into place, a cheer rose from the settlement. I stood at the helm, looking out over the people who had helped make this dream a reality. Their faces were flushed with exhaustion, but their eyes were shining with pride and joy.

"She's finally home," I murmured to myself, my hand caressing the smooth wood of the helm. "She's finally home."

"What do you think, Marcus?" Marina asked. "As good as you remember?"

I looked at Marina, a grin spreading across my face. "Better," I said. "She's stronger. We're stronger."

Marina clapped a hand on my shoulder, a proud smile on her face. "We sure are," she agreed. "The Iron Will has returned, and with it, our will to shape a new world."

And as I looked around, I could see that our vision for Atlantis was beginning to take shape too. All around us, the once desolate settlement was transformed into a vibrant community. Homes had been built, patches of land were being cultivated, and the cheerful sounds of children playing echoed throughout the settlement.

It wasn't just a ship and a settlement anymore. It was a symbol of freedom and a beacon of hope, shining out in a world once dominated by the tyranny of the Caretaker.

"I remember, when I was young," I started, looking at the bustling scene in front of us, "the stories they used to tell about Atlantis, the city beneath the waves, the city that was more advanced than anything else in its time, a city of dreams and promise. And now, Atlantis has risen again," I continued, "not beneath the waves, but from the ruins of a decimated world. We are the new Atlantis, a beacon of progress and freedom in a world once lost."

Marina was quiet, gazing at our people working together in harmony, each contributing in their own way to the rebuilding of our new world.

"Atlantis was a settlement where you were from? Did you live there?" she asked softly.

"No, no. Atlantis wasn't a settlement where I was from," I replied, laughing softly at the misunderstanding. "It's a legend, a myth from ancient times. It was said to be an advanced civilisation that sank beneath the sea in a single day and night of catastrophe. Some people believed it was a real place, while others thought it was just a story to teach moral lessons."

I looked out across our bustling settlement, the people working together to create something new and beautiful from the ashes of the old world. "But what's important is the idea of Atlantis, what it represented. A place of wisdom, of advanced knowledge, of a society that was more enlightened and just. That's what we're trying to build here."

Marina nodded thoughtfully, her gaze focused on the horizon. "A society that's more enlightened and just... I like the sound of that."

"Me too," I agreed, wrapping an arm around her shoulders. "That's why we're here. To build that society, to create a new Atlantis."

For a moment, we just stood there in silence, watching as our people continued their work. The sun was setting, casting a warm, golden light over everything. It was a scene of hope, of determination, and of resilience.

"But where did you come from then?" Marina asked. I could tell that she didn't want to ask the question in case I was upset by it, but I didn't mind really; there was only once place I ever thought of as home: The Iron Will. Well, that was before my new Atlantis had appeared that was.

"I was born in a place not unlike this world," I began, remembering the grand estates and cruel practices of my early life. "I was the son of a wealthy lord, and we owned many people who worked for us. Slaves," I added, seeing Marina's puzzled look. "It was common back there; people were traded like objects and although it wasn't in the pursuit of power, like the Entropics, the result was the same. My father was a harsh man, a man who valued power and wealth above all else. I was supposed to be his successor, to carry on his legacy. But I didn't want that. I didn't want to be a part of a system that took away people's freedom, their dignity."

I paused, taking a deep breath as I recalled the defining moment of my life. "One of those slaves was my friend. His name was George. He was killed by my father as an example to the others... and me. That's when I knew I had to leave, to find a different life. I ran away when I was just ten, stowed away on a pirate ship. The Captain became a kind of father to me, taught me about life on the sea, about freedom and friendship. When that ship was sunk by the Royal Navy, I was just eighteen, but I set out to gather a crew of my own. Friends from the last ship, people I met in towns and ports... we came together, stole a ship that was still under construction, and named it the Iron Will. That ship, and the crew I shared it with, was my first true home. But now... now this is home. Atlantis. A place where we're free to be who we want to be, where no one owns anyone else, where we can build something better."

I turned to Marina, my eyes meeting hers. "That's my past, Marina. And it's why I'm here, why I'm doing all this. I never want anyone else to go through what George did, or any other slave for that matter. My whole life I worked to free people from their shackles and this place has taught me that it doesn't matter who you are, where you're from… everybody deserves to be free. I want to create a world where people are free, where they're safe."

Marina was quiet for a moment, absorbing my words. Then, she reached out, placing her hand over mine. "And that's why we're here with you, Marcus," she said, her voice firm. "We believe in you, and in this dream of yours. Atlantis... it's not just a place. It's a promise of a better future. And we're going to help you spread that word."

Chapter 23 – The Future

A thought had occurred to me after I'd spoken to Marina about my past. It was that the kids, although resourceful, strong and resilient, had no form of schooling. Of course, they had their inherited memories and skills from the Caretaker and his genetic experiments – they were clones after all – but if they wanted to break out on their own and survive to lead long lives in this world, I was sure that I had things I could teach them. Especially once they were free of the Caretaker's dominance.

"I want the kids to have a school," I announced to Marina through a mouthful of mushrooms. I hadn't got around to actually liking the slimy things yet, but Marina and Guy simply insisted that I eat them every day. I think it was their way of having a practical joke, so I didn't begrudge them their little game.

"What?" Marina asked.

"A school," I repeated, setting down my fork. "They have the skills and memories they inherited from the Caretaker, but there's so much more to learn. Things that aren't about survival or fighting, things that are about living. About understanding the world around them, about how to think for themselves, making their own choices. They deserve that."

Marina was quiet for a moment, considering my words. "You're right," she finally said. "They're not just fighters or workers. They're kids. They should have the chance to learn, to grow." She looked at me, her eyes serious. "But how do we do it? Neither of us are teachers."

"We don't have to be," I replied, shaking my head. "I had teachers when I was younger, and we both know things about the real world, right?"

"Right," Marina agreed, but still looked unsure. "But it's not the same thing, is it? Teaching is a skill, just like anything else."

"True, but if we think about it, we're already teaching them every day," I said, gesturing at the bustling settlement around us. "Every time we teach them a new skill, every time we talk about our past or discuss ideas for the future, we're teaching them. We just need to formalise it a bit, give them a more rounded understanding of the world."

Marina frowned, deep in thought. "Maybe you're right. We've already been teaching them so much, just by being here and living with them. And I bet there's still a lot we could learn from them, too, if we just took the time to listen."

She looked at me, a new determination in her eyes. "Okay, let's do it. Let's set up a school. It doesn't need to be anything too fancy. Just a place where we can gather to share knowledge. We'll figure it out as we go."

I nodded, feeling a warm sense of satisfaction. "That's the spirit. We'll start with the basics, and we'll build on it. There's no limit to what we can achieve if we work together. These kids are the future of this world, Marina," I reminded her. "And the more people we save, the bigger this place is going to get. I want Atlantis to give every one of its citizens the best chance they can get."

"You're right, Marcus," she said, her eyes lighting up. "These children aren't just our responsibility; they're our hope for a brighter future."

She started to pace, her mind clearly whirling with ideas. "We need to provide them with a broader education. Not just how to survive, but how to live. How to think critically, to solve problems. To create and innovate. We need to teach them about the history of this world, and the lessons we've learned."

I nodded, impressed by her passion. "Exactly. And we also need to teach them about compassion, about fairness and justice. We want to create a world that's different from what they've known before. A world where everyone has the opportunity to thrive, no matter their origins."

Marina stopped pacing and looked at me, a small smile tugging at her lips. "That sounds like a world I want to be a part of."

"Then let's make it happen," I said, "But first, I need to eat something that isn't god damn mushrooms. I know I've seen the rest of you eat something else around here…"

"No," Marina said. "First, why don't we have a little practice session? It's been a while and I feel like with the settlement growing, our chances of being found are going to get higher and higher. I don't want to be caught out unprepared." Then she added thoughtfully, "and maybe the kids can start building things to defend ourselves with too, like that giant crossbow thing."

"The ballista," I couldn't help but correct. "And you're right. We need to do whatever we can to prepare everyone. And we also need to think about how to let this world know that there's another choice, somewhere safe to go."

"Yeah yeah," Marina replied sarcastically, then took a hold of my arm and pulled me into a punch, which I swiftly ducked under. "Let's fight!" she announced.

I grinned at her enthusiasm. It was infectious. Marina was always full of life, full of energy. It was one of the things I admired about her.

"Alright, alright," I said, raising my hands in a defensive position. "Just remember, you asked for it."

Our first moves were cautious, each of us testing the other's defences. Marina lunged at me, trying to catch me off guard with her speed, but I was ready for her. I stepped back, avoiding her strike and retaliating with a swift punch of my own. But she dodged my attack, a grin spreading across her face.

"You're going to have to do better than that, Marcus," she taunted, dancing lightly on her feet as she prepared for her next attack.

She lunged again, this time aiming a kick at my midsection. I blocked it with my arm, feeling the impact reverberate through my body. Marina was strong, no doubt about it, but something felt... different. I felt lighter, more agile. My movements were more fluid, my reactions quicker.

With a swift counterattack of my own, I aimed a punch at her stomach, pulling back at the last moment to reduce the impact. But Marina wasn't there. She'd moved, her agility matching mine. I spun on my heel, tracking her movement, and found her behind me, a look of surprise on her face.

"You're faster," she said, eyes wide.

"I... I don't know," I replied, equally surprised. "I feel... different. Stronger too."

And I did. I could feel it coursing through me, a raw, potent energy. It was as if I had tapped into a wellspring of power that had been dormant within me. It was exhilarating, empowering. I felt invincible. Had I always been like this, or had something changed?

With a newfound confidence, I lunged at Marina, my movements this time a blur. She tried to dodge, but I was faster. I landed a gentle hit on her shoulder, pulling back before I could do any real damage.

Marina stepped back, her eyes wide with shock. "Marcus," she said, panting slightly. "That was... incredible. I've never seen you move so fast. And you hurt me!"

I looked at her, my heart pounding in my chest. I couldn't explain it, but I knew one thing for sure: I was stronger than I had ever been before.

"Sorry, Marina," I apologised genuinely. "I guess I don't know my own strength."

Marina simply nodded, a touch of awe in her eyes, but quickly replaced it with a determined spark. "Again," she ordered.

I blinked in surprise, but I respected her too much to question her decision. The next battle was a whirlwind of rapid-fire movements and reflexive dodges. I was faster, I was stronger, but Marina was every bit the experienced fighter she'd needed to be to keep just out of my reach. She adjusted to the change in our dynamic quickly, anticipating my moves with a keen eye and retaliating with swift, calculated strikes of her own.

"I guess we're even now," she teased, dodging another of my attacks with a graceful spin.

"You wish," I retorted, a smirk playing at the corners of my mouth. Our banter added a light-hearted element to the intensity of our fight. I ducked under her incoming punch, retaliating with a swift, gentle tap to her side.

"I've been going easy on you."

And the truth was, I had been.

I dodged another of Marina's lunges, though this time I landed a fist on the back of her shoulder before she could move herself out of the way. It was the first time I'd actually tried to use whatever this newfound speed was, and it didn't disappoint.

"Okay, okay, you're still the better fighter," she admitted with a playful roll of her eyes, "For now." Her grin was infectious, and I found myself laughing despite the gravity of our situation.

Despite my surprise at my newfound abilities, I was already beginning to feel a sense of control. Every movement that followed felt calculated, every punch and kick precise. It was as if my body had awoken from a long slumber, embracing its potential with a newfound vigour.

Marina was readying for another strike, her eyes focused on my every movement. But I was already two steps ahead. As her punch sailed towards me, I grabbed hold of her arm with a swift motion. Using her momentum against her, I ducked under her arm and rolled forward, pulling her along with me.

Our bodies were a blur as we tumbled on the ground, a cloud of dust rising around us. In the blink of an eye, we had swapped positions. Marina found herself flat on her back, blinking up at me in surprise as I held her arm firm, effectively pinning her to the ground.

The fight was over.

I stood, offering her a hand to help her up. Marina grabbed it, pulling herself to her feet with a grunt. She was panting heavily, her face flushed from the exertion. But her eyes... her eyes were gleaming with both respect and excitement.

"That was... incredible, Marcus," she breathed, brushing off the dust from her clothes. "I've never seen anyone move that fast. You've got a real gift."

"I suppose I do," I replied, unable to hide the surprise in my voice. There was a time when I would've brushed off such a compliment. But now... now I was beginning to believe it myself.

Marina looked at me, her eyes serious. "Don't underestimate this, Marcus," she said. "You're strong. You're fast. You're a natural leader. And you've got a good heart. Don't ever forget that."

"Don't listen to any of that crap!" Guy's voice met my ears and I turned to see the young boy punching a fist into his open palm. "I beat you before, and I'll beat you again!"

Of course, the boy was only young, and not particularly stocky or anything but he was right, the last time we trained, he'd bested me. If I'd have known that he'd been genetically enhanced and given inherited memories at the time, then perhaps the thought of it would've hurt a little less.

Marina chuckled beside me, her gaze filled with amusement as she watched the determined youngster. "Go easy on him, Guy," she teased, before sauntering off to the side to watch the spectacle.

Guy wasted no time, lunging at me with a flurry of fists. I nimbly sidestepped each punch, weaving my body with the rhythm of his attacks, using my newfound speed and agility to effortlessly evade him.

Unlike my match with Marina, I made no move to strike back. I simply parried and defended, allowing Guy to use up his energy as he attempted to land a hit. The sparring match quickly turned into a cat-and-mouse game, with Guy growing increasingly frustrated with each passing minute.

"Stand still!" He grumbled, throwing a wild haymaker that I easily juked beside. I couldn't help but smirk at his frustrated expression. He was a skilled fighter for his age, but his inexperience was clear in his reckless attacks.

Instead of striking back, I chose to coach him. "Focus, Guy. You're swinging too wide. Keep your punches tighter, and don't forget to breathe."

He gave me a frustrated scowl but took my advice to heart, his punches becoming more controlled as he aimed them at me. Despite his stubbornness, he was a quick learner. Each round of attacks was more calculated, his punches coming faster and sharper.

Yet, I continued to dodge and parry, my movements fluid and graceful. I could see the fatigue starting to set in, his punches losing some of their initial fervour. But his determination was admirable, and he refused to give up, throwing punch after punch despite his exhaustion.

Finally, after what felt like hours, Guy's movements slowed considerably. His breathing was ragged, sweat trickling down his forehead as he took a step back, panting heavily.

"You're... you're not even... tired..." He huffed, throwing me a glare that would have been intimidating if it wasn't for his heaving chest and flushed cheeks.

"Not this time," I said gently, keeping my stance relaxed. There was no gloating, no pride. Just a calm understanding that this was all part of his learning process. "You did well, Guy. Remember, it's not always about landing the hit. Sometimes, it's about knowing when to conserve your energy and when to strike."

"But seriously, I don't know what's happened to me… I feel amazing!" I said with a smile.

Guy, now bent over at the waist and panting couldn't help himself. "It's the mushroom you great idiot! We've been crunching Cores up into them for weeks now and you ain't ever noticed!"

"GUY!" Marina scowled. "We said we weren't going to tell him until he figured it out on his own!"

"WHAT?" I practically screamed. "That's why no one else has been eating them and what, you just wanted to experiment on me like some… some lab rat?"

I was incredulous, my mind racing to process the information. The strange bouts of energy, the speed, the strength... it all started to make sense now. But the fact that they had been secretly feeding me this substance without my knowledge... it stung.

"Marcus..." Marina started, her tone apologetic, but I wasn't ready to hear it.

"No, Marina," I cut her off, my voice icy. I felt a swell of betrayal wash over me. We were supposed to be a team, a family, but they had kept me in the dark, using me for some experimental purpose.

"I can't believe you'd do this to me," I said, my words heavy with disappointment. I turned away from them, feeling the need for space to process everything.

In the silence that followed, I could hear Guy's heavy breathing slowly become more regular, and the rustling of Marina's feet as she undoubtedly exchanged worried glances with the others.

Feeling a potent mixture of anger, hurt, and confusion, I walked away from the training area. Despite the incredible feeling of power still coursing through me, the bitter taste of betrayal was hard to swallow.

I had a lot to think about. Trust had been broken, and whether it could be mended... that was something I'd have to figure out.

I walked away from the settlement until I reached the forest and took a good few steps into the vegetation before I placed my back against one of the trees and slid down to the ground. I placed my hands on my face and realised that my eyes were wet with angry tears. How could they have done this? Wasn't I their friend? And they what? Just wanted to use me to see if they could make some weapon to fight off the Entropics? The Caretaker?

As I sat there, lost in my thoughts, I heard a rustling nearby. I looked up to see Yari appear from wherever she had been, her projection as bright as ever, standing a few feet away.

"Marcus," she began to say softly through our mental link. "May I sit with you?"

"Fine," I grumbled, not really in the mood for company but not wanting to chase her away either. After all, she hadn't been a part of this.

She flapped her wings and leapt a few feet into the air, taking a perch on my shoulder. There was silence for a moment before she spoke again.

"I'm sorry, Marcus," she said, her voice almost a whisper. "They should have told you from the beginning. I know how it must feel…"

I snorted derisively, my anger flaring up again. "You think?"

"Yes, I do. It was wrong of them to keep this from you, especially considering what it could do."

"So why would they do it, then?" I shot back, my voice laced with bitterness. "Do they not care if I just died? If I went away?"

I could tell that Yari was uncomfortable, that she needed to say something but that it could hurt my feelings. I didn't encourage her, but she spoke anyway. "I suppose they were curious… to see how the Cores could affect you. Maybe they hoped they could give us an edge against our enemies… against the Caretaker…."

"That doesn't make it right," I spat.

"No, it doesn't," she agreed. "But Marcus, understand this. They didn't do it out of malice or desire to control you. They did it because they thought it could be beneficial, for all of us."

"Beneficial to turn me into some... some super soldier?" I spat, my anger giving way to hurt. "Just point me at the enemy and let me attack?"

Yari looked at me, the tone sent along our mental connection serious. "Not a soldier, Marcus, but a protector. A survivor. We all need to be as strong as we can be in these times. It doesn't justify what they did, but it was done with good intentions."

I was quiet, taking in her words. They did nothing to quell the betrayal I felt, but it gave me a different perspective to consider. Maybe they had meant well, in their own misguided way.

Yari placed her head softly down onto my shoulder. I couldn't feel the physical touch, but the thought was there. "Marcus, we're a family. We make mistakes, yes, but we also learn from them."

I sat in silence for a moment, trying to arrange my thoughts, then something occurred to me.

"Yari, did you know what they were doing?"

Yari was silent for a long moment and in truth, that told me everything I needed to know.

"Not at first..." she replied slowly. "I could feel the power enter your body and the changes that were being made. I thought you were doing it at first, ingesting more of the Cores. Then I saw them later, crushing the Cores up and giving you the food. You didn't seem apprehensive about it at the time, so I didn't want to ruin what was a good thing... I'm sorry Marcus. I betrayed you."

"No," I said, my voice coming out choked. I couldn't believe what I was hearing. "No, Yari. You wouldn't... You couldn't..."

There was a lump in my throat, making it hard to speak. Even Yari... Even Yari had known.

"I should have told you, Marcus," she said, her mental tone heavy with regret. "I know it now. I should have told you the moment I found out. I... I just thought it was for the best."

"For the best?" I echoed, laughing bitterly. "For the best? Yari, how could keeping this from me possibly be for the best? How could any of this be for the best?"

"I... I don't know, Marcus," Yari admitted, her mental voice trembling. "I thought... maybe if the Cores could make you stronger, they could help you protect yourself... help us protect each other. I didn't think... I didn't realise... You haven't done anything since you've freed yourself from the mines Marcus!" Yari's tone changed to a much more defensive stance. "The children were all free anyway and the Sylph helped you escape! We need to fight the Caretaker and unless you get stronger I don't know if there is anyone else that can do it!"

My mind was a whirl of emotion: confusion, hurt, betrayal. But at the core of it all was a deep-seated sadness. I felt as if I'd lost something precious, something I'd never be able to get back. Trust. But beyond that too, I knew that what Yari was saying was true. I hadn't done anything.

"I trusted you, Yari," I said, my voice barely a whisper. "Out of everyone, I trusted you."

"I know," Yari said, her mental voice again filled with a sorrow that mirrored my own. "And I failed you. I failed to protect you, not from physical danger, but from the betrayal of those you considered family. And for that... I am truly sorry, Marcus."

I sat in silence. The sting of betrayal was still fresh, too fresh for me to consider forgiveness. And yet...

I looked at Yari, the familiar golden glow that surrounded her. She had made a mistake, a terrible one, yes. But she had also been there for me, through thick and thin, ever since the day we had formed our connection. She had been my friend, my confidante, my support. Could I really cut her off for this one mistake?

"I... I need some time, Yari," I said finally, my voice hoarse. "I need some time to think."

"Of course, Marcus," she replied softly. "Take all the time you need. I'll be here when you're ready."

With that, she took off from my shoulder and disappeared into the sky, leaving me alone with my thoughts. As I sat there in silence, the full weight of the day's revelations pressing down on me, I knew one thing for certain.

I was going to do something. I had to.

Chapter 24 – Make a Difference

I sat for a long time before I felt the need to move. The hurt and betrayal didn't leave my system and I continued to feel used. Had all of this simply been an act? Had Marina pretended to be my friend all this time just so that she could turn me into something useful for her and her people? The thought alone made me feel sick to my stomach.

But Yari's admission had surprised me. She was supposed to be a part of me, linked to my consciousness and yes she was right that the Sylphs had helped me, but without me being there, without our persuading, they would still be at the mercy of the Caretaker, or perhaps even worse: bonded for life with a newly of-age Selari.

I thought about my role in this world for a long time. A stranger, but also what I truly believed that I had been all this time, even if I hadn't really achieved anything I had set out to do: a beacon of hope. Everyone and everything I had encountered had been capable, and when given a little ray of hope, it allowed them to achieve what they wanted on their own, without help from some Core-enhanced soldier.

And then it hit me. That was exactly what I needed to do: give the Selari and the Sylph alike hope that change will come, but also the knowledge that it won't just be handed out; change is taken by those deserving of it, those who strive to make a difference.

With that revelation, I stood up, brushing the dirt from my trousers. The feelings of betrayal and hurt were still there, but there was also a new thought process along with it. I had a purpose, a clear vision of what needed to be done. And with that, I started to walk back towards my settlement.

As I neared, I saw Marina. Her gaze met mine, her eyes filled with guilt and regret. She opened her mouth to speak, but I held up my hand, stopping her. I didn't need apologies, not now. There was work to do.

Without a word, I passed by her, heading towards the centre of the settlement. A glance to my left showed Guy attempting to make himself scarce. The guilt was written on his face too.

"Yari," I called out mentally, and she appeared beside me, her ethereal form glowing faintly. "Gather the Sylphs. I have a task for them."

Marina tried to approach me again, but I kept moving, not giving her the satisfaction of my attention. Right now, it was the Sylphs that were crucial to my plan.

Within moments, the settlement was filled with the faintly glowing figures of the Sylphs, all of their eyes focused on me. I could feel their curiosity, their anticipation, their willingness to help.

"Listen to me, all of you," I began speaking and mentally told Yari to relay my orders to the birds in their own manner of speaking. "We've freed you from the Caretaker, but now there is a greater task. I need you to spread a message, far and wide. To every Selari, every child and every Sylph you encounter."

"Wait," I paused, turning to Yari. "Can the Sylphs even communicate with the Selari?"

Yari hesitated before answering, "On a basic level, yes. They can relay emotions, ideas... rudimentary concepts."

"Good. Then they need to spread hope. The idea of a home... Atlantis, our settlement here. This is a place of refuge, of freedom. It is here that we will stand against the Entropics. Here, where we will reclaim our homes, our lives. Here where we will build and rebuild, bigger and better than this world has ever seen."

The Sylphs all watched me, their eyes wide and shining. I could feel their resolve, their willingness to help, their desperation to do something, anything, to fight back.

"Go," I told them. "Spread the word. Let everyone know that we're here, that we're fighting. Let them know there is hope."

One by one, the Sylphs rose into the air, their beautiful forms disappearing into the sky, off to fulfil their mission.

I watched them go, feeling a strange sense of satisfaction. I may not have had control over my own circumstances, but I had just given everyone else a chance to control theirs.

I wasn't a weapon. I was a beacon. And I would continue to shine, no matter what.

"I'm going to stay in the Iron Will for a while," I announced. It was for Marina's benefit more than anyone else's; in truth, I doubted anyone cared if I slept on the ship or in the settlement, but I wanted her to know more than anyone else how hurt I felt.

I turned on my heel and strode away from the settlement, heading towards the place I had once considered my home: The Iron Will. It lay not too far away, towering beside our newly finished wooden wall, an impressive spectacle. It had been carefully restored, its tall masts reaching for the sky, sails neatly folded. Of course not that they were needed on a vessel never to sail the high seas again, but they'd been restored nonetheless, a small act that made me smile.

As I approached the makeshift boarding ramp onto my ship, I ran my hands over the new wood, taking in the smooth, gleaming surface. The salty smell of the ocean clung to it, despite never having been submerged in the water.

The intricate carvings on the exterior of the hull were testament to the skill of the Selari who had rebuilt the ship. Every inch of the Iron Will was proof of the hard work and dedication that went into our home, the very spirit of Atlantis.

I climbed aboard, my footsteps echoing through the silence. It felt almost like walking through a ghost ship, so still and quiet. But the gleaming floors, walls and polished cannons served as a reminder that this ship was far from a relic of the past; it was a symbol of hope, of defiance.

I passed by the rows of gleaming black iron cannons, each one restored to its full glory. The storehouse below deck was a sight to behold, filled to the brim with cannonballs and cutlasses. No pistols, unfortunately, but enough weaponry to hold our own should the need arise. Almost instinctively ,I took one of the myriad of cutlasses and tucked it into my belt. I always felt naked without one.

I wandered aimlessly through the ship for a while before I found myself in front of the Captain's quarters. The polished brass handle seemed to gleam invitingly. With a deep breath, I pushed the door open and stepped inside.

The room was just as I remembered it, save for the distinct lack of the sea's continuous sway. My chair, the one I used to sit on while resting or planning was there, as if waiting for my return.

I walked over and sank into it, the familiar creak of the wood beneath me oddly comforting. I allowed my eyes to drift shut, my senses heightening as I focused on the smell of the ocean that lingered in the room. I could almost hear the gulls squawking, the waves crashing against the hull of the ship and the soothing rocking of the tides.

A bitter smile tugged at my lips. It was here that it had all begun. The confusion, the fear, the feeling of being utterly lost. But it was also here that I had found purpose, companionship... and betrayal.

I was not the same man who had sailed on this ship all those months ago. I was stronger, both physically and mentally. But the hurt was still fresh, the sting of betrayal still a sharp pain.

I shook my head, banishing the thoughts. There was no room for regret or sorrow now. There was work to be done. The beacon of hope had been lit, and it was my responsibility to ensure it never dimmed.

The silence in the room became my companion as I opened drawers, pulled out almost entirely ruined maps, charts, and relics, but they held no interest for me, even if they hadn't been terribly water damaged. It was like I was looking for something, an answer perhaps, but what the question was, I didn't know.

After what seemed like an eternity, I pulled open one last drawer. My breath caught. In the dim light of the room, a single gold coin gleamed from within. It was one of the Sirens, the magic token that had brought me, and presumably the Iron Will, along with her crew, to this strange new world.

I reached in and pulled it out, the cool metal sending shivers up my spine. The intricate design was unmistakable. This was the item that had caused the crew of the Iron Will to mutiny. The item that had ripped my old life away from me.

The beauty and mystery of the coin mirrored the world around me from when I first arrived here.

With a thumb, I began to trace the outlines of the engravings on the coin as I had done so before. It would be so easy to activate the Siren, to let the beautiful, haunting song fill the air and pull me back home - well if that's how it worked anyway. Back to a world I knew, back to a place where I didn't have to fight for survival, where I wasn't constantly in danger, where I hadn't been betrayed.

Though that's how I'd chosen to live my life aboard the Iron Will, wasn't it? Constantly fighting for the little guy, against danger and oppression.

The thought of leaving this place was tempting, almost intoxicating. But as quickly as it had come, I pushed it away. I couldn't abandon this world, not now. Not when there were so many counting on me, not when there was so much at stake.

I clenched my hand around the coin, feeling its edges dig into my palm. This was a reminder, a reminder of why I was here, of what I was fighting for. I had a purpose, a duty to fulfil. I couldn't let personal feelings or my own desires cloud my judgement.

Slowly, I unclenched my hand, looking at the coin one last time before slipping it into my pocket. It would stay there, a token from another world, a beacon from my past.

My past, my present, my future... they were all tangled in a complicated web. I couldn't change the past, I couldn't predict the future, but at least I could control my present.

I sat back in my chair, my eyes staring blankly at the ruined charts and maps spread across the table. The Sylphs were spreading the word, Atlantis was being fortified, and slowly but surely, we were becoming a force to be reckoned with out there. These things before me were relics of the past and they had no use anymore, so I bundled them up into one big pile and pushed them to a corner of the room.

Just as I was about to doze off, a soft touch echoed in my mind, a sensation like a whispering wind that was distinctly familiar. It was Yari. Her voice echoed softly in my head, gentle and concerned. "Are you okay?"

"I'm okay, Yari. I just... I need some time," I replied, pushing a soft reassurance through our link. I felt her mental nod of understanding before the connection dimmed, leaving me alone with my thoughts.

Sinking into the comfort of my old chair, I allowed the weariness of the day to pull me into a restless sleep. It wasn't the kind of restful sleep I yearned for, but it was enough to recharge me, and to prepare for whatever the new day would bring.

I was woken sometime later by a soft knocking sound. Blinking the sleep from my eyes, I rose from my chair, confusion drawing me to search for the source of the noise. It took me a moment to realise where I was and what I was doing – the familiar surroundings of the Captain's quarters almost had me believing that I'd been in some fevered dream this entire time. But I quickly shook that feeling off when I felt the weight of the Siren in my pocket.

Standing up, I shook my head and moved to investigate the knocking sound, and as I approached the boarding ramp outside the Captain's quarters, I realised it was coming from outside.

I walked down the ramp to find a wooden bowl filled with something that immediately made my mouth water. It wasn't mushrooms; it was something much better. A medley of grilled fruits and vegetables, their vibrant colours striking even in the dim light. The sweet scent of caramelised fruits mixed with the earthy aroma of charred vegetables wafted up, making my stomach growl in anticipation.

I picked up the bowl, the warmth seeping into my hands. I couldn't see anyone around, but I knew who it was from. Marina. Despite everything, she still cared. And this was her way of saying that she was sorry.

Sitting down on the ramp not wanting to waste time taking the meal back to my lair, I dug into the food. The fruits were soft, their sweetness amplified by the grilling process, complementing the slight bitterness of the charred vegetables. It was simple, but it was one of the best meals I'd had in as long as I could remember.

I savoured each bite, letting the flavours dance on my tongue. Each morsel was a small piece of solace, a momentary escape from the harsh reality I found myself in. I closed my eyes, basking in the comfort the food provided.

As I scraped the last bit of food from the bowl, a sense of warmth spread through me. It wasn't just the food, it was the gesture. Despite the pain, the hurt, there was still a sense of community, of care. I wasn't alone, and that thought brought a genuine smile to my face.

Once I finished, I set the bowl down, taking one last look around the silent ship. It was quiet still, but it was a comforting quiet. It was a quiet that promised the possibility of a better tomorrow.

But there was something missing. I hadn't realised it before or perhaps I chose to ignore it, but each time I'd eaten the mushrooms and the grated Cores that they had been infused with, it felt good, like I was stronger afterwards. With this though, the food had been delicious of course, but without the growth that the Cores had afforded me, eating it just felt kind of pointless. Empty.

So I did something about it. I swallowed the anger, the feeling of hurt and betrayal, and walked back into the settlement.

With a thunderous expression on my face, I held the empty bowl in my hand like it was a weapon as I stalked through the settlement. Marina was near the centre, talking with a group of children. When she saw me coming, she paused, her eyes widening slightly at my approach.

"Is this your idea of a joke?" I demanded, holding up the empty bowl. She blinked, taken aback by my sudden appearance and accusation. "Do you think I want your sympathy?"

Marina flinched at the venom in my voice. She looked around at the gathering crowd, then back at me. "I just wanted to... I thought you might…"

I threw the bowl to the ground with a clatter, the harsh sound echoing through the silence. The crowd gasped, some retreating back while others looked on with wide eyes.

"Because if you really want this place to become something more, if you really want to fight back against the Caretaker..." I paused for dramatic effect, "...then you better bring me out one of those Cores. So we can really see what they can do."

"But I... wait, what?" Marina paused in her defence. Then she saw the wide smile on my face.

"And here I thought you had been listening to me," I teased, seeing the spark of comprehension ignite in her eyes. My thunderous expression had turned into a smirk, the anger from earlier now completely gone.

A quiet ripple of laughter spread through the gathered crowd, relieving the tension that had been mounting since I arrived. Marina looked shocked, the silence stretching on for a moment. She seemed to have been prepared for an argument, for another round of heated words and accusations. She hadn't expected this.

"Okay, okay," Marina finally said, breaking into a reluctant smile. She shook her head, her earlier nervousness fading away. "You certainly know how to make a point, I'll give you that."

"The point, Marina," I responded, gesturing towards the crowd of awestruck Atlanteans who were now watching us with eager anticipation, "is that when you thought we needed to do more than just survive here... you were right. We need to make this world ours, just like we made the Iron Will ours. And to do that, we're going to need to use those Obsidian Cores, no matter how much it hurts me. But this time, I want to do it properly. I want us to do this together, as a team."

Marina's smile grew more confident as I spoke. She understood now, that our goals had been aligned. It wasn't just about the food or the simple comforts of life. It was about taking control of our destiny, about making this place a home. And to do that, we needed to unlock the power of the Obsidian Cores.

"Alright," Marina agreed, a sparkle of determination in her eyes. "Let's do it. Let's show this Caretaker what we're made of... uh… you're made of."

The crowd erupted into cheers, their expressions filled with a newfound hope and determination. Marina turned towards me, her eyes filled with gratitude and respect. Together, we would stand against the Caretaker, against the Entropics. We would make this world our own, not just survive, but thrive. But there would be no more secrets.

With a nod, Marina turned and headed towards one of the houses, presumably to retrieve an Obsidian Core. I couldn't help but smile as I watched her go, feeling a surge of hope. Maybe this crazy, upside-down world wasn't so bad after all. Maybe, just maybe, we could make something great out of it.

"Oh and as for the rest of you," I turned my attention to the kids and the Selari workers. They all turned their attention to me, but I could see in the milky white eyes of the workers that they weren't exactly listening to me. "I want you to start preparing for war. I want catapults, ballistae, spears, swords, anything you can think of that we might need, and I don't just mean to fight off the Entropics, I mean to keep ourselves safe for the long run. Just… do what you can, I trust you."

Chapter 25 – A Core Belief

I looked at the Obsidian Core in my hand for a long time. It was a deep, shining black and I could almost feel the energy that it contained. I knew that each time I had ingested the things, I had experienced more and more pain as my body had tried to deal with the power – and the last time, Yari had tried to deal with it herself on my behalf, and it'd put her out of action for a long time. This time, I knew that I had to man up, step up to the plate and do this for the good of Atlantis.

The Obsidian Core lay heavy in my palm, a tangible reminder of the responsibility we all shared. Its black surface reflected the light around us, its smoothness almost ethereal. This small piece of whatever it was held the potential for so much more, a force that could change everything.

I turned it over in my hand, staring at it with awe. Each time I had used these cores, I had felt my body grow stronger, capable of feats that I hadn't thought possible.

I took a deep breath, my gaze never leaving the Core. My crew, the Atlanteans, Marina... they were all counting on me. I couldn't let them down.

"And you can stop looking at me like that," I announced without taking my eyes off the Core. I could see just at the periphery of my vision that Marina was staring at me with wide eyes and a deep grimace. "It's just another Core, same as any other, same as the mushrooms," I said quietly but it was more for my benefit than anyone else's.

Marina didn't reply, but she made a definite effort to amend her expression.

With a resolute nod, I stood up, the Obsidian Core clutched tightly in my hand. "Alright, let's do this," I declared, my voice echoing around the settlement.

And then I placed the entire Core into my mouth.

I was afraid, there was no denying that. But as I looked around at the faces of my crew with the Core sat defiantly on my tongue, I felt a surge of determination that washed away the fear. This was more than just a personal journey; it was a chance to create a brighter future for everyone in this world.

The Obsidian Core was smooth and cold against my tongue as it had been the first time the Caretaker had once force-fed me one of them, but this time its weight wasn't strange and unwelcome. This was my choice, my power to wield, and I welcomed it.

Once more I could feel the power pulsing from the Core, filling my mouth with a tingling energy that was again both invigorating and terrifying. But this time I didn't try to spit it out, I let the Core sit on my tongue, doing exactly what it was supposed to do, its power transferring to me as it did its work.

The Core began to dissolve, once again its power seeping into my body.

I could feel the power spreading through my entire being in an instant, my veins growing white hot with unused power and energy. My muscles seized and relaxed in rapid succession, my vision blurred, and the world around me began to spin. Marina had once told me that nobody could use the Cores except the Entropics. But I had proven on so many occasions now that this simply wasn't the case; the Entropics weren't the top of the food chain in this world; I was.

Then the Core was gone, dissolved completely, and I was left staring at the wide eyes and open mouths of the Atlanteans.

"What?" I tried to say, but it was immediately clear that my ability to speak, or even move had been soundly removed from my control.

I watched Marina take a tentative step closer to me.

"Marcus… are you OK? Your skin… it's… glowing…" she said.

Again I tried to move to look down, but I couldn't. I was entirely paralysed. Though in hindsight, I would've preferred that to what came next.

An explosion of pain inside my chest

As I clutched the area above my heart as it tightened, a roar of pure agony erupted from my throat. It was unlike anything I'd ever experienced, worse than all the previous ingestions combined. I could feel the energy within me burning, tearing me apart from the inside out.

The last sound I heard before everything went black was Marina's desperate cry, her voice tinged with fear and distress. I couldn't respond, my world reduced to the overwhelming pain consuming my very being.

The darkness didn't bring relief. The energy within me kept lashing out, raw and powerful. It felt like my very cells were being broken down and reconstructed in rapid succession. I tried to fight it, tried to stay conscious, but the energy was too much. It was like trying to hold back a tidal wave with my bare hands.

And then, as suddenly as it had started, the pain receded. I was left in darkness, my body feeling strangely numb. I tried to move again, but it was as though I was suspended in space, my body refusing to respond to any of my commands.

Then something new filled my vision. It wasn't the dim light of Atlantis that greeted me. It was a universe filled with stars, galaxies, entire worlds that I hadn't known existed. I could see the strings of energy that connected everything, the bonds that held the universe together.

But then as quickly as they had appeared, they disappeared once more and my world was again filled with darkness. But I'd seen for a second. I'd known.

The darkness stretched on, a seemingly endless void. A sense of fear crept over me as time stretched on, and I couldn't tell if minutes or days had passed. I was stuck in a limbo, unable to move or speak, trapped within the confines of my own mind.

Then, something changed. I could feel a strange sensation coursing through my body, like my senses were being reawakened one by one. It was a gradual process, a slow reconnection with my physical self that was both overwhelming and relieving.

As my senses came back, so did my perception of my surroundings. There was a cool stillness around me, the feeling of rough material under my fingertips. A light flickered behind my closed eyelids, signalling that I was not in the total darkness I had been in before.

It was time to open my eyes, to return from the darkness. As my eyelids fluttered open, the world came back into focus. The flickering light I had sensed turned out to be the dim illumination of the sun rising outside of the room I was lying in. Marina's face loomed over me, a mix of relief and concern etched on her features. And then anger.

"Five days Marcus!" she punched my shoulder. "Five damn days!"

I wiped my forehead with my fingertips as though I was trying to coax my mind into understanding what the Selari woman was on about. And then I sat bolt upright.

If I had been paying attention, I would've noticed that Marina was rubbing her knuckles; apparently when she'd hit my shoulder, it'd hurt her.

"Are you OK?" I asked, gesturing to her hand.

"Am I OK?" Marina repeated. "Me?" she looked me up and down. "You're such an idiot!" she announced, threw her arms around me and I felt her cheeks wet with tears.

It was odd though, the weight of her body didn't feel right – like she was no heavier than a bird sitting on my shoulder.

And that reminded me.

"Yari?" I sent the question through our mental link. "Are you there?"

"Marcus," Yari's mental voice was a comforting balm, yet somehow filled with an undeniable power. "I'm here."

I smiled. But Marina and Guy looked shocked, their eyes wide. Then it hit me: They could hear Yari.

"I can hear her," Marina whispered in disbelief. She turned to me. "Is this the Obsidian Core's doing?"

"What? I asked in disbelief. Are you sure?"

"Yes, Marcus. I heard Yari, we both did," Marina said, her gaze moving over to Guy, who was slowly nodding in agreement. He looked so stunned and his face was pale. It seemed he too had heard Yari, and that meant the Cores had made a change, a big one.

"I... I don't understand," Guy stuttered. "How is this possible?"

"It must be the Core," I concluded aloud, letting the enormity of the situation sink in. Yari was no longer just a voice in my head, a creature linked solely to me. Through this new power, she could now communicate with everyone, and that was something that I honestly hadn't been expecting to ever happen. The implications were far-reaching and not something I could completely grasp just yet.

"How far do you think she can communicate for?" Marina asked.

"With Marcus it seems like the link is further than ever, I can feel it," Yari answered on her own behalf. "But for everyone else… I have to be very close. I get the feeling if I leave this room then you won't be able to hear me at all."

"I see," Marina said, her gaze distant as she processed this new information. "Well, we'll just have to test that theory later. For now, though..." Her eyes glinted with a familiar challenge. "You look like you've recovered, Marcus. How about a little sparring match?"

I grinned. "Are you sure you're ready to lose again?"

In response, Marina merely smirked and stepped back, giving me plenty of room to stand. Then she led me back outside to the place where we'd already sparred a number of times, and took up a ready stance.

"I have to warn you," I said with a cocky smirk. "I think the Cores have changed me a little more than the last time. I think… I think you're going to be surprised."

It was true that I'd been out of action for the best part of a week, but I didn't feel groggy or sluggish, I felt good. Really, really good.

Marina's gaze hardened, the playful banter not diminishing her focus. "We'll see about that."

Our match began quickly, the air around us charged with anticipation and many of the Selari kids pausing their tasks to watch as I miraculously felt well enough to fight even after being out for the last few days. This was a dance we had danced before, but now the music was faster, the rhythm more intense.

Marina moved first, lunging at me with an agility and speed that spoke volumes of her combat experience. She was a skilled fighter, a force to be reckoned with. But I was different now. Enhanced in a way that nobody had been expecting.

I sidestepped her lunge effortlessly, a blur of motion that even Marina's experienced eyes had trouble tracking. I could hear gasps from the kids as I moved behind her, a slight push to her back sending her stumbling forward.

Undeterred, Marina spun around, her fists raised in a defensive stance. She attacked again, a flurry of punches and kicks that would have overwhelmed any normal opponent. But I was no longer normal.

Each of her attacks were telegraphed in my heightened perception. The way her shoulders moved, the shifting of her weight, even the direction of her gaze. I dodged and parried her attacks as if I was dancing, turning what was meant to be a fight into an elaborate choreography. And I was fast. So much faster than I could've even imagined – but that speed was morphed into a perception of the world around me somehow moving slower than normal.

Then, I counterattacked.

My punch came out lightning-fast, too quick for Marina to fully dodge. She managed to deflect it slightly with her arm, but the force of it still sent her skidding backwards, her feet digging into the sandy ground to bring her to an eventual halt.

Marina stared at me, her chest heaving. Surprise and shock reflected in her eyes, but not defeat. She was a fighter, and I could see the resolve hardening in her gaze.

But before she could retaliate, Guy leapt into the field of battle and stood between me and Marina.

The young boy was small, but from our last few sparring matches, I knew that his own enhanced body was not to be underestimated.

I held out a hand and beckoned the pair of them to advance. They had nothing compared to my new power.

Guy was certainly stronger, but like Marina, he was no real match for me. I danced around his attacks as he lunged at me, my newfound abilities making it seem like I was in two places at once. He swung his fists, tried to grab me, but I was faster, ducking and weaving, my own parries a whirlwind of strikes that left him reeling. I was relentless, pressing my advantage, leaving Guy with no room to breathe. But I never hit him. It really didn't seem like the right thing to do.

Instead, as I had done so before, I used his own momentum against him, blocking his attacks and deflecting them in ways that took advantage of my strength. When he tried to use his strength to try to force me onto the defensive, I'd effortlessly slide around him, or turn the direction of his attacks around to send him sprawling to the ground.

In the meantime, Marina regrouped and lunged at me again, her mouth set in a grim line of determination. I could see her trying to anticipate my movements, to predict where I would be. But I was too fast, too unpredictable. One moment I was in front of her, the next I was to her side.

I watched her eyes widen in shock as I dodged her attacks, her arms and legs moving in a blur as she tried to land a hit. But it was to no avail. Where once she took pride in her speed and agility, it was all too clear now that she had nothing compared to me.

In a swift movement, I swept her legs from under her. As she fell, I caught her in mid-air, setting her gently on the ground before swiftly turning back to face Guy.

The young boy stared at me, his eyes wide. But I could still see the determination there, the unwillingness to back down. He came at me again, his moves more reserved than before. It was clear he was trying to formulate a new strategy, to find a way to counter my speed.

We engaged in this dance, our movements synchronised in the rhythm of combat. But no matter how hard Guy tried, no matter the combination of punches and kicks he threw my way, I was always one step ahead, parrying and redirecting his attacks, leaving him off-balance.

As we continued, I could see Marina starting to get up, brushing off the sand from her clothes. With a glint in her eyes, she once again joined Guy. Now, it was two against one again, and if they had any chance of getting anything out of this fight, then they needed to work together.

Marina and Guy sensed this, and worked in tandem, coordinating their attacks, trying to box me in. But it was like trying to catch smoke. I was everywhere and nowhere at once, a ghost that they couldn't pin down. Their punches met nothing but air, their kicks hitting only the empty space where I had been moments before.

Despite their efforts, neither of them could land a hit. Not a single one.

The frustration was clear on their faces, but so was their determination. They refused to back down, refused to admit defeat.

But in the end, it was pointless. Their efforts were commendable, but in the face of my enhanced abilities, they stood no chance.

After what seemed like an eternity of sparring, I finally decided to end it. In a swift, fluid motion, I swept both their feet out from under them at once. As they fell, I moved to catch them, setting them both gently on the ground before stepping back.

They lay there, panting heavily, their clothes stained with sweat, dirt and sand. There was a stunned silence from the crowd that had thickened, every pair of eyes wide in shock and awe. And in that moment, I knew without a doubt, I was not just a regular human anymore.

I stood there, panting slightly, but not from exhaustion. It was exhilaration that filled me, a sense of power and potential that was as intoxicating as it was terrifying.

But as I stood there the clear victor, I couldn't help but feel a pang of concern. These enhancements, this power... it was unnatural, unpredictable. I couldn't help but wonder what the cost would be in the end. But for now, I stood victorious.

For now, I was the top of the food chain. I was ready.

"Marcus, that was..." Marina started, sitting up and staring at me in awe, "That was incredible."

Guy, who was slowly pushing himself to his feet, let out a breathy chuckle. "He's not wrong. You're a completely different person. It's like... it's like you're something else."

I held out a hand, helping Guy up from the ground. "I'm still human, Just... a little different now. Stronger."

Marina too then accepted my hand, pulling herself to her feet and brushing the sand off her clothes. "No, not stronger, Marcus. You were faster. Faster than I've ever seen anything move before. Like... it was like you were a blur sometimes."

"Just like the Caretaker," I muttered. "But then... I do feel stronger, not just faster."

Looking down at my hands, I flexed them, feeling the raw power coursing through me, the heightened senses, speed, and strength... it was intoxicating. Yet, at the same time, it was terrifying. It felt like a heavy responsibility, a power that needed to be handled with extreme care.

The crowd of kids slowly began to disperse, returning to their duties, whispering amongst themselves, and casting glances my way. I could hear their whispered conversations, their awe and wonder, their fear.

But amongst the whispers, there was one voice that rang out clear and loud in my mind.

"Marcus," Yari's voice echoed in my thoughts. "You were amazing out there."

I smiled at her praise, feeling a warmth spread through me at her words. "Thanks, Yari. It's good to have you back."

"How strong do you think…" Marina said quietly, clearly not wanting to believe that I could have made so many improvements in such a short space of time.

"Test my strength?" I asked, raising an eyebrow as I turned to face her.

"Yes," she nodded. "Something more than sparring, something that can really give us an idea of what we're dealing with here."

I considered for a moment. I felt powerful, yes, but I also felt a certain sense of control, an innate understanding of my abilities. It was as if my body and mind had adapted, had evolved to accommodate the power coursing through me. "Alright," I agreed. "Let's test this."

We began to walk towards the edge of the Selari settlement, some of the others following behind us. The sun was low in the sky, casting long shadows across the ground and painting the sky in hues of orange and red. The air was crisp and cool, the taste of salt heavy on the tongue from the nearby sea.

Finally, we reached the cliff that overlooked the sea, the waves crashing against the rocks below. It was a sight I had seen many times before, yet now it held a new significance.

I bent down and picked up a stone, feeling the weight of it in my hand. "You want a demonstration of strength?" I asked Marina, my gaze shifting towards her.

Marina nodded, crossing her arms over her chest. "That's the idea."

I looked at the stone in my hand, then out at the endless expanse of water. I took a deep breath, and then, with all the strength I could muster, I cocked my arm back and launched the stone as far as I could.

It cut through the air like a bullet, the force of my throw sending it hurtling far and fast. It went so far that we lost sight of it, the stone disappearing into the distance, swallowed up by the sea and sky. The sound of it hitting the water never came.

There was a moment of stunned silence before Marina finally spoke. "That… that was…" She stumbled over her words, her gaze fixed on the point where the stone had disappeared.

"Incredible?" I finished for her with a huge grin on my face.

"Incredible doesn't begin to cover it," Marina murmured.

As we both stared out at the sea, I turned and walked back towards the settlement, leaving Marina to absorb the magnitude of what she had just witnessed.

And all the while, Yari's voice echoed in my mind. "Incredible, Marcus. Truly incredible."

My response was a simple nod. It was incredible. Terrifyingly so. Because with great power, comes great responsibility.

I sat in my little house alone. Marina had a lot to think about and by all accounts so did I. The time was soon approaching that I would have to use my new power to actually achieve something in this world.

But then...

"Yari," I announced through our mental link. "What's been happening in the settlement since I was out? Have you managed to find anything out whilst I've been practising?"

"Yes," Yari's voice came through, carrying a sense of urgency that put me on edge. "Something... interesting has happened. The Sylph have been doing their work, spreading the word of hope and safety as far as they could travel, and it seems that people are beginning to believe. Every day more and more people are arriving, searching for the place that promised them hope. And with the arrival of new Atlanteans and Sylph, the dynamics of the settlement are changing. It's... it's incredible, Marcus."

My heart raced at her words. That was certainly news. And it was exactly what I'd wanted. But how had I missed all of this when I'd been out in the settlement just now? Had I been so focused on what I was doing that I hadn't realised the changes that had been made?

"So the Sylph..." I said, my mind reeling with the implications.

"The Sylph have been invaluable," Yari continued. "They've helped expand the settlement, and they're still going. But..."

The pause was a sharp hook in my attention. "What is it, Yari?"

"I've overheard some conversations. Some of the new arrivals who are... uncertain about the direction we're taking. They're wary of what the Caretaker will do if he finds out about our increasing number, or of the rapid changes happening around them. I think they're afraid, Marcus. I think they hoped that the Caretaker would be removed as a threat sooner than this."

I sighed, running a hand through my hair. Fear could lead to division, to dissent. It had to be quashed.

"How many are there?" I asked. "How many have come in search of hope?

Yari paused for a moment, as if trying to calculate the exact number. "There are now over a hundred Atlanteans in the settlement, Marcus," she said finally. "And the number is growing every day."

I let out a low whistle, both astonishment and concern colouring my tone. "That's... that's more than I expected. And all because they heard about a place where they could be safe, where they could belong? They must be so desperate, so in need of help and a change in this world."

"Yes," Yari agreed, her voice tinged with sorrow. "They are desperate, Marcus. Desperate for safety, for hope, for a place where they don't have to hide who they are. And we've given them that. But now, they are afraid. They've found what they were looking for, but the threat of the Caretaker is still hanging over them."

The gravity of the situation hit me hard. I'd known that the Caretaker would be an issue, of course. But I hadn't realised how much fear he was still inspiring, even from afar.

"We need to address this," I said, determination clear in my voice. "We need to reassure them. To show them that the Caretaker can't harm them here, that this place is as safe as we can make it."

"Agreed," Yari said. "But how do you plan to do that, Marcus?"

"It's simple," I replied. "I'm going to kill the Caretaker."

Then I had a thought. "Can the settlement cater for that many people?" I had some experience in looking after a handful of people, but a hundred was a lot, and if we kept accepting more every day... "And are more still coming?" I asked.

"We're managing for now," Yari replied. "The new Selari children have been a huge help in expanding the settlement quickly, and we're making use of the natural resources in our surroundings as much as we can. But yes, more are still coming. If this continues, then Atlantis will be less of a settlement and more of a city in no time. And that's a risk in itself."

My heart thumped in my chest at her words. As wonderful as it was that our haven was growing, it was also terrifying to realise the responsibility we now carried.

"We're going to have to find a way to sustain this in the long run," I mused out loud. "We need to think about food, water, and housing. And we're going to need a system in place for decision-making, for conflict resolution, for... well, for everything."

"You don't need to worry," Yari said matter of factly. "The Selari... they're managing. The settlement is growing under their influence and so far it's been working very well. You just need to concentrate on that one thing…"

I nodded, grim foreboding seeping into every pore. "Yes. I do. The longer he's out there, the longer our people will live in fear. We need to eliminate that fear."

"But Marcus..." Yari's voice wavered for a moment, but she forced it steady. "Killing the Caretaker won't be easy. He's... he's so powerful. Are you sure you're ready for that? You saw what he was capable the last time you met him."

I opened the door to my shelter to the long, ominous shadows over the settlement, which I now took the time to appraise properly. "I'm not sure," I admitted. "But I'll do whatever it takes. For our people. For Atlantis. And if I die, Marina will carry on our resistance. This isn't all just about me."

Yari didn't respond, clearly not wanting to think about that outcome. When I had said the words, I had forgotten that if I did die, then Yari would go down with me. It was the way the Sylphs were bonded to their hosts. I didn't bring up the issue.

"Anyway," I said in a completely different tone. "It's about time we spoke with everyone, to put to bed any worries they might have, right?"

And with that, I walked through the open door and out into Atlantis. This time really seeing all of the changes that had been made.

I gathered everyone around the firepit in the centre of the settlement. It wasn't difficult in truth, most of the Atlanteans were already there, getting a hold of their usual meals. I stared at the faces around me, most of them just happy to have company, though I could see a lot of anxiety in a lot of them, and that was something that I wanted to pacify.

"OK, listen up," I announced loud enough for everyone to hear me. "Once, back when I was the Captain of the Iron Will, my crew and I landed in a place where we didn't know what was going to greet us. We had no choice. We were forced into docking outside of the normal places, the safe places... I won't go into detail why. Anyway, when we walked ashore, we were greeted by a group of native people who don't speak the same language as us... and we had a treasure chest of gold coins with us. We were all worried that what we had, these people were going to try to take from us. The situation was tense, and nobody really knew what was going to happen."

I noticed the slightest squeak from Yari as she recognised this as the very story that had led to me giving her her name.

"We had to trust each other, because if we didn't, it would mean a fight. And with our power and their numbers, a fight would've meant the loss of so many lives. Too many. So that's what we did. We trusted each other."

I paused for dramatic effect and took a deep breath.

"The natives gave us shelter, food, clothing and warmth, and asked for nothing in return. We had assumed the worst of them, and that was our mistake to make; to assume something of others never really works out. But eventually, we discovered that their settlements and communities were terrorised by some great beast. Something they couldn't seem to catch, as it worked in the night and when they tried to hunt it, they were killed. I made a promise to help them. If I didn't, the beast would keep taking from them, night by night, week by week until they'd eventually run out of the food they harvested."

I closed my eyes at the memory. It was not a pleasant one for me.

"We went out one night, the crew and I. We went looking for whatever this creature was and to help our new friends. We waited in the darkness, silent and alert. The tension was like a thick fog hanging over us. We had no idea what we would be up against - the natives described the beast as monstrous, huge, a being of nightmares. We were armed to our teeth with pistols and cutlasses, but that did nothing to quell the fear bubbling under our calm exteriors. We were in an unknown land, surrounded by unfamiliarity and uncertainty, and we were hunting an unknown creature."

I opened my eyes, glancing around at the crowd gathered around me. Their eyes were wide, their faces reflecting the fear, curiosity, and the anticipation I had felt that night.

"Hours passed, the darkness of the night turned to an eerie twilight. The stillness was broken by a rustling in the trees nearby. We steeled ourselves, weapons at the ready, as a group of shadowy figures emerged."

I paused for a moment, letting the suspense build again.

"They weren't monsters. They weren't beasts," I continued, my voice growing soft. "They were men, like me. Soldiers from a foreign land, who didn't speak our language. They'd been raiding the settlements, using the cover of night to steal and kill. They were the 'beast' the natives feared."

There was a collective gasp from the crowd.

"We fought them off. The fight was brutal and fierce, and we managed to kill most of them. The survivors fled. We let them go. We had defended our friends, and defeated the beast."

I saw relief in some eyes, and expressions of shock in others. This was not the story they were expecting, but it was important they heard it.

"We went back to the natives and told them the beast was defeated. That they were free. But we didn't tell them it was just men, soldiers like us. We didn't want to change them, make them fearful, suspicious. They were kind, hospitable people, and we wanted to keep it that way. It would do no good to spread a fear of men to these natives."

I cleared my throat, surveying the crowd once more.

"But there's more to the story," I said, my voice taking on a grave tone that caused any chatter to cease immediately.

"We eventually left that place, sailing off to continue our journey, our mission. But we didn't forget our friends. We didn't forget their kindness, their hospitality. So, a year later, we decided to visit them again."

My voice hitched as the painful memory resurfaced, my mind filled with the images of that fateful day. I swallowed hard, pushing through the pain. This was important. They needed to know.

"But when we returned, we found... destruction. Our friends, the natives, had been wiped out. Every single one of them, killed. Their homes burnt down to the ground. Their smiles, their laughter, their kindness... all gone."

Tears welled up in my eyes, but I blinked them away, my gaze firm on the crowd in front of me. "The soldiers we had fought off... they returned. They returned with more power, more men. And our friends... they didn't stand a chance."

The crowd was silent, the impact of my words hanging heavy in the air. "I realised then that we had left them vulnerable. By sparing those men, we had left our friends to be slaughtered. And I vowed... I vowed then that I would never again leave anyone to gain power unchecked. I would never again leave a job half done."

I could see the dawning understanding in their eyes, the realisation of why I was sharing this story.

"This is why we must stand against the Caretaker. This is why we are here. This is why I will fight for each and every one of you. We are not power-hungry warmongers, we simply want to survive, to live without fear, without constant threat. And we will. I promise you, we will. Not just because I say so, but because we all will it."

There was a pause, a silence that seemed to stretch on. Then slowly, one by one, the Atlanteans around the fire pit began to exhale. I could tell that they had understood now, and in their eyes, I could see trust. Trust and hope.

Chapter 26 – One of Many

Once the kids had all absorbed my story and had realised what the moral of it was, the new arrivals became far keener to show me what they'd managed to achieve in the time they'd been a part of Atlantis, and far less concerned for their future.

"Come and have a look at this!" one of the younger kids announced, practically bouncing up and down on the spot in anticipation of my attention.

"No look at this!" another cooed.

I followed the first child, grinning as I saw the enthusiasm in his eyes. Besides, if I didn't follow him I was worried that he was going to explode. When we reached a large clearing, my breath caught in my throat.

Lined up in front of me were several large, wooden structures, each one more formidable than the last. There were ballistae, powerful crossbows ready to launch large bolts far into the distance. Catapults, capable of flinging heavy objects over large distances stood tall and proud. The designs were intricate, efficient, their construction a testament to the ingenuity and skill of these mere children. I mean, I'd seen them use a ballista before but these… these were just something else.

I turned to look at the excited faces of the children, my heart swelling with pride. "You made these?" I asked, and they nodded eagerly. "These are incredible."

One of the older children, a boy with a serious expression and an intelligence in his eyes, spoke up. "We remembered," he said. "From the old times. We knew how to build these."

I knew what he was referring to - the genetic memory that the Atlanteans had inherited from their ancestors. It was amazing what they could recall when they put their minds to it.

"And these..." I began, gesturing towards the war machines, "these will be incredibly helpful in defending our home."

The kids beamed at the praise, their chests puffing out with pride. "We thought we could mount the ballistae on the towers, and the catapults on the walls," the older boy suggested. "They would give us a range advantage over anyone wanting to come close."

I nodded, impressed by their strategic thinking. "That's a great idea. We'll start implementing it right away. I'm proud of you all, this is outstanding work."

Their smiles grew wider, their eyes brighter. They had stepped up, used their skills and memories to contribute in a significant way. I felt a wave of affection for these children. They were brave, resourceful, and determined. I knew then that our settlement stood a real chance. We had the power, the knowledge, and most importantly, the will to defend our home, our family.

"Alright, let's get these mounted," I said, clapping my hands together. The kids cheered, their earlier fear forgotten in their excitement. The mood in the settlement had shifted and now there was a renewed sense of purpose and optimism.

As I helped them roll the first ballista towards its tower, I couldn't help but feel a sense of pride. We were strong. We were united. And we were ready to stand our ground, no matter what came our way.

After a few steps, I looked around at the kids and noticed something: I was the only one doing any pushing.

I stopped, putting my hands on my hips and turning to face the group of youngsters. They were all standing back, watching me with wide grins on their faces. There was a twinkle in their eyes that suggested they were holding back a secret.

"What's going on?" I asked, my gaze darting from one to the next. There was a hushed whisper that went through the crowd before the same older boy who had spoken earlier stepped forward.

"Well…" he kicked the floor. "When you push, it's like we don't help at all. You're… you're too strong."

I couldn't help but laugh, rubbing the back of my head sheepishly. "I guess I forgot my own strength there for a moment, didn't I? But this isn't just my job. It's our job, as a family."

They seemed taken aback by my words, their eyes wide and mouths slightly agape. I think, in that moment, they finally understood. We weren't just a group of survivors; we were a family, and we were in this together.

"Alright, let's do this the right way," I said, moving to the side of the ballista. "Everyone gather round, find a spot, and on my count, we'll push together."

The children moved quickly, finding places on the massive war machine.

Some of them barely reached the middle of the wheels, but they were determined to help. I watched with a soft smile as they jostled and giggled, their previous sombreness replaced with lively energy.

"Ready?" I asked, my voice booming above their chatter. A chorus of eager "Yes!" answered me. "Alright, one... two... three... Push!"

It didn't matter that I was barely touching the thing. The kids felt like they were helping, so they were happy.

Eventually the day dragged on and I felt myself helping less and less. I wasn't being an ass, it just seemed like when I did help, I just tender to take over and most of the time, the kids felt like they were of more use when they were doing things on their own.

They were little geniuses though. I had wondered how they were going to hoist the defensive war machines atop the towers and walls, but with a series of makeshift winches and cranes, they managed it, and it made me so proud.

Dinner time came around quickly again and I took the time to chat to as many of the Atlanteans as I could. Predictably, the adult workers from the mine came, took their food, ate, then left and went to sleep. I felt bad for them, but it was all they knew, and there wasn't anything else I could do for them. Their Sylphs had bonded for life and the Selari's bodies had reacted to the constant punishment-reward cycle they'd been put through for far too long. I did wonder if one day I'd be able to help them, but I had no idea when, or even how.

"Marina," I said quietly. "Tomorrow is the day. I'm going to go to the Caretaker and only one of us is going to come out of it alive."

"What?" she looked back at me with wide eyes. "Can't you stay and try to take in more of the Cores? Get stronger?"

It was something that I'd already thought of, but there were two reasons why I had decided against it.

"No... I can feel it inside me like before... I can't take in any more of the Cores, it'll just make me sick. And I don't know how long that's going to last for. And every day we risk being found out by the Caretaker. Every day he could simply appear and take all this away from us. But also... What if too many of the Cores kill me? I've got a good chance right now, I'm strong and fast... but if I die before facing the Caretaker, then what does that mean for the rest of you?"

Marina was quiet, staring down at her plate, her eyebrows furrowed in thought.

"You're right," she finally said, her voice barely above a whisper. "It's...

it's just hard, you know? Seeing you risk your life like this."

"I know," I replied gently, reaching out to squeeze her hand. "But it's something I have to do. For us. For all of us. We all knew that this was coming, that this was always going to be something that I had to do."

"I want to come with you," Marina said abruptly, her gaze snapping up to meet mine.

"What?" I asked, taken aback. "No. Marina, that's not happening."

"But Marcus…" she began, but I cut her off.

"The Caretaker is dangerous," I told her, my tone firm. "He would use anything I care about against me. I can't risk you, Marina. I won't."

Marina looked at me, her eyes filled with a mix of fear, frustration, and determination. "But I can help," she insisted. "I've been practising, too. I can fight."

"I know that," I said, giving her hand another squeeze. "But it's too risky. I can't... I can't lose you, Marina. Not when we've come so far."

Marina fell silent, her gaze dropping back to her plate. But I could see the stubborn set of her jaw, the way her fingers twitched as if longing to do something, anything. I had the feeling that this wasn't the end of our conversation. But she didn't say another word.

As we finished dinner in silence, I couldn't help but feel a twinge of worry. Marina was headstrong and independent. She wasn't used to sitting back and letting others take risks for her. But I couldn't let her face the Caretaker. I just couldn't. If he took her, hurt her even… I didn't know what I would do.

Tomorrow was going to be a long day. And as I watched Marina walk away, her shoulders stiff with unspoken frustration, I couldn't help but feel a sense of dread. I was about to face the most dangerous adversary I'd ever encountered, and there was a chance I wouldn't come back.

But the thought of Marina, of our people living in fear... I couldn't bear it. The Caretaker had to be stopped. For Atlantis. For our future. For Marina.

I slept well surprisingly, given what my plan was the next morning. But I wanted to give the day the fullness of my attention and also I wanted to be as well-rested as possible.

In the morning, I walked out of my shelter and to the fire that seemed to be perpetually burning to get some breakfast. It took me a while to decide what I was going to eat, the mushrooms looking as unappetising as ever and somehow I knew that even though they weren't Core infused, if they were it wouldn't make a difference to me. I was past all that now.

I caught sight of Marina, but she didn't look me in the eye. She didn't even smile.

She looked as though she had been crying, and it was clear that she was upset. The cold reception I received was unexpected, but not undeserved. I had decided to face the Caretaker alone, after all. To risk my life and to possibly leave everyone else behind. Including Marina.

As I sat down to eat, I found that I couldn't taste the food. My mind was filled with thoughts of the battle to come. The Caretaker was powerful, more powerful than I could even comprehend. But I was ready. I had to be.

I finished my breakfast and stood, my gaze scanning the crowd of Atlanteans. They all avoided my gaze, their faces full of fear and uncertainty. They knew what was coming. They knew I was about to risk my life for their freedom.

"I guess this is it," I said, my voice barely more than a whisper. But it echoed in the silence, reaching every ear before me.

Everyone looked at me, but there were no words. No goodbyes. Just silent nods, and a few teary eyes.

My heart clenched in my chest as I stood up and turned away, the weight of what I was about to do settling heavily on my shoulders. I took a deep breath and started to walk away from the settlement, towards the looming threat that was the Caretaker.

As I was walking away, I heard a noise behind me. I turned to see Marina running towards me, tears streaming down her face. She ran straight into my arms, wrapping her arms tightly around me.

"You'd better come back alive," she whispered fiercely into my ear, her voice choked with emotion. "Because if you don't, I swear to the Gods, I'll find a way to bring you back just to kill you myself."

I held her tighter, my own tears starting to well up in my eyes. "I'll do my best, Marina," I said softly, "I promise."

And with that, I pulled away and turned back towards my fate, leaving behind the home and the people I had come to love. As I walked away, I felt a newfound determination. I was going to defeat the Caretaker. For Atlantis. For our future. And especially for Marina.

By my side hung my cutlass, a reminder of who I was and where I'd come from, but I carried nothing else of note, I didn't need silly trinkets to weigh me down on the journey ahead.

My footsteps echoed eerily across the empty expanse separating Atlantis from the Caretaker's realm. My heart pounded in my chest, a beat in time with each step I took closer to the looming threat. I focused on my breathing, taking slow, deep breaths, feeling the cool air fill my lungs before slowly exhaling.

I had made this journey before, and I knew that I wouldn't encounter any wildlife or threats along the way, but that didn't do much to settle my anxiety and nerves.

After a long while, a sense of calm washed over me, a calmness born of acceptance. I had done all I could to prepare for this moment. There was nothing left to do but face the beast itself. Thoughts of failure, of defeat, I pushed them away. They had no place here, not now.

The landscape started to change, becoming more barren, more desolate. The greenery of Atlantis and the forests beyond were replaced by the stark, grey lifelessness that marked the edges of the Caretaker's realm. As I ventured deeper, I could feel the pressure build, a tangible manifestation of the Caretaker's oppressive presence. It was like walking into a storm, the tension in the air palpable.

I gripped the hilt of my cutlass and held it tightly, ready, drawing strength from its familiar presence. The weapon had been my companion for only a short time, but it was a symbol of my resilience, a testament to my determination to survive and protect those I cared for.

The Caretaker's fortress loomed in the distance, a monstrous edifice built into a sheer mountainside. The closer I got, the stronger the oppressive energy became. It was as though the very air was saturated with the Caretaker's malevolence, making every breath a struggle, every step a battle.

But I kept moving, propelled by thoughts of Atlantis, of the people depending on me. The image of Marina's tear-streaked face was burned into my mind, her whispered words a mantra I clung to. I was going to come back alive. I had to.

Despite the heaviness in the air and the darkness surrounding me, a small flame of hope began to kindle within my heart. I was not alone in this fight. The Atlanteans were with me, their hopes and dreams fuelling my footsteps ever onward.

"Are you sure this is the right thing to do?" Yari's voice shocked me and I almost reached for my sword.

My Sylph companion had projected herself out of my body and had fluttered up to sit on my shoulder. I glanced at her flowing golden wings, and she was as beautiful as the day I'd met her.

"I..." I began, then stopped, realising that Yari was just voicing the fear that had been gnawing at my own heart. "I have to be sure, Yari. There's no other choice."

Her small, graceful features twisted into a frown, and I could feel her worry emanating in waves. "I don't want you to die, Marcus," she said quietly.

"I don't plan to," I reassured her, my voice barely more than a whisper against the wind. "I plan to come back. I have to... for Marina, for you, for all of us."

Yari didn't respond, her dark eyes filled with an unspoken sadness. She seemed smaller, more vulnerable and I wondered how much of that was just her mirroring my own feelings. We had been through so much together, she was as much a part of me as my own heart.

We walked in silence for a while, each lost in our own thoughts. The Caretaker's fortress loomed ever closer, a reminder of what awaited us.

"I'm scared, Yari," I confessed, the words seeming to hang heavy in the air.

"So am I," she admitted, her tiny wing reaching out to touch my cheek. "But we're stronger together, remember? We can face anything."

I nodded, feeling a warmth spread through me at her words. "Yes, we can," I echoed, gripping the handle of my cutlass tightly. "But I need you to stay here."

Yari reeled, clearly not entirely sure what I was saying.

"I know that if I die, then you die along with me..." I said slowly, choosing the direct approach. "But nobody's ever experienced the link we have before. No Sylph has been able to project themselves out like you do... so if there's any chance that it could save your life..."

"But Marcus..." Yari's voice trembled with emotion. "I can't just stand by and let you do this alone. You've already turned away Marina, you can't push me away too. We're partners."

"I know, Yari, I know," I replied gently. "But this... this is something I must do alone. The Caretaker... he's powerful, and I don't want him to use you or Marina against me. It's the only way I can protect you. The only way I can protect everyone."

Silence fell between us. Yari didn't say anything, but I could feel her confusion, her worry, and a hint of anger. But underneath it all, I also sensed her understanding. She didn't like it, but she understood. She knew how much I cared for her, for Marina, for all of Atlantis. And she knew I would do anything in my power to keep them safe.

"Promise me you'll come back," she finally said, her voice barely a whisper. Her wing brushed against my cheek again in a gesture of comfort. It was as though I could feel it. "Promise me, Marcus."

"I promise," I told her, feeling the weight of those words settle in my heart. "I promise, Yari."

With a nod, Yari spread her wings and glided down off my shoulder to stand on the ground a few metres away.

"I'll be waiting right here," she said. She was putting on a tough front, but I could feel the fear and sadness radiating through our bond.

And that was it. I was finally alone.

I watched her standing there, the ethereal glow of her wings casting a soft light behind her. A symbol of hope. Then I turned away, pulling my focus back to the task at hand.

As I approached the base of the steep hill that led up to the entrance I'd once escaped from, the very ground beneath me seemed to hum with the Caretaker's power. The cave entrance loomed ominously above me, carved from stone and covered in ancient, winding plantlife. That too radiated an ominous energy that sent a chill down my spine.

With a deep breath, I pushed onwards and upward. Alone. I reached the entrance to the cave without anything surprising happening. Darkness enveloped me as I stepped inside, and for a moment, all I could hear was the echo of my feet against the hard stone floor.

The Caretaker was here. I could feel him, his presence a pressure on my mind, a heaviness in the air. The fortress was vast, a maze of corridors and rooms cut from the stone, but I'd been here before, and I had the feeling that the Caretaker knew exactly where I was, and what I was doing.

"Hello," a devious sounding voice came from behind me. I wheeled around just in time to hear the Caretaker follow up with: "It's so nice of you to join me in my humble abode again."

The Caretaker had well and truly blocked off my only route of escape, and I hadn't even heard him coming. Not that I needed some way to escape, but I usually liked to have options at least.

I studied him, a shroud of darkness in the barely lit cavern. His eyes glowed, a chilling luminescence that made my skin crawl. Even in the poor light, his grin was visible - a cruel twist of lips that barely hid his malevolence. The metallic *whatevers* on his head shone dimly, and his eyes were an ethereal blue.

"It seems we're in the habit of repeating ourselves, Caretaker," I replied, letting a touch of bravado creep into my voice. "And you should know by now that I don't scare easily." Then I added almost as an afterthought: "And this being the third time you'll have tried to kill me, you should know that I'm not so easy to put down."

His grin widened. "Oh, I know. That's what makes this all the more fun." He spread his arms wide as if welcoming me. "You've come a long way, only to die here."

"I didn't come here to die," I retorted. "I came here to end this. To free this world and the people who live here from your tyranny."

The Caretaker let out a hearty laugh, his voice echoing ominously in the cave. "You think you can defeat me? A mere human?"

"I'm not just a human," I declared. "I've found the power of the Cores, and that's how I plan on beating you."

The declaration rang in the air, my words a challenge to his authority. The Caretaker's laughter died down, replaced with a steely silence. His eyes narrowed at me, a gleam of intrigue - or was it anticipation? - sparking in his eyes.

"Then by all means," he replied, his voice dripping with arrogance. "If you think a few tiny Cores can change who you are so drastically, so much that you think you can stand up against me… Show me what an enhanced human can do. Perhaps then I'll see about bringing more of your kind through to this world to work in my mines."

Drawing my cutlass, I squared my stance and prepared myself for the fight of my life. One way or another, this would end here and now. I was done talking.

The moment hung in the air between us, a slice of silence that marked the beginning of the end. I flexed my grip on my cutlass, my heart pounding an erratic rhythm in my chest. He was a giant against my mere mortal frame, an embodiment of power and malevolence that made every survival instinct in me scream to run.

But I was not just a human. I was an Atlantean.

With a burst of speed, I charged him, my blade flashing through the air with deadly intent. The Caretaker barely moved, simply watching me as I lunged at him. I aimed for his midsection, hoping to end it quickly. I was so sure I'd connected until I felt a jarring shock against my blade. I watched in disbelief as the cutlass simply bounced off him, the sound of metal against his skin as hard as steel ringing out and echoing away into the darkness.

I barely had time to register the event when the back of his hand connected with my body, sending me flying back across the cavern. I crashed against the stone wall, the breath knocked out of me. I gasped, trying to regain my footing, to push through the pain. I managed to stand, staggering slightly as I tried to regroup.

Ignoring the stabbing pain in my side, I ran at him again. I managed to dodge his retaliatory blow, and I swung my cutlass again. But it was like attacking a stone, each strike a futile attempt that did nothing but drain my energy.

With an arrogant laugh, the Caretaker swiped his hand in a dismissive gesture. I was thrown back, tumbling out of the cavern and rolling down the hill end over end. Pain exploded in my body as I hit the bottom, my breath knocked out of me.

I groaned, my body aching from the impact. My cutlass lay a few feet away, glinting mockingly in the sunlight. But I wasn't defeated, not yet. I could still feel the residue of the Cores pulsing within me, their power a beacon in the darkness. They were my only hope, the only chance I had to beat this monstrous entity.

Ignoring the pain, I pushed myself up. I was battered, bruised, and on the verge of collapsing, but I was far from beaten. I would fight. I would protect Atlantis. And somehow, someway, I would find a way to beat the Caretaker. No matter how fast or strong he was.

I had to. There was no other option.

"This is foolish," the Caretaker laughed as he sauntered down the hill towards me. "You are a nothing, not even an annoyance and yet you still think that you can stand toe to toe with me."

His words, meant to degrade me, only served to stoke the burning defiance within. There was no room for doubt, no space for fear. I knew who I was, what I was capable of.

Standing tall, despite the pain, I picked up my cutlass again. I knew that I couldn't use it to harm him, but it was a part of me, an extension of my will. A familiar companion on my hand.

"You underestimate me," I said, my voice echoing through the silence. "You underestimate the power of the Cores. But most importantly, you underestimate the power of the human spirit."

His laughter echoed off the mountains, a cruel, mocking sound that bounced around us. "Human spirit? You really think that can defeat me?"

"Yes," I answered, my voice steady despite my trembling body. "Because unlike you, I'm not fighting for power or control. I'm fighting for something much more. For the people who depend on me. For freedom. Those are things you'll never understand, Caretaker. And that's why you'll lose."

A cruel smile twisted his lips as he stopped a few feet from me. "We shall see, human, but before you take another step, I have something to show you, and we shall see how resilient your spirit is, and then you shall die."

"There's nothing you can…" I started to say, but my sentence was cut off when from behind the Caretaker walked two adult Selari holding the arms of Marina and Guy, who looked like they were struggling very hard to escape.

"Let me go!" Marina cried, but then she looked up and our eyes met. My heart sank.

Time seemed to slow as I took in the scene before me. My worst fear had come true. My friends had been taken captive. A cold wave of fear washed over me, the gravity of the situation weighing heavy in my chest.

But what were they doing here anyway?

"Release them," I demanded, my voice strong despite the fear clawing its way up my throat. "They have nothing to do with this."

"Oh, but they do," the Caretaker replied, a malicious grin playing on his lips. "They are your friends, are they not? And that means they are part of this."

Rage bubbled within me, hot and furious, but I tamped it down. I couldn't afford to let my emotions get the better of me, not when Marina and Guy's lives hung in the balance.

"Let them go," I repeated louder this time, meeting the Caretaker's gaze head-on. "This fight is between you and me."

The Caretaker chuckled, his eyes glinting with amusement. "Oh, this fight involves all of us now. Your determination... your human spirit as you call it, it's intriguing. But let's see how strong it really is."

The threat hung heavy in the air, a sharp knife-edge of tension between us. The Caretaker was clearly a master manipulator, using my friends as pawns in his cruel game. But I couldn't, wouldn't, let him win. I glanced at Marina and Guy, seeing the fear in their eyes but also the determination.

"We're not afraid of you," I said, addressing the Caretaker but keeping my gaze locked with Marina and Guy's. "And we won't let you win. These are my friends, my people, and I won't let you hurt them.

The Caretaker's smile didn't waver. "We shall see," he said, "but I hoped you say that. I hoped you'd tell me that these are your people... because if that was such a definite truth, then why do you carry the very item that can free you from this place and leave this all behind. Sat neatly in your pocket, always within reach. Your escape plan may be kept hidden from your people, but I see it there. And I know why you keep it."

It took me a moment for my mind to catch up to what the Caretaker was saying, and then it focussed on the small golden coin in my pocket. The Siren that could transport me back to my home world, the Siren that I had found in the Captain's Quarters of the Iron Will. The Siren that I had placed in my pocket and forgotten all about.

"Yes, you remember now don't you, and now your friends see who you really are."

"Marcus you... you were going to leave us?" Marina asked in a very small voice. "But you..." she trailed off and held my gaze, not able to speak any more.

"And that's why you never trust anyone," Guy announced in a huff.

"So why don't you try to use it now?" The Caretaker asked me. "See if you can get back to your home. But then... you don't actually know what that is do you? Or even less what it was designed for?"

"It's to bring slaves through to this place so you can put them to work in your mines!" I spat. "And Marina, Guy, honestly I forgot I found that thing. I never wanted to use it, I promise."

"No!" The Caretaker bellowed. "Let me enlighten you… if you think that your spirit is so unbreakable, then there are a few truths you must learn."

I didn't take my eyes off the Caretaker as he spoke, but something deep down inside me feared what he was about to say next.

"You believe you're special, don't you? That you are some kind of chosen hero, destined to bring an end to my rule and free the people of this world," the Caretaker began, his voice oozing mockery. "But what you don't understand, Captain Reid, is the true depth and complexity of the game you're playing."

His gaze locked onto mine, a cold, gleaming focus that sent shivers down my spine. "The Siren is not just a tool for transporting slaves, it is a gateway that connects all of the worlds under the control of the Entropics. We control thousands of worlds across the multiverse, worlds which we fight over, hoard, or ignore as we see fit. In our past, we have fought amongst ourselves, but this solution has given us the ability to control where we wish, including your own world."

His words landed like a blow, forcing me to reassess everything I knew. My world, which I'd always thought of as free, was just another cog in their immense, colossal machine. And the implications of this reality were staggering.

"Every world that has been enslaved by my kin is different. Each of them is controlled by a Caretaker that spreads his influence as far and as wide as he sees fit. The world you come from for example…" he paused for dramatic effect. "The Royal Navy? That is a machine, built by the Caretaker that governs your world. I believe you have had at least some dealings with the one who calls himself Commodore Henry Atherton?"

My stomach dropped. The note I had received along with the Sirens in the first place… that had been from the Commodore.

"He grew tired of trying to sink your little ship… so he sent you here, to a place where he knew that power was not so evenly spread amongst the enslaved. You are not unique, Marcus," the Caretaker continued, a cruel smile on his face. "Your world was just another link in our chain. And the Iron Will, the ship you fought so hard to protect, was nothing more than a playing piece to us, to be moved to and from wherever we saw fit. When your Navy failed to sink it, we decided it was best sent here. To me."

A cold feeling of dread was beginning to seep into my bones.

"Your 'noble' fight, your struggle... it was all part of a larger game," the Caretaker continued, still grinning. "A game in which you are merely a pawn. You, your ship, your crew... everything you've fought for... was nothing more than amusement for us."

I couldn't believe what I was hearing. My world, my fight, everything I held dear was being twisted and manipulated by these Entropics. The sheer scale of their power, the immensity of their influence was beyond my comprehension. But in that moment, one thing became clear.

"My world... my fight... my people..." I began slowly, my mind racing to comprehend the depth of the manipulation. "You think of us as pawns, playthings for your amusement. But that's where you're wrong, Caretaker."

"Is that so?" He replied, chuckling at my defiance.

"Yes," I said, clenching my fists. "Because we are not your playthings. We are not your slaves. We are not your pawns. We are people, with fight in our hearts and spirits that you will never understand or control."

My words echoed around us, a bold proclamation of defiance. Marina and Guy, still held captive, looked at me with awe in their eyes. The Caretaker, for the first time, seemed taken aback by my words.

"No matter what you say, no matter what you do, we will never bow down to you or the Entropics. We will fight. We will resist. And one day, we will be free," I concluded, a fierce resolve burning in my heart. "But more than that, one day I will use the Sirens to go back to my home, and I will sink every ship the Royal Navy has on the seven seas and I will tear the power from the Caretaker there piece by piece until there is nothing left for him, just like I will in this world, from you."

But then a thought occurred to me: There were no Obsidian Cores where I came from, so what did the Caretaker there actually want? It was a question that I couldn't answer, so I asked it.

"Not all power is equal, and it comes in many forms," the Caretaker answered cryptically. "And I beg you, try to use the Siren but it will not answer to your call. It will simply transport you to a new world, controlled by another Caretaker and you will not know where you are or how to return. You will be lost, Captain. Not that it matters anyway. You gave a touching speech, but words are wind. And I don't see any sails attached to you."

"Then I will travel the multiverse, and kill every single Caretaker I find," I replied simply.

"And so, the pawn dreams of becoming a king," the Caretaker sneered, "but you forget your place, Captain. You are not the first to voice such threats, and you won't be the last. All who dared to challenge us have fallen, and you will too."

"Maybe," I admitted, "but I'd rather die fighting for freedom than live under your rule."

"Oh will you just SHUT UP, Marcus!" Marina shouted and it snapped my attention right around to her. "You come here with grand promises but you never had any idea what you were messing with, did you? Marcus, you lied to us. You betrayed us. You were going to leave us here. And now you talk about freedom?"

The Caretaker raised an eyebrow, clearly interested in the unfolding drama. I was momentarily taken aback, but quickly realised what Marina was doing.

"Marina, I…" I started, but she cut me off.

"No, Marcus. Don't you dare try to make excuses now," she shouted. "You've shown us what kind of man you are."

The Selari workers holding her and Guy began to stir, their attention drawn to the shouting. They started to loosen their grips, clearly confused with what was happening.

Guy was the first to seize the opportunity, using the disarray to push away his captor. "You're right, Marina," he added, feeding into the act. "We were fools to trust him."

"No more," Marina declared. "We fight for ourselves now." And with that, she elbowed a startled Selari in the stomach, and Guy landed a punch on another's face.

The worker that Guy had punched fell to the ground with a thud, but Marina had to land a second elbow to drop her own target.

But then, the Caretaker was there, materialising in front of me as though he'd simply stepped out of thin air. He was so fast. So much faster than I was, even with my Core-enhanced strength and speed.

He reached out and picked me up by my throat. His grip was iron, his eyes full of malice. "I am afraid that this time, Captain," he said, his voice a chilling whisper, "there will be no escape."

"Marcus!" Marina and Guy yelled simultaneously, but I knew that there was nothing I could do. This was finally it, my end.

But then a flash of bright golden light lit up the world around us and I saw Yari, flying at breakneck speed directly behind the Caretaker. And then it happened. Yari impacted the Entropic and where I would've expected my little Sylph friend to pass right through him, the Caretaker dropped me to the ground and stiffened as though he'd been shot in the back. I couldn't see Yari anymore, but I could see the effect she'd had. The Caretaker was frozen in place.

"Marcus, here!" Guy called as he threw my discarded cutlass over to me, having picked it up from the ground. I caught it by the handle and wasted no time in forcing it into the Caretaker's chest. Where once his skin had been like stone, the blade now slid in easily and in that moment, I felt the life begin to leave my enemy.

I had done it. I had won. But I couldn't have done it without my friends, these three people, Marina, Guy and Yari by my side. And that was a lesson that I wasn't going to forget any time soon.

I fell to my knees and before the Caretaker had even hit the ground, his lifeless body no longer a threat to this world, Marina and Guy had both rushed over to me and wrapped their arms around my body.

"You did it…" Marina said quietly. "You actually did it."

I looked at the Caretaker's lifeless body, my heart pounding in my chest. It was surreal - the mighty foe that had ruled with an iron fist was no more, and we were free.

"I didn't do it," I replied, my voice hoarse. "We did it. Together."

Marina pulled back, her eyes shining with tears. "Marcus, I… I'm sorry for what I said. I just wanted them to…"

"I know," I interrupted, giving her a small smile. "You were great. Both of you were."

I turned to Guy, extending my hand to him. He grabbed it firmly, pulling me into a rough hug. "I never doubted you, Captain," he said. "You're a true hero."

Then my expression turned harsh. "And what the hell were you doing out here anyway?" I asked.

Marina looked sheepish. "We couldn't just leave you out here alone… we…"

"We knew you'd need our help," Guy finished with a smirk.

And then Yari's golden projection floated out of the Caretaker's body and she flapped her wings, coming to rest on my shoulder.

"Yari!" I exclaimed, my eyes wide with surprise and relief. I reached up to her, half-afraid that she would disappear. But she was real and remained in place, the light emanating from her body warm and comforting. "How… how did you do that?"

Yari chirped, a golden pulse of light radiating from her, but she didn't say anything. She had flown directly at the Caretaker, somehow had entered his body and disrupted his power from the inside.

"Thank you," I said softly to her, my voice choked with emotion. I looked up at Marina and Guy, my gaze shifting between them. "Thank all of you. I… I couldn't have done this without you. I think I wouldn't have made it back…"

"You think?" Guy shot back, but then there was a long pause as we took a moment to let everything sink in. We had faced the Caretaker, one of the most powerful beings I had ever known, and we had won. Against all odds, we had survived and prevailed.

"Alright, let's not get all sappy now," Guy finally said, breaking the silence. He had a goofy grin on his face, and there was a twinkle in his eyes. "We've still got a lot of work to do."

He was right, of course. The Caretaker was defeated, but the path to freedom was still long. The Selari needed help to regain their independence, to rebuild their lives, and we were going to be there to support them every step of the way. We also needed to fortify our settlement and ensure that we were prepared for any other threats that may arise in the absence of the Entropic.

But for now, in this brief moment of respite, we allowed ourselves to celebrate. We had won a major victory, and it was a testament to our strength, our unity, and our unwavering determination.

We were stronger than we had ever been, and together, there was no challenge we couldn't overcome. As Yari let out a joyful trill, a burst of golden light enveloping us, I felt a surge of hope. I was ready to face whatever came our way. For the first time in a long time, I felt genuinely hopeful about the future.

We were free. We were together. And we were ready to take on the world.

Epilogue – A Brave New World

The Iron Will. My home for as long as I could remember was awaiting the three of us when we returned triumphant. It still stood resolute on the outskirts of Atlantis, providing protection and hope to all who would approach.

As we saw the Iron Will, a thought occurred to me. The ship was now our symbol of defiance and hope, but it could be more, it could be a beacon of unity. And the key to that unity was still within our grasp.

I turned to Marina, who was looking at me expectantly. "Marina, do you think we could use the Siren to travel different worlds with the Iron Will?" I asked, thinking about Siren's purpose and how the Caretaker had told me I wouldn't be able to use them the way I wanted.

Marina's eyebrows rose, but then she nodded slowly. "It's possible. But I wouldn't know where to start… and don't we have enough to do here first?

"I'm not expecting it to be easy," I replied with a small smile and I decided to keep my idea on the back burner for the time being. Marina was right, we did have a lot to do.

"OK, let's forget that for now, let's concentrate on doing what we can to free this world. The Sylphs and the kids are easy… but the Selari still in the mines, I bet they're still working, not realising that their captor has been killed."

Marina frowned in thought. "You're probably right, Marcus. The Selari likely have no idea about the Caretaker's death and even if they're simply told, I doubt the Sylphs bonded to them would believe it. The Entropics held them captive for so long... I don't know if they would even be able to lead a normal life anymore."

I looked around Atlantis at some of the Selari workers we'd already freed. Marina was right, they had no personalities and they couldn't even talk. They just worked and worked and appeared to care for nothing else.

But that didn't make it right to simply leave them where they were, working in mines that no longer served a purpose.

"We need to convince them," I announced. Even if they just come and work here with us. I want them to know, even if they don't comprehend, that they're free. I don't want them to have to work the mines for a captor that no longer exists."

Marina nodded. "And we have Yari. If there's a Sylph out there who can convince the Selari that they're free, it's her."

"Exactly what I was thinking," I agreed. Yari can go and spread the word to any mines she finds out there and we'll do what we can to make this place a real home for everyone who needs it.

Marina gave a small smile and nodded. "Then that's what we'll do. Yari, are you ready?"

Yari, who had been quietly listening, projected her golden light brighter in affirmation. The little Sylph was ready to fulfil her part. I didn't know why she wasn't speaking right now, but I hoped that by not bringing any attention to that fact, it would soon resolve itself. Besides, I could still feel the emotions that she projected through our mental link, and right now, she wasn't worried.

With our plans laid out, we wasted no time. Yari was sent off to the Obsidian Core mines, her primary goal to communicate with the Sylphs bonded within the Selari workers. Meanwhile, Marina, Guy, and I focused on improving the conditions of Atlantis, making it a home not just for the us, but for anyone who needed it.

But again, I didn't really need to oversee anything, because the kids knew exactly what they were doing, and the Selari workers although they didn't seem conscious to me, seemed to be able to carry out helpful tasks too. I did sometimes lend my strength and speed to some of the larger projects, but in the end, I was happy for the most part to leave people to do what they would.

Besides, I had something else on my mind.

I'd discovered quickly that my body didn't seem ready to ingest any more of the Cores whole – and I didn't know if that was something that was ever going to change – my body simply rejected them, and violently. What I could do though, was take in tiny amounts of crushed or powdered Cores in the form of mushrooms courtesy of Marina. I didn't know if it was a cruel joke on her part that she couldn't seem to crush them up into anything else, but I tried not to argue too much about it. If it was making her laugh, then so be it.

The crushed Cores did do something though. I got better at planning.

I had spent a lot of time in the Iron Will thinking and planning. Predominantly about how to manage an entire world and its inhabitants, but also of my own world because back home, there was another Caretaker, and that was something that I couldn't ignore.

I knew that the Cores would be the key to unlocking something about the Siren to allow me to use it, but it was after ingesting them in their tiny, crushed up form did I always seem to have the best ideas. The Sirens had been designed to bring people through to other worlds, and that is exactly what I wanted to happen. But that would have to be something for the future, and I hoped that after a little more time, I would somehow gain a better understanding of the intricacies of the powers that I held in my hands.

As the years passed, Atlantis changed. From a settlement of a shattered and fragmented people, it grew into something spectacular. The first few years were challenging as the growth brought something new with each day, but every effort was worth it.

In the first year, we focused on the city's infrastructure. Buildings were built, streets laid, and decision-making systems formed. The Selari, who once worked under the cruel regime of the Caretaker, laboured willingly alongside the children. I knew it wasn't much better, but now at least their work meant something, and slowly, Atlantis grew to accept them for who they were, rather than trying everything we could to bring them out of their shells. I learned that the Selari were an industrious species, who for the most part enjoyed the monotony of routine tasks and found peace in their diligence. Though I only had the workers and the kids to base that on, and by all accounts the kids could've simply been genetically modified to enjoy their work.

In the second and third years, we saw the city's population grow exponentially. Word spread across the world about the city that offered safety and sanctuary, and more of the Selari workers we had freed from the mines had found their way to us. The children though, that was the mystery. I didn't know if it was because the Caretaker had been actively doing something to them when he was alive, but none of them aged. Not a single day.

The fourth and fifth years were a period of tremendous growth for Atlantis. The city was booming, and so were its people. The Selari, now free from the Caretaker, began to develop their own culture and traditions and many broke away from Atlantis to forge their own paths in their freedom. Some even painted murals on the buildings, depicting their journey from captivity to freedom, giving our city a unique charm and personality.

Marina worked tirelessly to integrate the new arrivals into our community. She organised festivals, communal and gatherings. The bond between our settlement and the world strengthened, and we all began to see ourselves as free people, not just slaves, Sylph, children or workers.

By the sixth and seventh years, Atlantis had become a bustling metropolis, home to thousands of Selari and Sylph. The city was vibrant and full of life, a testament to the resilience and unity of its people. We established schools, libraries, and even a council comprising a cross-section of the settlement to make decisions for the city.

Ten long years passed, and for the first time in a long time, I had become happy with myself.

But there was always something there, in the back of my mind, nagging at me.

Throughout the years, I had continued ingesting crushed Cores and contemplating the other worlds that the Caretaker had spoken of, the Iron Will, and the Siren, which I had placed back in the drawer in the Captain's quarters back on the ship, right where I had found it so many years ago. I couldn't push the oppression and the slavery that the Caretakers across the multiverse were inflicting on millions of sentient beings and no matter how happy I felt in Atlantis, I knew that I would never allow myself to rest while there were people out there striving for freedom, but being kicked back down at every turn.

On the dawn of our eleventh year, as I stood on the deck of the Iron Will, I marvelled at the city that had risen from the ashes. Atlantis was a symbol of hope and unity, a beacon for all who sought refuge. The Iron Will, which was once a mere ship, was now the heart of Atlantis, pulsating with the energy of thousands of lives that called it home.

"Marina," I said as we sat and watched the sunset. "I need to ask you something."

She turned to look at me but didn't say a word.

"Atlantis is home to so many people. They know what they're doing and I think… I think it's time I moved on, found a new adventure and lent help to those who need it."

Marina looked at me, a small frown marring her features. "You mean... leave Atlantis?"

I nodded. "Not for good, just... we have the opportunity to do more, to help more people. We've always known that the Caretakers have enslaved other worlds too. And we have a tool that can potentially help us get there. I think it's time to test out that theory."

She studied me silently, her eyes scanning my face as if trying to read my thoughts. "You mean the Siren?"

"Exactly. We've been sitting on this possibility for years now. The Siren, if I can figure it out, has the potential to take us to those worlds. We can stand against the Entropics, we can free more slaves. We can give them a new home, a new life, just like we've done here in Atlantis."

Marina was silent for a long moment, the setting sun casting an orange glow on her face. I could see the gears turning in her mind, the hesitation, the uncertainty... but also the resolve.

"You're right, Marcus," she finally said, turning to meet my gaze. "We've done great work here in Atlantis, but there's more to be done. More worlds, more people in need. If we have the means to help them, then we should. And I suppose... it would be a new adventure, wouldn't it?"

I couldn't help but smile at her words, feeling a sense of relief wash over me. "Yes, it would. It would be a chance to see new places, meet new species, and most importantly, make a difference. We've been able to make Atlantis into a symbol of hope here, but it's time to extend that hope to other worlds."

She returned my smile, and for a moment, we sat in silence, staring out at the city we had built from ruins. The sight of Atlantis filled me with pride, and the prospect of the journey ahead filled me with excitement.

"Alright," Marina said at last, turning to me with a determined look in her eyes. "Let's do it. Let's start a new adventure." Then she added: "Do you know how to make the Siren do what you want? Will we be able to come back?"

I shook my head slowly. I had been thinking about this for a long time and the answer that I gave to Marina is the one that the Cores had eventually allowed me to see so clearly.

"The best I can say is that where we go will be random," I said. "But that's exactly how it should be, isn't it? I mean should we get to decide who we help and who we don't, or in what order?"

Marina considered my words, her eyes slightly narrowed as she thought about it. Finally, she nodded. "You're right. Choosing who to help based on where they are could lead us down a dangerous path. If we can help, we should, regardless of where or who they are. And coming back?" she asked, a hint of worry in her voice.

"That... is something I don't know," I confessed. "I hope that we can, one day. If the Siren can take us to other worlds, I think there should be a way to come back as well, but I can't promise it. That's why I wanted to talk to you about this, to make sure you understand the risks."

She nodded slowly, taking a deep breath. "Okay. I understand. And I still think we should do it. Atlantis has grown, it can survive without us, and there are others out there who need our help."

"Thank you, Marina," I said, relieved. "We'll make preparations then, ensure Atlantis can manage without us, and when we're ready, we'll start the next chapter of our journey."

As we began to plan for our new adventure, I couldn't help but feel a sense of anticipation. While there was uncertainty and fear of the unknown, there was also hope, the hope of helping those who needed it, of bringing liberation to those oppressed by the Caretakers. Atlantis was proof of what could be achieved when people stood together against tyranny, and now, it was time to spread that hope to other worlds.

"So you know how to make the Siren take the whole ship through?" Marina asked as we stood behind the wheel of the Iron Will, looking at Guy and a crew of the kids who had chosen to accompany us.

I nodded. "I think I've always known. I just didn't want to accept that we might not come back," I replied. "That's what I've been looking for this whole time."

Marina's hand found mine and she gave it a comforting squeeze. "You're not alone in this, Marcus," she said, her voice firm yet gentle. "We're in it together, no matter where we go, no matter what we face."

I looked over at her, her determination was reassuring, her presence comforting. I squeezed her hand back, my mind buzzing with the enormity of the decision we were about to make, yet calmed by the firmness of her conviction. "Together," I echoed, drawing strength from her.

The kids, under Guy's watchful eyes, were busy preparing the ship for the journey, their youthful energy and enthusiasm filling the air. Some of them glanced our way occasionally, their eyes filled with curiosity and anticipation, but also a bit of uncertainty. They were relying on us, and we had a responsibility to ensure their safety, a responsibility that had felt overwhelming at times, but one that I was determined to fulfil.

"I guess this is it," Marina said, her voice barely above a whisper. "Once we make the jump, there's no turning back."

"Yes," I agreed, steeling myself. "But wherever we go, we go to bring hope, and to help anyone who needs it. That's worth the risk."

With a final glance at Atlantis, the city we had built from nothing, the symbol of hope we had created, I pulled the Siren from my pocket.

"Ready Yari?" I asked the Sylph sat softly on my shoulder.

"I'm ready Marcus, and I'm with you, no matter what happens," she replied.

I held the Siren in my hand, the same coin that had taken me on such an agonising journey before. The memory of the pain I felt last time was somehow still fresh in my mind, but I was ready this time. This was what I wanted.

I traced the markings and etchings of the Siren with a single finger, the ancient artifact that had opened my eyes to the existence of other worlds, its familiar presence somehow calming in the face of the unknown. A gentle melody began to rise from the coin, a beautiful harmony that seemed to sing of ancient mysteries and cosmic journeys.

The tune filled the air around us, its enchanting melody seeming to resonate with every fibre of our being. As the music continued, I felt a surge of energy coursing through me, an invigorating vitality that seemed to emanate from the Siren itself. But unlike last time, the pain was absent.

The white-hot searing pain I had endured before was now replaced by a gentle warmth that spread throughout my body, leaving me feeling invigorated rather than agonised. It was as though the Siren recognised me and knew what I wanted from it. We were working together now somehow.

My knees buckled as the sensation overtook me, but it was a feeling of awe rather than agony. The energy around us seemed to pulse in time with the music, the walls of the Iron Will seeming to dissolve into the song. I felt as though I was being condensed, transformed, but the process was gentle this time, a gradual merging with the music rather than a violent rending from one place to another.

As the symphony swelled, our reality seemed to fracture and warp, a brilliant array of colours and sounds enveloping us. It was as though we were stepping into the heart of a cosmic symphony, the very fabric of reality bending to the will of the Siren's song.

And then, with a final crescendo of sound and light, everything changed. The world as we knew it fell away, replaced by an endless expanse of swirling colours and melodies. I felt as though I was part of something much larger than myself, a tiny speck in the grand symphony of the cosmos.

Then, silence. The melody faded, the light dimmed, and a new world slowly appeared. We still stood on the deck of the Iron Will, but all around us, a whole new landscape unfolded. A deep blue sky stretched out before us, strange and beautiful.

"We did it," I said, looking at Marina.

"Is this where you're from?" she asked.

My mouth hung open, but I couldn't answer Marina's question. We had materialised in the entrance to a cave and the Iron Will was in just a few feet of water. It could have been my home, but there was no way to be sure.

Desperate to know, I lowered a rope from the deck and descended carefully, feeling the familiar thrill of uncertainty wash over me. Each fibre of the rope grazed against my palms as I slowly made my way down. The world around us was silent except for the gentle lapping of water against the hull of the Iron Will.

Finally, my feet touched the water. The sensation was electric, a shocking reminder of what I had missed during our time in Atlantis. The cool, soothing feeling of the sea swirled around my ankles, taking me back to countless memories of exploration and adventure. For a moment, I closed my eyes, savouring the feeling, the smell of the sea filling my lungs.

I stepped away from the rope and waded deeper into the water, making my way towards the mouth of the cave. The soft sand and mud under my feet felt oddly comforting, and I paused, looking out at the horizon, trying to piece together where we could possibly be.

Suddenly, I felt it. A strange vibration, a barely perceptible trembling in the water around me. I turned, peering back towards the Iron Will. The water began to ripple slowly over and over, each ripple growing larger and larger, cascading outwards in a growing circle. The rhythm of the rippling water seemed to quicken, like the beat of a heart racing with fear.

Yari then spread her wings and flew back to the Iron Will from my shoulder, apparently able to sense the same danger that I could.

As I squinted at the ever-widening ripples, a shadow began to form far away from the mouth of the cave. I froze, my heart pounding as the water outside began to churn and foam. Then, with a sudden, heart-stopping rush, a gigantic head emerged from the depths sending water cascading for miles in all directions.

It was a creature the likes of which I'd never seen before. It was blue, the colour of the deepest ocean, with eyes as bright as the sun and as orange as the most vibrant sunset. Its head was massive, mountainous even, dwarfing anything that I'd ever seen before and making me feel utterly insignificant.

And then it stared at us, its gigantic eyes seemingly filled with curiosity and intelligence. A chill ran down my spine as I realised it was looking right at me, right at us. Was this the Caretaker of this world? Because if it was, then I'd vastly underestimated our capabilities to help people out there in the wider multiverse.

In a surge of panic, I turned and ran back towards the Iron Will, my heart pounding in my chest. I frantically scrambled up the rope, climbing as if my life depended on it. I barely registered Marina's alarmed face as I sprinted towards the helm, towards the Siren.

I clutched the artefact, pressing my fingers against its etchings and pleading for it to work, for it to take us away from this alien and terrifying encounter. But the Siren was silent. There was no melody, no surge of energy, nothing. My pleas echoed emptily in the silence, swallowed by the vast expanse of the alien world.

And the creature was coming towards us.

In my desperation, I begged, I threatened, I coaxed, but it was no use. The Siren was dormant, as though I somehow sensed that it had used up all its energy bringing us here. We were stuck on an unknown world, with a sea creature as large as a mountain about to put an end to our adventure.

"Please," I begged the Siren, but nothing happened.

"Marcus?" Marina asked. "What is that?"

"Please..." I continued begging but it was no use.

I turned my attention back to the creature, which was now so close that any second it would be upon us. And that would be our end.

The monstrous being lifted a hand from the water, its form so colossal it dwarfed the Iron Will, making it look like a toy ship in comparison. Its fingers were like hundred-foot ships themselves, coming towards us with a deliberate but terrifyingly swift motion.

"Hold on!" I shouted at Marina, bracing myself at the helm, one hand still clutching the Siren and the other wrapped tightly around a rigging line. The giant hand was mere seconds away, the world around us seemed to go silent, as if everything was holding its breath for the impending impact.

Suddenly, the Siren began to hum. It was so soft at first, I thought I had imagined it. But then the hum grew louder, vibrating in my hand like a tiny heartbeat, syncing with my own racing pulse. The Siren was coming back to life.

"Work, please, work!" I pleaded. "Get us out of here!"

The etchings on the Siren began to glow, a faint iridescent sheen that quickly intensified, quickly bathing the deck of the Iron Will in a brilliant light. A feeling of relief surged through me, followed by a sudden, jarring wrench in my gut as the world around us began to blur and warp once again. The Siren's melody filled the air, louder and more triumphant than ever before, drowning out the alien world and the monstrous being that had come within mere inches from ending us.

As the melody swelled, our reality seemed to fracture and distort. The giant hand that had been coming towards us seemed to dissolve into the iridescent hues of the Siren's song, the deep blue sea, the sky, and the creature's enormous orange eyes melting into the riot of colours and sounds.

Then, with a final crescendo of sound and light, we were engulfed by the multicoloured abyss once more. We were back in the cosmic symphony, a vibrant world between worlds, safe from the gigantic creature and the unknown alien world.

Everything was shifting and changing, spiralling colours and sounds enveloping us. I turned to Marina, her face illuminated by the swirling, dazzling light. She looked back at me, her eyes wide with shock and relief, and I felt a sudden rush of gratitude. We were safe, we were together, and we were on our way to another adventure, riding the Siren's song into the unknown. But perhaps that place was somewhere we simply weren't ready for. Not yet at least.

The End

Bonus – The Adventures of Marcus Reid

Thankyou for reading Atlantis Rising. As a continuation of the story, I am writing episodes of the adventures that Marina, Marcus, Guy and Yari embark upon through the multiverse, and these are available for FREE on my website, www.davidlingard.com. All you have to do is sign up to my newsletter for access to the (FREE) members section.

Episode 1 - Stranded

"Marcus!" Marina shouted at the top of her voice as the wind billowed against her face, sending her red hair cascading away from her head behind her. "I don't care how strong or powerful you think you are; you can't just take the Iron Will wherever you like and expect there to be no consequences!"

I could say nothing in return to object to Marina's statement, but there was one thing that I could do, and that was smile.

I'd fought tooth and nail to have my fearsome ship, the Iron Will returned to me. I'd killed men I'd once called friends, and I'd stood face to face with beings that most men would see as Gods.

But I survived.

I endured.

I had won.

And now, the universe was my playground.

Well, strictly speaking, it was more of a multiverse than a universe, from what I could gather, but who really cares for semantics?

"Marina," I began, my voice steady against the howling wind but also carrying the hint of a smile, "I understand your concern. But you must understand, I didn't fight for the Iron Will just to let it sit idle in a dock, or on some cliff edge. I fought for it so I could explore the unknown, so I could chart my own course and so that we could free any world we came across from the oppression of the Entropics and their Caretakers."

Marina's green eyes flashed with anger, her hands clenched at her sides. "And what about the people you've left behind, Marcus? What about the worlds you've disrupted with your reckless journeying?"

I paused, considering her words. She was right, of course. My adventures had not been without their consequences. But I was not a man to be tied down, not a man to be confined by the rules of others. I was a sailor, a wanderer, a seeker of the unknown. But above all else, I was a free man, and that was all I had ever wanted.

"I've always tried to do right by the people I've met, Marina, you know that," I said, my gaze steady on her. "But I can't stop exploring, can't stop seeking. It's who I am."

Marina looked at me, her expression softening slightly. "And what if your seeking leads to destruction, Marcus? What then?"

I shrugged, a small smile playing on my lips. "Then I'll face it head-on, just like I always have. I'll fight, I'll endure, and I'll survive. Because that's what I do. And besides. If an enslaved world is destroyed, is it really the worst thing to happen?"

Marina was silent for a moment, her gaze locked with mine. Then, slowly, she nodded. "Just promise me one thing, Marcus."

"Anything."

"Promise me you'll be careful."

I smiled, reaching out to take her hand in mine. "I promise, Marina. I'll be careful."

Then I turned back and heaved on the large wooden wheel that once upon a time would've been the only way to get the huge galleon to change direction. But now, it was more of a symbol. I had no idea where the ship would take us; in fact, all I did know was that by changing course, we would end up somewhere entirely different and new to us.

A second later, the world before us morphed and distorted; nebulae of pinks, purples and yellows filled the world around us, and the Iron Will floated onwards, ever onwards, towards the horizon and the nothingness that expanded away from us.

Then it faded away to nothing.

Suddenly, the ship lurched violently, throwing me off balance. The nebulae vanished, replaced by a harsh, blinding light. I squinted, trying to make sense of our new surroundings. The Iron Will groaned and creaked, its hull scraping against something hard and unyielding beneath.

"Marcus!" Marina cried out, gripping the ship's railing as the Iron Will shuddered beneath us. "What's happening?"

I didn't answer, my eyes scanning the landscape. We were surrounded by towering mountains, their peaks lost in the clouds. Below us, a vast desert stretched out, its sands gleaming under the harsh sunlight. The Iron Will was stuck, half-buried in the sand, its sails flapping uselessly in the dry, hot wind and there wasn't a drop of water to be seen for miles around.

"Is this... is this where you're from?" Marina asked, her voice barely audible over the wind.

I shook my head slowly, my gaze never leaving the desolate landscape. "No, I don't think so... This is something else." I didn't know how I knew, but this place just didn't smell right to me. Of course, I was far more used to the beautiful open oceans of my world, but there was just something about this place, something not quite right.

Just then, the door to the lower decks burst open, and a small figure emerged. My young, ten-year-old crew master looked around in confusion. His eyes were wide and his face pale.

"What 'happened?" he asked, his voice trembling. "Why have we stopped?"

"We've landed, Guy," I said, turning to face him. "We're in some strange desert."

"A desert?" Guy repeated, his eyes going even wider. "But... but the Iron Will is a ship, not a... a..."

"A land vehicle," I finished for him, a wry smile on my face. "Yes, I know. But the Iron Will is more than just a ship, Guy. It's an explorer, a wanderer, just like us. And right now, it seems it's decided to explore this desert."

I didn't know how to respond in truth. The way that the Iron Will worked, the way that it sailed from dimension to dimension, was beyond my understanding, and I didn't know if it was something I had done specifically to bring us through to this place or not. The ship used the small golden coin which I always kept in my pocket - a Siren - to travel the multiverse. A gift from the Caretaker of Marina's world. A Caretaker that I'd bested.

"But... but what about the crew?" Guy asked, his voice barely a whisper. "What about us? Is there any food around here? Water? My men are hungry, and if there ain't no food around in this place, it's best we just get on and leave."

"We'll survive, Guy," I said, my voice steady. "We always do. We'll just have to wait for the Iron Will to get moving again, and we'll continue our journey. Because that's what we do. We explore. We endure. And we survive. But honestly… I don't know how long any of that'll take."

It was the truth. Each time we'd leapt from world to world, I could feel when the Siren - and in effect, the Iron Will was ready to move on through the cosmos. It was like a power that the coin, the ship and I shared, but when it'd been used once, I never really knew how long it was going to take until it was ready to be used again.

And with that, I turned back to the desert, my gaze fixed on the distant mountains. The multiverse had thrown us a curveball; we had no water to sail upon. But we would face it head-on, just like we always had. Because we were the crew of the Iron Will, and nothing could stop us.

As if to punctuate my thoughts, the Iron Will gave a sudden, ominous groan, and the ship listed heavily to one side. The cannons, once our formidable defence against the unknown, now hung uselessly, their muzzles pointing at a downwards angle towards the sand. Marina gasped, clutching the railing for support again as the deck tilted beneath us.

"Marcus!" she cried, her eyes wide with alarm. "The cannons... they're useless now!"

I nodded grimly, my gaze fixed on the now useless artillery. "I know, Marina. But we'll find a way to right the ship. We always do."

Just then, Guy piped up, his voice cutting through the tension like a knife. "Well, while we're stuck here, how about some lunch? I've got a nice batch of mushrooms stewing below deck."

I turned to look at him, my eyebrows raised. "Mushrooms, Guy? Seriously."

Guy shrugged, a mischievous grin on his face. "Well, beggars can't be choosers, Marcus. Besides, they're good for you."

I sighed, shaking my head. "Alright, Guy. Mushrooms it is." I hated mushrooms.

As Guy scampered off to fetch our meal, I turned back to the desert, my mind already working on a plan to get the Iron Will moving again. We were stuck, yes, but not defeated.

But all that could easily change. And it did, no more than ten seconds later.

From the corner of my eye, I caught a flicker of movement. I turned quickly, my hand instinctively going to the hilt of my cutlass. A short distance away, the sand was shifting, rising. And then, with a sudden burst, a skeletal figure emerged, its hollow eye sockets glowing with an eerie, unnatural light.

"Marcus!" Marina cried, pointing at the figure. "What. What is that?"

I peered at the creature, but it was clear to me what it was. "It's a skeleton," I said, my voice steady and flat. "Stay here."

I did my best to act as though this was the most normal thing in the world, but every part of my body was shaking, begging me not to confront the creature.

And by all accounts, I didn't have to. I could simply stay up here on the ship and forget about the demon on the sand below. But it was just one, and what possible threat could it pose to me? My body was stronger and faster than it had ever been, thanks to the enhancements I'd gone through thanks to the Obsidian Cores in Marina's world.

"But Marcus..." Marina began, but I was already moving, descending the rope ladder that hung from the side of the Iron Will. I landed lightly on the sand, my boots sinking slightly into the hot, dry ground.

The skeleton turned to face me, its jaw clacking ominously. It was armed with a rusted sword, its grip firm despite its lack of flesh. I drew my own sword, the steel gleaming under the harsh sunlight.

The skeleton lunged at me as soon as I had drawn my sword, its movements surprisingly swift. I parried its opening attack, the clash of our swords ringing out in the silent desert. I counterattacked, my sword slicing through the air, but the skeleton deftly dodged, its bony frame surprisingly agile. It was fast. and strong.

We danced around each other, our swords clashing again and again. The skeleton was relentless, its attacks never ceasing. I was forced to go on the defensive, parrying its strikes, looking for an opening.

Suddenly, the skeleton lunged, its sword aimed at my chest. I sidestepped, but not fast enough. The blade grazed my side, ripping through my shirt and drawing blood. I grunted in pain but didn't let it slow me down. I retaliated with a swift strike, my sword slicing through the skeleton's arm. It clattered to the ground, but the skeleton didn't seem to notice. It simply continued its assault, its one-armed strikes just as fierce as before.

If anything, the devious grin on its face seemed to goad me into further action.

I was panting now though, sweat trickling down my face. The skeleton was stronger than I'd anticipated, its relentless attacks pushing me back and the heat of the desert was oppressive. But I couldn't afford to lose. I had a crew to protect, a ship to save. And above all else, if I turned and ran now, I'd look like a damn idiot.

So with a roar, I launched myself at the skeleton, my sword raised high.

The skeleton tried to parry, but I was faster. My sword sliced through its skull, splitting it in two. The creature staggered back, its glowing eyes flickering. And then, with a final, echoing clatter, it collapsed, its bones scattering across the sand.

I stood there, panting, my sword still raised. I was covered in sweat, my side throbbing with pain. But I was victorious. I had faced the skeleton and survived.

I turned back to the Iron Will, my gaze meeting Marina's. She was watching me, her eyes wide with relief. I gave her a small nod and threw in a cheeky wink for good measure.

It was more than that, though; it was a silent promise. I would always protect them, always keep them safe. Because we were the crew of the Iron Will, and nothing could stop us.

But as I turned to climb back up to the ship, a sudden, sharp pain erupted in my back. I gasped, my hand reaching behind me to find the hilt of a sword protruding from my body. I stumbled, my vision blurring as I turned to see the skeleton, now whole again and standing behind me, its hollow eyes glowing with an eerie light.

"Marcus!" Marina's scream echoed through the desert, but it sounded distant as if coming from underwater. I fell to my knees, my hand still clutching the hilt of the sword in my back.

But then, with a battle cry that would have made any seasoned warrior proud, Marina quickly descended from the ship followed by Guy, their own weapons drawn. Marina's sword clashed against the skeleton's, the sound echoing through the desert, while Guy, with surprising agility for his age, darted around the creature, his small dagger slashing at its bony legs.

The skeleton tried to fight them off, but Marina and Guy were relentless. With a final, powerful strike, Marina's sword shattered the skeleton's skull, sending bone fragments flying. The creature collapsed, bones scattering across the sand, this time for good.

I watched as Marina and Guy rushed over to me, their faces pale. "Marcus," Marina gasped, her hands hovering over the sword in my back. "You're hurt..."

I tried to laugh, but it came out as a pained grunt. "I've had worse," I said, though I wasn't sure if that was true. But as I looked up at them, I could see the fear in their eyes, and I knew I had to reassure them. "I'll be fine. The Cores... they'll heal me."

The Cores, the source of my enhanced power, had a strange effect on me, but only me. They could heal wounds, even ones as severe as mine, though the process was not instantaneous. But I could already feel the warmth spreading through my body, the pain in my back slowly receding.

Marina nodded, her hand gripping mine tightly. "You better be right, Marcus," she said, her voice trembling. "Because we need you. The Iron Will needs you."

I squeezed her hand in return, managing a small smile. "Don't worry, Marina. I'm not going anywhere."

And as I lay there on the hot sand, with Marina and Guy by my side, I knew that we would face whatever the multiverse threw at us head-on. Because we were the crew of the Iron Will, and nothing could stop us.

"More are coming!" The cry came from above, and I shuddered at my lack of ability to rest after such an ordeal.

The call had come from Yari. She was a Sylph – a small golden bird who had once lived inside my consciousness – but that's a story for another day. Yari could talk, and by all accounts, was an amazing asset to have for a free man and his ship.

"What do you mean 'more'?" I grunted.

"Look!" Yari squawked, her golden wings flapping as she pointed with her beak towards the horizon.

I followed her gaze, my heart sinking as I saw what she was pointing at. Emerging from the base of the mountains, a horde of skeletons was charging towards us, their hollow eyes glowing with more eerie lights. There were hundreds of the, maybe even thousands of them, their bony forms kicking up a cloud of dust as they raced across the desert.

"Back to the ship!" I shouted quickly, pushing myself to my feet. The pain in my back was a dull throb now, the Cores' healing power slowly mending my wound. Marina and Guy helped me up, their faces pale as they glanced back at the approaching horde.

We scrambled up the rope ladder, the ship's deck tilting beneath us as the Iron Will groaned and creaked. The cannons were still useless, their muzzles pointing towards the sand, but we had other defences. We just needed time.

"Why do we do this, Marcus?" Marina asked as we reached the deck, her voice barely audible over the wind. "Why do we keep throwing ourselves into danger?"

I looked at her, her green eyes filled with fear and uncertainty. But there was also determination there, a fierce resolve that I had come to admire. "Because we have to, Marina," I said, my voice steady. "Because there are people out there who need our help."

"The Entropic," she said, her voice barely a whisper.

I nodded. The Entropics were a powerful and ruthless empire that spanned across the multiverse, enslaving countless worlds and their inhabitants. They were the reason I had fought so hard to get the Iron Will back, the reason I had made so many enemies, the reason I had lost so many friends.

"They have slaves throughout the multiverse," I reminded her, my gaze meeting hers. "And it's our duty to do whatever we can to free them. That's why we do this, Marina. That's why we keep going, no matter what."

Marina was silent for a moment, her gaze locked with mine. Then, slowly, she nodded. "Alright, Marcus," she said, her voice filled with resolve. "Let's do this."

"Hey, you think we can take them all?" Guy asked with a smile. I knew there were more kids down below deck, but as usual, even though they were skilled fighters, genetically enhanced to be stronger, faster and smarter, I couldn't help but want to protect them.

"Probably not without the cannons," I said dryly. But then I thought of something. Something that might work.

"Listen, we don't have much of a chance against that many of these things," I announced. I ignored the looks from Marina and Guy, who both said they didn't seem to have as much trouble with the last one as I did. "But I've got a plan. Guy, get down below deck and tell the crew to man the cannons."

"But they aren't facing outwards," Guy replied in almost a whine.

"We don't need them to face outwards, do we?" I replied with a smile. "The skeletons are coming towards us, right? So they're going to run under the Iron Will."

"They'll run right into the barrels of the cannons!" Marina practically squeaked.

"It'll be too close to fire," Guy said, shaking his head. The blowback could damage the ship."

"Nah," I replied cockily. "The Iron Will's taken far worse than that."

"And besides," I continued, my gaze fixed on the approaching horde, "we don't have much of a choice. It's either this, or we let those skeletons overrun us."

Guy looked at me for a moment, his eyes wide. Then, slowly, he nodded. "Alright, Marcus," he said, his voice filled with determination. "I'll tell the crew."

With that, he turned and scampered away, disappearing into the lower decks. I turned to Marina, my hand resting on the hilt of my sword. "You ready for this?"

Marina looked at me, her green eyes filled with resolve. "I was born ready, Marcus."

I grinned at her, my heart pounding in my chest. "That's what I like to hear."

As we waited for the horde to reach us, I couldn't help but think about the journey that had led us here. The battles we'd fought, the worlds we'd seen, the friends we'd lost... It had been a long, hard road, but it was one I would walk again in a heartbeat.

As the skeletons drew closer, I could see their grinning skulls, their rusted swords. I could see the death they brought with them. But I would not let them take us. Not today.

I turned back to the approaching horde, my hand gripping the hilt of my sword. "Then let's give them hell."

And with that, we braced ourselves for the onslaught. The skeletons were almost upon us, their hollow eyes glowing with anticipation. But we were the crew of the Iron Will, and we would not go down without a fight.

Boom.

The first volley from our cannons rang out.

The sound was deafening, a thunderous roar that echoed across the barren desert. The ground shook beneath the force of the blast, sand and dust billowing up into the air. The front lines of the skeleton horde were instantly obliterated, their bony forms disintegrating under the sheer power of the cannons.

But the horde didn't falter. If anything, the destruction of their comrades seemed to spur them on, their hollow eyes glowing brighter as they charged towards us again with renewed vigour.

"Again!" I shouted, my voice barely audible over the din of the battle. I didn't need to give the order, though, because with a practised ease, the Iron Will belched its second volley of cannonballs into the horde.

Another wave of skeletons was obliterated, their remains scattering across the desert. But still, the horde pressed on, their numbers seemingly endless.

"Marcus!" Marina called, her voice strained. "We can't keep this up!

"Keep firing!" I ordered, my gaze fixed on the approaching horde. "We just need to buy some time!"

The third volley hit the horde like a tidal wave, again sending bones and dust flying into the air. But still, they came, their hollow eyes glowing with an eerie, unnatural light.

"Marcus!" Guy's voice came from below deck; his voice filled with panic. "The cannons don't have much more to give!"

I cursed under my breath. This was bad. If we stopped firing, the horde would overrun us.

"Keep firing!" I shouted back, my voice echoing over the din of the battle. "We can't let them reach the ship!"

And so, we kept firing, the cannons roaring as they unleashed volley after volley into the horde. The desert was filled with the sound of clashing steel and the thunderous roar of the cannons, the air thick with dust and the smell of gunpowder.

But despite our efforts, the horde kept coming, their numbers seemingly undiminished. I could see them properly now, their grinning skulls and rusted swords, their hollow eyes glowing.

"We can't hold them off much longer, Marcus!" Marina shouted, her voice filled with desperation. "We need to do something!"

I knew she was right. We were running out of time and options. But then, an idea struck me. It was risky, but it was our only chance.

"Marina, Guy," I called, my voice steady despite the chaos around us. "Get ready to abandon ship."

"What?!" Marina exclaimed, her eyes wide with shock. "But Marcus, the Iron Will..."

"I know," I said, cutting her off. "But it's our only chance. We need to lure the horde away from the ship, give the cannons time to cool down before they overheat. If we lose one... Anyway if things get too dangerous, we can use the Siren to escape."

"But Marcus," Guy protested, his voice trembling. "That's suicide!"

"Maybe," I admitted, my gaze fixed on the approaching horde. "But it's our only chance. Now, let's move!"

I had no idea how long we would need to hold out, and judging by the sheer speed of the skeleton horde, they could run a lot faster than we could.

When the ship was ready to jump again, I'd know, but something deep down inside me always told me that we wouldn't jump until we'd done what we came here to do: to free the enslaved people of this place, whoever or wherever they were.

But I still didn't know who they were. By all accounts, the skeletons themselves could've been the enslaved race in this place... but judging by how they reacted to our presence, I doubted it.

With a heavy heart, I turned to Marina and Guy, my gaze steady despite the fear gnawing at my gut. "We need to free the enslaved people of this world," I said, my voice barely audible over the din of the battle.

"But Marcus," Marina protested, her eyes wide with fear, "we don't even know them!"

"I know," I admitted, my gaze drifting to the horde of skeletons. "But we have to try. It's what we do. It's why we're here."

Marina was silent for a moment, her gaze locked with mine. Then, slowly, she nodded. "Alright, Marcus," she said, her voice filled with resolve. "Let's do this."

With that, we prepared to abandon the Iron Will to face the horde head-on. It was a desperate plan, but it was all we had. And as the skeletons drew closer, their hollow eyes glowing with anticipation, I knew that we would face them head-on, just like we always had.

Because we were the crew of the Iron Will, and nothing could stop us.

As we descended the rope ladder, landing on the hot sand, I couldn't help but feel a sense of dread. The horde was vast, their numbers seemingly endless. But we had faced worse odds before, and we had always come out on top.

"Stay close," I instructed Marina and Guy, my hand gripping the hilt of my sword. "And whatever you do, don't let them surround you."

They nodded, their faces pale but determined. We moved as a unit, our eyes scanning the horde for any sign of weakness. But the skeletons were relentless.

Suddenly, a loud, thunderous roar echoed across the desert, the sound so powerful it shook the ground beneath our feet. I turned, my eyes widening as I saw a massive, skeletal figure emerge from the horde.

It was easily three times the size of the other skeletons, its bones gleaming under the harsh sunlight. In its hand, it held a massive, rusted sword, the blade glowing with a deadly light.

"Marcus!" Marina cried, her eyes wide with fear. "What is that?!"

I didn't answer, my gaze fixed on the giant skeleton. It was unlike anything I had ever seen before, its size and strength far surpassing that of the other skeletons.

In fact, as it approached, it was pushing the smaller skeletons out of its way, sending their bodies flying to the left and right.

"It must be the leader or something!" I shouted. "Take it down, and the rest will fall! It could be the Caretaker!"

"Take it down? Are you insane?" Marina shouted back.

"Don't worry, I've got an idea!" I shouted and shot Marina a wink. "After all, they don't call me Captain Fantastic for nothing."

"Nobody calls you that," Marina sighed. "And they'll call you Captain dead if you think you can fight that thing."

"That's a terrible name," I laughed, then turned my attention to Yari, who had taken up residence on my shoulder. "Go tell the crew to load the cannons with the chain-linked shots. Then tell them to try not to kill us when we pass within range."

"No problem," Yari replied. "But isn't it normal to not shoot your own crew?"

"You'd think, but the last crew of the Iron Will didn't really share in that sentiment..."

"What ARE we doing here?" Marina pressed as she watched the flow of skeletons ebb closer towards us, but still being periodically decimated by the Iron Will's powerful canons. I could see, too, that some of the skeletons had made it through the kill zone and had started clawing at the hull of my ship. We didn't have long before it would be too late.

"HEY GUYS!" I shouted to the horde, waving my hands back and forward. "I'VE HAD TOOTHPICKS WITH MORE MEAT ON THEM THAN YOU!"

Marina placed a palm on her forehead.

"You're an idiot, you know that, right?" Guy said.

It didn't matter; my words seemed to have the desired effect. The horde of skeletons as one turned their attention towards me, and the huge leader seemed to double his efforts to push through the crowd to get to us.

"Run!" I shouted, turning on my heel and sprinting back towards the Iron Will. Marina and Guy were right behind me, their footsteps pounding against the sand underfoot. The horde was hot on our heels, their skeletal forms clattering as they charged after us. It seemed that now they cared much more about getting to us than tearing into the ship.

The Iron Will loomed above, its massive hull casting a long shadow over the desert. The cannons had stopped firing, the only sound our sprint across the barren landscape. But the horde was relentless, their numbers seemingly undiminished despite the onslaught.

I could see my crew scrambling to load the cannons, their faces pale and sweaty. Yari was fluttering above them, her golden wings glinting in the harsh sunlight as she relayed my orders.

"Almost there!" I shouted, my heart pounding in my chest. The horde was mere feet behind us now, their bony fingers outstretched with anticipation.

Then we turned the corner around the Iron Will, placing the ship between us and our pursuers. But we kept running. We had no choice.

Suddenly, the ground beneath us shook, a thunderous roar echoing across the desert. I turned, my eyes widening as I saw the massive skeleton leader bearing down on us, its rusted sword raised high.

"Marcus!" Marina cried, her eyes wide with fear. But it was too late to stop, too late to turn back. The leader was upon us, its massive form casting a long shadow over us.

If the skeletons could breathe, I would've felt hot breath on the nape of my neck, but I daren't look back again. We were so close.

We rounded the corner at the far end of the Iron Will again and then again, and I could see the tail end of the skeleton horde disappearing around the Iron Will in front of us. We'd rounded the entire ship, and now every single skeleton was trying to catch us.

But they were faster than us.

I chanced a look back and caught a glimpse of the huge skeleton now mere inches away from me. Its weapon still raised high in the air above it, and I knew that if my plan didn't come off, this would be the end of all of us.

Just as the creature swung its sword, a deafening boom echoed across the desert. I turned, my eyes widening as I saw the cannons of the Iron Will firing one by one behind us, the chain-linked shots whistling through the air.

The chain shot tore through the leader, its massive form disintegrating under the sheer force of the blast. The rest of the horde was caught in the following blasts, their bony forms scattering across the desert.

We were thrown clear of the devastation, but if we'd been just a few feet back, the shots would've taken us to the grave along with the skeletons. I silently thanked my crew for their precision, they may only have been kids, but they were the most loyal crew I'd ever known.

For a moment, everything was silent. Then, slowly, the dust began to settle, revealing the devastation. The horde was decimated, their skeletal forms scattered across the desert. The leader was nowhere to be seen; its massive form was reduced to nothing more than a pile of bones.

We stood there, panting, our hearts pounding in our chests. We had done it. We had faced the horde head-on and survived. We had protected the Iron Will and each other.

But I was still expecting the tailings of the horde to arrive, the ones who hadn't been caught in the initial blast. But they never did. Either they'd turned and ran at the fall of their leader, or through some divine miracle, they'd fallen along with him.

I turned to Marina and Guy, and a cocky smile spread across my face. "We did it," I said, my voice filled with false bravado. "Told you."

Marina rolled her eyes, but I could see the relief in them. "You're an idiot," she said, but there was no heat in her words. She was smiling, too, a small, shaky smile that spoke volumes.

Guy, on the other hand, was beaming. "That was amazing!" he

exclaimed, his eyes wide with excitement. "Did you see how they just... exploded?"

I laughed, clapping him on the shoulder. "I did, Guy. I did."

We stood there for a moment, just taking it all in. The desert was eerily quiet now. The horde was gone, their skeletal forms scattered across the desert. We had survived.

But our mission wasn't over. We still had to find the enslaved people of this place to free them from the Entropics' grasp. And I knew that we wouldn't rest until we had.

As we turned to head back to the Iron Will, I couldn't help but feel a sense of pride. We had faced the horde head-on and survived. We had protected the Iron Will and each other.

"There!" Yari cried, and I inwardly cursed, turning to see what the next thing was that was going to try to kill us for absolutely no reason.

But it wasn't a new enemy, and I sighed in relief.

People, clearly an oppressed populace, were slowly emerging from the landscape around us. I didn't know if they'd been hiding or had been working in some underground mines, but by the look of how they moved, I could tell they hadn't seen daylight in a long, long time.

And with their apparition, I could feel deep down inside myself that the Iron Will was ready to jump again.

On to another place.

Into another adventure.

To free anyone the Entropics had enslaved anywhere in the multiverse.

Because we are the core of the Iron Will. We are Free Men. And we will stand up for the little guys.

"You want some mushrooms?" Guy asked with a cocky smile. "Got you a whole bowlful below deck, thought you'd be hungry."

My name is Marcus Reid. And I hate, hate mushrooms.

A Thankyou

Again, your investment of your own time and money is always well appreciated and again, I ask that you **rate** and **review** everything that you read – and not just this book, so that lesser-known authors can grow their audience and gain the credibility that they deserve for their hard work.

Also, check out my website, it's usually kept up to date with current works, reviews and a few extra little bits. You'll find it at:

www.davidlingard.com

Thank you